THE ARCHIVIST

THE ARCHIVIST
A black romance

Gill Alderman

UNWIN

HYMAN

LONDON SYDNEY WELLINGTON

First published in Great Britain by the Trade Division of Unwin Hyman Limited, 1989.

UNWIN HYMAN LIMITED
15/17 Broadwick Street
London W1V 1FP

Allen & Unwin Australia Pty Ltd
8 Napier Street, North Sydney, NSW 2060, Australia

Allen & Unwin New Zealand Pty Ltd with the Port Nicholson Press
Compusales Building, 75 Ghuznee Street, Wellington, New Zealand

British Library Cataloguing in Publication Data

Alderman, Gill
  The archivist.
  I. Title
  823'.914 [F]

ISBN 0–04–440399–2

For John

Contents

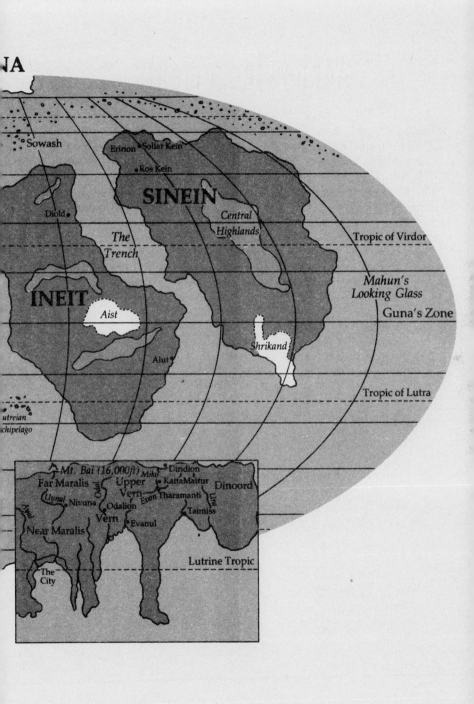

Acknowledgements

The lines from Constantine Kavafis's *The City* and *On a Ship* (pages 312, and 344) from *The Penguin Book of Greek Verse*, edited and translated by Constantine A. Trypanis, 1971, are copyright © Constantine A. Trypanis, 1971, and reproduced by permission of Penguin Books Ltd. Thanks to the shade of T.H. White and Alan Sutton Publishing Ltd for permission to quote the line (page 350) from *The Book of Beasts*, translated, made, and edited by T.H. White, 1984; and grateful thanks to my friend 'Angharad' for the translations from Pindar and Plato.

Translator's Note

The travelled reader may find anomalies between the languages of Mahkrein and English; some interpretations are a matter of opinion rather than of scholarly precedence.

The Archivist had a superficial knowledge of some archaic Gaian myths and certain images in the text may be his own, or they may be intrusions of my grandmother's. In her later years she studied Universal Cults at Sollar Kein.

My grandmother's text gives many verbatim examples of Cal's polyglot idioms: I have removed a number of obscenities for which English has no equivalent and modified others.

ODM III,
London, 657AR, 6088AD

PART I

HIGH LIFE, LOW LIFE

The City is fairest of all. A crescent bay embraces her and her three hills arise crowned from the depths: see the black towers of Learning, the blue towers of Faith and, upon the highest hill in the gardens of Delight, the white towers of the ruling women.
The Travels of Huyatt Tayal

1

The City

Cal opened his eyes. Everything flowered: the purple heads of the zy trees, the hanging baskets, the red and blue cotton tight on the arse of the street sweeper. He had flown high, above the bay, on the wing with the grey fishing swifts. He had looked down on the tops of every one of the City's twenty-nine towers. The sweet taste of anise lingered on his tongue, but the rahi bottle by his hand was empty and the fold of paper which had contained oblivion was twisted and rammed into its neck. His head was so clear, it rang.

He sat up, alarmed to find himself on a bench in na Hinoor Circus. Naturally, there had been few women at Dromio's party. The musicians had been sober when he left, the blue bottle of spirit in his pocket. As he went out, shouldering aside the canvas door of the pavilion, Dromio had pushed the paper of husk into his hand with a cheery 'Happy Birthday'. It was a two-minute walk from the Quarter to the circus: he had lain at least five hours in the open, out of his mind, ripe prey for any patrol. He looked down at his left arm: the skin was golden, innocent. It should be tattooed with the Mark of his class, the black tree of a Beggar perhaps, or the wheel of a Trav. His life, begun on the hard City pavement, had escaped registration. He was on no file in the Archive, he did not exist. Chance and accident had no place in the immutable laws of the Gynarchs. He pulled down his sleeve.

The huge circus, with its alternating border of derelict and well-tended houses, was empty. He saw the sweeper, her basket high on her back, leaving by Dyers' Street. Tyler would have opened his shop. He pulled a handful of coins from his pocket, and counted them. If he bought bread from Tyler, he could use the small back room where there was a cracked mirror and, usually, a razor abandoned on the grimy basin. He touched his chin, testing the stubble.

When he left Tyler's, cutting through the narrow alleys behind the Lily Exchange, Cal remembered that tomorrow the Red Wind would blow, gusting from the distant Tayaal, laden with ruddy dust. This, the last day of Isk, was a public holiday. On the corner by the gaming hall a group of Ironmen lounged and he saw their leader, Bale, a militant threat. Their iron staves were piled against a wall and two of them, heads back, were folding husk.

He had no wish to linger, but Bale had seen him from the corner of one malevolent eye. He whistled and half a dozen of his creatures followed suit. If he had worn motley and capered past them he could not have been more conspicuous. He turned about, down Copper Street, towards the metro. One of Bale's beaters was following him, no need to respond. He swore softly, repeating a portion of the rosary of obscenities which was his inheritance as one of the City's poor. Once, he turned his head and saw his pursuer Stoker, the odd one, the correction freak whose job was to harry the shay drivers and take a tithe from their foreign currency earnings. It was too early in the year for tourists: the Ironmen had time on their hands. Stoker delivered his lewd message beside the entrance to the Bicamera building and then, a charge on his own account, said, 'Want to earn some Sineinian redbacks? Straight road, do me a favour?'

Stoker was famous for his maladroit passes and he could recognise a come-on. He shook his head. Like him, the Ironmen got their husk illicitly in the Quarter where it was cheap. Who wants to shop in a drugstore with housemen and maids, buying ecstasy on their afternoon off? But he could not cross Stoker; so, 'Thanks,' he said, 'I'll come by.'

Stoker remained where he was, still as a mantis, canting his bulk over his graceful prey, holding his stave at an ambivalent angle: prop or weapon. Passers-by eddied around them.

'Ten tonight?'

'Make it nine.'

He would have to hide, concealing himself in one of his secret retreats – when he had visited Tarla under the close anonymity of darkness and got husk from her. Then he would hide. In the cellar, no one would find him and security and celestial beauties would be his until the streets felt safe again.

'Make it nine sharp,' said Stoker and turned away.

Husk, smooth brown powder, spores to grow visions, detritus manufactured from a noble plant, grit. . . . Husk would calm him, soothe and protect him. One of the pleasures the tourists came for, folded in an authentic setting, the old cafés on Goat Street, or the central plaza in Kiden Parks where all the world gathered under the rain trees. In Sinein and Ineit, husk was sophistication served up at a fashionable party, an expensive stimulant with its own set of boxes and scoopes. The crafts-women in the Old Market made sets of these implements from gold and tortoiseshell, ivory and silver: to own such work must be proof in the east of a pilgrimage to the City. He used litter, scraps of paper discarded by the tourists themselves; they lived their lives differently in the prosperous developed world. He knew that his dreams were sweeter, his sensations sharper, his illusions complete. In his world, the dream was all.

It was too early in the year for the tourists. When they came he would make easy money carrying parcels, opening doors, lending the beauty of

4

his face to street artists in return for sketches he could hawk around the hotels. He would have liked to lend the tourists his body too, as some of the portraitists did, screwing rich women in exchange for cash. He dreamed of that with the piety of a clairvoyant: new clothes, a soft bed, plenty to eat. In Sinein and Ineit they would be buying their tickets and booking their passages: the swamps of Southern Ineit, the birds of Lutra, the luxury steamer to bring them over the blue seas and into the beauty of the Bay, the picturesque, the only, way to approach the holy City, her temples and her famous Quarter. Today was for the citizens, a holiday before the storm. After the Red Wind, the shopkeepers said, the fat cats came out to play.

The street was crowded. People liked to ride out to Space Park for a day amongst the antiquities. Most of the crowd about him were Artisans of one grade or another, every left forearm marked with the indelible class distinction. He passed for an Artisan himself, in his thin grey shirt and slops. The women wore the maral, the long cotton kilt of the City and of its first province Maralis; some, the young and the unfashionable, were barebreasted, with a scarf or a string of beads for adornment; others wore the short traditional jacket or, a style imported from Cheron, a loose blouse of glittering weave; a few, the rich or the religious, were swathed in hooded cymars and veils. Rolled sleeves revealed the Marks of the men: shovels, picks, burdens, scissors and comb, the odd pen. He could read and write and he would have liked a pen himself, the Mark of a literate man, but since he had missed out, been missed out, he kept the cuffs of his shirt fastened.

Markchecks were made infrequently, at well-defined places such as the City hospitals, the shopping malls, and the waterfront. The authorities were complacent and slack. Government, armed with the Security Corps and the Overseers of the Mark, the camels and lice of idiomatic City speech, had become an exercise in administration. In the courts, the Archive provided precedent and solution in every case. There was no originality and he was safe enough in a holiday crowd. The pillared entrance to the metro lay ahead, the station sign in bold red lettering: 'Globe'. The globe itself loomed above the street, held aloft on the hand of a colossal statue of his deity Mahun, Mother of the City, precursor, giver of life and the Law.

Long ago the thief, Swan, had named him Cal. Before that nomination, a dim memory of childhood, which made him an honorary filcher, he had not given his identity a name, feeling his substance to be as the shadows of the great buildings or as the nimble sewer rats. And like a rat, he knew the refuge of the sewers intimately; in the days to come they would be his haven from the Ironmen and the dry dust the Red Wind brought. Now he was grown, adult and adept; yesterday, the thirty-ninth day of Isk in the cool and breezy season of Alcuon, had been his birthday.

Failing to find a woman at Dromio's party, he had celebrated with the bottle of rahi and the paper of husk. He was eighteen, or seventeen, or nineteen.

Like a cat, he preferred to walk by himself. But he had a few friends, and numerous acquaintances in the Depths among the half-settled itinerants for whom travel had been declared illegal: the Beggars, the Prostitutes, and the Tribers, those rebellious Artisans who had formed their own distinctive groupings. He drank rahi with Dog of the Faces, smoked tobacco with the Fister, Dile, had once pleasured a Rosy. Like everyone else he feared the Ironmen, like everyone else, he crossed the street when he saw a Dismemberer. Beggars, Tribers, Travs and Strays made, with the Prostitutes, the five classes in the group known to every other citizen as the Depths. But as a stratum of mud may lie below the ocean floor, another class lay below these: the Dismemberers, taboo, whose butchery released the soul from its prison, the body, and sent it on its way to Paradise. From them, Cal had heard, the rich could buy new skin or a young breast to replace one devoured by cancer, could buy cheap. A legal transaction recorded in the Archive was dear.

His gossip was the old Prostitute Tarla, past it but still earning, the puffy flesh of her face hidden under white make-up which cracked when she smiled, the sagging flesh of her body concealed by a scarlet cymar. 'My poor boy,' she would croon as she stroked his hair and the inside of his thigh, while her pink-crested cockatoo screamed in its cage. The bird was named Tifon after her most exalted client, long dead. When trade was slack Tarla and Cal sat late, over a pitcher of sweet beer, talking till the last lights went out, talking till the Rosies came out to rob the spent clients of the whores and studs, discussing the politics of their subworld until the Beggars woke and crawled from their wrappings like diseased spiders, spindly as their Mark, the twisted Tree. When night fell he would go to Tarla, but first, he would enjoy the day. Meanwhile, let Her shit fall on the Ironmen and odious Stoker. He was charmed: Mahun held him in Her arms. Swan had said that when he slipped and recovered himself on the roof of the Lily 'change. He had no Mark yet he had survived, from the unknown time when he had been expelled from his mother's body on to hard stones, born like many others a pavement child. Hundreds died after such a beginning. He had beaten it.

No one (but him) escaped the Mark, no one who was caught erred without punishment – but he did not intend to die for a long time yet. He loved the City and avoided and despised her institutions and civil precepts. He was lucky like a Matriarch, as blessed as one of the Gynarchs with their golden lily Marks and their golden drug, dust, the dry and pulverised lily flower, which the holy women and their Dancers used in the Temple. No base fantasies for them, but quality visions to go with their silks, perfume and gold. He looked up. Here and everywhere, throughout the City, the Temple on its hill dominated him and his fellow citizens. Only Paradise Hill was higher.

The crowd pushed through the narrow space of the metro entrance, jostling the Beggars who crouched there. He was carried along with it and boarded the train for the ride to Space Park. Travel was free within the City; without, it was forbidden. The Hill people, they said, were given passes, small plastic wafers which enabled them to leave the City. He leaned against a window, looking incuriously at a husker. The woman was asleep, her flight over; when she woke she would cover seat and floor with her vomit. One in fifty thousand became addicted, an acceptable risk. They were the chosen, marked by Mahun and sentenced to gorge themselves on Her flower. The train stopped, Quarter End. A big Artisan woman shouldered her way among the painted drolls and drakes. He feared big women, and the crowd pressed her against him so that the flesh restricted by her tight maral touched his slender hips. He kicked her sharply, his hard bare foot encountering a leg like the trunk of a tree. She looked down at him, and he turned his head aside to avoid her hungry eyes.

At the next station, a weaver left a seat vacant and he beat the big woman to it. He took his ease there while he watched irritation pinch her face until she forgot him, shuffled her heavy body into a new posture, and turned her attention to a picture paper. The highly coloured strips depicted women whose bodies dripped with jewels; sumptuous flesh oozed from dresses tight as sausage casings, scarlet mouths devoured slim young men. Cal stared at the woman and her fantasies. The pictures were satirical: she read them as the truth. She was a joiner and she wore a wedding ring. Her life must be dull and comfortable: a house near the Old Market, a husband to cut and plane for her, five children (the average) and one servant.

As a child he had watched people, always waiting for his fortune to fall on him until he learned to go out and look for it; watched, waited, and hoped.

The glowing coals of a cooking-fire heated the warm night: the Beggars who crouched around it were holding a feast. He did not know what they celebrated, nor why, when so many Depthers were ill or dead of the sweats which this year had come early and vicious. The Beggars had guests – a famous thief or two, a few Travs, the girl from Paradise Street – to enjoy the lamb they must have been given and the spicy daash which simmered in a pot big enough to swim in. Meat came rarely to Beggars: a condemned carcass dumped by a careless butcher or, a conscience salve, the gift of a Hill queen or a holy from the Temple, such bounty it might have been dropped from heaven or by the hand of Mahun Herself.

7

He watched the girl making the rounds of the diners. Zalcissa. Her mother had the first pavilion on Paradise Street and she wore her mother's earrings, a black Sineinian dress, too big for her, earrings, bangles, and high-heeled shoes whose straps were pulled tight about her thin ankles and whose toes and spindly heels were scarred and pitted from hard wear on the broken stone setts of the City's streets. The pink flower was her own touch. She was growing breasts, he observed, shifting and absently scratching his crotch, those soft excrescences which nourished babies and made women more important than men. Mahun had them: he had seen them pushing out from the chest of the image in the Temple yard where men and Depthers were allowed to rest. M'nah had breasts, pliant and soft. On cold days she let him rest his head against them . . . he must not think of M'nah. He shifted again and settled in his cardboard shelter. The Beggarwomen stroked Zalcissa and kissed her on the cheek; the men were more familiar. Diment laid a calloused hand on her leg and walked his fingers up it like a spider until they disappeared under the hem of her skirt. Zalcissa giggled. She got meat from everyone.

That lamb. It spat and dropped its grease into the fire as the feasters broke it apart with fingers and blunt knives. The spices in the daash were a sauce to his hunger. His mouth was full of spit. He dribbled, put up his hand and wiped it away. He was not a baby. They were passing a big spoon around, sucking the juices from it. The one-eyed Trav looked up from it with a mouth stained yellow by the spices, leered at the girl, and took a swig of rahi. He could almost taste the aniseed, just by thinking. . . . And rahi gobs. Once, M'nah had bought him one. In the centre of the little world whose sugary skins you could suck away, changing their colours from yellow to pink and white, was a fennel seed and biting into that was as good as a long scratch at a flea bite.

They were singing. The song about the boy. He liked the catchy tune, everyone in the City knew it, and he tapped his fingers on his knees. 'There he stood, the pretty little boy – ' They sang the verses raucously together, but on the strong beat which marked the first word of the chorus they fell silent and listened to Zalcissa crooning in her high child's voice.

> Boys, boys, boys, boys,
> Teasing, pleasing,
> Charming, flirting,
> Always, ever, never-ceasing,
> I wanna MAN!

(Well he was a man now, Zalcissa had learned her trade, and he had learned from her what women were and what men did, but not by watching. In the comic strip of his past the language and the pictures were simplified, the image of himself as a child an outline, the buildings

8

raw, in primary colours. His ability to recreate his past like a legend amused him and he smiled while the train hummed and the fat woman looked at her magazine.)

The food was finished, gone. Tears rose, but he swallowed them. That man there, he was Swan the famous filcher. He could climb anything, houses, chimneys, towers, the towers of the Temple and the University, probably the Octagon itself. Swan was looking in his direction, his small, neat head craning over one narrow shoulder. Swan in one swift and graceful movement had risen and was moving towards him. He cowered and tried to hide himself among the boxes. Now, he should run. But Swan blocked the way, extended a long and muscular arm, and extracted him.

At the fire the Beggars stared at him and one of the women felt his forehead.

'He's all right. Cold as last night's piss.'

She held a bone in her other hand. Juicy lumps of meat clung to it. She held it out.

'Go on,' said the thief, Swan.

He took the bone, too hungry, too frightened, to thank her. He choked on it, spat, gnawed, chewed and swallowed.

'Who is he?'

'M'nah's bit of candy,' said Swan. 'One o' the orfants from Daid's Ground. Got no Mark.'

'Shame!'

'Poor little dud!'

Swan, by birth and training, was a crossing sweeper; if his inclination was towards higher things, no one here blamed him for it. The pretty blue and gold tattoo on his arm was his cover; it was one of the oldest and most sacred of the Marks, a wisp of a broom as graceful as the man himself or one of the cherry trees which, in Alcuon, filled the Botanic Gardens with scented white lace. It was almost as old as the Beggars' Mark itself. M'nah, displaying hers proudly, had told him it proved how important Beggars were. It was a picture of the very first plough, she said.

'Come yer,' said Swan. The bone was dry and tasteless. He had sucked every last scrap away. Swan held him and tilted the blue bottle against his lips. Rahi. It was cold, and sweet like the gob, icy and burning – the heat, as it went down, made him cough. 'That's enough. You're only a nip. Come here, that's right. Sit down.'

He crouched in the ashes near the thief, wary and still ready to run, afraid of the deep voice and the sinewy arms, the supple fingers and what they might do if he didn't behave. The girl Zalcissa stared at him, her expression saying clearly that he was a little boy. (But she had praised him well, after that first ecstatic time.)

The thief spoke gently to him.

9

'Where's M'nah? Too busy on her pitch to see to you?'

He sniffed. The tears formed again. He was afraid to say it, but he knew from past experience what the silence of the curled-up body meant. He was alone. He was lonely and his mind and body ached for the shabby woman who had tried to fill the place of his unknown mother.

'By the new fly tip. She's dead,' he said, and couldn't swallow any more tears.

Swan's arms were gentle about him. His chest was not soft but it was warm and solid, resistant to terror. He smelled of the lamb, spices, rahi, and – this was a new perfume in his short life – pungent male sweat.

'Cusha,' he crooned. 'Stay with me. You and I'll get on fine. You can be my cavvy, keep a lookout 'case the camels come, whistle if you see one. I bet you can climb.'

That night he had cried again for M'nah. The picture was so strong he could feel her now, beside him on the worn seat. She had always worn a chequered scarf which had golden threads in it. He used to wonder why she didn't unravel the gold and turn it into money. He had nothing of her, nothing to remember her by. Once again he wished he had taken the scarf from her body. She hadn't needed it. The vultures must have torn it to pieces. When he had dared return to the place, the body was gone as if she had never been. He poked about in the boxes which had been their home but there was nothing beside two frags, tucked under the rags they slept on, and Swan claimed these when he saw them. For the first time he saw how shabby the boxes, printed with red and blue symbols, were and kicked out at them. His foot, meeting with a broken staple, hurt and he yelled and punched the boxes. They swayed and crumpled and he, kneeling on the pile of cardboard, wept and hammered it with his fists and forearms.

M'nah had dreamed of a house. Sometimes she talked of a wooden house at one side of a dry pasture where hens ran and scratched and the forest encroached, its outrunners thorns and spiny laurels. Forest birds came boldly to the verandah of the house for scraps. He did not know if this peaceful house was a memory or a story; he hoped Mahun had given her a proper house now that she was released. The train, braying its position in the tunnel, made him start. He shed his unhappy memories and looked at his reflection in the window. Surely he was handsome enough to prosper? He didn't care: in the City he had many houses, rooms with roofs of clear skies and hangings of early morning mist, ruined palaces, castles with shattered windows. He had gardens, fourteen of them. The train was drawing to a halt. Here was one of his houses, a white mansion where anyone could sleep or walk. SPACE PARK said the illuminated signs. The wrought iron gates at the top of the escalator led to his favourite pleasaunce.

*　　*　　*

10

The big woman, pushing, shoving, and waving to the friends who had come to meet her, blocked his way on the stairs and in the turnstile at Space Park. He had hoped to attach himself to the party in front of her and get in for nothing, but he was forced to pay. One precious frag. His money was running low. He took swift revenge on the woman, extracting her guide and a candy bar from her open bag in one silent, dexterous movement. As he walked he ate the sticky confection and scanned the guide.

The open air museum was vast, the exhibition areas surrounded by groves and thickets, by water and formal gardens. As well as the much-restored starships and the halls displaying relics, clothing, and pictures of that time, there were giant wheels, carousels, and aerial rides, twisting arcs of metal along which small cars sped and bucked. He heard the riders' screams, which despoiled the quiet of the place and drowned the birdsong, as he walked from the entrance through the Sculpture Garden, where he paused to look at the stone aliens among the nudes.

Beyond the statues was an area of booths and stalls, where cold drinks and souvenirs were on sale. Children rushed about trailing silver balloons overprinted with cruisers and stars; park employees dressed as starsailors mingled with the crowd. A slender captain approaching Cal offered lottery tickets, but he grinned and waved her away. Everyone was smiling. It seemed as though a day at Space Park exploring the past confirmed the rightness of the present.

Cal took a side path which meandered about plantings of pseudo-boheas, far prettier, with their pale green fronds, than their prosaic relative whose dried leaves made the City's staple drink. The sacroids were in bloom, red flowers heavily scented, and strange yellow blossoms sprang from the bare wood of the tumour trees. Ahead of him, he saw the elegant silver column of the *Daystar* tethered, earthbound, to her launching gantry, and hurried to join the queue at her entrance port. In the guide he read,

> *Daystar* Fleet Cruiser, Star Class. Her sister ship, *Evenstar*, perished with a thousand souls in the tragedy of 3999 (before the Reformation), metamorphosing fifty-six seconds after lift-off into a bright and short-lived star. 'My love, my people, suspended an instant, time, life and space held up/Before incandescent death made of you ten thousand meteors falling': Shelda Hinoor M'una, fl.3974-50AR.

Shelda had written in Maralay, the language of officialdom and the ruling classes, and the translation into Citycommons was poor.

> *Daystar* in her heyday carried a crew of five hundred women and men ratings, one hundred officers, and two hundred passengers

and technicians. After her initial experimental exploratory cruises she became a transgalaxial cryomorph transporter and was grounded in 1AR to be preserved for the City.

Visitors are asked to refrain from depositing litter and to KEEP MOVING while aboard.

Disobeying the last instruction he went as quickly as the slowly moving queue allowed to the captain's recliner where he lay back and, closing his eyes, flew the *Daystar* a light year or two until the clamour of a group of children made him give up the command.

The companionway leading to the cargo holds was empty, and he bounded down the steep metal stairs. 'Hold No 1' he read on the first hatch, 'CMT 1#/Gai'. A wide doorway for visitors had been cut beside it in the bulkhead and he glanced at the display outside it. Inside, the huge hold was illuminated with blue light, and the air was chill and moved softly, adding verisimilitude.

On the first level, where he stood, most of the body bays were empty, but an exhibition had been arranged depicting, with models, *Daystar*'s last outward journey, and two of the bays were occupied by the wax replicas of a male and a female cryomorph, based on two actual travellers of eight hundred years ago. A tall man stood near the display, apparently sketching the cryomorphs. The cut of his dark shirt emphasised his physique.

Cal gazed at the male cryomorph. He lay naked on the white bench, his brown skin veiled in frost. His eyes, curiously, were open, bright blue, the lashes furred with ice. So his first sight after thawing, on waking, would be of the blank ceiling of his bay and the globular light in it. Or possibly of some attendant leaning anxiously over him. But suspension of animation was not sleep, although it was loss of consciousness. Cal pondered on the paradox. What happened in the solidified brain, its circuits in stasis? What would his first thoughts be, when power was restored?

Appropriately, the male cryomorph was called Hero; the woman's name was Chiara. He juggled the names in his mind. He knew little of marriage, and these two had interrupted theirs to make the seventy-five year journey. When the ship reached Gaia, Chiara had failed to wake; it was the perfect tragedy and if he had been a rich man, he would have written a play about it.

The Galaxy Show was still running; Cal took the lift up to the theatre. This time, the images were even hazier, as if the projection equipment needed not just maintenance, but replacement; the slides were dusty and discoloured, yet he thrilled to the replicate galaxy, a pinwheel in space, and to the image of the planet with her three great continents and the necklace of islands strung across her northern seas.

He joined another queue and got bohea and a pasty from the food dispensers; the crew of *Daystar* had not enjoyed such plebeian food, but a meal in their eating hall was a popular attraction, an easy money-spinner for the amusements administration. From a separate table, the dark-haired artist of the body bays stared frankly at him. Leaving his meal half eaten, Cal got up and went below to explore the restored living quarters.

Here, more wax figures in varying attitudes portrayed shipboard life. A paper-covered diary lay on one of the bunks, open at the date 40 Isk in Alcuon, 3701; on another bunk was a hairbrush and strands of red hair were caught in its pale bristles. Many another such item made the ancient ship seem peopled and on course.

In the ship's library, the books were cased in plastics. There were very few. He supposed that many had been burned. The little room was forlorn and unvisited, superfluous when so few could read more than basic Citycommons. The place irritated him, the books untouchable behind glass. He climbed down the ladder which led to the empty drive chambers. His footsteps echoed on the metal floor; he could not imagine what power might have driven the ship.

Daystar invariably claimed the whole of Cal's time. The other displays, the Battleclass fighter *Xenon*, the pictures and models of Gaian athletes and circus performers, the tiny floaters, moulded to fit a single pilot, had no romance. Park wardens were beginning to close doors when he descended from the ship and marshals leading guard dogs shepherded the crowds towards the exit. He had stayed too long. But the Markdykes never came out to Space. The crowd made way for a group of men carrying tarpaulins to protect the statuary from the coming storm. When they had passed, he allowed himself to be hemmed in and surrounded. He smelt scent and sweat, the edge of a bag jabbed him; people shuffled and sighed impatiently.

White-clad figures were at the gate. The crowd pressed him. He tried to turn around and a large woman trod heavily on his bare foot. 'Shit,' he said aloud. He began to rehearse a tale.

An overseer stood either side of the narrow gateway, chaser dog at heel, and a small knot of troopers were grouped about an officer, beyond the gate. They were questioning a prisoner. The metro entrance, dark refuge, was unguarded. The crowd divided into two columns and as each person reached a 'seer, she grasped the marked left arm and scrutinised it. The woman in front of Cal was Artisan Rank X, a nailmaker, and the long mark on her freckled forearm looked like an absurd scar. She looked tired. He shoved her hard, and she fell.

He was running, dodging the woman who came at him, fast and down, into the metro. He took the empty stairs, for the moving ways were choked with people. Plunging through the crowd at the platform edge, he leapt on to the track.

He pulled out the torch necessary to his troglodyte existence. Now he had to exercise extreme care or he would be dead under a train or on the central high voltage power-supply. The citizens on the platform stared at him, but made no move. He heard suppressed shrieks and also the pursuit. He bowed to the crowd and with a wave of his hand disappeared into the tunnel.

Soon they would turn off the power, stopping the trains. They would release chaser dogs into the tunnel. He thought he knew the metro better than any Marklouse dog, but he wished he had a knife. He sped along the drainage trough beside the track, the light of the torch running before him and showing him scummy puddles, which he jumped, paper, and more sinister rubbish. He heard the rumble of a distant train, the hiss of its brakes, a whine as its engine died. Now the dogs would come. He trod carefully: the journey under the river was perilous and dim with only the smell of the seeping water and the small pools of light from his torch for company. At last, he reached the old junction and scrambled through a gap at the top of the wall which closed off the old network. Here he rested, his breath rasping; a few seconds. He ran again, swift and safe along the disconnected line, turned left and right at junctions and came to a metal ladder. He climbed. A crawl in a pipe led him to another ladder and he descended. He was above a sewer, standing on the ribbed metal of a storm drain. He lifted the cover and stopped, landing in the slime at the edge of a small river of slurry.

He was certain of his whereabouts, smelling perfume in the warm effluent flowing at his feet: beneath the Glass Mall and Hotel Z in the prosperous eastern precinct. At least the scented bath water diminished the stink. He lowered himself into the deep channel, torch in teeth, and waded downstream.

He threaded the sewermaze for perhaps an hour, imagining the pursuit far above him in the metro, pausing to avoid a ratcatcher who tramped by clad in shiny black, and reaching at last familiar territory, the storm drain beneath Vern Street and the drugpackers. The bonfire scent of husk and the flowery odour of dust, the trumpet-lily drugs, came through the gratings; Cal breathed deeply and bit his lip. For the first time since the chase he noticed his fatigue and filthy body. He guessed it was dark outside.

Turning aside, he climbed down a ladder, crossed an abandoned cellar and arrived at his refuge, which had a bolthole, a bed and table and a proper lamp. He would not be entirely alone. A big rat, recognisable by a cluster of white hairs on one shoulder, shared his quarters and what food he had, allowing him to watch its elaborate washing and grooming ritual in return for crumbs. But the rat was absent, away on an errand of its own. Only a set of narrow footmarks and swirls made in the dust by its tail showed where it had come and gone. Cal lit the lamp and stripped,

14

mopping the filth from his limbs with a blanket. The bed he had assembled from junk stood against the wall. Spare clothes hung from nails above the bed. He leaned to grab a shirt, slipped, and fell heavily, striking the wall with a shoulder.

The flaking brickwork trembled. He heard the patter of mortar falling on the other side of the wall and hurled himself backwards. Several bricks fell into an unseen space behind the wall. He heard them strike a hard surface, except for one which seemed to fall further before silence returned.

Curiosity banished his fatigue. Taking the torch, he looked into the hole. Sweet cold air rose to him; the cone of light showed a flight of stone stairs leading down.

Carefully he removed more bricks, and climbed through the hole. The stairs were of ochre-coloured marble, dusty, and he felt a metal handrail on his right. Directing the light, he saw bronze balusters, a stairwell and a marble floor a drop below. The staircase turned through ninety degrees; the second flight ended at the marble floor. He stood in the buried hall of an ancient house, speculating that he had descended from the old street level, for the site was hilly and the only doorway led into a vast room with bricked-up windows. This room too was panelled in marble but of several colours, and each differing panel was framed by pilasters. Rubble littered the floor. He scuffled in it but, finding nothing of interest or value, left the room.

In the doorway, the torchlight glinted on metal. He bent and picked up a twisted spike not more than half a finger's length.

The hall, likewise, was empty except for a marble bench built against the wall opposite the staircase. One corner of this was broken and scratched and a niche in the wall above the bench contained a shattered foot of green stone.

Under the stairs, he found a small open door, sagging, for its hinges had rusted away. The cool current of air blew in his face and he heard water running as he went down a flight of steps into a cellar. Here was a range of slate slabs and narrow shelves which looked like wine bins; he found an empty bottle and a broken corkscrew. A low-arched door led out of the cellar, a second flight of steps, twisting and rough, led down.

He stood still, arrested in horror; he felt his heart hammer and tried to stop breathing. Two figures stood in the centre of the chamber. He watched them for several minutes before he saw that they were lifeless: statues standing in a pool which took up most of the floor. Stepping nearer, he saw that water flowed into the pool from a vase held by one of the figures, spilled from the pool into a channel, ran out through an arch into a low tunnel.

She. The standing figure was Mahun, Her right hand extended in blessing, Her face familiar in its eternal welcome. Her acolyte was a man

15

who knelt and looked reverently up at Her while he unloosed the knot of Her maral. The water of life cascaded between them.

Cal put the torch on the floor. Its beam lit up the water, and he waded into it. He knelt at the feet of the deity. The bitter water fell upon his head and shoulders, coursing down his back. He lifted his face and prayed to Mahun.

Her blessing hand was smooth, its detail kissed away. He, too, kissed the hand.

An intemperant bather, he emerged chilled and foolish from the water. His fears began to return, mixed with others of the place. He took up the torch, shone it briefly once more round the domed chamber and retreated.

Above, in his room, he closed the gap in the wall with the retrieved bricks. By the light of his oil lamp, he examined his find. It was an old piece of jewellery, an amulet. In shape, it was exactly like the Beggars' Mark, a tree with two twisted branches, and a curving trunk. It was made of a brassy alloy, not valuable, and the face of it was enamelled black. Some of the enamelling had gone, leaving an empty honeycomb of cloisons. A ring on one of the branches was worn on one side, by the chain or thong from which it had depended. Amongst the litter on the floor, he found a length of string from which to suspend it and hung it round his neck.

The room was warm but he shivered from his wetting below and from exhaustion after his flight. The order he had imposed on his life was shattered, his plans spoiled. So be it. He rolled his damp body in a blanket and lay down on the bed. Images of black dogs, Mahun, and silver starcruisers chased about his mind. He slept.

While he slept, his head pillowed on his arm and his hair over his eyes, concealing his long lashes and smooth eyelids, the rapid movement of his eyeballs when he dreamed, the rat descended from its run along ancient pipework and crouched beside him, extending its long body over the space between them while it sniffed. No food was proffered, there was no movement. It went away again, scampering up the brickwork as rapidly as a thief.

When Cal awoke he ate bread and cheese from his store and went out as far as the sewer to piss in the dark tide, returning by the alternative entrance to make sure he was safe. Again, he slept.

Later, he dressed and made a second sortie as far as the drain below Vern Street. He heard the rattle of the Wind at the drain covers. The smell of meat roasting mingled with that of the hallucinogens, husk and dust, but the familiar humidity had gone. He cleared his throat of the dry air. Clouds, drifting in the access shafts, turned the clear beam of the torch back at him. He blinked and rubbed the sand from his eyes. He was hungry; he went back to the cellar and finished the bread. As he lay in the dark – alone – he thought of teeth and chaser dogs, and his sleep was fitful; he dreamed he had husk and was floating with *Daystar* among the planets.

The empty street was red; every ledge and shutter was lined with the desert's jetsam. He had been below for the entire five days and now, just before dark, when the provident citizenry was still shut up, he had run out of food. To eat was not a necessity; but it would be a pleasure and, besides, he wanted a drink. He had money, but he would not waste it on food. Every window was close shut. The swifts were out, he and the swifts. A flock of them veered against the clearing sky. He trudged up Citadel Street, his feet slippered by the dust, and sidled into the yard behind Hotel Z. He was lucky. An overalled chef banged out of the kitchen door and flung food into one of the bins. When she had gone, he helped himself to a portion of spiced lamb. Eating as he walked, he set out for the wasteland by the City wall, on the skirts of which the tribe of disaffected Artisans, the Faces, lived.

This perimeter of wasteland was scattered with dwellings built of anything that had come to hand, the houses huddling close to the city wall, just beyond the range of the arclights. Its grimness was not alleviated by bright tags of flame from occasional fires, around which squatted groups of Beggars sorting rags. A small pack of ribby dogs snapped over a remnant of flesh. He stepped over some broken pieces of wood which had been deposited by the Wind. The smoke from the fires obscured the last of the daylight. Several men with hammers and stones were trying to straighten the contorted sheet of metal which was somebody's roof.

Dog's house was mostly made of tin, the sheets tied down and anchored with stays made from the wire he had removed from the fence of a chair factory. Its door had been reclaimed from a derelict building and cut down to fit the doorway. Outside, Dog had planted an old electric streetlamp to which someone had affixed a notice saying 'DOG's piss here'.

Cal knocked and lifted open the door. The room within had been made comfortable with hangings, and furnished with table, bed, and shelves. A large number of wigs on stands were ranged along the shelves and an erotic print was prominently displayed over the bed.

Dog was having his face painted. He sat on a wooden chair, his shirt protected by a towel. Tubes and boxes were laid out on a table beside him, · nd a large mirror leaning against the wall reflected the scene back at him. The Bitch was working on his left eye, and cursing him for blinking.

Cal stood and watched them and himself in the mirror until Dog, screwing an eye open, saw him and raised a hand in greeting.

17

'Long time,' he said laconically.

''time,' echoed Cal.

'You look farackin' rough,' said Dog, opening his other eye, and evading the Bitch's laden brush. 'Got any husk?'

'Get you some from Tarla.'

''s null. Have a drink. Bitch.'

'Ow Deog,' she said in her inimitable shrill tones, carefully laying down her brush and handing Cal the squat blue bottle of rahi.

'Health!' He gulped a dose and passed Dog the bottle.

'Heart!' replied the Facer king.

Bitch finished painting his eyelid. She had used purple, but the left eyelid she had painted white, so that Dog's gaze had become startling, asymmetrical. The rest of his face was polycoloured and striped; the waves began at his nose, the centreline, swept outward across his cheeks, brow and shaven scalp, and met in tight convolutions on the back of his head. Bitch was proud of her skill in painting, and Dog prouder still. She had worked as a tattooist before he, reversing, as did all the Faces, the custom of the City and the Law of Mahun, had taken her to live with him. The livid green Mark on her left arm, a coiled dragon devouring its tail, was that of an Artificer, the first rank of Artisans.

The Bitch's own face was as remarkable. Her paint was cakeflour white and thick, not unlike Tarla's; but the Bitch was young, with a firm canvas to work on, and high and prominent cheekbones. She had filled in her lips with scarlet and rimmed her dark eyes with black, but her shaven brows were defined only by the bone beneath. The bare skin of her scalp gave her the look of a half-finished doll. Later, she would select a wig from her fantastic collection. She was slender and wore the uniform tight black maral of the Facer woman.

'Do you next,' she said to Cal, but he shook his head.

Dog stood up, confronting Cal, who, a head shorter than the king of the Faces, stood his ground and looked up.

'Stoker's after me,' he said, answering the unspoken question. 'And I had to sidestep the Marklice. If you wanted a good knife, Dog, where would you go?'

'Markdykes and Stoker,' said Dog, sensing an entertaining story, or several. 'What's happened to put you in the eye? Inherited an estate?'

'A knife, the knife? – I might go and help myself – if I needed the exercise – in the Mall; or I'd go to Glaver. Camel knives are the best, and the dearest. And some pretty ones come in from Vern: they use them there to cut down the lilies. Big. You want one you can hide.'

'I'll take you round to Glaver's if you wait. We're expecting some friends.'

'Welcome to join us,' the Bitch put in. 'Go on Cal. Let's do your face.'

He smiled at her, assenting.

18

'A bit,' he said.

She made him sit in Dog's vacated chair and picked up a pair of scissors.

'Got hair,' she said. 'Don't fret, my love. I'm just tidying it.'

'Mahun! I don't want to be noticed any more,' he said, but she was already snipping and he had to shut his eyes to avoid the falling hairs.

He kept his eyes closed. The snip snip of the Bitch's scissors ceased, and he felt her blow the cut hairs from his face. She unbuttoned his shirt and stroked the muscle of his chest. Gently, as if he were a small child, she removed the shirt.

'What's this?' Her sharp voice startled him. She held the Beggar's Tree he had found between finger and thumb, rotating it around its string so that she could examine it. He was shocked into a bold reply.

'Leave it alone.'

'But what is it?' The Bitch was nothing if not persistent.

'I found it.'

'Look Dog, it's a Tree, quite pretty. I don't think he should have it. He isn't a Beggar. It looks very old. It might be a relic.'

'You're a superstitious cunt, Prenta,' Dog growled. 'Leave him be. If you want to tart him up, get on with it.'

'Sit up straight,' she said to the boy, in subdued tones. Dog only used her real name if he was rattled. The golden boy relaxed and closed his eyes again. He heard her pouring water and felt the wet kiss of a shaving brush. When she had shaved him she began to smooth a soft cream into his face. She worked around his chin for a long time and he dozed, entranced by her touch. The paintbrush began stroking across his skin, sweeping around and down his neck and chest, caressing his back.

'Look now,' said the Bitch, eventually.

He stood up. From the mirror, a moonstruck figure returned his gaze. She had trimmed his untidy hair, combed out its muddy density, and dishevelled it again by artifice; she had made a forested tapestry of his face and body. Tigers and sambur pursued each other round the trees.

He yelled, twisting in front of the mirror, craning to see the animals chase each other across his back.

'Work of art,' said Dog, pausing in his task of setting out bottles of spirit.

'Won't come off,' Bitch laughed, winking at Dog. 'You'll have to join us now, become a Face.' She crossed the room and took a white wig from one of the stands, easing it on. She put on her shoes, with their thin, spiky heels.

'Ready.'

The first to arrive was a big black man called Horse, who manoeuvred a tall drum before him through the doorway. Then came Ax with talking drums, and Malkin and her man Cat. Jill came alone, for the Hob had recently been killed in a fight against the Ironmen, and Tod and Vixen were late, speedily drinking to keep pace with the others. The Vixen was a large white woman who wore a ginger wig and carried a stole made from two dead foxes over her arm, since in the City's heat, she could not wear it. They were desert foxes from the Tayaal, their glass eyes sorrowful, their huge and delicate ears seeming to strain for vanished sounds. A silken cord joined them in a deathly tie. She kissed everyone and settled beside Cal, stroking her foxes and occasionally pawing him as if he were another fur. Because he had already downed three doses of rahi, he endured it.

Ax and Horse began to drum, beating out a complex rhythm to which the Bitch danced alone. Cal told his tale with many exaggerations and the Faces gave him his own bottle of rahi. Malkin stood up to sing. She wore her own hair, but it was bleached and dyed like watered silk, or a tabby cat. She sang unaccompanied, her powerful voice filling the small room. Famous for her coloratura screams, she sang tragically of love and death. Then, pausing only for a dose of rahi, she sang lewdly of death and love.

When the night was past its best and Dog snored, while Ax and Horse leaned sweating on their silent drums, there came a commotion at the door. A small Facer woman pushed past the musicians into the room, soliloquising as she came.

'Bleedin' Rosies oh beg your pardon didn't know you had visitors all over the street can't get down Paradise without falling over them stupid bitches sorry Bitch ought to learn who their friends are that Morn she. . . .' She paused to breathe.

'My little sister,' said Bitch to Cal. 'Mouse.'

He had seen Mouse in the street and been fascinated by her walk, by the fact that she managed to walk at all in the tiny tight maral which scarcely covered her round arse. He became suddenly and desperately afflicted with a problem: he must discover what she wore under the silky bandage.

'Rahi, Mouse.' Tod passed the bottle.

Mouse drank, kicking off her shoes as she did so. Her facepaint was mouselike, grey and dainty; she did not drink daintily.

'Mouse'll get your paint off,' said the Bitch, giggling. 'Won't you, Mouse? This is the real visitor; he's waiting to go out with Dog, but I couldn't resist all that golden skin.'

Mouse looked at her sister and then at Cal.

'Null,' she said. 'Anything else you want?'

'Just go and enjoy yourself.'

Mouse pulled Cal to his feet.

'Hope you haven't had too much,' she said, leading him out by a doorway at the back of the room.

The doorway led into a kitchen of sorts. A kettle stood on an oilstove, and torn bags of bohea lay among some dirty food trays; several cockroaches were breakfasting there. Mouse took a towel and a bathplug from a hook. She picked up a bar of yellow soap and pushed Cal outside.

It was day. The new sunlight fired the red dust. In the middle of the littered communal space a bathtub stood forlornly beside a standpipe and a copper. A low fire burned beneath the copper and the whole arrangement was screened with canvas and old carpet nailed to poles.

'Public bath,' said Mouse. 'Fill up the copper and stoke the fire when you leave.' She drew water and began to fill the bath. 'Get in then.'

'It's a shame to destroy them,' he said, turning his head for a last glimpse of the rioting deer. As the picture dissolved the paint ran in coloured rivulets down his body and the water in the bath turned the colour of mud. Mouse took off her clothes and got into the bath with him.

When they returned to the house, the visiting Faces had gone. Dog lay on the bed looking at a picture paper, and the Bitch was setting out four paper trays of food on the cleared table. She looked at Cal and laughed.

'Pretty boy,' she said.

An underground news-sheet lay on the bed beside Dog. The black headline said 'ARREST'. Cal picked up the paper and read of the trial of a Fister for unlicensed husk dealing; he was expected to die unless his arbiter was eloquent. He turned the page, and studied a cartoon showing the usual lice and camels engaged in ingenious and unnatural practices. Advertisements underneath it offered services from sex to laundry.

Nadar. Linen returned, ironed and folded, within two hours.
Tarla. Tarot and other services.

Pulchrinella has no need to advertise.

He grinned. Dork, the bastard, made a good living as a woman.

'Food,' announced the Bitch.

They ate a greasy daash and drank imported beer, the traditional antidote to an overdose of rahi. Dog belched his appreciation and stood up.

'Business,' he said. 'Glaver.'

The house stood in Facer territory, the old market quarter, its white walls shadowed by dark balconies. They alighted from the shay Dog had insisted on and he paid the driver.

A knock brought a pallid man to the door, Miel, Glaver's assistant. He led them through a room full of glass statuary and bowls and brightly painted boards advertising 'Shiron, Knife Thrower to the Known Universe'.

Glaver herself was at breakfast on a verandah overlooking a court where children played noisily in and out of lines of washing. She sat, slicing a peach, at a table beside an urn full of flowers.

21

'Please, sit,' she said. 'Miel, some bohea. Food'

'It is good to see you, Dog.' She kissed him. 'Who is this?' Her accent betrayed her origins among the nomadic boat people, the Tlivoorn.

'Friend of mine. Cal.'

'Please, sit down.' She smiled at Cal. Her skin was brown, smooth, oiled.

They sat with her and ate another breakfast. She poured bohea for them, but would not touch it herself for, she said, it would make her hands shake.

'Not good for Miel,' she laughed. 'What are you doing nowadays, Dog, my friend?'

'A little trading.'

She laughed again.

'And him?'

'He's a bum, too.'

When the visitors had eaten their fill, Glaver clapped her hands. Pale Miel came scurrying from the door where he had waited and cleared away the dishes. The knifethrower put her hands firmly on the table.

'Have you come to buy, Dog? You?'

Cal listened as Dog told her sufficient of his tale.

'Can he afford one?' said Glaver.

Cal put his hand in his pocket and felt for the bar which lay there amongst the small change; but Dog, glancing sideways, stilled him.

'No,' said Glaver. 'No bargaining. I like his face. He can have one for seven frags.'

Dog whistled.

Five knives were laid before Cal. Dog hefted a heavy vinegrower's knife from Baia, Cal picked up a glistening blade with initials engraved on the hilt.

'This is the one you want,' said Glaver. 'This camel knife. It's the real thing.'

He closed his fingers awkwardly around its hilt.

'My chick. Like this.' She arranged his fingers correctly. 'Now try and stab me.'

He made a clumsy feint, frightened of injuring her. She caught his empty left hand and pressed it to her; instead of a soft breast beneath the cotton, he felt the hard shell of a ceramic bodyshield. They both laughed.

'Last year, as I sat here, a man came over the balcony rail with a lily knife in his hand. If I had not been cleaning my blades – the Domes for me. So I got this from Cheron.'

'You had better come for lessons,' she continued, caressing his hand. 'Let me see, today is – first day of Lilb, tomorrow I must go into Maralis; then, a performance . . . come to the Shack on the fifth. At eleven. I give a party for my friends. Enjoy yourself, and I shall see you there. I'll bring your knife.'

'But I need it now.'

'A murder to commit, mm? You've survived until now, what is five days more? This knife needs sharpening. I shall bring it for you; then you pay me.

'You, Dog, come along – bring your woman.'

She smiled at Cal.

Dog stood up. Cal said goodbye to Glaver in Tlivoornal and she, in reply, let loose a string of clicks and rapid sibilants; the words he could understand made him blush. The door closed behind them. They stood in the street and watched a woman pass by.

'I bet you could have that as well,' said Dog, slapping Cal's shoulder. 'See you.'

He strode off to lay a bet on the barefist match which was to take place, illegally, in the men's bath house on Goat Street, and Cal, turning south, went out of the old quarter by one of the gaps in its broken wall. He walked the two miles to the beach slowly, reflectively, multiplying hours by days.

The Ironmen were denied the Pleasure Quarter by a combination of camel vigilance and the flails and knives of the Fister and Facer tribes; fists and faces were pulped, fingers smashed and facepaint scarred, if ever a confrontation occurred, on the black iron staves; sometimes the camels' own staves were broken and several constables of the Security Corps accordingly kept watch at the junction of Gold Street and Trial Lane on the eastern margin of the Quarter. He could see five of them now, louche in their whites, lolling against a shopfront because it was midday and the streets were quiet. Therefore he too walked carelessly.

Nevertheless, he turned by habit into Cut Alley and the yards beyond it, avoiding the camels and emerging in the heart of the Quarter. The gaudy canvas of the whores' pavilions hung heavy and still; cats slept, one curled tightly in a broken pot, another stretched full length in the shade of Ala's pavilion; a pair of kittens nestled together on the hot bare earth in Kondar's doorway. Surely the whores and studs slept too? Ala's screams told him trade was brisk.

The Ironmen had their own base practices. Tarla had told him they drank the blood of menstruating women at their initiation ceremonies. He knew this was heresy. No one's safe from them, she'd said, so watch your back when you're east of the Quarter. He had prayed that Stoker had forgotten about him; half asleep, he had caught himself wishing he had kept the enforced appointment. He might have gained something, cash at least, for a few minutes' abasement. But he did not relish life as Ironmen's tissue, Stoker's piece, one of the crowd of beautiful boys and girls which followed the Ironmen and seemed to delight in their cruelty.

Tenders was another Deep term for them, service tugs to attend to the cruising Ironmen and pander to their whims, weak wills with tender flesh. He needed to make his own way – but he did like the loose draperies the tenders affected, white versions of the Rosies' picturesque pink tatters hanging in folds from straight limbs, tissue borrowed from antique statues and a wild contrast to the Ironmen's sombre suits. He was dreaming again. He was a loner; he came and went when he chose. He had no Mark so he could not conform.

Tyler's was full, of weary people, a battle of voices and the clatter of crocks. There were no seats. He went in and leaned on the counter, tapping it softly with his last remaining bar. He must be frugal: he owed Glaver. Eventually, Tyler got to him and raised heavy eyebrows, barely parting his lips to murmur, 'Health.'

'Heart,' he responded. 'Rahi.'

He drank it down and pocketed his change. He could afford another but he hesitated. Someone might come in and treat him. He did not put his glass back on the counter. The someone came in: it was Zalcissa. She saw him and made a beeline, coming to rest against the counter and wiping her face on a handkerchief edged with a length of the lace she crocheted between clients.

'Those early-morning creatures,' she complained. 'Where do their wives sleep? And I've had a regular in. I'm worn out, and not a bloody seat in the place. What's yours?'

'Rahi,' he said. She would not expect a return. She would drink one imported beer and then two beakers of bohea while she scanned the room for replete diners. After that, she would order bread, pickles, and sliced sausage, claim her seat and sit down to consume them. Her head would nod, she would doze a little, wake with a start and call for bohea. At five to two she would take out her mirror and lipstick, wipe her greasy lips on her handkerchief, apply a new coat of red grease, comb out her hair, study her revised reflection and, at two, depart for the second stint in her pavilion. He studied her pretty face. She must be twenty-four or -five, a mistress of her trade. For old times' sake he smiled his best smile, and she smiled back. She was pert and provocative, assured of her looks; she was a favourite with the hardworking husbands of Artificers and Weavers, sharing the sexual burden, good at flattering depressed personalities.

'Well, we've survived so far, you and me,' she said. 'If we haven't grown rich; and we've seen some strange sights. Remember the snake woman? And that Hill tiger that ran mad on Cat Street? And, tell you what, if you want to see a strange sight, go up to the Garland this afternoon. There's a travelling woman there, a real travelling woman come by ship from Ineit. She's showing the Queen of the Rats, a proper beast my regular told me. He saw it on his way to work.'

24

'I might.'

'Oaf. What's the matter?'

'Nothing much. Dreaming.'

'As usual.' She patted his arm and planted a succulent kiss on his lips. 'Get along, do.' He stepped back, resenting the fact that an hour of intimacy three or four years ago seemed to have given her a licence to kiss him in public. He scowled.

'Oh, run along, do,' said Zalcissa.

He imagined the monster as he walked, the Queen of the Rats, rodent ruler, a mighty and invincible sleek brown rat which fed only on the tender parts of corpses – but it was caged. He supposed. Did it have to be muzzled? Maybe you could tame a rat and train it to be fierce on demand. His own rat, the benign denizen of the cellar, was circumspect. It would take food from a piece of paper if you held it out, but not from a hand. Maybe it wasn't a rat at all, but some other rodent, something from the Ineiti swamps, something which rose out of the mud to snap at unwary turtles, fish, and feet. The tinsmiths called the Tlivoorn swamp rats. Maybe the monster was a mad Tlivoorn like the tiger Zalcissa had spoken of, naked and full of uncontrolled anger, smashing his fists into anything that hindered him as he ran. A beast like that would have to be caged. Or it would be a cat which had killed a thousand rats, a thousand notches in her once-smooth and perfect triangular ears . . . the women would love such a cat, the doyenne of felines, favourite and sacred animal, a super-clawed destroyer, the death and devourer of a mountain of rats . . . but rats were pleasant enough. Making a living in humanity's ordure, they were neat and clean, always washing and polishing themselves, always alert.

In the window of Zircon, the big grocery store, a pile of sugar cakes rotated slowly, each one decorated with a different flower. He wished Zalcissa had bought him a meal.

The Garland had been built as a theatre in the days when strolling audiences were popular. They used it still for displays of provincial dancing, for middlebrow art auctions and lowbrow mud wrestling. He knew which entertainment he preferred. It was funny, it brought on hysterical belly-aching laughter, to see two strong men lose their grip because they stood and tried to grasp each other's slippery bodies in a sea of yellow river mud. Such anarchy was strange in the ornate surroundings, all polished wood and garlands of ceramic flowers, tiles painted with lilies of every kind, tiger daisies and libbards' tongues. Today the shiny floor was hidden, the flowers masked, by a dense crowd. Rich and poor rubbed shoulders and jostled each other. He was tempted to abandon his quest for the Rat Queen to pick pockets and filch from a few of the open bags which hung unregarded from shoulders and arms. He touched the smooth flank of a young Matriarch as he wormed his way in, delectable yielding flesh under the silk, and she looked wildly round. But the shrieking came from deep in the crowd.

There was a clear space in the centre of the crowd: a barrier of painted boards made a temporary ring and in it stood a big blonde woman wielding a miniature whip. The source of the shrieks was a pile of rats leaping and tumbling over one another as she goaded them with the silver tip of her cane. He was immediately cast down. He had expected an animal with two heads at least. And then the rats were still. The woman had ceased to torment them. There were nine rats, fat and sleek. They sat in a circle, facing outward, their nine times thirty whiskers twitching, their nine bald tails stretching out behind them, the tips joined in an inextricable tangle in the centre of the circle, a knot of monstrous proportions, an obscene weld of flesh and animal freedom. He admired rats: they played and carried out the business of their daily lives beside him, and he was sickened, not with nauseating sympathy for the animals' plight but with the chilling clutch in the belly which is loathing and fear. Yet the individual rats were sleek and well-fed. He stared at them and tried to overcome his disgust, while he wondered how the knot had been tied.

Obviously the rats were trained, well-trained, or they would not have been so still. Some lay quietly down, two sat up and nibbled at some pellets the woman gave them, two others washed their faces, kneading and shining their cheeks with dexterous paws like little hands – and the woman had noticed him. She came over, moving lightly and with purpose. Her costume had a military feel: tight red cloth over long legs, high boots – mirrors these and he saw his face in the toecaps – a braided jacket, gaudy brooches jingling on her breast, a red jap jaunty on her curling hair. She smiled at him, looked down, assessing him and his potential.

'Like a turn, my pretty?' she said, and held out her whip.

He shook his head and the crowd laughed. Something in her professional smile was genuine: he should play up.

'Afraid are we?' Another laugh. He took the whip and while he stepped across the barrier and stood at her side, 'I like rats,' he confided. 'So do I dearie,' she murmured. 'Go on, tickle them up. Ladies and gentlemen, the Rat Queen of Alut, sisters and brothers these, joined with Mahun's untiable knot. I found them myself, rampaging in the President's wine cellars last Alcuon!' He tried to be gentle, touch the animals softly; in fact, a gesture was enough and the squealing confusion occurred again, inches from his bare feet. 'Now put up the whip.' The animals were still. He bowed and smiled, she applauded him and as she walked him back to his place at the barrier, 'I like a neatly packaged boy,' she said. 'As long as he knows what's expected of him. The Lunar Hotel after nine tonight?'

'I'll try,' he said, lame and (he felt) impotent before her assurance. The cherished dream was impossible: he could not aspire. He left her to her rats and expectations and shouldered his way towards the exit. Showing the Rat Queen by day, she his queen by night, the first big woman who had not instantly inspired him with dread, he her king, kneeling before her amplitude on a soft bed . . . such were fancies, nothing to do with real life in which Glaver had summoned him, and Stoker. . . . The entrance to the Garland was on Vern Street, another edge of the Quarter, but the exit gave on to Spital Way in Iron territory. He emerged in afternoon heat and there stood reality, Stoker looming out of the sun.

'Hey, you!'

The adventure was over. Lady, he only asked for peace and quiet, a return of his monotonous food-gathering existence. It was the birthday, that was it, his birthday had begun a new year and it was ill-starred. He must get Tarla to deal the cards – as he took off at top speed he hoped there would not be a hue and cry.

'Hey, cully!'

The hue and cry was composed of the Ironmen who had been lounging in the street. Other citizens saw it as a private quarrel. No one interfered.

He would lead them a dance. If only it was evening, nightfall, cooler. He ran well, he was light and nimble; he was amazed at Stoker's speed, briefly glancing back at the black lightning as he rounded the corner by the bank. He would head for Spinners Flat and the roadmenders' yards, where he could get away beyond the piles of stones and reclaimed setts, from which he could climb . . . Stoker was gaining on him and the others were not far behind.

He slipped in dog crap and fell flat on the broken ground. He knew he was bruised, grazed probably; Stoker would have him. Springing up from such a tumble was impossible: he dragged himself upright. They must have lost him – there they were. In the last yard he had his revenge for the gruelling run and the shit on his feet: he climbed the wall. It was about fifteen feet high, a broad top. He ran along it and began on the foundry wall. The building was derelict: he knew it intimately and was safe. He sat on the apex of the roof to get his breath and savour Stoker's defeat. Below him the heavy man was jumping vainly at the first wall. Bale, behind him, swore and called him off, bringing his chief cur to heel. Grudgingly, Stoker obeyed his master. It was Cal's turn. He whistled piercingly from the safety of his perch then, letting his slops fall about his ankles, turned about on the rooftop, an unrefined and refractory putto, and displayed the twin golden globes of his buttocks to the enraged Stoker.

'Bugger you, Stoker,' he shouted over his shoulder. His voice echoed over the rooftops. He covered himself and disappeared behind the ridgetiles.

Early on the fifth day of the month, Cal walked through the arched gateway into the old market quarter, passing Glaver's House, where the balconies were now bright with pots of flowers. Things were better. His shadow skipped before him. He looked up at the windows with their faded and pierced shutters, wondering which room she slept in, on what white bed she stretched her dark limbs. The involuntary salute his body gave her, the flush of blood to the groin, elated him; but he walked on quickly to kill it. Deferred pleasure was usually no pleasure but, anticipating her, he had enjoyed four huskless dream-haunted nights: he had neither wanted nor needed the drug. He paused to look at the goods on display in the open-fronted shops. A horse hide belt from Zalcasia attracted him, but it was long enough for a giant. He examined inlaid brassware from Odalion, dusty books. Fruits and sticky sweets were laid out in patterns. On the fish stall the snappers and grobies gleamed silver, green, and rose. Outside the curio shop he opened a tiny inlaid box and sniffed at ghostly husk. The figurine of a Temple Dancer stood nearby. He picked her up. She was tiny, the height of his forefinger, her perfect detail modelled in porcelain, the glaze partially rubbed away. Her scarlet skirts were tight about her hips, belling outward to her bare feet, her silken scarves floated. Almost, he expected the bells on her costume to chime.

A thin old woman smiled at him as he held the little Dancer in the palm of his hand.

'That is Mayuna,' she said. 'She was the best in her day.'

'Want to buy?' The shopkeeper loomed over him, and he quickly put the Dancer down.

He entered a basket dealer's and paid five bits for a street sweeper's basket. At this time of year the waters of the Ayal, the western river where he was heading, yielded good pickings, the banks littered with debris brought down in the fast meltwater from Mount Bai and the Zalcasians. Anything he collected could be sold in the junkyards which bordered the Uynal and the lower Bania.

He left the last house behind him and, clambering over the decayed wall, came to an area of scrubland. This was the place where the City jettisoned her rubbish and smoky fires burned under the debris. He heard the laughter of the children who were scavenging there. In the distance before him, dark green trees defined the river's course. The road petered out, becoming a network of muddy tracks which led to squatter shacks, unlicensed brothels, drinking houses and cock pits. Every hillock was occupied by grazing goats; the vegetation at the roadside half concealed discarded bottles. He picked some of them up.

He made his way along a narrow track between the trees. The passing of the Red Wind had tattered the Alcuon leaves on the branches, but already the new growth was opening and some of the trees were in flower. Striped birds flitted from branch to branch. He jumped the twisted roots in his path; the tall basket bounced on his back and the bottles, which he had forgotten about, rang. He came to the river. To reach it, he had to climb along a branch and slide from it to the shore, startling a crested rat which was feeding on a fallen blossom. It scampered away.

The Ayal was wide. It was the wild canal which watered his parkland, and he was going hunting. The snowmelt had passed and the slow-moving waters glittered in the sun; he could just make out the low shapes of some Tlivoorn dwelling boats against the far bank. A rich man could expel such nomads from his land, or make friends with them. He dropped back into reality. He liked the Tlivoorn. Glaver was one.

The Tlivoorn were wandering boat dwellers, an annoyance to the Security Corps, who could only control them when the raised river waters allowed their patrol boats passage in Alcuon and Udan. Usually, the patrols were searching for fugitives who crossed the Ayal in both directions. The Tlivoorn traded in such passages; some desperate fugitives tried to cross alone.

A bright bundle of cotton rags on a mudbank was the decaying corpse of such a fugitive, and he hurried to pass it.

He dropped every useful article he found into the basket on his back: shoes, bottles, good garments, a complete wooden rake from one of the fruit gardens upstream. Other items were rejected: a shallow broken basket, the fragment of a flag torn by the Wind from the towers of City University, rotten pieces of fishing net. He found a long filmy scarf and rinsed it in the water. It had been washed downstream from the Mamelon gardens, the blue scarf of a Temple Dancer, exactly like the one he had recently admired on the figurine. He wound it round his neck to dry.

A dead monkey lay at the water's edge and he picked it up by the tail: monkey penises, excised and dried, were valuable. In the Quarter they were sold as charms, and quacks powdered them for sale as an aphrodisiac. The belly of this monkey had been eaten away by a sucker fish. As he looked at it, the sucker emerged from the rotting flesh and dropped at his feet. He flung the body away from him into the water. The sucker slithered after it, passing near his bare toes.

He heard the distant shouts of children, and presently came to a mooring of Tlivoorn dwelling boats, roped to the bank and to each other. Narrow planks made paths from boat to boat. Two of their light fishing boats were there but the rest, he knew, would be out in the bay. Naked brown children played in the water, shrieking and splashing each other. When they saw him, they crowded around, and their mothers and sisters, aunts and grandmothers, leaned chattering from the boats. Tlivoornal was a hissing, clattering language, full of sharp consonants and sibilants. As he had demonstrated to Glaver, he understood it fairly well, although he could not follow every hurrying word. The pretty women gestured towards him. Obviously their remarks concerned his appearance. He stood calf-deep in the yellow water, his shirt open, the blue scarf about his neck. Looking up at them, he guessed the words he did not know, imagining Glaver here. Their marals were loosely tied, without the wide hip band; some of them wore cotton slops like his.

At length one asked in Citycommons, 'What news?'

He spoke in their language of the closed days of the Red Wind and of the day of holiday before it when the City was alive and vibrant with enjoyment. They cried out and laughed, thinking he had understood all their words. One woman took the flower from her hair and threw it to him. He tucked it in his own hair. Again the women laughed, but they, who controlled the money and marketed the fish their men caught, did not ask him, an obvious Depther, to buy. An old woman handed him a sweet rice cake, and he ate it while the children pulled at his scarf and his basket, and one boy showed him an orange flapping fish which he had just caught.

He left them, following the river towards the sea, taking the eastern-most stream where the river entering the tidal flats, divided into many streams. The branch that flowed west disappeared into the tree-lined swamp to flow around the low headland where the bodies of every woman, Gynarch or Beggar, were broken on death. Men got the same treatment without the ritual; their deathground lay beyond the Domes. The structures were hidden from him by trees but he saw the circling and ever present kites and vultures riding the thermals at the edge of the land.

It grew hotter. He walked in the water. Soon he would be unable to walk long distances in the morning heat. The crescent bay was polished like a mirror and, far out, a Sineinian cornbulker lay at anchor, its vast sides and aerofoil sails silver, its flexible chute probing the interior of the smaller carrier which would bring the grain into the City. The fishing boats of the Tlivoorn were dwarfed beside it, their brown sails hanging limp. Out there the fish were feeding, and being drawn up in nets. Here, sand borers wriggled between his toes and the water covering his feet was warm and clear. He moved his toes and stirred up a cloud in the water.

A group of fishermen shouted to him as they drew clumps of oyfish and weed from the shallow water. He greeted them in return. A handful of the fat shells were cracked open and offered to him. He ate the liquid flesh eagerly, tipping it to the back of his mouth.

A long walk lay before him, three-quarters of the curve. The City was a far-off dream of coloured towers. He walked in the water again and, casting his basket high up the beach, went seaward until the shallow waters deepened and flowed about his thighs. He lay down, wetting his head, splashed, rolled, and swam out. Floating in the blue water, he watched the gulls soar.

The sun dried the clothes on him. When he had walked half the distance, he heard the clock on Citybank strike ten. He came to the wooden sheds of the City fisherwomen; several of them looked up, away from the gear they were preparing, at him. One of them whistled, two of them yelped. Their calling had given them huge muscular arms, their diet of fatty fish had increased their already stupendous waists. But he did not hurry away. He turned around and gave them a mouthful of invective in Deep.

Cal sat on the beach and counted the money he had made: eighteen bits. A long wooden jetty shaded him; it would be pleasant to read. He opened the most precious book in his tiny library, *The Travels of Huyatt Tayal*. 'I journeyed West for two days,' he read, 'and where the forest met the sea, I found a hut made of palm leaves. A white woman, like the face of Eshtur by day, sat outside it. She beckoned me.' He checked the horizon for threatening shapes, rolled under the jetty, pillowed his head on the book, and slept.

Long ago, he had learned the places in the City where food was to be had, where there was fresh water, shelter, and shade. The other pavement children relied on him. Then M'nah died and Swan came. He learned to pick pockets and look at his victims with devastating innocence. He learned what it was to shape his own life.

One day Swan brought home a bag of dirty linen. The ink-stained contents, linen handtowels, less useful than clothes, were washed and sold to a barber and, from the bag, Swan made him a shirt. It was vast and baggy and stencilled across the chest were the words 'City Archive LAUNDRY'. The garment kept him warm at night; any humour that might have been derived from the legend was mitigated by the child's sorrowful stare. Soon the boy was known in the Depths as Cal.

Swan died. He became his own master, hiding his grief (he was much older) in a passionate hunt for companions and food. For a time he rejoined the hosts of the pavement children until, finding them less adept than he at survival and thieving, he went to live alone and began to occupy his kingdom, the sewers and buried cellars beneath the City of Mahun. Climbing about the old and derelict manufactories on the east side, he discovered an elevated world of ruined towers. An old clock tower became his Vern residence; during Udan and the Death Days, he lived in the sewers.

When Cal was about nine years old, he found a book in a gutter, a book with a red cover and golden lettering on its spine, the book on which his head now rested. He sat in the gutter with the book, turning it this way and that, and assessing its value. He knew that books were important and perhaps held the secrets of life because the prices of new volumes in the big city stores were phenomenal: tens of frags.

The pages of the red book were crowded with symbols. There were no pictures. Inside the front cover was a row of symbols written in black ink.

A Lector passed by and, taking Cal for a Beggar child and because it was a holy day, stopped and bent over him, her blue gown surrounding her like folded wings. She spoke to him in Citycommons.

'Do you know what that is, child?' she asked and, without waiting for a reply, grabbed the book. Cal cowered.

'No, no,' said the Lector crossly. 'Look. This black writing says it belongs to Magon Nonpareil. He has been careless enough to lose it, so you may keep it. It is worth three bars.'

She handed him the book.

'Aren't you a lucky boy?' continued the Lector, slipping into her customary Maralay without a pause. 'That book is about a great man's travels – Huyatt, one of the Tayal. It is well done; some of it is true.'

'True man book,' repeated Cal in Citycommons.

The Lector stared. Her brow creased. He had repeated three words from her speech in his own dialect; these words had roots in common. Curious. Or coincidence. Her subject was Comparative Language.

'Come,' she said suddenly, grasping his arm with the same sweeping movement with which she had first taken the book. 'I hope you are free of lice.'

He resented the slur: did he not swim in the clear blue sea; did he not buy a bath when he was in funds? But he went with her, because she had the key he wanted.

She led him to a hot drinks stall and, seating him on one of the high tables before it, plied him with sticky cakes and hot honeyed bohea. He was full, he was warm – in cool Alcuon breezes from Zalcasia tempered the air to a mean sixty degrees – he was grateful. The Lector, for her part, was fascinated by the thin boy. She looked at him. His eyes were the colour of the yellow river mud; his hair was mudlike, brown and greasy. He stared back at her, his gaze accusing and acute. She wished that even two per cent of her students were as intelligent; she wanted to take him home so that she could measure his IR. The little beggar boy learned as others eat, hungrily, and with a good digestion. In the short time – perhaps three hours – of their acquaintance he had learned the basic grammar of Maralay and a certain amount of the vocabulary, also the thirty letters and most of the sound combinations required to read his book. (But he would sell the book, and be unable to use the language among his illiterate peers who spoke only Deep, the dialect of the lowest classes, and Citycommons.)

'You are extremely bright. Quite amazing,' said the Lector, finishing her bohea. She had given alms on a holy day, she had some material for an article in a learned journal, she had amused herself by allowing an expensive book to continue its downward journey: nothing more could be done. The child was a Beggar. Cal, seeing the finality of her last sip, the way she wiped her mouth on a lacy cloth, smiled.

'Goodbye,' he said, in the high language.

'Goodbye, my clever lad,' she replied. 'Look – take these.'

She gave him a handful of coins. She wiped her mouth again and walked rapidly away.

Cal remained, clutching the book and the money. He opened his hand: one bar, five frags and five bits. Yes! And he was 'extremely bright'. The Lector had a clipped tone and rolled her 'r's.

'Extrrremely bright,' he said aloud in her accents, and went to buy another cake.

The stallholder had been watching the small drama.

'Ain't you done well?' he said. 'Must be your lucky day.'

He gave Cal two cakes for the price of one.

Cal sat down, opened his book, smoothed out the sheet of paper the Lector had written the alphabet on, and began to learn to read. The first word he deciphered was strange to him: 'elephant', which he chose because of its irregular shape on the page. Then he slowly unravelled the meaning of the nearby words, discovering that the elephant was an animal and reading about its huge size and marvellous moveable nose. He found a tiger in the next paragraph, read of its stripes and teeth and was sorry that the man Huyatt had found it necessary to kill the tiger. He read of the mandrill, thinking of it as a kind of man, like those about him, like himself, and read on, growing puzzled.

In the afternoon he went away and hid the book in one of his lairs where he took great care of it, wrapping it in a news-sheet, and storing it as if it were precious food; in time he had read it all, even those parts which he was too young to understand.

For some weeks after his encounter with the Lector, Cal frequented that part of the City. He followed several blue-gowned figures to the gates of the University but he did not see her again. Most of her gift of money had to be spent on food, but he kept three frags, hiding them away with the book, and he carried them three years later when, on a stall, he saw a broken-backed book called *Languages High and Low*. It had been a student's primer and a scent of flowers rose faintly as he turned the pages. The author was V. Tain. He read the preface hearing the rolling 'r's and precise vowel sounds of his Lector as he read.

The rudiments of language are soon grasped: at the nurse's knee, in the mother's study, at play with other infants. The student passes to higher matters, to Initiation, to Examination, to Matriculation. She succeeds; perhaps she excels. She enters University. She is

33

familiar with many a technicality; within her own discipline she may become a neologist. She begins to be educated.

With her fellows she uses another language: the vernacular of the young woman. It is a language which follows fashions and is soon outdated and unintelligible.

This volume is dedicated to her, for she will need to be a skilful communicator when she leaves the sheltering towers of her foster mother. It may also be of interest to those who are studying Comparatives in our City.

V. Tain, M.L., D.P., SSc., C.Soc.Lex.,
Lector Comp. Lang., City University

Cal paid two bits for it.

By this time he had read and reread Huyatt Tayal's book of traveller's tales, besides every news-sheet, official and underground, he happened on, and every hoarding, package, sign, placard, public notice, and advertisement in the City. He had dared the forbidding entrance of the central library and found it a haven, quiet and cool, discovering that the Beggars, too, knew this. The anterooms were filled with sleepers. He roamed its peaceful halls and explored its tall shelves, devouring chunks of text at random. Three times, finding himself alone amid the book-shelves, he had torn pages from books, augmenting his own library with an account of the founding of the City, a description of the Tayaal by a traveller from Maralis and a wad of erotica from a salacious novel. By imitation he had taught himself to write, somewhat awkwardly and untidily, but with speed and verve. He found new employment in reading to Beggars, who paid him in food or favours, and in filling in official forms for illiterate Artisans or applications for trading permits for stallholders. By now he knew certain Travellers well, and was permitted to learn their language. He delighted in their songs and learned some of them, imitating their wailing voices and adult gestures. He learned their dances and gave his own performances at their firesides, moving his supple child's body in the exaggerated rhythms.

In City Library, he read Mahun's Law. There, too, he found dictionaries and books in the languages of the provinces and the client states, and he learned, without much difficulty, to read them, practising his new skill on any visitor he happened to meet. He dreamed of distant lands and Huyatt's book was his constant companion. He grew, but not tall, and Tarla mothered him when she had time. When he was fourteen, she collected money from her friends and, after a ceremonial dose of rahi, they sent him in to study life with Zalcissa.

He lounged under the jetty and read Huyatt's story of the Blue Falcon. Huyatt had caught and manned the bird when he travelled in Vern and she had taken the golden-eyed cat from which Huyatt obtained his magic

34

Ring. Despite his knowledge of the Depths, of human avarice and misery, Cal had believed this tale of Huyatt; only lately had he begun to ask questions of it. Its fantastic events fascinated him. He began to play with the text, to regard the Blue Falcon as Reality, perhaps, and the cat as Fiction; the Ring might be Truth or Reason.

Huyatt had made his journey three hundred years ago. In the City a post-technological Silver Age was beginning but in the Tayaal, a thousand miles away, people lived as they had always done, in stone houses amongst the rocks, by hunting with bird and dog. The Tayali worshipped Mahun, and yet their society was dominated by men. The concept worried Cal until he thought of the Faces. Tayali women made fine embroideries, and these were still sold at the Alcuon market in Maralis; but they were costly.

Huyatt was a cultured man, a falconer and an archer, a musician and a poet. He was rich enough to have two wives; but he left them both to go journeying, taking with him his favourite falcon, Sarak, and his best horse, the white mare Alna.

His travels occupied many years, yet he did not seem to age. They told of his journeys by sea and by land, his exploits in the mountains, his capture by and escape from pirates, his visit to the City, his hunting of the leopard and the tiger, his sojourn in Evanul, his meeting with Balkiss, their love, their idyll, and their parting. When Huyatt came home no one scolded him for being absent for ten years; his wives served up the evening meal as if he had just come in from the hunt.

He closed the book. It was mid-afternoon; children were running on the hot sand, chasing each other into the shallows, and men and boys were flying kites, multicoloured wings, high above the blue water. The ships in the roads awaited the tide.

He opened the book's cover. The black characters had not faded: Magon Nonpareil. He studied the two words, the precision of the pen strokes, the elegant letters. Taking a pen from his pocket, he wrote his own name underneath, with a flourish: Cal. It was a mean signature so he gave himself a surname and wrote it there: Citizen. He put the book in his pocket.

Leaving the beach, he walked gingerly on the hot stones of the promenade. The slack time and tide were propitious. He could make his way to the tower through the shipyards. At the last set of steps he went down again, on to the shore, and made his way across the broken land on the margins of the Uynal. The tide was turning; soon salt water would sweep inland, reversing the flow of the rivers while it ran, washing the yellow silt back towards the land.

Cal turned inland, paddling across the river, across the yielding mud itself, succulent and oozing under the shallow water. He looked up. Arbitration Bridge loomed, a huge structure of steel girders, which pivoted to allow ships into the river. Below it the river ran in a deep trench walled with stone. Dwarfed, he followed the wall until he came to a stair. Halfway up, an arch led to a small chamber. He never looked into it for fear of what, debris of the river, he might see but passed through a doorway beside it and climbed weed-covered steps. He emerged in a derelict building at the edge of the shipyards.

The place was still in the heat. The men were drinking bohea in their rest huts and one of the forewomen lay asleep by the water, her legs spread wide. The idling steam engines hissed.

A wooden ship was under construction in the nearest dry dock. He walked in its shadow and slowly threaded his way between great basins full of green water, his shadow extending over the brick surround. A pair of rose-winged gulls were courting on one basin, raising their wings to each other. A salt-water rat sat boldly nibbling its catch.

Cal walked unchallenged from the open shipyard gate, lifting his hand to the gateguard who tilted her wooden chair in the shade, her eyes on a news-sheet.

The landward side of the docklands abutted the old industrial area, disused, now the haunt of the Fists. A Fister sunned himself in a doorway, his leathers unbuckled; he grinned at Cal and sucked on his weed. The smoky tang of it reminded Cal of husk; he thought of the Quarter and of the knifethrower, and in his mind the night took shape.

B ANTS EADS O ISS he read. He had often tried to reconstruct the ancient message from its cryptic remains. Behind the broken metal billboard lay a wasteland. He crossed cinders and broken glass. A thousand golden dandelions shone there, the lilies of his paradise. He avoided them, padding in the shadow of a broken wall; a striped cat turned its head to regard him; he climbed through an empty window-frame and ascended half a stairway. Passing, on charred beams, old hearths suspended in mid-air, he slid in through the annular window of a ruinous chantry, and found his desert inhabited.

Holiness smote him. He looked down from his perch on the high sill and saw a group of men heretically at prayer.

The sacred central circle had been desecrated by a line drawn across it in paint. A table had been placed there. The men surrounded the table and a priest, for such he must be, spoke to them. A glass chalice stood on the table, a holy book, and an unshaded lamp from which a flame sprang high.

Most of the men wore their street clothes; one or two of the older ones had on grey robes. They were absorbed in the ritual. A little way behind them stood a tall man, the man from *Daystar*. His dark hair moved in the breath of air which crept through the broken windows. He, too, was intent on the ritual.

The old chantry still had 'Pray for the Soul of Hibornal na M'un' in blue and gold across its vaulted ceiling, but the statues of Mahun, excepting one headless figure affixed to the wall, had been removed when the doors were locked long ago.

The priest lifted the chalice of water and chanted a prayer.

'Lord of the Skies, Master of the Four Winds, Monos, we greet thee.'

With ceremony, he handed the chalice to the first worshipper, who drank. The water passed among the worshippers, the dark man taking the last draught.

Frowning, Cal watched him for a while: prayer had washed the cynicism from him and his face was that of an ascetic, if a man could be such a thing. Cal swung up and out of the window, forced by the new presence to climb the chantry's outside wall. He crossed the roof, a girder, a parapet, and dropped into the tower room, annoyed to find himself trembling.

The base of Cal's tower had been part of a dyeworks. It was bricked up below and shuttered, but the high tower top was a clockroom, empty now of sound, full of the rusty clock mechanism and its double dial. There was no way up except by his aerial route. The stair hole, to one side of the room, opened above giddy darkness, and he had covered it with a board. Here he was lord of all and could watch the clouds form about the distant Baian range; the Zalcasians, beyond them, would – had he the eyes of the clouds – be grey spikes, hard and inaccessible towers of rock. Kites soared, spiralling upward above the heart of the City, feral pigeons flew below him, and the hunt, stoop, and kill of the bat falcons which nested on the building opposite was his entertainment. The chittering cloud of swifts mounted upward, far above the tower tops.

The tower had four windows, beside its two clock faces; an ornate stone balcony surrounded its pointed roof but it looked unsafe and he had never tried it. From the seaward windows he could survey the ocean and the south; from the landward, the City. Cal looked out.

Left and westward, on a low hill about two miles inland, stood the towers of City University, black granite pinnacled in gold. Today, red pennants flew. He did not know what they announced, but had observed that they differed every day. There were six towers, and he wondered briefly which housed Lector Tain.

Beyond the University and also on a low hill, he saw the enclave of the Gynarchs, five blue towers irregularly placed about the white dome of the Temple and the golden dome of the Mamelon. At this distance, moments before the sun dropped into the trees, the blues began to merge with the darkening sky and their fine lines melted behind the stark frame of the black towers. The juxtaposition of the black towers of Learning and the blue of Faith was a sight many, including Huyatt, had travelled from afar to behold, and it was the favourite subject of the City's painter, Crinon M'una.

The outpourings of the manufactories and foundries in the west

37

contributed to the haze; a jumble of low buildings and tall chimneys, they lay in their own enclosure and the dull gleam of two ditches intersected the area. Directly before and below Cal the chaos of the old manufacturing quarter gave way to the conical roofs of the Pleasure Quarter pavilions, their gaudy colours muted. Beyond Broadwalk lay the Fairground; the brownstone bulks of the Law Courts and the House of the Mark stood on Broadwalk with grey Citybank and the Block. The Lily Exchange glowed, white marble and glass. Newer buildings east of these were housing for the well-to-do, streets of shops and the Glass Mall.

The Uynal bisected the City and a wide canal, the Bania, separated Space Park, its gardens, and the western beaches from closely packed buildings. On this side of the City, the sluggish waters of the Ayal took the place of the Wall.

The swifts dived below him and vanished inside the tower.

All was darkness beyond the Wall, where lay the market gardens and the dairies which daily supplied the City.

A third hill, Mahun's Belly, commonly Paradise Hill, in the east, carried the Octagon and the soaring white palaces of the Matriarchy, their feet hidden in a dense growth of trees. From these might issue Bella and her transformed beast, Mahun's sister, pale Eshtur, or dark Balkiss herself. Silver cars dangling from a high wire floated towards the hill. A precipitous outcrop guarded the hill, the old citadel atop it. The first lights to show in the City sprang up, the arclamps which surrounded the great Octagon of the Archive. The lights of the Pleasure Quarter were the next to appear, multicoloured. He recalled the crude joke which asked its hearer the difference between the women of Paradise Street and Paradise Hill.

Cal went to the ledge where he kept food and took down a saffron bun, speciality of the tinsmiths' bakeries out at Worldsend. It was stale, and he chewed it thoughtfully, staring from the seaward window.

The tide was high, filling the trench below Arbitration Bridge, where he had recently walked. Even in the gloom, the stain of the Uynal's burden was clear, a bar dividing the crescent bay. West Beach was dark now, but lights on the private east beaches marked bathing belvederes, each sheltering a damp Matriarch and her daughters, returned from their evening bathe. For a moment he thought of them as naked wet women and not as hierarchs.

The sun had declined, its red rim just visible in the west. He would sleep now and wake at midnight.

Waking, he heard the changed sounds of the City at night: the constant insect song from the gardens and waste places, the voice of a fruit hawker, music, the braying of the temple trumpets marking the hour of prayer. A pack of prowldogs bayed.

He equipped himself, changing his clothes and taking his money, his

38

torch and, an afterthought, his *vade mecum*, the book of Huyatt Tayal. The enamelled tree hung around his neck. He descended, careful in the dark, relieved to see no glimmer of light from the windows of the chantry. He climbed through the round window and shone his light along a ledge.

Wide and safe, it was a convenient path between two windows. To step on to it he had to swing around the headless image of Mahun, and usually he touched her raised hand in passing for luck. The torch slipped from his grasp and fell to the floor.

'Mahun,' he said aloud. He would have to jump down to retrieve it, or leave it. It was valuable. He stepped forward and down on to the broad sheaf of wheat the Lady held under her left arm. The torch had rolled into the central fane: he saw its beam illuminating red tesserae. He peered into the gloom, looking for a place to land.

A beam of white light dazzled him. He put a hand to his eyes, trying to see from behind the lattice of his fingers who stood below.

'Come down.' The voice was commanding but it did not have the parade-ground bark of a camel. It was cultured.

Cal panicked. Edging backwards, he attempted to regain the ledge. The light advanced and a hand gripped his ankle.

For a moment they struggled, Cal resisting and the hand below gripping his ankle, threatening his balance. Tugged from his perch, he fell into the arms of the dark-haired worshipper. He aimed a clumsy boy's punch at the handsome face, but it was intercepted and he was forced back against the wall.

'I mean you no harm,' said the man. 'But I am curious about who disturbs my peace, a thief perhaps, but there is nothing to steal, or a pickpocket looking for a haven in which to count his takings.' He released Cal. 'What are you doing here?'

'Mind your own business.'

The man grasped his left arm and, pulling back the sleeve, bared his Markless flesh.

'I'm a Traveller,' lied Cal. The man changed his grip and bared Cal's right arm.

'I see. And you have no Mark and no papers. Inconvenient.' He released Cal again. 'On your way.'

Cal stood up. The stranger was a powerful man. He was dressed in the best and wore two rings, both gold, one with a great carved stone. Conscious of his sardonic gaze, Cal retrieved the torch, shone it upward, looking for a foothold.

'The door is open,' said the stranger. 'Farewell.'

Outside in the street, Cal suffered a reaction. His legs gave way and he sat in the gutter. He wondered why Mahun was angry with him, and muttered one of the five Apologies.

The street was dark and silent. He took one of the alleys which led

39

from it into a lighted shopping street. On Citadel Street, many of the shops and all the cafés and bars were open; citizens strolled in the cool night air, an emerging crowd of theatregoers filled the pavement. There were no Ironmen. He rounded the corner and entered Broadwalk, stepping into the roadway so that he could grab and hang from the back of a market cart loaded with fruit. As it approached the long slope leading to the fruit market and, ultimately, Temple Hill, he dropped off and turned into the Fairground.

The Shack was nothing more than a huge pavilion, its roof a canvas rainbow, its walls sectional boards on which were painted the disgraced companions of Mahun, the creatures and spirits whose existence had been denied at the Reformation. He saw Garissa, the Elephant of Plenty; Sailsh with her splayed legs and inviting bush; the red and evil Tycee, bringer of storms.

'It's a private party.' A bruiser in evening dress stopped him at the entrance.

'I'm invited.' He produced the card Glaver had given him, and was admitted. Someone offered him a bottle of rahi and a glass. He refused the glass and took the bottle, drinking two, three, doses, until the naked girl dancing in the ring assumed a pleasant perspective.

Dog and the Bitch were there, amid a crowd of Faces and Fists. They loudly applauded the dancer. Tumbling from hands to feet and cart-wheeling back to hands again, Meleager entered the ring. Cal half watched the old and classic act. The white-faced clown was merry and sad by turns; he sang a plaintive song and was abused by the augustes. A group of Rosies sat together; the red spun sugar they sucked seemed a proper food for such vampires, like crystalline blood. He recognised Morn in her tight pale gown, and Luce with her rosebud mouth and yellow curls. A man was stripping in the ring, peeling off a trooper's uniform to strident drumbeats. He looked ridiculous, strutting and exercising his muscle while the music played, but the women screamed and clapped. On a bench below him Cal saw the transformed Dork, Pulchrinella, seductive in a gold and white maral, stand up and scream, 'Encore!'

A silver trapeze descended, and the gymnast, stepping on to it, became an acrobat. Elevated in the spotlight, he was a thing of beauty, hurling bone and sinew from bar to narrow bar. Cal, tilting the bottle, gazed upward to see him fly. Near him a woman folded husk; he smelt its smoky smell. He glanced at her, but she was too big for him. The acrobat spun in space.

No act could follow his, and the ring filled as guests met there to take drinks and husk. Malkin stood in the orchestra to sing. He watched her toss her mane of hair.

Trumpeters cleared the ring and silenced Malkin. Enveloped in a white cloak, Miel came on to set the stage. He put up the targets, scarred from the thud of Glaver's knives, placed her table, set out her broad and shining blades. Taking up one of these, he opened his cloak and drew the knife across his chest. A bloody furrow appeared and the audience howled; spinning like a top Miel displayed his cut.

'Shiron!'

She walked into the centre of the ring. She had freed her hair. Her breasts were bare, the brown flesh pressing against a bandolier of sheathed knives. Luce stood up, clasping her hands together; Cal put down his rahi bottle.

The knifethrower turned about, acknowledging the applause. Taking a blade from the bandolier, she drew it contrawise across Miel's chest, marking him with a scarlet cross.

Glaver began to fling knives. She filled a board with them, hitting the animals drawn there dead centre. She cut paper and cloth. Miel placed cigars and cigarettes, diminishing in size, between his lips, and she cleaved the cylinders in two.

The drums signalled the climax of her act. Spreadeagled against a board, Miel turned his face aside and closed his pale-lidded eyes. Glaver picked up a ribbon and slowly made much of tying back her hair. She took hold of the first knife. It sank quivering beside the hooked nose. The blades flew, outlining him in steel. The last knife thudded, pinning his loincloth to the board. Gracefully, he divested himself, stepping from his silhouette and leaving the white cloth impaled. As one, the audience sighed, and burst into applause. The knifethrower took her bow: hers was the ultimate performance.

Then came dancing for all and the ring became crowded. Cal rubbed his eyes. The rahi, the entertainments, the encounter in the dark chantry conspired to exhaust him. He wanted husk.

But Glaver was moving through the crowd. The Rosy, Luce, behind her pushed at unyielding bodies so that she could grasp and enfold Glaver and cover her face and neck with hungry kisses. There was a swift scurry of movement; he saw the Rosy's face contort in pain. Glaver moved on. She came to him and sat beside him, her thigh against his. He reached out and touched the cloth which covered it.

'I have your knife,' she said. She took it from her belt and folded his fingers about its hilt. 'This is how you use it. This is how you thrust.'

They laughed and he put his hand inside her jacket and his tongue inside her mouth. She had not resumed her armour.

The Rosy fell on him like a cat, biting and clawing. The knife was on his knees; he gripped it and pushed. Luce screamed and fell over, her pink mouth gaping. He looked down. The cloth of her dress was impacted by his knife into a spreading bloodstain, the shiny blade and steel hilt an absurd ornament in her breast. He looked at Glaver: the

41

Rosy's blood ran down her arm, across her wrist, dripped from the ends of her fingers.

She screamed at him.

'Run, you arsehole, run!'

He obeyed her, dodging the party guests. Outside, in the dark, he fell his length over guy-ropes. Men and women were shouting.

Cal went silently in the shadows, but once on the lighted Broadwalk he had to run, pounding like an athlete down the centre of the road. Carts and shays passed him. Someone called out, 'Seen a ghost, mate?' He came to Citybank and turned into an alley. Here was concealment and darkness once more; he leaned against a wall and panted. He spoke another of the five Apologies to Mahun. In his mind's eye he saw Tarla, fat and white, soft and comforting. She smelled of husk. He breathed deeply until he was calm; he walked on.

Cal entered the Pleasure Quarter. By night the place became enchanted. The streets were hung with coloured lights and a bright flare burned outside each pavilion unless its proprietor was inside plying the trade. Those awaiting clients sat outside; a few wore transparent garments, but most were draped in sleeveless silk or satin cymars, relying on the paintings outside each booth to attract custom. They idled and gossiped like Hill people. A group of drakes stood talking at the entrance to Paradise Street. Cal could not discern their gender beneath the androgynous clothing, nor did they attempt to detain him for they recognised the slouching haste of one in search of husk.

Tarla was not outside her pavilion and her light was doused. He waited, listening with amusement to the sounds of exertion from within, and to the screams of the cockatoo, until a man emerged and hurried away. Lifting the doorflap, he entered the pavilion. The bed was neat and Tarla was feeding Tifon with nuts, which the bird took in a claw and nibbled at.

'You!' she said grumpily. 'I've got a living to earn, belly of Mahun!'

'You've been fighting, boy. Look at your face.'

He glanced in the nearest mirror. Claw marks and bites crisscrossed his chin.

'Rosy marks,' said Tarla. 'Who was it? Luce?'

He nodded.

'She's a cow, that one,' said Tarla as she put away the bag of birdseed. 'What were you doing to fall foul of her?'

He told her, and she chuckled and patted his cheek when he related Glaver's part in the tale. He looked at his hands. The left hand, which had caressed the knifethrower's satin skin, was clean, the strong familiar fingers exactly what they always were, his to use. He put the hand to his nose and smelled the perfume with which Glaver must have anointed

42

herself before she came to him. On the palm of the right hand, the one which had wielded the knife, was a smear of the Rosy's blood. Both hands trembled and he held them out before Tarla as if he hoped she could remove the stain.

The old woman wiped his hands and held the sponge against his hot face. He looked at her through a haze; she made him lie on the bed and brewed bohea. When he had drunk a beakerful, he recovered.

'Poor dear,' said Tarla, fussing with the sponge.

He told Tarla how he had run through the streets and waited until her client left. And then, because he needed to master his environment once again, he told her how he had outfaced and outwitted Stoker. He told her about the Rat Queen: she invoked Mahun. He showed her the Tree he had found beneath the City: she blessed herself and muttered a prayer. He told her of the marklice and the pursuit in the metro, of the beauties of *Daystar* and of the old men who prayed to Monos, but of the common factor in these two disparate locations, the dark-haired man who had pulled him from the ledge, he said nothing. Tarla was too fond of invoking fate and drawing ominous conclusions; he believed in her powers of second sight and was afraid of them.

'There are several congregations of Monoclid heretics in the City,' said Tarla. 'A whore hears things. Strife will come out of it.'

'But,' he said, a theological paradox striking him, 'Mahun must want it so.'

'Who knows? Who knows the soul's secrets but Mahun?'

He lay still and looked at the pavilion roof. The canvas stirred slightly, its once bright hue faded and stained by the rains. He heard Tarla counting her takings.

'I need husk. I've needed it for days,' he said presently. 'I can pay.'

She grunted. 'Why don't you go to Jakes?'

'Because, dear Tarla,' he caught her hand as she passed the bed, 'he mixes bran with his husk, but I know that yours comes from Toomy in the depot.'

'What if I haven't any?'

'You've never failed me.'

The old woman smiled. She sat down at her table and shuffled in the upholstered chair until she was comfortable. He got up and put his arm round her. Now she would do it.

'Deal me the Cards, Tarla.'

'Well, well.' She tugged a lock of his hair. 'Even wild boys grow cautious.'

The old woman opened a drawer in the table and extracted a tin box, her tarot pack, and a framed photograph from its crammed interior.

'Me when I was young. When I had Tifon,' she said.

He had seen the photograph many times, but he never failed to study it and to compliment her. It showed Tarla in a coy pose, her generous body not much hidden by a gauzy cymar, her scarlet Prostitute's Mark seeming, like her lips, to glow with promises.

'You were beautiful,' he said. 'Like a ripe mango,' he added, amused at his easy flattery.

Tarla laughed. 'And now you've got yourself in Tarla's good books, I suppose you're expecting a free fold?'

He shook his head and gave her two frags in exchange for a paper of husk from the tin box.

'The stuff of dreams,' she said. 'I will deal and, afterwards, you can lie on the bed and fly where you will.'

She laid the card pack face down in the centre of the table and shuffled it with a circular movement of her right hand. Then, taking up the cards, she began to deal, laying down four cards in the shape of a cross. Her Depthside accent disappeared and she began to speak in a monotonous drawl.

'I use this draw,' she said, 'because it is the Beggar's Draw and the Tree has come into your hand.'

The backs of the cards were printed with a design showing Shelda, the sun, supported by Mahun, and by her sister Eshtur, the moon. Tarla turned up the first card and revealed an old woman with lantern and stick; the second showed Shelda in her glory; the third, a naked man with cap and bells; and the fourth, a proud woman with a lion. Tarla studied the four cards and, riffling through the pack, took out a fifth. It showed a queen riding in a triumphal chariot.

'Prudence. Happiness. Inconsistency. Trust. With Triumph. He has many gifts. He is bold, intelligent, violent maybe. He will be disappointed in love, be in danger, fail. Now he is vital, in good health; but he will sicken. He will live a long time. . . .' She picked up the chariot again, muttering, 'Change, change,' and came out of her oracular trance. He thought the reading could apply to many; she, troubled, said she could only see generalities, nothing specific. She scooped up the cards, and returned them to the pack.

Cal opened the fold of husk. The powder fell from the creased paper to the back of his throat and he closed his eyes and breathed deeply, already feeling as though he floated.

'Come. On the bed.' Tarla led him there, and he stretched his limbs, on the wing. His body stopped floating upward, he began to dive and wheel; he became a swift. He dived through space, through galaxies and nebulae, through a mesh of dark hair in which he struggled, shedding feathers, moulting his wings, dissolving.

He awoke weak, wanting to vomit and with a foul mouth. Languidly, he observed that he was naked under the bedsheet and supposed that Tarla had used him. Memories of his dreaming returned to him, of the woman in the photograph, of dark curling hair and strong hands, of Glaver, of the stars. His head ached.

Tarla, dressed now in a wrapper of red velveret, threw him his clothes. She made bohea and they drank the hot and bitter brew, their talk of no consequence. At daybreak she sent him away, and he walked slowly through the muted streets of the Pleasure Quarter, blinking in the new daylight.

He looked about for Rosies as he walked, careless now, the pain in his head his only concern. The light grew strong; too strong for the she-cats and too strong for his weak head. He shaded his eyes: the last sated clients were leaving the pavilions.

Cal passed into Cat Street; some of the boys were playing fivestones in the dust. He stopped and spoke to Dromio, complaining of his head. Dromio laughed and recommended food, showing the handful of money he had made in the night.

'I'm eating at Tyler's when he opens,' he said. 'Come with me. I had a good night.'

Cal shook his head, instantly regretting the movement.

'I want to throw up,' he said. 'Sooner or later.'

He walked on, carefully, the motion interfering with his equilibrium. A red pavilion marked the end of Cat Street. It belonged to the exquisite, Achille, who was known to model on Palace Hill for the sculptor Amarant. A painting of Achille in the guise of Erotic Love hung in City Hall and his stone image was part of the spectacular fountain in the beach gardens, pinned face down beneath the waterfall. As Cal passed the red pavilion, a man stepped from it on to the street. Cal watched him retreat into the distance. The broad shoulders were hunched and tense. It was the heretic. So, ho – but his head ached too much to permit him to figure out the puzzle.

Cal went into the bath house and spent five bits on cleansing himself. He dried his hair on the damp and threadbare towel, filled his mouth with clean water and spat into the drain. Still his head throbbed and nausea washed over him.

He came to a metro entrance and went down into the dark. The dim white lights in the passageways echoed the nebulae in his head. He walked in the labyrinth of corridors, hearing hollow footfalls and the faraway trains. The mosaics on the walls were crumbling and defaced, hoardings and boards covered the worst holes.

When the train arrived, he fell into a carriage and rested his head on his hands. He sat there hour by hour while the metro rumbled around its circular route: Quarter End, Space Park, Arcade, Broadwalk, Bank, Mall, Globe, Quarter, Quarter End again. No one regarded him: many others slept on the Ring, not a few lived there permanently. He dozed

45

under the permanent sun in his head, seeing the nebulae, the women, and, always, the dark curls.

At length the sun turned black and extinguished itself in a blaze of roaring. His ears popped and rang, while nausea gathered itself in a tight ball, crouching in his belly. He fell against the window glass and vomited brown bile.

'Bloody Husker,' said the man next to him, shifting away. No one else moved and Cal, snoring, travelled another four circuits of the Ring. Between Broadwalk and Mall the train stopped, silent, dark. Another breakdown. The passengers, resigned to the frequent breakdowns, hardly moved. Eventually the train began to hum and judder and moved forward to stop at Mall station.

He awoke with a jolt. The platform was brightly lit and crowded. He saw the white uniforms of the security corps and marklice everywhere; chaser dogs were being held on tight leashes. The camels entered the train and began to move along its length, evicting the passengers on to the platform. There was nowhere to go. He stumbled forward in the crowd and as he looked wildly around, still dazed from the drug, an overseer grabbed his arm and roughly pulled back his sleeve.

'Just come ashore, have we?'

Cal's tongue came out to wet his dry lips. He nodded.

'Other arm.' It was grasped. 'And still nothing. Don't you know the port regulations?

'Or swum ashore, is it? Jumped ship?'

Cal nodded again.

'Madam,' the overseer shouted to an officer. 'Another one here.'

She walked briskly, her smart white shoes tapping on the platform. 'Sailor?'

He nodded for the third time; speech could betray his City origins.

'These merchant fleeters. Why don't they obey the Law, Sergeant?' she complained.

'Says he's jumped ship, Ma'am.'

She took hold of him herself. Odd to see the bright unchipped lacquer on her nails. He thought of kicking, but she was propelling him towards a windowless, white kiosk, and two of her women had fallen in behind. He rehearsed the story he would tell.

Inside the kiosk stood a desk with a pile of charge sheets and a pen on it. The officer sat on the only chair. The two troopers forced him to kneel on the spotless white floor and held him there.

The officer read him the regulations in three languages.

' "It is the Law in the City of Mahun that all citizens bear the Mark of the appropriate Class and Rank where this is also appropriate. There are no exemptions.

' "Every person entering the City to trade, to study, for recreation or for whatever purpose shall be at the point of entry marked with a secondary Mark on the right arm. In the case of sailors a secondary Mark is to be applied by the ship's captain or his agent, using the dyes supplied by the Archivist of the City of Mahun. Regular visitors may apply for a tertiary Mark.

' "It is a capital offence to evade this Law or to forge or attempt to forge any Mark. In the case of foreign nationals the sentence may be commuted to transportation to a penal colony and release (dependent on good behaviour) in six months.

' "You are required to answer any charge made by the officer reading these regulations. She or her subordinates may use force to obtain an answer. Silence in the face of interrogation may be interpreted as guilt. You may ask for an arbiter if a charge is preferred by the officer." '

The officer took up the pen and poised it.

'Do you understand Citycommons?' she asked.

He nodded.

'Do you understand Maralay?'

He shook his head.

'You are a male?' A nod.

'You are a sailor?' A nod.

'Name?'

'Ennal T'or,' he lied.

'Age?'

'Eighteen.'

'Ship?'

'*S.V. Telvar.*' He had seen the coaster yesterday afternoon, lying at anchor in the roads.

'Cargo?'

'Timber in, cotton and damask out.'

'Home port?'

'Taimiss in Vern.' He had read these details in Dog's news-sheet. So far so good.

She laid down the pen and looked directly at him. His shoulders were growing numb from the pressure of the troopers' hands.

'Well, Seaman T'or,' she said. 'You will be glad to know that the *Telvar* sailed on the tide this morning. So you are free of her.

'Are you married?'

'No.'

'That is fortunate. No grieving wife, small children, unpaid debts. When did you last fold husk?'

'Last time I was in City. Five months ago.'

'Your pupils are still dilated. Bad try.'

'Last night.'

47

'Good. As you know, it is an entirely legal substance here. Why did you jump ship?'

'Couldn't stand the conditions. Not enough food. And I'd only signed on to Odalion.' He gave her some lurid details of rats, flour weevils, and shipboard sex to support his story. It was a fascinating tale, and she listened appreciatively until he had finished.

'Right, Seaman T'or. I want to search you.'

The troopers took his shirt off. She glanced briefly at his torso, came over and minutely examined his hands and arms. One of the troopers took away his possessions, money, book, Tree, knife, and piled the objects neatly on the desk. The officer tilted his head, pushing the hair out of his eyes with a cool manicured hand, and examined each eye. 'Open your mouth.' By the thin light of a pencil torch she studied the inside of his mouth and his tongue.

'Had a lot, didn't you?'

He nodded, tongue out.

'Been in a fight?' Her voice was soft and cynical. 'Rosies don't usually leave money behind; but maybe you satisfied her?'

'All right. Subs.' They gave him back his shirt. 'At the prison you get a full body search.' She went back to the desk. 'I am going to charge you, Mr Fascinating T'or; your trial should make extraordinary precedent.' She picked up the pen, writing as she spoke the charge.

' "I, Hyason Sarin M'unah, charge you, Ennal T'or, alias – name or names as yet unknown – with the first degree crime of residing in the City of Mahun for eighteen years without being Marked or seeking to be Marked. Other charges may subsequently be preferred." '

'You have a beautiful body and an exciting voice.' She stared at him. Her eyes were blue, her blonde lashes blackened with dye. 'And you have a Depthside accent, however you try to disguise it. I nearly believed you.'

'By the way.' She screwed the lid tight on her pen. 'Sailors never read literature.'

One of the troopers took the handgrips from his belt and locked them on Cal's hands, securing the chain that ran from them to his partner's steel wristband. They led Cal out and put him with the other lawbreakers they had caught.

M'untal's Tale

1 Lilb in Vern, 486

Today, the first holy day of the dek, she was four years old. She could not yet write her name, but she knew it. She was Mahuntal Kiden M'una. Her mother's name was Malajide and her father was called Olthar Oyno. He was a soldier in a country called Cheron. Sometimes, he came to see her and brought her presents; today, because he could not come, he had sent her a belt of silver bells and a kitten. The kitten was very different from the striped kittens and cats in the Temple; she was dark brown and her eyes were bright blue. She had come all the way over the mountains from Cheron, her basket tied to the saddle of a pack-horse. M'untal had wanted to call her Mahun after the Lady of the Dance but her mother had told her to show respect and the kitten was named Plama after the leopard who lived in the Temple. Plama played with M'untal's rope of silver bells.

The bells had been made for her to wear in the Temple. She was a Dancer. Her mother was a Dancer too. She danced for Mahun every day; M'untal had danced once, on the last holy day before the Red Wind, but every day she went to the big room in the Temple garden and learned new movements.

She ran to her nurse and clasped her about the legs. Alna was with her always. 'Where are my other presents?' she asked.

She wrote steadily in the commonplace book her father had sent her:

1 LiV 492

My birthday. I am ten today. Father sent me this book and he is coming next month to see me dance. Mother gave me a new yellow maral, a picture of herself painted by Zaithe, a book called *Fables and Legends of Far Maralis*, and a box of candied cherries. These grow in Sinein. There is a picture of a cherry tree on the box, a small tree shaped like a fan. Taressa gave me an elephant made of ivory, his tusks are painted red and he is called Noor. Aunt Lonie came to dinner and she brought me bells for my ankles. These are not from Cheron like my others but are made in the City by Slake Amskiri. Alna gave me a blue scarf.

I can do the new steps; they are an exercise to prepare the feet for the Wheel. Sunna complimented me. Someone brought a boy to class today. He had to sit and wait while she talked to Mm. Yalt. Boys can't dance.

Uncle Gildo brought me some Vikkutrian raisins. He has been married again although he is very old. I think he is thirty-seven. He has a new baby, I mean his wife has. I shall never marry anybody.

Going to bed at ten tonight because it is my birthday. My hair reaches to the hollow bit at the back of my knees.

3 LiV 496

Dear Father,
Thank you for the pearl, it is so beautiful. I look at it and think of the sea at Roakn. Is it as blue as the sea in the Bay? I think I will have it set in silver, then it will remind me of you, white and gleaming like your dress uniform. If I had two, I could have them made into earrings (yes, I am greedy!).

I met a boy from Cheron yesterday. His name is Osi and he comes from Vern. He is fourteen too. There was a reception for your president.

Now that I am grown up I must go into the Mamelon. It's frightening, so dark; I wish I knew what the She looked like without her mask. We have learned the Wheel for ordinary Temple use, the figure Mother liked best to dance before she became one of the soronai.

Mother says I should marry; she says it is best to marry young and get it over especially the babies. She says she has her eye on someone. Please tell me what you think. I don't believe I am ready for all that.
M'untal

My hair almost reaches to my feet. It has to be in a plait all the time now.

10 Ah in Vern 496

Dear Father,
I will take your advice, and I will obey my mother and the Gynarchs. It is just that he is so old: twenty-six.

I received the skin safely, so soft, so pale – poor leopard. I found the hole your weapon made in her neck – and you are only three deks' journey away. When I look at the hazy blue line of the horizon I imagine you sitting on a rock in the Zalcasians with your rkw across your knees, or perhaps giving orders to the men to hurry up with your supper! Can you see the Bay and the City?

50

Your (not very happy)
M'untal

39 AiV 496

Dear Father,
There will be a pile of letters from me when you get home. I hope
you are reading them in the right order.

I haven't written anything about the Dance for a long time. I am a
pattern leader now, and still only fourteen – what a clever girl! I
have learned all the dances.

I have saved my best news for last. Two days ago Tellon was
promised to me and the ceremony of Confirmation is tomorrow.
He is quite different close to; we have been to so many places
together in the last two deks. Parstrie is my chaperone. She is all
right but Aunt Lonie would have been better, or even Tressa. We
saw *The Tragedy of Vikkut* at the Drum Theatre, attended a dinner
and a party held in Hotel Z by the silkweavers, two other dinners,
one an informal buffet on the beach, an exhibition of big blobby
paintings by Xharam'un', and a very grand reception given by the
Archivist. Now I will describe my man: he is a fine athlete and a
good archer and horseman. His family are not part of the mercenary tradition; they used to be lily refiners but they have recently sold
their business.

We are to be married in Hibornal; Grandmother wanted us to
wait until next Vern but Mother and I both agree that I must not be
kept from the Dance any longer than is customary.

M'untal

2 Hibornal 496

Perhaps this book with all my childish thoughts should have been
offered with my dolls to Mahun; this is the last entry I shall make –
on my wedding eve.

I could be a mother this time next year. My daughter will be a
Dancer too, how could she be anything else? My family's love for
the Dance and Mahun has come a long way, down through twenty
generations. I wish Tellon was a big younger and had not been
married before. I saw one of his former wives yesterday, walking in
the gardens with her children. I should think the second smallest –
a pretty little girl – was Tellon's, as she married again at least a year
ago. I wonder why she divorced him? I wonder if he will be kind and
might even love me. He says he does. All my fears will be answered
tomorrow.

A real writer would deposit her work in the Archive. I shall hide this book and read it when I am alone. Just once a year – on my birthday. When my daughter is ten, I will give it to her with a new book of her own to write in. My own secret tradition. Praise Mahun.

Mahuntal Kiden M'una

Malajide put the baby into her daughter's arms.

'You are making it harder for yourself,' she said. The women stared at M'untal and her new baby boy.

M'untal looked intently at her baby's face. His new blue eyes stared at her. She unfolded the cloth he was wrapped in and marvelled at his tiny perfect hands, his minute nails. She put him to her breast and he nuzzled and sucked. So new, so clever: the sensation calmed and excited her. Soon, he slept.

'He's called Luth,' she said, defiantly.

The women humoured and tended her. Later, she lay in her own bed with Luth in a cradle beside her. She was deeply happy, and desperately afraid. In seven days the boy would be taken from her; they had told her nothing, the bitches, her mother the chief bitch among them. If she had been less practical, she would never have spoken to Malajide again. This was how they revealed the Gynarchy's vile law, with hurried explanations when she was tired and full of the triumph of giving birth. In seven days her baby would be sent to some Artisan woman and she, one of Mahun's Dancers, would receive a workwoman's girl in exchange. She would not cry; she would not give them that satisfaction. She bit her lip and drummed her fingers on the frame of the bed. They only subjected Dancers to this, so that they could preserve the Wheel. If she had been a plain matriarch, some useless archivisit or official, her son would be hers; why, many of them used a syringe to get their heirs, instead of a real man. Her two loves divided her, the Dance inspiring her soul, the child her heart.

Tellon came to visit her, relieved and embarrassed. Every one of his other children was a girl. She protested to him but he misunderstood and tried to comfort her. She grew angry and sent him away.

The Archivist entered, his quiet assistant at his heels. The younger man carried the latest volume of the Register and an inkstand. The Archivist, smiling, made her sit in a chair and fetched a chair for himself. He set his writing materials out on the table. She noticed his hands, large and fine, the nails carefully trimmed, and the dark hair on his forearms under the black sleeves of his cymar.

Luth began to cry, and M'untal fetched him from his cradle. The Archivist, with his frank and direct gaze, watched her.

52

'I have to feed him,' she said.

He waved a hand at his assistant, who blushed and left the room.

'You won't embarrass me,' he said.

'You might embarrass me,' she returned. 'It would be unusual, and might be compromising for you to be found here with a half-naked woman.'

'Ah, but I occupy a position of privilege.'

Provoked, she wrenched the cymar from her shoulder, sat down and applied the infant to her breast. He sucked loudly. Still, the Archivist regarded her.

'Shall we begin the registration?' he asked. 'You must give me your name.'

'Mahuntal Kiden M'una,' she said. 'And my husband is Tellon Celth M'unor. The name of my son is Luth Kiden M'unor.'

The Archivist wrote steadily.

'It's not usual for a Dancer's boy to be named by his natural mother,' he said, as he signed his name and blotted the record.

'You haven't missed it out?'

'I have written it. Look.'

The name was written there, with the other names and the date of birth, 14 Ah in Vern, 497, in his beautiful flowing hand. She smiled but her hands, supporting the baby, were tensed. Luth finished sucking. She released her tight hold of him and stroked his tiny face with the tip of a finger. The Archivist extended one of his long fingers and touched the baby's hand.

'You are alone?' he asked.

'Why shouldn't I be? Yes. My maid has gone for fresh flowers; she won't hurry, for the gardener is a friend of hers.

'You and I and Luth are the only ones here – and your assistant outside the door, I suppose.'

'He has gone back to the Octagon.'

'It is the fourth day,' he continued. 'In three days' time you will surrender your son to the Gynarchs, and they will carry him away. Your daughter will be brought in and named, your heir in the Dance.

'How are you prepared for this?'

'I am resigned,' she replied dutifully. 'I have prayed.'

She pulled the hood of the cymar across her face. The Archivist watched her.

'Mahun is not vengeful,' he said. 'Why should she treat her daughters so?'

'She only punishes her Dancers!'

'I know. It was a custom of friendship which was wrongfully made law – because of the passage which begins, "All my dancers shall be the daughters of dancers." ' He spoke gently. He leaned towards her and

53

lifted the hood from her face. She started, too surprised at the incredible breach of convention to protest.

'You must have patience,' he said.

'I've many years for that! And many for anger, too. Why don't you write it in your book? "She was upset when they took her baby away."?'

'Have patience,' he said again. 'He will go to a Weaver.'

'So? Some hideous shed off Broadwalk. Why tell me? Perhaps you hope to be invited to my bed?'

He laughed. An expression of tired cynicism replaced the openness in his face. He closed the record book and put away his pen.

'I shall come back – I must, in any case, to record the Exchange.

'Why should I tell you anything? Why should I prejudice my position? All I have to do is ensure that the record is kept.'

Her tears came after he had left. Whatever it was he offered, it could not comfort her. She did not recognise it as friendship. She sat still and thought of the other mother, the woman she had abused, waiting to part with her baby.

The seventh day came. M'untal woke calm, sleepy, forgetting the day. She got up and fed the baby, remembering halfway through. She thought of concealing a letter to his new mother in his clothes, but probably the Gynarchs changed the clothes as well. She called Alna and put Luth into her arms.

In the gardens, everything was still. She walked by the Long Lake and watched the ducks; she walked up the hill to Shekarah's folly, climbed its crazy steps, and looked out over the sea. The ships were toys on a pond, and the City herself was a model. If she could pick up the buildings and move them around! If she could stop time! She walked slowly down the stairs and stood among the alien pines breathing in their scent. In the hollow below the hill, Crinon M'una's house, surrounded by its own small forest and its intimate garden, looked like a refuge from life. She heard birds calling in the garden. It was unfair that a painter should have such a house; paintings needed no mother, no home. She went quietly by the narrow garden gate and turned a corner; there was the painter, up a ladder, a saw in her hand, trimming the branch of a tree. A straw hat was crammed on her untidy hair.

Crinon looked down.

'My dear!' she exclaimed, dropping the saw. Her long legs in their practical green slacks moved down the rungs.

M'untal felt her hand taken by this unnatural woman who had forsworn motherhood, men, and position for paint. Crinon gave her a white handkerchief, enlivened by smears of paint and smelling strongly of linseed and turpentine.

'Come,' she said, 'into the garden: Xhara' will take care of you and I'll take you home later. When it's all over.'

54

It was early in the morning and she was feeding Fiora when the Archivist returned. This time he was alone, carrying the book and the pens and ink himself. She sent Alna out of the room. He was a little breathless, excited like a boy; strange to see in such a big athletic man. He had forgotten to put on his black robe.

'I came straight from the butts,' he said. 'I had a letter – he has gone to Far Maralis, to the hills below Mount Bai. They are Weavers, but they have a farm. Cattle, many sheep, a fruit garden – and sheds full of silkworms.'

The picture he wanted her to see came: of a sturdy little boy in a fruitful place amongst gentle animals. She cried for a time, and he took a handkerchief from one of his pockets and gave it to her. The cloth smelled like him, of books and leather dressing, and faintly, almost imperceptibly, of the fragrance called Youth.

'And are they gentle people?' she said.

'I am sure they are. I will have more detail in time.'

'When?'

'You must do as I say, and possess yourself in patience – infinite patience. How is she? Why, she has eyes like yours. You haven't handed her over to the nurse.'

'How could I give my son's sister to Alna?'

He came a third time and a fourth, while he made, with minute care and while the baby cried, the needle marks of the golden lily tattoo. She learned that the name of Luth's new mother was Lorilla; she learned that Luth would grow up as Ister. Lorilla, said the Archivist, was a skilled craftswoman, beautiful, kind, intelligent. In return, she spoke of her father in Cheron, of her childhood and, at last, of her marriage.

'You drew a low card,' he said. 'Next time you'll be dealt an ace.'

'I shall never marry again,' she said.

She was restless when he had gone, thinking over the shortcomings of her ten-months' husband. She knew now that the older women called Tellon the Teacher; an early divorce was expected, but the hags could wait and he could wait, until it pleased her to pronounce the words of dismissal.

Transition

The white tiled room smelled of disinfectant. There were four cages, the crowded men in each one each occupying his allotted space of eighteen inches by two feet six. Cal was freed from the handgrips and thrust into the second pen. A Fister with a cut over his eye made room for him on the narrow bench and gave him a cigarette.

'Been at the fight?' he said, staring at the Rosy marks on Cal's face.

'I was the fight.' He leaned against the horizontal bar which, cemented at each end into the wall, represented a seat. He was tired; his shoulders ached and his mouth still tasted foul. A void hung open in his mind.

'What time is it?' he asked.

The Fister shook his head. Someone shouted, 'Four o'clock,' and the gap closed up. He remembered. He had been riding the metro since early morning; it must have been afternoon when the blonde cunt charged him. The light on Broadwalk had been full, the pavements crowded. He grinned at the Fister.

'Been on the wing,' he said.

The Fister smiled lazily. His lips were soft and broad. He smiled around the black weed stuck between them.

'They don't grip you for that,' he said. 'Me, I was the finish of the fight; you were the lucky fucker that began it?'

'Luce was jealous,' he said. 'And Shiron had just given me a knife.'

It was a better reason for being where he was than the pallid crime of having an untattooed left arm.

'They're looking for a rapist,' said a Trav opposite him. 'That's why they took all the men off the train; that's why we're in here.'

A boy in the corner said, plaintively, 'There's nothing about rape on my charge sheet.'

The Traveller laughed.

'What's on a charge sheet is of no account,' he said.

Cal, with the capital eighteen-year-old crime of omission on his, listened to them. They had found a victim, a butt, and they began to torment the boy with half accurate tales of rebellions, of the Burnt Lands, of torture and castration.

In the tiled chamber, the light women's voices of the warders were distorted into harpy screams.

'You,' they shrieked, 'and you, boy; and you, the pretty one with the Rosy marks.'

He followed five others into a bare room. A warder ranged them in an untidy row. A veiled woman was brought in and they were paraded before her. The woman left the room. One of the men spat on the floor. The clock on the wall ticked loudly; six twenty-four.

They kept him back, and took the other men away. He had a warder to himself, his own personal guard. He thought about rape. He had been raped five years ago and he had no illusions; it was a hazard of life on the streets. An officer with a gold flash on her shoulder came in. She whispered with the warder. He thought about castration, naming its hideous names: unman, emasculate, geld, neuter, cut, maim, mutilate. The dictionary's bland definition floated before his eyes: 'to cut away the testicles, to deprive of generative power'. He was close to panic and he shut his eyes and silently recited the first page from Huyatt's tale to calm himself.

'You're wanted upstairs,' said his warder. 'Come on.'

The office was small. On the bookshelf, the books stood upright in order of height. A tray of pens and a white folder lay on the table next to five stems of sweet-scented mountain narcissi, confined in a pot. The warder told him to sit down and retired to the back of the room.

The chair was soft. He rested his right elbow on its arm and his head on his hand. He started to fall asleep, but a woman came briskly in and sat down opposite him. She wore a grey cymar over a neat jacket and skirt. When she opened the folder, he saw the charge sheet with Hyason Sarin's writing on it. She smiled at him.

'Ennal T'or,' she said. 'Your crime is so unusual that we would like to investigate you thoroughly, if you have no objection.'

He read the label on her cymar: L/P. X.T. M'una. Had I wealth, freedom, status, had I choice, he thought. 'Go ahead, Lector,' he said, and shrugged. But this one was not Verelustra Tain with her lace-edged handkerchief and sentimental conscience. She made a note on the charge sheet. 'Permission given,' he read. She looked at him and they shared the secret, both aware of his ability to read her handwritten Maralay upside down.

'Good,' she said. She spoke to the warder. 'Regulation search. After that, he can begin his statement and we'll make a start on the assessment tomorrow.'

She stood up and the warder came forward and prodded him with her cane. He stood up, but slowly so that she would know it was his choice to stand.

This room contained a hard couch, an empty bath, and a urinal. The tiles gleamed. His escort had increased to three; one of them was a physician. He knew she was a physician because the label on her overall told him so; but her initials were YK. One of the warders bent over and

57

put a plug in the bath. The water ran and steam hazed the tiles.

'Undress,' said his warder. He wasn't wearing much, just the grey slops and a blue shirt; a black singlet underneath. He undressed quickly. The warders had to put him on the couch; their hands were soft, and cold. The physician looked annoyed and consulted her wristwatch. She looked into his ears, his eyes, and mouth; she raped him with gloved fingers. He tried to make a mask of his face.

'All right. You can bathe,' the warder said.

He sat in the warm water while the two warders watched him. Afterwards, he had to use the urinal; they did not take their eyes off him. He put on the clothes they gave him; like everything else they were white.

Another bare room, an unshaded light, two hard chairs and a table. On the table, a pile of paper and a pen. They sat down, the warder preparing to write. 'Provisional Statement, MS14/MP479', he read.

'Begin at your birth,' she said, pen poised.

Most sailors could not write, or wrote indifferently. Why should he be so remarkable? Nor was she Hyason Sarin. He swung his chair back on its rear legs.

'I wasn't born, so much as hatched,' he said. 'My mother had so many children, it became easy for her: she had one a year for fifteen years. My first brother is named Vai-ess, my second Tornmor; as for my sisters, Elieta was the first, then Zelsa, then – ' He saw the warder compress her lips. Her hand, with the pen, moved quickly. He would make it ache; and it would take them hours to check all the names in the Archive. He continued to list Ennal T'or's siblings, and named his parents, grand-parents and great-grandparents. He gave the warder a detailed descrip-tion of the woman to whom he was promised. He started to tell of a dockside childhood in Taimiss.

The warder stopped him when she had covered seven sheets.

'Lock-in time,' she said.

His room. White again, windowless, a heavy door with a shutter in it. A bed. He lay still, curled up against the silence.

Soon after dawn, when the lamp in the ceiling came on, a vibrant bell rang in the corridor outside his cell. He heard a heavy door being opened, the warders coming, two of them. They hit each cell door as they passed. His shutter was slid open and he saw the eyes of his warder. She looked at him coldly.

'It took them five hours to check your lies, you little sod,' she said. He pretended not to hear her, and she went away. The thuds continued, decreasing in volume.

Later, the warder returned. She took him out of the cell to a washroom, never leaving him alone. He noticed that the other prisoners did not have a personal warder, but one to ten; nor were they watched so closely. He did not know if it was a good omen, or a bad. When he had

58

eaten a breakfast in his cell, a better one than he got on the streets, bohea, bread, rice, and vegetables, his warder took him back to the bare interview room. This time, there were three chairs. He sat on one of them and the warder stood by the door. She had no name, just 'Warder 5, Stratum II' on her lapel badge.

'What's your name, 5?' he said.

'What's yours?' she returned. She opened the door and admitted Physician YK. Now he was afraid. The physician smiled at him.

'I'm here as an observer,' she said. She sat on the third chair.

His seven sheets of fiction lay on the table beside a fresh pile of paper. The warder sat opposite him.

'Shall we continue?' she said. 'Who are you today?'

He hesitated. The game was over; it could not be prolonged because the Archive had found him out. If he chose a new identity, it would be discovered false, even if the checking took five hours. But who could check his true identity? He pulled the blank pages close and picked up the pen. The two women watched him.

'They call me Cal,' he wrote, 'I know nothing of my birth and I remember little of my early years. When I was three years old, the Beggarwoman M'nah took care of me. She died in Ah, 487. There was a bad outbreak of cholera. The main drain was blocked and the Uynal polluted above the purification plant. I remember the stench and the shit in the streets. One or two Hill people died; it was the talk of the Quarter.

'I never had a Mark. I suppose M'nah didn't have the money to register me, or maybe she was afraid. She was a sturdy Beggar, not deformed, or ill until the cholera. Her pitch was outside the Glass Mall, but she moved about because she had no licence money either. I think she had a licence in '85 or '86 because I once saw her looking at a printed form. Swan looked after me next.

'Swan was a good man. He made a living and was never arrested. His best filch was on the big house on the corner of Silk Street; we lived on the proceeds for ten months.'

He wrote for several hours, stretching his hand at intervals to relieve the stiffness. They brought him a meal. He continued to write. He had reached his eighth year. The physician watched him and made notes on a pad; the warder looked bored. Twice, the physician went away, to return after a short interval. He laid down the pen when he had had enough.

'Have you finished it?'

'No. My hand aches.'

They brought him a mug of bohea and he wrote another page before he was stopped, taken back to his cell, and locked in. So far, he had written only of himself and of people who were dead. He thought of Tarla, of Dog and the Bitch, of Glaver. Next day, he refused to write anything. When the warder saw that he was determined, she took him

59

back to his cell. That night he was unable to sleep; something without definition existed in his cell; it kept him awake and made his head ache. Perhaps it was in his mind. It was still there in the morning, throughout the day, the next night. He could not sleep. There was noise in his cell, continuous noise. He sat still, holding his breath, trying to hear the sound that was not a sound. And while he strained to listen, it ceased. The warder looked through the hatch. He did not look up.

He was taken into the bare room, where he sat before the pile of paper, his hands on his knees.

The physician visited him in his cell. She was unsubtle.

'Why have you stopped writing?'

'I've told you enough.'

'What you tell us may make the difference between life and death.'

She went away. He tried to think of dying, but in this unnatural environment he could imagine nothing. It was the negation of reality. Dawn was a lamp, night was when the lamp went out. Food came regularly in large portions; they made him bath and a woman came and shaved him every day. No sound from the world outside the prison penetrated to him. The noises were all metallic, keys, metal doors, steel tables. The cell was clean, the smells antiseptic. He was the pollutant. He inhaled the air he trapped between his hands, trying to recall Glaver's perfume and the potent smell of her aroused body.

That night he heard a man scream. The noise woke him. In the morning, when the lamp was lit, he thought that the sound had been engineered to frighten him. Silence may be interpreted as guilt.

When he had made the decision to continue with the statement, he called for his warder. No one came. He sat on his bed, frustrated. Now that he had decided to name them all he wanted to finish it.

The warder came into his cell next day.

'I'll finish the statement,' he said.

He wrote swiftly, guiltily, naming everyone he knew. It was easy to gloss over the illegal worship in the derelict chantry. He made no reference to it, nor to his tower, nor did he mention his cellar, describing instead another which was a common haven. When he had finished the statement, he signed it and threw the pen on the table so that the ink splattered from it. The warder mopped up the ink and looked relieved.

He entertained another visitor: XT came with four books under her arm. They were written in different languages. Yes, he said, he could read them all, and his Huyatt written in Maralay, he could read that. He demonstrated his skill.

He was a celebrity, with his own personal physicians and attendants. He slept at night, his sleep a total, dreamless, entity. His last meal of the day, he was sure, contained a sedative. He was tested with puzzles, anagrams, ink blots, shapes, concepts, riddles, numbers, coloured blocks; he was questioned about his abilities, the fact that he could read and write, his sexual experience, his huskings, his religious allegiance. A small crowd of experts gathered in the gymnasium to watch him climb, to see his heart rate and breathing tested. In the surgery, they measured every inch of him and connected him up to various instruments to see if they could find any fault with the well-regulated machine that was his body. He was photographed, and his voice was recorded. No one mentioned rape and he thought of the uneasy boy in the pen, of the Fister and the Trav. He saw no one but his captors.

A day came when they left him alone for hours; but after the midday meal, and he was given meat and fresh fruit, the warder took him back to the interview room and told him to strip. The warder held him while an auxiliary plunged a hypodermic into his flesh. They placed a chair in the centre of the room and made him sit there, vulnerable, exposed. The Lector and the physician came into the room, with a veiled Gynarch; the women sat in a row opposite him and his warder read his long statement. It had been added to: it contained other statements, the words of his friends and enemies; his frankness had been suppressed and made to seem like guile; they accused him of asking the questions only an atheist would dream of; of indifference toward Mahun. His lack of a Mark was a sin against Her. He answered their questions dreamily, because of the drug; he signed the pages as they were passed to him.

The veiled Gynarch came to his cell. He looked at her hands. The skin had yellowed and become wrinkled and dry. He wondered if the sacred dust clouded her mind as much as the veil clouded her face. But her voice was kind.

'I am here,' she said, 'to tell you that your trial will take place in two days' time. Arbiter Mahud will speak for you: you will see her tomorrow. Meanwhile you are permitted stimulants and reading material. Can I order anything for you?'

'Husk,' he said.

A warder brought it and he lay on the bed and tapped the fold. Weak dreams came, of empty spaces among great hills, of closed doors, but there was no flying nor any ill effect when he awoke. He supposed the fold to have been adulterated with a harmless filler.

The Arbiter-at-Law came. She congratulated him on the completeness of his statement, she told him how she would represent him, of the circumstances in which sentence would be mitigated, of the lethal injection of lily milk. He was suspicious and she friendly. He asked her to get him a copy of *The Travels of Huyatt Tayal*.

The book arrived with his evening meal, a better drug than the substitute husk. He opened the book. In Commons the prose lost its stateliness. He began to read as if the tale were new to him. He read the book three times and the eve of his trial arrived. He fell asleep but awoke in the dark screaming. He got up and banged on the door. Two warders arrived with YK and they held him down while she injected a tranquiliser.

He was woken, given a second injection and a good breakfast, and taken to a bathroom. There was an argument and he hit out when the warders tried to take off his clothes; eventually he relented and undressed himself. He bathed while they watched him. When he was dressed they locked his hands in grips and led him away down the corridor and up a narrow flight of stairs. A door at the top led into the court and into the separate enclosure which held the prisoner's chair. Arbiter Talamun Mahud stood at a desk near it, her lawbooks and papers before her.

Cal looked about him. The courtroom was high and vaulted, painted in white and gold. The public gallery was full; a steel lattice before it protected the spectators. He glimpsed slim hands adjusting veils: a party of matriarchs was in court. Before him curved a semicircular dais and on it were seated the nine white-shrouded judges.

He sat, as he was directed, in the high prisoner's chair and the warders locked the chain of his grips to it and stood, one on either side. He watched his hands with interest and detachment: they shook as if he had a bad attack of sthenics like a husker. Close to him was another high seat and on it sat a Gynarch, invisible under her blue veil. She raised her hands and spoke a prayer to Mahun.

The chief judge struck her block, the signal for the start of the trial. Its hollow note echoed like a whiplash. She spoke.

'In the name of Mahun, our Lady and Protector, I call on you, Prisoner 479, captive of Our Mother, to answer these charges.

' "First, that your body is innocent of a Mark. Second, that you have lived illegally within the City limits for eighteen years. Third, that you have wilfully continued Markless for eighteen years. Fourth, that your birth has not been recorded in the Archive. Fifth, that, while you are not a heretic, you have been heard to question the sacred words of the Law. Sixth, that you took part in an illegal affray and display at the Fairground on the fifth day of Lilb in Vern, 500 After Reformation. Seventh, that at this fight you maliciously assaulted Artisan Luciana Tisal M'una. Eighth, that you are guilty of maliciously wounding Luciana Tisal. Ninth, that you possess and carry illegally a security corps knife, obtained illegally. Tenth, that you had on your person, when arrested, stolen property: a book, *The Travels of Huyatt Tayal*, the property of Magon Nonpareil."

'Arbiter Mahud will answer the charges for you.'

Talamun Mahud began to speak. The Law allowed her one hour to make her assessment, and she spoke for fifty-four minutes. He watched the gilded hands of the great clock above the Nines.

'We have heard your argument, Arbiter Mahud, and will consider it,' said the chief judge. He was taken out to a rest room. An attendant brought food and drink, but he could only sip water.

'Three abstentions,' the judge announced. Talamun Mahud turned round and smiled at Cal. 'Five Guilty. I am not required to vote, since the decision of the judges is clear.

'We find you, Prisoner 479, captive of Our Mother, guilty of the ten charges read and recorded.'

The Arbiter looked at him again, but he would not return the look. The nine judges stood up and removed their veils for the sentence. They were all middle-aged women, mothers themselves.

'We ask your forgiveness, prisoner of Our Mother, and pass sentence on you: you shall be taken out from this place to the place of execution and there be put to death. In the name of Mahun.'

The Gynarch prayed for his soul. She came to him and put a white cloth over his head. He was taken out by a different door. He heard a murmur in the court behind him as he was led away.

Someone removed the cloth from his head. Two Gynarchs stood in an otherwise empty room. One of them held a blue cymar. She put it over him and adjusted the hood so that it hid his face. She took his chain from the warder and put it in his hand. The other Gynarch laid her hand on his arm; her nails were painted silver.

'Don't let the chain rattle,' she said. 'Come.'

She kept a hand on his arm. They hurried him along corridors, outside and across stone slabs, across grass, and through a gateway. He lifted a hand to the hood and saw a closed carriage. 'Ssh!' said the women. They got into it, and the horses moved off at a trot.

The pace of the horses slowed. The carriage was climbing. He smelled hibiscus and frangipani. The carriage moved evenly on to gravel. He heard the small stones scrunch, and a peacock screamed.

The carriage halted. He was helped out and led up a broad flight of steps. He felt currents of cold air, neatly shod feet hurried past, as he was led along echoing corridors, up flights of stairs, and into a lift. Beyond the lift were soft carpets. They halted before a panelled door, and he tilted his head to see the three words painted on it: 'Magon Nonpareil. Archivist.'

One of the Gynarchs opened the door, the other gently pushed him.

Paradise

He pulled the hood from his head. He stood alone in an elegantly appointed office or study. The walls were alternately panelled or book-lined, and he faced a tall window. The room was cool, shaded by a half-drawn crimson curtain. Near the window hung a huge oil painting in which a man with attenuated limbs and a stricken face knelt amongst rocks. Immediately below the painting stood a small table on which three small bronzes, two of horses and one of a naked man with a helmet-shaped head and polished blinkers in place of eyes, had been carefully placed. A desk and chair of redwood stood near him and some of the objects on it, a blotter, a pen tray, a letter knife, an inkwell and paper clips clinging to a magnetic icosahedron, were tools of the Archivist's trade, but two others, the silver figure of a boy leading a greyhound, his garments spread by the wind, and a tiny carving in ivory, of a worm devouring an apple, had no use.

His possessions lay on a second table beside the window. He moved across to count them, the chain of the grips dangling to his knees: his torch, his Beggars' Tree, the camel knife, spotless and shining, cleaned of the woman's blood, seven triangular frags and eighteen round bits, and the book with the Archivist's name in it. Beside the coins lay a key and he tried unsuccessfully to fit it to the lock of the grips.

The window would not open. He leaned against the glass and looked down a giddy distance into a courtyard, where a fountain splashed into a stone bowl and careful planting made a shadowy grove. They were lemon trees and the fruit glowed. An open archway in the courtyard wall gave him a view of blue distances.

The door opened behind him, and he swung round to regard the Archivist, tall and dark, the man aboard *Daystar*, the heretic, Cat Street's guilty predator and the owner of his book.

The Archivist crossed the room and picked up the key, towering over Cal like a soldier over a girl. But his touch was light as he unlocked the metal gloves and drew them from Cal's hands. Cal looked at his fingers: each felt as though it had been broken. He began to flex them carefully, his hands trembling like an athlete's body after exertion.

Magon Nonpareil, the Archivist, watched his protégé. The boy was thin after his privation in the gaol. His golden skin had a sallow cast, and his cheekbones had assumed undue prominence under the yellow eyes.

Three fading scars spoiled his chin. Magon touched them.

'The asylum doctors get tired of stitching up Rosy bites,' he said.

The boy continued to stare at his trembling hands, and the tremor spread upward through his arms and into his shoulders. Magon stretched out his strong right arm. The boy's head rested against his chest and he held it there, his strength a support. He put him in the chair.

The boy squatted there, on the chair's edge, his face hidden by his hands. He sobbed as a child does, without inhibition. When he was quiet, the Archivist spoke.

'I expect, since you find yourself here, that this is superfluous information – but you have been reprieved.'

The boy stood up and wiped his face on his sleeve. Restlessly, he walked round the desk, and came to the window. The light outlined his slender body. He began to laugh as intemperately as he had lately wept.

'What do you know of the world on the streets,' he said. 'Confined in your white tower until your body cries out for relief?

'Look at these.' He picked up the handgrips. 'Devised by a woman to be used by women. They should be in a museum. "The Security Forces under the Gynarchy" – there's a title for a history, something else to bury in the Archive. You are a part of their system.

'What do you want with me?'

'I need you,' said the Archivist bluntly. Cal saw no trace of lust or ambition; the fine features were calm.

'I had you tested,' he said. 'Build on it. The First Officer was fascinated, the Prison Lectors curious. I hired the best arbiter for you, but even Talamun Mahud cannot work miracles. Why, in God's name, did you not go to the House for registration?'

'I preferred not to waste my money; I could easily avoid the camels and the Markdykes.'

'But you were caught. Too much husk and too little care. It is a capital crime.'

'I'm not afraid of dying.'

'Come: to allow you to die would have been an act more heinous than any you had committed, or than any I might commit in releasing you.

'Besides, you found my *Huyatt*.

'I lost the book ten years ago, on Vern Street. It must have slipped from a bundle of several I was carrying, and it's an edition I have valued since childhood.'

'It was in the gutter beside the statue of Eshtur. So,' Cal handed him the red book, 'here it is.'

'Keep it. It has been your elementary school, your primer, tutor, and academy.'

'Your name is written in it.'

'Your name is also written in it; and I think your name has superseded mine. At least where that book is concerned.' He smiled.

'I am sorry you had to undergo trial and sentence, the last exit, for the sake of the Archive. But you are a good actor – flying colours, no less than I expected. What is life but a comical tragedy: the street boy has died, but you live.

'How would you like to be a rich man?'

So he had dreamed on long, hot, afternoons.

'There is a part ready,' said the Archivist. 'The role of a lily trader, dramatic justice. Rafe Dayamit is his name. For the sake of the Record, you understand? The original is dead.'

Cal shrugged, aware of his debt. He could not resist any use to which the Archivist chose to put him, owing him a life which, if it was no longer his own, belonged to this newborn Rafe, the flight farmer, the Hill tiger, the creature of Magon Nonpareil.

'Tomorrow is a new day,' the Archivist said. 'You need nothing now but sleep. The Octagon is closed, and there are no late readers today. I will show you a place where you can sleep without fear.'

In a dusk lit only by dim security lamps, he led Cal about the silent building. The Octagon after dark was a mystery of great spaces, lifts and stairwells, of many looming shelves and library ladders ascending into darkness. Unlocking a door, Magon ushered him along a corridor and into a small white room. An electric lamp burned there, and a narrow bed waited.

'Sleep,' said the Archivist. 'Nothing else matters in the universe.'

He left, closing the door softly behind him. Cal took off the Gynarch's cymar and dropped the prison garments on the floor. He lay down.

Sleep came at once, before he could compose his limbs or draw the bedsheet over him.

He lay unmoving. Cal, the sewer rat who swam in ordure and feasted on it, was dead, his nimble paws stiff, his tail rigid. He lay on the slab, unable to stir. He felt the knife of the corpseman begin to section his body.

When he opened his eyes, he remembered that he was translated, that the base street boy had been transmuted into the dealer in golden lilies, Rafe Dayamit. But why? The ceiling above him was pale blue; a clerestory window showed him a halcyon sky. Yesterday's fears had gone.

The rest room was small, but it contained, beside the bed he sat on, a chair, a washstand, and a low cupboard bearing the physicians' snake. He was covered with a sheet and a thin quilt. His prison clothes were gone, only the blue cymar they had hidden him beneath remained. It lay neatly on the chair. Someone – a servant? The Archivist? Magon? He spoke the name aloud. Someone had entered the room while he slept. He sat up and grinned at the wall. An insulated jug and a tall white beaker stood on the cupboard. A line of print ran down the side of the jug, and he got off the bed and read it. In Maralay, it said 'Property of the Octagon'. He unscrewed the lid: the scent of hot honeyed bohea flung him back down the years and into the company of Professor Tain. He filled the beaker and drank to her.

The door was broad and made of pale wooden panels. He hitched up the voluminous cymar; the door swung open when he touched it.

He stood in the hushed Library. Tall windows flooded the great room with new daylight. Soft and pale, the carpeted floor spread out, an ocean into which hove multicoloured shelves of books and island tables. A hungry man at a feast, he hesitated between the shelves and the nearest set of windows, walking eventually to the windows. They reached from floor to ceiling, and formed one wall of a courtyard like the one below the Archivist's room. He looked up and down the glass walls for a crimson curtain before he realised it was a different court, the floor of it completely occupied by a wide tank of water. He thought he was on the fifteenth or sixteenth floor of the building; even from such an elevation he could clearly see the gold and white carp which swam in the tank. The arch which pierced the outer wall of the court showed the sun risen over a distant wooded hill. Nearer, the woodland thinned and he saw deer browsing in glades, and the sloping roof of a wooden house. Outside, the birds were singing, and he heard an eldritch scream, but whether it came from a peacock or a silktail monkey he was uncertain. Within the building, the silence was profound.

Stairs climbed up and down within a shaft of glass. He came to them. Beyond them, the building was pierced by a greater shaft: a huge octagonal well of dusk. Dark shapes at the bottom were probably trees.

A table stood near the stairs. Along one edge of it was a loose bar, and when he pressed this, a light came on illuminating plans under glass: a guide to the Octagon. Schematic blue women showed him his position in the room and in the building. He was on Level 15. He studied the plan, finding the four rectangular courts which bit into four of the Octagon's faces, and the great central well behind him. South Court contained the entrance to the building, and the three others were named Fountain Court West, Pool Court, and Fountain Court East. The four triangular areas of Library floor on this level were named according to their orientation, but there was no indication of their book content on the plan before him. He supposed that some system of classification existed.

Without troubling to search for further guidance, he went back to the books. 'H' confronted him and he scanned rapidly along the book spines searching for 'Huyatt' (but perhaps his work was shelved under 'T'?). Soon he found five shelves on each of which the name of the traveller was printed in gold.

Numerous, differing, editions of the *Travels* filled the upper shelves; below them were editions of two other works by the Tayali. He did not know which work to examine first. Diridion was mentioned in the *Travels*, but here was a whole book on it: *The City in the Cleft*. Opening a copy, he read the subtitle, *Diridion of the Desert*. *Ethos* was the name of Huyatt's third work. Philosophy, he could see that at a glance, the musings of a man who had left his own people.

A shelf and a half was devoted to commentaries on the three works; one chosen at random was a collection of essays about the city of Diridion. Professor Tain's name headed the list of distinguished contributors. He scanned it; amongst the names towards the foot of the list, the names of men, was Rafe Dayamit's. He turned to the essay: the voice was distinctive and spoke to him from the page.

I came late to Huyatt, encountering him in the last Academy year before Matriculation. Huyatt can be read too early: a level of maturity is required for true appreciation of his style and content. I was lucky to read him first in the original Tayali; in Maralay his prose acquires a glossiness foreign to the harsh syllables of the desert. The Tayaal is an unforgiving land: why should the reader be lulled into believing it and Huyatt's other landscapes to be Arcadia?

The dead voice continued to speak to him as he read the printed page. Was it old, or young? It had vigour and style; the personal idiom of the essay gave it an attractive intemperance. Maybe he had been quite young and died of some accident or fever? He read the whole of the essay.

Then, ignoring the other shelves, he knelt to examine the load on the lowest. All were large volumes, and they proved to be atlases of the regions Huyatt had visited. He chose one and, carrying it to a table, spread it open at the first map, which showed Diridion of the Tayaal. The cartographer, named Glisa, had been a neo-technocrat, working in 400AR; her maps were not enhanced by irrelevant drawings of mythical beasts, nor by quaint footnotes, and Diridion was marked by a dot surrounded by brown contour lines. Diridion lay high in a cleft in the promontory of rock called the Mahkra, an outcropping of Baian limestone beyond Vern. A neat road of dashes wound towards the City, but passed on the 5000 foot contour without encountering it. The key to the map told him it was a road 'without metalling'. The desert to the north of the Mahkra was lemon yellow, but only one small area of it bore the legend 'dunes', and crescent dunes, he believed, made a desert. The rest was an enigma of watercolour. He turned to a map of Vern. As he expected, most of it was coloured green. He looked up, seeing the stiff green stems and straplike leaves of the lily fields, as depicted in so many paintings and posters about the City.

A woman approached, stepping resolutely across the carpet, her breasts bouncing merrily beneath her brown librarian's cymar. She smiled and passed him by. Beyond her, he saw the Archivist, the vigour of his step muffled by the carpet and concealed by his black robe. His strong voice rang out:

'Good morning!'

'You slept well?' he asked, arrived at the table. 'Ah! Glisa.'

'It's a hideous atlas,' said Cal. 'But I suppose it is accurate.'

'Alas, no,' said Magon. 'She made a fundamental error of conversion. A Diridian yelt equals two miles exactly, not four, so all her distances should be halved.

'No. Filka will tidy up. Come and eat.' Cal followed him. The Archivist led him into one of the lifts, and pressed the control marked '27'. The lift soared.

They walked beside a glass wall near the top of the central well, the arched tops of the windows of the eastern Fountain Court on their right. The well was lit now and Cal saw a rectangular tank and fountains far below; entire forest trees ringed the water. Creepers and ferns grew along the stone ribs of the windows; by craning his head, he could see a parapet at the top of the shaft.

'You shall see the City from the roof!' Magon touched his shoulder. 'After the formalities.' He withdrew a key from a pocket in his robe, and unlocked a door of banded woods, hardly visible in the striped wall of panelling.

Beyond lay a rectangular hall, where the peace and stillness of the great library was converted into intimacy; it was a chill intimacy, the air colder and drier than that of the Library. The walls of the hall, like those of an art gallery, were covered in paintings. A silver calendar clock on the wall told them the hour was seven and the day the twenty-second, Eshtur, of Lilb, 500. The newborn Rafe had been alive eleven hours.

The Archivist held out his right hand in a theatrical gesture.

'Welcome,' he said. 'This is mine.'

He lead the way through a second anteroom. Several paintings hung on its walls. They passed into a large study crowded with books and pictures, pieces of sculpture and deep chairs. Breakfast was laid on a table before the window and a thin man wearing spectacles stood with his back to the view, smiling hesitantly.

'From Vern,' Magon introduced them. 'Rafe Dayamit, Silvanor Cudbeer, my personal assistant.'

They took the places he indicated, and he poured bohea.

'Vern,' said Cudbeer in a surprisingly deep voice. 'A province I long to visit, were it permitted.' He glanced at the Archivist. 'Tell me about the Alcuon feast.'

The imposter saw before him the green of Glisa's map and frowned before Rafe, aided by Huyatt, took command.

69

'It's not so very different from the description in Huyatt. Country places develop slowly,' he said. 'The feast is one of the high points of our year – after the lily planting, before the Red Wind. The women. . . .'

Cudbeer's face glowed.

'You should visit the Quarter,' the man from Vern said enthusiastically.

'You've been to the City before?' said Cudbeer politely.

'A trader has his privileges. Yes, many times. I am usually relieved to get away from home. My mother is a hard driver, except at feast time naturally. That's when the women and the men change places; the men can order the women about for a day. They call it Allfools day in Odalion.'

He saw the man's face suffuse again, as he described a composite and generalised woman in whom parts of Glaver, Filka the librarian, and the Bitch were welded indiscriminately together. He talked on, describing the women the lily trader might be supposed to have enjoyed. The Archivist watched him, with a half-smile on his lips.

Cudbeer, his face still scarlet, said, 'In the Octagon – it's impossible. They're not interested in men, or they're married.'

'It's seven-thirty, Cudbeer,' said the Archivist, his voice sudden and authoritative, 'Would you please place those new files on my desk as you pass?'

Cudbeer's normal pale complexion returned.

'Yes, Archivist,' he said. He drank down the last of his bohea, and left the room rapidly.

Magon leaned back in his chair and laughed.

'He is five years older than you,' he said. 'And he has worked in the Octagon since his fourteenth year. His mother and grandmother were both archivists. I don't believe he goes out much – but a brilliant numerist and a methodical worker. Incidentally, it was he who discovered Glisa's error: the Diridian cleft would be a mile deep if she were correct.

'He is terrified of women.'

'I'd send him to Zalcissa, or Pulchrinella.'

'No doubt your knowledge of the Quarter is encyclopaedic.'

They fell silent, staring at each other. Cal, looking past the Archivist, was dazzled by the sunlight reflected from the windows on the far side of the court outside.

Magon smiled at him.

'There are several biographies of Huyatt up here, but you had better spend the morning studying Rafe's file in the Archive. It contains information vital to your characterisation. A creditable performance, if extempore.'

'You set it up!'

'I enjoyed the play,' said Magon. 'Now since you are – or he is – my guest, please go to your room and put on something more suitable. The double doors by the entrance, and follow the corridor.'

Cal did as he was told. The corridor bent left and right, continuing for a short distance beside the windows overlooking Pond Court. A redwood door on the right stood open and, at the end of the corridor, a door of ebony inlaid with squares of pale wood was closed. Obviously the chequered door led to Magon's bedroom, so he opened it. The room was spacious. On the opposite wall hung an unframed canvas the height of the room: an abstract of jagged colour. Placed centrally, so that the occupant could overlook the courtyard, was a vast antique bed, with a short wooden post at each corner. The wooden floor was bare of covering. He withdrew, and went into the room beyond the red door.

This room was lit by windows high in the wall abutting the corridor. The bed was not vast, merely large. A door near it led into a bathroom. A bedquilt was rolled at the foot of the bed, and a painting of the Tayaal hung above its head. He lay with his head on the roll of fabric and stared at the red and black painting. The sameness retreated to infinity, but far back in the fiery distance a minute trail of men and horses passed by.

On the wall to his right hung one of Crinon M'una's City paintings. It was a panorama taken from the viewpoint of an observer on the shore. He wondered, as he had in the City's galleries, how she made light with paint. He got up from the bed and looked closely at the painted surface and at the firm brushstrokes of the painter's signature: CHM.

Turning, he saw his reflection in the mirror at the end of the bed, a fallen spirit. He laughed. His possessions were arranged on the bedside table; the door of a clothes cupboard beneath the windows stood ajar, inviting his curiosity. The artisan slops he customarily wore were here transformed: he chose the black and a vermilion singlet and went through to the bathroom, to finish the conversion there. He was clean, his clothes were clean; the contrast of the heraldic colours with his golden skin gave him a fresh identity. He pushed his hair into the style the Bitch had cut.

A second door in the bathroom led (where else?) back into the Archivist's bedroom. He felt dwarfed by the giant abstract but the painting on the opposite wall was a masterpiece, foreign, strange. A bound and naked man, pierced by the arrows of his enemies, faced them amongst antique stones. Before the painting stood a prayer stool with an open book on it. 'Lord of the Skies, Master of the Four Winds, Monos we greet thee,' he read. It was the heresy he had heard spoken in the desecrated chantry.

Regaining his own room, he looked again into the mirror, and grinned at his reflection. In the study Magon, seated at the desk, was writing, and a pile of documents lay on his left. Cal stood close behind him.

71

'There is an open book in your room,' he said cautiously.

Magon laid down his pen, and turned round.

'Thief's eyes,' he said, smiled, and opening a drawer in the desk, took out a brass and mahogany box.

'Rafe had a permanent visitor's Mark.' He began to mix inks, and selected a tattooing needle.

'Right arm. Citizens are the only people to be marked on the left.' The Mark he outlined was a green reversed V.

'For Vern,' he said. 'I'm sorry, if it's painful. That's one way of telling a true ink; the forgeries have no sting.

'And it is an ugly Mark; the older symbols, pre-Reformation, are much more picturesque.'

The marking made slow progress: his hand was steady and the needle sharp. The green V grew like the crown of a trumpet lily emerging from the ground.

Magon held the arm out and moved it from side to side as if it were something he had made.

'I told you he was dead,' he said, looking into Cal's face. 'In fact, he took the milk: he was executed. A group in the City had begun to assume that every future lily harvest would be as abundant as that of 499, and to sell on that basis. In Sinein and Cheron one may do business in this way. The Law forbids it in the City – only Mahun has foreknowledge. It was an excuse to break up a troublesome group.'

'How can I play the part of a dead man?'

'Rafe Dayamit is still alive. The traitor they executed yesterday was the City boy, Cal.

'You must think of yourself as Rafe, or you may forget who you are.'

He paused, let go the hand.

'He was brilliant,' he said. 'Almost as remarkable as you.

'Come on. I promised you the view from the roof. There is just time.'

The way up involved a climb through the pipework of a service shaft, the ladder ending below a trapdoor. Magon pushed it open and they climbed out on to the roof.

Five flagpoles stood in the centre of the roof, where a small viewing platform had been constructed. The huge roof stretched away in all directions, its dull ribbed surface a trap for particles of red sand dropped by the Wind. The blue and gold flags of Mahun dipped and fluttered in the warm capricious air. They stood on the platform.

Magon, his black robe flapping, stood with his hands spread out as if he had conjured the City. Her streets and waters, the bay a smooth blue demilune, were revealed, her buildings shrunken by distance. The three Domes of the Sleepers were distinct above the trees by the Ayal, the attendant scavengers drifting above, an argent sea west of them. Cal turned his back on the City. In dreams, he had not seen so far. The magic gardens on the Hill continued for miles, until they encountered the sea. The coast of Vern was faint, ghostly. On the horizon a smudge, a misted apparition of red and gold, floated.

'It is clear this morning,' said Magon. 'That cloud is the Mahkra; that way lies the Tayaal.' He made a signpost of his arm. 'Next year, I must go into the Tayaal; you will come with me.'

His dream was being constructed without his permission; he turned to face the south. A green island lay across the line between sea and sky.

'What's that? There's no continent south of Mahkrein.'

'The Island,' said Magon. 'One of the Gynarchy's three prisons. You can't see it from the shore although they would be pleased if it were visible. Even they cannot decrease distance.'

'Who is sent there? Might I have been sent there if the Arbiter had succeeded?'

'No. It's a place for lost souls, for heretics, huskers, and those rapists who are too sick to be castrated. They used to send pederasts there before the Edict of Practices was issued in 484, Old Style of course. . . .' He spoke diffidently.

'And was it once Huyatt's blessed isle?'

'No; it has always been a convict colony. Look, green flags on the university today: the new term.'

The wind rattled at his robe and whipped his hair into a frenzied black cloud. The wind excited Cal. A sheet of paper lodged against the parapet, rustled, and was whisked away. Cal walked to the edge of the roof and stepped on to the parapet. The hot air pushed him; it was often windy among the tiles and ridges of the rooftops. He leaned on it and extended his arms; he had walked two sides of the eight before Magon pulled him back.

'You're mad. The wind would take you like a rag.'

'It's too weak today; you forget who I am. Rafe was a creature of the soil, a lily grower. I am at home on rooftops and towers: I consume the lily.'

'You have gone mad.'

'It's the wind. Listen! You can hear the cogs of the clock on the Bank; it's the only one which tells the correct time.'

'I can't hear them,' said Magon. The clock, confirming Cal's announcement, struck nine times. Then the other four chimed the unsynchronised hour in their separate tones.

In the Archive, the hush was even more reverent than that in the Library; breaking it with the assurance of his position Magon introduced him to the Assistant Archivist and left him. Estila Morion was a thin, elderly, woman who looked carefully at him before she took his hand and shook it. She escorted him into the recesses of the Archive. Desks stood in partitioned alcoves, private booths. He sat in one of them and Estila brought him a sturdy green file which she unlocked before leaving with the key. As he confronted it, the ease with which a determined reader could remove material and conceal it occurred to him. Then he looked up and saw the glass eye of a camera lens watching him.

He opened the file. The pages were loose, contained by a set of metal rings. (His own photograph was glued to the paper, his face, startled, against a seething background of metro passengers and overseers; he had not even been aware of a camera.)

RAFE DAYAMIT M'UNOR

BORN 9 Verrun in Udan 477AR (4477OS)

Of Odalion in Vern, Lily grower/trader, linguist, student of Huyatt Tayal, author.

MOTHER Melada Dayamit M'unah of Odalion, farmer. B. Odalion, 37 Hibornal in Udan 461AR.
FATHER Siamon Hennist M'unor of Illt in Baia, viticulturist.
SIBLINGS 2F 1M (Dayamit 0 2/3F, 2M/V)
PHYS. CHAR. Hair, lt. brown; skin, lt. brown; eyes, yellow/green. Ht. 5.6. Wt. 9.4
INT. RAT. Ceiling (500)
POL./REL. Neutral/Mahun
DRUG PROF. Med. Husk no dust.
CRIM. REC. Neg.
CRED. RAT. Solid
CREAT. RAT. High+. Vol. in prep., prov. title 'Huyatt Revisited'

Cal smiled, but uncertainly; the creature was a compound of himself and Dayamit surely, an inch taller, several pounds heavier, a similar hair colour, the same eyes.

MARIT. STAT. Neg.
SEX. PROC. Grade C

So much was obvious, but he swore for the sake of it, a pithy blasphemy in the ordered sanctuary for books and records. But, Mahun, his wages were already more than Dromio's.

CHILDREN Negative
SPERM BANK Two deposits (SP V201, V403), Bey 495 and 498
PROF. QUAL. Cert. Lang., Odalion 492; Cert. Matric., Odalion 492; Bat. Lang., Triple Hon., City, 494.
MARKS/PERMITS Tertiary, Vern. Annual trading permits. Permanent visa: 22 Lilb in Vern, 500.

He turned the page. Two sheets covered in blue handwriting detailed the history and geography of his body, the measurements and profiles they had taken in the Block. The four photographs were clear and clearly of him, verified by a corner of Y.K. Munah's skirt and white uniform coat. He looked closely at them as if he were an art student studying in a museum; he admired the stark photographs which made his familiar body into a beautiful object.

Clipped to a separate sheet of paper was a copy of Dayamit's will. He had owned a house in Roakn, eleven horses, and a third share in his mother's business; his personal estate was worth 29,731 bars. Curiously, he had left everything but one of the horses to his mother; the horse, specified as a grey registered mare, he had left to Magon Nonpareil.

A fish out of water, he stared at the booth wall in front of him. He imagined the body of Rafe Dayamit, the man who had unknowingly become himself, floating face downward in the Uynal or the Bania, one of the ubiquitous suicides. Who would miss him? Tarla perhaps. Amita, if she had not died. Was there a file on the traitor, Cal, in this cenotaph?

A lesser archivist had replaced Estila Morion at the desk, and he handed her the folder saying carelessly, 'Wasn't there an execution yesterday?'

'Yes, there was.' The girl smiled at him. 'Don't you have them in Vern, Mr Dayamit?

'He was some kind of Depther, I believe. Anyway, his file is with the rest from the Block. I'll fetch it for you.'

He studied the details of his former self. The pages were bound into this file. The photograph showed his double in prison clothing; a likeness was apparent, obscured by the inaccurate focus and a trim beard. A note scribbled across one of the documents in the handwriting of Arbiter Talamun Mahud read, 'Tenth case in twenty-one years. Beautiful boy.'

Dayamit had died at eight in the evening – yesterday; at about the time sleep had overtaken him. He remembered Magon's comfortable evasion, 'The original is dead,' and his subsequent declaration, 'He took the milk; he was executed.' He shivered as he read, trying to compel his intellect to subdue the superstition he had imbibed in the City streets. The Travs said that a soul could pass from one body to another. He looked at his hands, at the same strong and slender fingers which had served him for eighteen years. He touched his chin and closed his eyes, remembering the time when he had been Cal. He thought of Glaver, the smooth skin of her breasts, the second skin of cotton tight over her beautiful thighs; of Amita. Certainly, these were never the thoughts of Rafe Dayamit. He began to read the copy of his statement appended. With his finger, he traced his signature on every page. The record was completed with a laconic scribble, 'Last words before brain death: "Damn him." '

He slammed the file shut. At first, he took the lift but it was too slow, too mechanical for his anger: he left it and ran up five flights of stairs, sprinting unceremoniously through the marble galleries, and noisily throwing open the door of the Archivist's office.

Magon was standing by the window, refreshing himself with a cold drink. He looked down at the flushed and angry boy and raised his eyebrows.

'What have you done with him?' Cal demanded.

'The body has been disposed of, as is the custom after executions.'

'Where?'

'It no longer exists.'

'Is there nothing left of him?'

'Deposits V201 and V403 in the sperm bank; his wordly goods. Otherwise, no.'

'But he only died yesterday; when I was asleep. I thought he had been dead a long time.'

'It could have been you. I chose that he should die: I have replaced him with a better version.'

'That doesn't excuse you.'

'Morally, no. Logically, it does. Amazing that you both had such a rare eye colour – there is one other in the Archive.'

'Amazing,' said Cal in his accents. 'If his eyes had been blue, or brown, he would still be alive.'

'No.' Magon continued to stare out of the window.

'Look,' he said, gesturing towards the courtyard below.

A silktail monkey had climbed into the court from the gardens without. It was leaping from branch to branch in the lemon trees pursued by two gardeners with a butterfly net. One of the gardeners chased it through the fountain as it leapt, shattering spray. The water moulded the yellow cotton of her maral to her body.

'Has it never occurred to you,' said Magon, 'that women are ungainly? Look at those arms, distorted by disharmonious muscle. It seems obvious that their bodies had to be conditioned to toil; that their social and material advantage owes everything to the goddess and nothing to physical suitability. Consider the body of a man – how much more apt it is to heavy labour, how much in tune. Wasted here.'

The second gardener began to climb the tree in which the monkey was temporarily lodged and it watched her, chittering, ready to flee.

'It won't harm the tree,' Magon said. 'My sister and I had a silktail when we were children. Mother brought him in one day; she had bought him in the old market. We called him Tsiksik. Onomatopoeic, but also Tlivoornal for chatter.

'Come, Rat.' He placed a hand on Cal's shoulder, and turned him from the window. 'You have a book to write, have you not?'

Cal, his metamorphosis incomplete, went up to Level 15. Amusement mingled with irritation replaced his anger as he climbed the stairs; as he

76

and Magon both knew, Rafe was an Odalian matrionymic, often used as a given name: it meant rock, and raef were tree rats from the forests of northern Vern. He wondered if Magon had given Dayamit the same punning diminutive.

The buxom librarian, Filka, was cataloguing books. He sat down at a table, she brought him paper and pencils; she brought *The City in the Cleft* and leaned over to open it for him. Her full left breast pressed his ear; she smelled of scented soap and, seductively, of books and printing ink.

'I can open a bloody book,' he snapped, the tension breaking. She laughed at him.

'You must expect attention,' she said. 'Educated men are a rarity. From day to day we often only see the Archivist and poor Cudbeer – one inaccessible and the other inept.'

She retreated. He watched the movement of her hips; then, opening the book, plunged into Huyatt's clear prose. The first page of the book was a general description of the Tayaal and the location of Diridion in the Mahkra on its southern fringe; as he read the description of the road thither he grew unreasonably annoyed and paused to scrawl 'visit' in large letters on one of his sheets of paper. Now that his name was Rafe, he supposed he might do anything. Huyatt, who had first opened the window into his world, beckoned to him from without.

He read half the book, and walked the coloured rocks and narrow streets of Diridion with Huyatt. Filka reappeared.

'If you would like to join me, Mr Dayamit,' she said, 'I'm going down to eat now.'

'My name is Rafe,' he said, smiling at her. 'I'm sorry. I didn't mean to – ' (he almost said 'resist you') ' – er – be so abrupt.'

The dining hall was long, and furnished with separate tables. With the exception of Cudbeer, who sat in a corner reading a book, and an elderly man in the costume of Dinoord, the room was full of chattering young women wearing bright marals. Cymars were draped carelessly on chairbacks or laps. An occasional elegantly dressed older woman sat among the younger ones. He covered his face with one hand and groaned, peeping between his fingers at Filka.

'What's the matter?' she asked.

'Nothing. Nothing. Look, you sit here – get me some food. I must speak to Cudbeer.'

He strode across the room, conscious of a lull in the many conversations, and put his hand on Cudbeer's arm.

'Oh, Rafe,' said Cudbeer, startled.

'You were right. It's enough to make me blush,' said Cal, gesturing at the crowd of women. He squeezed the bony arm. 'Keep smiling.'

Filka had ordered. She itemised the dishes, dishes of which he had only read the names on menus outside expensive restaurants.

'Is that all right?'

He began to laugh, choking as he did so, and she poured water for him.

'You should have seen me yesterday,' he said.

'Why? What happened yesterday?' For a moment her eyes betrayed a kind of panic and he wondered if she knew who he was and was playing her part in the charade. She smiled, waiting for his explanation.

'Oh – I was drunk. Too much rahi. Yesterday I saw some Travellers imitating one of the Temple Dances; blasphemy but very funny.'

He told her tales of the City, as if from Rafe's experience, as they ate the food he was supposed to be familiar with. He tasted the wine she had ordered for him. It was sour.

'Don't you like it?' Filka asked, alarmed at disappointing her charge. 'The Archivist drinks red: Ceremana of course.'

'A bit early for it,' he said. 'Can you get rahi here?'

'Oh yes. Most people drink it as an aperitif.' She called a waiter who brought him one of the squat and familiar blue bottles and a glass. He poured himself a dose, caressing the waist of the bottle like a lover. Filka watched him.

'Health!' he said and raised his glass. Filka's face was a blank.

'Didn't you once have a beard?' she asked.

'Never.' He returned her challenging look.

He drank three doses of rahi and poured a fourth. Filka finished her multicoloured ice. A tall woman and another, whose red curls tumbled to her shoulders, were leaving a nearby table. Carefully they draped themselves in their cymars, casually they walked near and paused to speak to Filka while eying him under cover of the silken cymar hoods. Others followed them. He drank the fourth rahi, shifting uneasily in his seat. He yawned.

'Sleepy?' said Filka. 'We rest now, until the heat has abated. It's a habit that dies hard; the air conditioning is wasted on us.

'A garden shelter would be pleasant – let's find one for you.'

He followed her down the wide flight of steps into the entrance court of the Octagon and out through the great arch. Beyond the road and the floodlamps the pleasure gardens stretched away from them to the feet of the white palaces; the three towers were gilded by the midday sun straight overhead. There was shade only under the arcades of vines. Westward, the lawns were green; cascades and fountains jetted water everywhere. And there were women everywhere. The discriminate division was more obvious here than on the City streets where workmen, cooks, shop assistants and delivery boys mingled with the professional and businesswomen in the hurrying crowds. He wondered if it was evident to the small boys who played with their sisters and nurses on the lawns, if they knew who their fathers were, or that they had fathers, the rare and dead geniuses and beauties of past centuries. He wondered if they knew what they would become: the beautiful boys who paraded on Citadel Street and around the Glass Mall, eyeing the women and each other.

Filka led him over the grass, past flowering trees and bushes, by pleasaunces and bowers. They walked in an alley of arching branches and came to a green valley where two narrow lakes met at a fountain. The spray wet the statues by the water, making their green limbs glisten.

The rahi doubled his desire for sleep and his awareness of her attractions, veiled the valley in a delightful haze. Groves of trees spread close to the water and among them he saw the placid deer. If a unicorn had appeared in the midst of them he would not have been surprised.

They walked by the water, a paddling fleet of harlequin ducks following them, and came to an arbour within sight and sound of the fountain. A daybed stood here in the shade and he sank on to it. Filka arranged the pillows for him.

'Stay,' he said, reaching out. 'Lovely girl. Just what. . . .' He slept.

Filka stared down at him, frowning. He had long brown eyelashes, better than hers. His mouth was closed, the upper lip even and straight and the lower curved, bee-stung; she wanted to kiss them and she forced herself to think of the man she had chosen, a muscular shipwright. She thought of the Archivist and his proclivities. She replaced a fallen pillow and went away.

Cal, awakening, heard the falling water, the morning tide in the sewer, and sat up blinking in the strong light. As usual the rahi had left nothing but a sweet taste in his mouth. He remembered his spread of books and papers, he remembered his novel situation.

The androgynous statues wrestled in the fountain's spray; when he stood beside them he saw that they were, indeed, a pair of Dorinda's bronze hermaphrodites. Like them, he would become a creature which could only couple with its like, an earthworm, a leech, a barnacle, a crawling thing attached to the rotting ship of state; like Inana of legend who had been both woman and man. Undecided, unable to discriminate between the pleasures of both sexes, she had become both. He would become Rafe Dayamit.

But he lived; and he would live for many years though not for ever. Age made a jest of the beauty and the ambition of youth. He had no wish to see his hair grey and the fluid muscle of his body decay into tough elderly sinew.

From here the Octagon looked slender and graceful, its soaring arches deprived of bulk by the distance. The blue and gold flags fluttered bravely.

Magon's manservant served dinner promptly at eight; a silent man dressed in unobtrusive brown, he moved softly, visible but absent. Cal sat at Magon's right hand and watched a series of dishes come and go upon the long polished table; he ate hungrily and tasted the red wine Magon savoured. The white label on the wine bottle carried the single word 'Ceremana' like a signature across it. The bottle stood on the table between them, but the servant lifted the bottle and poured the wine into Magon's glass.

Two paintings hung behind Cal, either side of the door; he could see three more from where he sat. At the end of the room, to his right, hung the picture of a naked man and a fully clothed girl. She held two recorders and had just ended her tune; he held a recorder in his right hand. The landscape behind them contained other antique and symbolic objects: naked children, an old man contemplating a skull, a flock of sheep and their herd. Magon, seeing the direction of his look, smiled.

'It is the original,' he said.

The unframed painting at Magon's back, a neo-Minimalist abstract, was deliberately hung both as a foil to the ancient vitality of the figure painting opposite it and as a backdrop to Magon himself, a rich crimson rectangle, the colour of the curtain in his room repeated, but over gold. In one corner, an area of colour was turned back, peeled off, to expose the gold underpainting. He sat consciously before it, the reverse of the ascetic at prayer.

Opposite Cal, familiar tropical colours struck out: orange tigers hid amongst the dark and luscious greens of rhododendrons in flower, camellias bloomed, and the brighter flowers of isconas and naias hung down and mingled with tall bamboos; a brown man armed with a spear and a blue shield stalked the big cats through this zoologist's nightmare. It was a Silver Age painting, a City artefact. Below the painting stood a long narrow table of black and ancient wood and standing on it, not impinging upon the view of the painting, was a flat dish of silver shaped like a mighty starbeast.

Magon spoke of renaissance; he spoke of rebirth and change, illustrating his words with examples from the post-Reformation Silver Age, and introducing new concepts from faraway Gaia. Always addressing his guest correctly as Rafe, he invited participation and Cal became involved in the words.

Dessert was placed on the table, fruit on a footed wooden dish; Magon chose an apple and peeled it carefully with a silver knife. The red skin lay in a coil on his white plate; he bit into the flesh. Cal ate grapes like a votary.

When they left the table Cal, passing them, saw that the two remaining paintings were portraits. The one on his right showed a dignified woman and a small dark-haired girl; both of them wore the costume of the City. The other was of a man like Magon, a tall strong figure in the uniform of a Cheronese soldier.

The anteroom was in darkness; lamplight fell out of the open study door. He sat in a soft chair and Magon poured clear spirit into glasses. The study walls were covered in drawings, many small frames; some of the drawings were in ink and some in crayon. There were books everywhere, crammed in shelves, lying on tables, piled on the floor; that morning he had seen only the window, the breakfast table and the Archivist. Beside him was an alcove full of small objects of wood, ivory, and semi-precious stones, carvings like the worm-eaten apple on the Archivist's office desk. The statue of a naked athlete reached into the room with his javelin and beyond his arm was a second alcove. Here, a lily lay across the lower shelf and on the upper a large crystal gleamed like a diamond in a jeweller's window. Diagonally across the room stood the wooden figure of a man, lifesize, attenuated, and spiritual. Magon, standing next to it, looked into the dark courtyard.

'So,' he said, 'death levels all distinctions.'

'He is dead, not I.'

'But other people will see what they wish to see; and you have found a home.'

Cal drank some of the liquid in his glass. It tasted of nothing and had a heat like rahi.

'The City is my home,' he said and then, remembering their last encounter in the office below and their encounters without, in the City, 'Why were you in Hibornal's chantry?'

'It's an historic building and, while it is not my job to see that such are in good repair, they are all listed in the Archive. I like to visit them from time to time.'

'Perhaps you should tell those whose job it is to repair the chantry.'

'Perhaps I should.'

'And the other men?'

'I was alone.'

'The presence of twenty or thirty men and a priest caused me a lot of trouble when I first got to the chantry, about five o'clock. I had to climb over the roof.'

'As you mention a priest you can surely deduce the nature of the gathering.'

'It was a service.'

'It was a service.'

'It was a meeting of heretics.'

He shifted in the soft chair and rearranged his limbs and the cushions.

'I missed it out of my statement,' he said. 'Would it have gone against me – or you?'

Magon did not reply but he turned his dark head and looked at Cal. His face, beyond the lamplight, was in shadow.

'Why were you aboard the *Daystar*?'

'I go there sometimes.'

' – particularly to look at the cryomorphs?'

'No. On holidays, to look, to fly the ship, to explore her; I was imagining what Hero felt when he awoke light years from home.'

'I see. He got there, did you know that?'

'Yes. Can I have another drink?'

'Help yourself.'

Cal crossed the room and poured three fingers of the spirit into the squat glass. 'Vinefire' the label on the bottle said, 'Hennist, Illt, Baia'. Not just the grey mare but his spirits as well. He resumed his seat. Magon sat down opposite him and, leaning forward, spoke with sudden passion.

'Thirty-three years ago, when I was born in the Archivist's House on Broadwalk, Annalat Abayon was a pious templegoer, dutiful and efficient at raising funds. Five years later, she became a member of the Council.

'Her family are Artificers, silversmiths; Slake, my servant, is her cousin. Her real name is Heleth Amskiri. She has her position because the Gynarchy noticed her; first, for her piety and then because she was arrested and held in the Block for fraud: City Revenue found that her silver statuettes were made from thickly plated bronze and the assay marks on them forged. She might have escaped detection, because her work sold very quickly to tourists. She depended on their ignorance and forgot one of the first rules of survival: caution. A Surrogee was found and Heleth was altered by the surgeon. She was made Council member with special responsibility for Temple interests and funds while her *alter ego* was sent to the Island: she was already completely insane. Her doctors had withheld husk from her in an attempt to cure her addiction.

'Thus the Amskiri family suffered its first disgrace and a lunatic was safely disposed of without scandal. It's a system I use; I don't commend it.

'I, also, am fortunate; there has been no male Archivist since 2002, and he only lasted six years. I followed my mother. The Archive contains the City, every item of knowledge, free and suppressed, since Foundation and I,' he smiled, 'have access to it all, except for one small room in which the Gynarchs hide the secrets of their Dancers.'

'You have more power than the Council; more than the Matriarch and the Gynarch together.'

'That is so. I hold the key to the City; but I am the servant of the government, temporal and spiritual. I am known to be a devotee of the goddess and, if I cannot personally attend the midday service each Triple Mahun, I send a representative.'

'You're no better than Swan.'

'Your mentor?'

'Yes. He was as skilled at climbing as you are at manipulating facts.'

'Unfair! I have a great regard for the truth: the likeness, not the snapshot which satisfies most people.

'Supposing ... the City and the Hill were one; that there were no Beggars or pavement children, that everyone had enough. Supposing every man could read. If there were real schools! If the Academy was not an enclave of privilege! The City is wealthy, I am inexcusably wealthy: one painting would build and endow a hospice, would found a hospital, would build a house for every Beggar.'

'You'd give it all away?'

'I don't know. The Gaian paintings. . . .'

'If Mahun willed,' Cal said devoutly, 'everyone would drink Ceremana.'

'That's the voice of the pavement child, the cry of the hopeless. Mahun emasculates you all; the City sucks you dry.'

'Mahun wills it.'

Magon laughed, a short and derisive bark. He leaned back in the chair, stretched, and smiled at Cal. It was the smile of a friend and Cal, disarmed, smiled back. Magon looked at his watch.

'You had better go to bed,' he said, 'I must work. Goodnight; sleep well.'

Cal, dismissed so abruptly, wandered through the anteroom and the hall; along the wide corridor where, in the dim light, the paintings were undiscovered rectangles. He found his own room. The bedcover was spread out and two large saddlebags and a smaller bag stood in the middle of the patterned rug, covering the tree of life which was woven there. Dayamit's. His. He sat on the floor and opened them in turn, as if they were treasure chests.

The first saddlebag contained clothing. He lifted the garments out and laid them in a pile beside him; they were clean and freshly laundered but from them all arose a faint aroma of leather, horses, and Youth: once, he had found an empty bottle of the perfume in a bin, its fine notes trapped in the bottle, and traces of it scented the air outside the perfumiers on the corner of the Glass Mall. The clothing was of fine quality. He looked at some of the labels: they bore the names of the best tailors and designers in the City and in Odalion. At the bottom of the bag, underneath the last lawn shirt, was a magazine called *His*.

In the top of the second bag were the clothes which had been taken from Rafe Dayamit in the Block: a pair of sandals, white slacks, tight about the hips in the present City fashion, a white sweater knit in fine cotton and with a pattern of roses in the weave. The knees of the slacks were dirty, muddied as if he had fallen, resisting arrest, and on one leg, on the area of the thigh, was a smear of blood as if Dayamit had rested or wiped a grazed hand there. He found a note in one of the pockets: 'Out, sorry. See you later. Dork.' How is it possible (he formed the words into a question) that he was Dayamit's friend who was mine? A cotton bag, tied with a string, in the back pocket, was a lucky dip. He pulled out a silver cigarette case with the monogram RDM and thirty dark cigarettes, and an expensive gold watch on a leather strap. The strap fitted his wrist exactly. A chain of flat links of silver was better than a string; he removed the Beggars' tree from his own neck and hung it from the chain. Dayamit's ring was made of platinum and inside it was engraved, in characters large enough to read without a glass, the single word 'Vanity'. It fitted the third finger of Cal's right hand and, as he spread his fingers to admire the silvery band, he realised that he was putting a ring from the finger of a corpse on his marriage finger. Not for the first time; but those toys, Swan had taken from him to sell.

Underneath the clothing, he found a lined leather bag. He looked with interest at a toothbrush and grinned at himself in the mirror, seeing his own white teeth which were cleaned with zy twigs or not at all. And there was the square bottle of Youth, about seventeen bars' worth: two fluid ounces. Scissors and nailfile were monogrammed and so was a tortoiseshell hairbrush. He pulled a hair from it, tugged one from his own head and carried them both, gripped invisibly between finger and thumb, to the lamp. Dayamit's hair had been at least two shades darker than his own.

Two green towels were big enough to make garments from; one of them had been used and smelled more strongly of the perfume, of soap and its dead owner. The shoes were too large. In an outer pocket, he found a novel, an illustrated edition of Huyatt different from his own, and a battered guide to the City. There was a clothes brush and a silver and leather flask containing – he sniffed – rahi. He drank from it.

He turned to the small bag: cardboard files, documents, a certificate and notes on Dayamit's speculative and illegal trading in lily futures, trading permits and a brochure from Hotel Z. Pages covered in an untidy and sprawling script, the ghost of his hand, were Dayamit's notes on Huyatt, confirmation if he had not already found it in the Library, that Dayamit was a scholar of the Tayaal. Dayamit wrote that Huyatt, the man of the desert, had loved his own sex and that the whole of the *Travels* was an allegory of his search for the perfect lover; the beautiful and enigmatic Balkiss, he said, was a symbol. Cal laughed and drank the rest of his rahi.

In a polished wooden box were several pens and pencils with gold cases, each one engraved with the name of Rafe Dayamit M'unor. Here was a diary. He opened it and read. The listed appointments with buyers had passed but he saw, with some amusement, that in two days' time, he was to dine with M. On one page the names of City restaurants were scribbled, on another the best dance and drama theatres, on a third, notes on the harvest and three names which might be those of cafés, but were breeds of horses; against them was written a range of prices in credits and bars. The price of a barbon from the Tayaal would have paid ten street-sweepers wages for life. Dayamit had kept an irregular record of his weight which never exceeded 9.7. On the streets, his slender body would have been called compact. Fat fights fever, they said. Against the date 39 Vern, in two months' time, he had written 'home, or find house'.

A photograph fell out. It showed two girls standing under a tree, in the background a grazing horse. One held up a small brown rodent, a tree rat, a raef. The soft banded tail of the animal coiled about her left arm; her right was about her companion's waist. His sisters.

Two inner pockets held more valuables. The gold box set with a single diamond was a grit casket; inside it were paper folds and a small quantity of husk. He stirred the brown powder with the tip of his forefinger and the odour of the drug rose up, exciting his memory.

The contents of the last pocket showed Cal that he was a rich man: in a wallet were details of Dayamit's accounts at City bank and in Odalion, the security codes necessary to withdraw the money, identification and credit wafers, and four hundred bars in coin and notes. So, he had dreamed . . . long, hot afternoons. He sat on the bed, opened Dayamit's magazine, and leafed through it looking for familiar faces. The men were all foreigners, dark-skinned athletes from South Ineit and blond body builders from Northern Sinein, far continents, faraway perversions. There was no publisher's imprint, but the price on the cover was in the currency of Ineit.

In the centre of the magazine was an article on the City. The facile journo prose made of his holy and imperfect, everlasting, familiar City a picturesque relic, a cheap show for tourists from the East. He turned the page and saw, while a heavy foot trod on his shade, himself walking along the platform at Bank station, his dull Artisan slops emphasising the unusual colour of his eyes and skin; in the background, various Beggars and waifs squatted against the wall, their plight made more piquant and interesting by the ragged graffiti which covered the stones.

'Take the Metro,' the caption read, 'to capture fully the City's exotic blend of ancient technology and modern misery. And hang on to your purse!'

A second picture showed a group of Temple Dancers and a veiled Gynarch, stilled by the camera into a silken frieze; a third, the junction of Cat and Paradise Streets, the group of fivestone players in position on the pavement. He read of Dromio and Achille, unnamed but instantly recognisable; of the bohea halls and husk parlours, the pavilions and pleasure bars, of prices, commodities, buying and selling; of purchases.

The knock on the door startled him. He sat very still. The door opened softly, its red rim reflected in the polished floor: in his hands would be glasses, alcohol, even husk perhaps. But Magon carried only documents and a pen.

'I forgot,' he said, 'until I came upon it with the other papers. It needs your signature; here is a specimen.'

It was the application for the permanent visitor's pass whose issue had already been recorded in Dayamit's file. He practised the bold signature and wrote Dayamit's name as easily as if it had been his own.

Magon looked at the littered floor.

'I'll send you Slake in the morning. He knows where these things should go.'

'I detested his cat-house smell,' he said.

The noise the door made as he closed it sharply behind him was the only other sign of his self-inflicted wound.

Cal woke with the daylight and lay still, thinking of his hard and sweaty couch in the cellar and of his nest of sacks and tattered blankets in the clocktower, before he left the soft bed and ran hot water into the black-veined bath. This bath, in which one could sit like a storybook king on a throne or recline like the fantasy despot on his daybed, was raised on a dais. But the attendant women were missing, banished, if not from his dreaming, from the place. He tipped green powder from a tub by the bath into the water; the powder was scented like the struggling Zalcasian pine on the public promenade. He lay in the bath and moved his hands, cruisers through gem-hearted bubbles. Across the chequerboard floor, the bathroom furniture was monolithic, marble sculpture, and the towels on the rail were, like Dayamit's, huge and soft: no longer the threadbare hardness of the bathhouse rags.

He dressed in Dayamit's clothes, choosing a cotton sweater, blue as the maral Mahun was dressed in on the fifth day of each dek, Fiorin, the day of tides and rains; azure like her flags.

The courtyard below was hidden in vapour, the fountain silent at this hour. Slake had not arrived, Magon had not stirred. He wandered about the study examining the pictures and books. There were three City landscapes in pen and wash, the vigour of the line dominant, the architecture captured with bold, exact strokes, a drawing in crayon of the woman in the dining room; of another like her, and three pictures in which bound aboriginals struggled, which troubled him. Five drawings occupied a space of wall together. They had been made in pen and ink, the detail precise, one corner of each signed MN: a romantic landscape with horses grazing under a moon; a swimmer; the guts of a watch; his desk with an open register, the worm in the apple, pens, his hand writing flowing and flourishing letters in the book; the head of an old man. Above the desk was a sampler in ink of letters, beautifully executed in different scripts.

Some of the books in the shelves were locked, each one made safe from prying eyes by a band of pallid metal which seemed to have no edge and no opening. He fiddled with one of them for a time. Eleven books nearby had matching blue bindings and an octagonal imprint. He could not read them: the letters inside were from another world. Next to them were three newer volumes, the name of the author cut and gilded into the spines: Magon Nonpareil. *The Universal Museum,* published in 493, *Gaian Languages: A Primer,* published in 496, and *Dead Languages: Parallel Linguistic Evolution on Guna and Gaia,* published in 498: some of his knowledge encapsulated in concise prose, printed indelibly. Cal shifted from foot to foot, a novice traveller looking on the infinity of the starry sky.

On Magon's desk his pen lay where he had left it, slantwise on top of a pile of papers. The silver cap of the inkwell was shaped like a demon, the ink was black as sin. The twelfth bluebound book of the set lay on the blotter, its paper glossy and smooth, the characters ciphers. A sheet of paper marked his place and on it he had written a translation. The boy's eye travelled rapidly over the sentences.

> You ought to pluck the fruits of love at the right time of life, my heart, when in your prime . . . the eyes of Theoxinus . . . seethe with desire . . . I, by the grace of the goddess; seared with heat I melt like the wax of sacred bees whenever I see the fresh-limbed vigour of the boy. So too in Tenedos. . . .

He looked wildly round. The room was empty, still and silent, filled only with Magon's possessions. He put the book down stealthily, exactly where it had been before he read Magon's heart.

The crystal in the alcove gleamed; he became convinced it was a diamond. He stretched out his hand to grasp it and his fingers encountered plaster. The alcove was a delusion, a counterfeit in paint. He went to its fellow and picked up one of the carvings to make sure.

The diamond lay beside a clear glass of water on the top shelf. On the lower, an hour glass, half run, stood next to a yellowing skull and, crumpled in front of the skull, lay a drawing of a naked man with the words 'None Such' written across the painted page. Before these lay a white lily which projected from the alcove into the room. Deceived again, he tried to touch its painted petals.

He felt Magon's presence behind him in the room.

'When you know me better,' he said, 'you will be able to read it.'

Magon carried an unstrung bow and a quiver of arrows. He was without the severe black cymar of his office and offered no threat.

'I work from eight until six and the evening hours may be extended,' he said. 'Anything else must come before or afterwards; the compensation is that I have the gardens and butts to myself.'

Cal got up and followed him like a child after a circus.

*   *   *

87

The butts were half a mile away, a flat area of ground excavated from the hillside below the palaces and surrounded by a high hedge atop a bank; statues of Mahun's archers stood against the hedge, and four sets of steps descended to the field. But Magon ran down the bank. A target was set up, waiting for him.

Cal sat on the bank and watched him string the Talong bow. When he put a foot on the wood and pulled up the string, it formed itself into a double curve, a wave of the sea, a stave for the music of shooting. Long ago Cal had watched, with other pavement children, the Temple archers in their practice ground. The discipline was the same. He saw Magon negate himself and the face of the man lose all identity. The archer nocked an arrow, raised the bow above his head and smoothly drew down the string. The enclosing arcs of bow and string moved steadily into the lateral plane and were still in perfect tension, lightly held. Then the arrow was in the target, quivering on the margin of the red and the gold. With the same movement the archer drew his bow until five more arrows were in the target, all in the gold. Cal knew better than to applaud. The arrows were retrieved and the exercise repeated many times. He sat still, his eyes never leaving the figure of the archer; there was no need for a swift glance left to confirm the certain hit. No arrow missed the target, no arrow hit outside the gold; the exercise flowed on, monotonous in its rhythm.

Magon wiped his arrows and unstrung the bow. He looked up into the sky and, turning, looked at Cal. To speak would be to comment on a rite and Cal got up and walked with him from the ground.

On the hillside, they paused and looked seaward. A black swan flew east, fast and level, its wings beating steadily.

'Will you come with me into the Tayaal?' said Magon.

'I have wanted to travel since I first read Huyatt; in the City, I had no choice because it was impossible; now, I have no choice because my soul has been bought.'

'Is it so bad?'

'I don't know; I'll let you know.'

Cal walked on, up the hill; a man like Magon Nonpareil would never run after him. At the top, he turned. The Archivist was motionless where he had left him, his eyes and his attention on the sea.

In his room, the impassive Slake was hanging Dayamit's clothes in the cupboards. He entered the room cautiously and sat on the edge of the bed, watching the manservant.

'You've done very well, for a dead man,' said Slake gloomily.

'Have I?' The man had ears then, and the knowledge that comes from keeping them pricked.

'Better than I have, keeping house.'

'You came here from the City: you were an Artificer, weren't you?'

'Yes.' Slake's confidence lapsed. He turned to the clothes. Cal studied him; probably he was younger than he looked. His features were permanently creased, his attention permanently abstracted as he folded and laid away the garments like a born servant. Yet he had been a craftsman. He volunteered no more information and finished his task. As he turned from the cupboard, he stood still and considered Cal.

'You don't really look like him,' he said. 'You might have been cast from the same mould but finished differently; he was a proper piece of pig-iron.'

'Your hair's too light,' he continued. 'Make it darker or lighter altogether. And your voice is wrong. At least it's not a full-scale substitution, no surgery . . . there's no need. You'll be yourself again next year.'

He went out, leaving his mysterious words and prescience for Cal to ponder.

In the afternoon, Cal was taken deep into the Archive and shut in a room with a hand recorder and a notebook. Dayamit spoke to him from the box. Alone with the voice, he shifted in his chair, seeing his double in the same place, sharing his thoughts. Death had no dominion here; the boundaries had lapsed. Dayamit read expressively, with the rounder accents of Vern, a passage from Huyatt. It was the account of Huyatt's voyage from Taimiss to the Blessed Isle. The musical voice lingered, appreciating the words, without intimation of its coming journey. When the recording ended, Cal spoke into the box himself. Listening to his own voice, he heard the flat Depthside vowels and harsh consonants, the additional content of breath which made the voice distinctive. He listened again to the dead man, listened intently, again and again.

In ten days Cal was accustomed to luxury. The noisy City was a picturesque realm far below him where other lives continued separately. It was not individuals he missed – the Tribers and Glaver inhabited an old dream – but the unruly community where life was a frantic race. Here was silence and order; even music had its own place, as the plants in the gardens had their own beds, water, and food. He did not need to scratch for money, he did not need to hunt for the next meal. He ate well, learned to drink wine, and worked all day at his books and Dayamit's identity in the great Archive. Sometimes Rafe, sometimes Cal, he lost himself and became an actor in Magon's play. His entrances and exits were written in the text.

Three times he dreamed that the dead Rafe visited him, in every way like himself, in stature, in comeliness, with beautiful eyes and voice; and the clothes on his body were the same. He stood over Cal's head and spoke to him: 'You sleep, Cal. You and Magon have forgotten me. Give me a proper burial, build me a monument. I died for you. I might have lived a long time among my horses.' Cal stretched out his arms to embrace him; but he did not touch him for Rafe had vanished like smoke in the wind. He awoke shivering; when he told Magon of the dream, Magon laughed and told him he was superstitious.

Once, coming into Magon's room, he found him bowed over the prayer desk; above him the painted martyr looked up to his deity, mute, unmoving, the ten arrows implanted in his flesh like skewers in butcher's meat. He left the room without speaking.

Magon read a book of sermons; he read the lives of the Desert Fathers. Watching him, Cal thought of Rafe and of the manner in which his life had been taken away: he watched a murderer. The man was a murderer by proxy. So much the worse, he was culpable. He appeared easy in his guilt, assured in his concupiscence, yet he continually read of saints and martyrs. He prayed morning and evening, poised in nice equilibrium between his two worlds of body and soul. His mind, Cal saw, was exercised every day, a commonplace and unregarded tool. Cal ceased to fear the time when Magon would possess him, but he began to fear the time which would follow when guilt possessed Magon.

Cal spent some of Dayamit's money. He bought leather shoes. Measuring, as Magon taught him and with the help of Slake, the distance from his outstretched hand to the floor, he sent down to the City; the bowyer, when she received his order, came up the hill to him and measured again. When the bow was delivered, a quadruple running curve of laminated woods, a wonderful example of the ancient art, he went out to try it; his arrows were fletched with the cerulean feathers of kingfishers and his glove and bracer were the cinnamon colour of his own skin. In private, Magon ceased to call him Rafe, reverting to his own customary and meaningless name. They shot side by side each morning, separate in the discipline, Cal revealing another talent, perfect co-ordination of hand and eye, an archer without identity, the essence of the bowshot. Together, they walked in the gardens. Below them, the City's many towers struck at the sky and the crescent bay held off the bright sea; sometimes everything was concealed in mist but the gardens. Cal saw new truth and beauty on the hill; he began to be seduced by Magon's dream of concord. Magon gave him gifts: a commentary on *Diridion*, his own glass of spun crystal, a carved ebony rat which, cornered, reared up to bite.

Slowly, the withdrawn Slake revealed himself to Cal, as if the daily presence of another from the City gave him back his heart.

'You know what I am. There was no defence and no plea. The Archivist got me out, but not before Hyason and the surgeon had their way.'

He had adapted his skills to his new condition, learning a way to fill the long empty years which remained to him; instead of the love of women he enjoyed the spaniel love of a body servant; instead of polishing silver he polished floors; instead of drawing wire, he cooked; instead of engraving fine detail, he maintained the pattern in his employer's ordered life. Whatever he overheard, he learned to forget; much of it, scenes, words, attitudes, passions, was a revelation, yet, when he went home, he made his mind a blank. Yes, he had a home, a pretty little house close to his family home; he could afford comforts on his salary.

Now, he produced two brown glass bottles and requested Cal's presence in the bathroom.

The alkali took the mud colour from his hair and turned it bronze. Slake applied his liquids in such a way that his head was dark with pale guard hairs, like the coat of a puma or a desert cat. In the mirror he saw Slake grin uncharacteristically and move out of sight. He was left with himself, or Rafe Dayamit, who regarded him insolently from the glass.

Matrician women and their satellites passed by Cal every day. Whether true to Magon, fearful of retribution, or mindful of the fate of Slake Amskiri, he did not know; but he looked on them as untouchable, beautiful butterflies behind glass, until, going one day into Magon's office, he met a Temple Dancer leaving. She was tiny, fine and delicate like the figurine of Mayuna in the curio shop. The veil of her cymar was only half drawn over her head and he saw her gazelle's eyes and her mouth as she smiled up at him. She passed him, the top of her head level with his chin. The bells on her ankles and at her waist chimed as she walked away. His body, revenging itself on him for his new devotion, fired up; his heart and soul ran after her.

There was a theatre in the gardens, a circle of red terracotta tiles enclosed by a high bank where wooden seats could be placed. Dressed as Rafe, he went there with Magon. An evening of classical dance was promised and he, who loved the rhythms of the Quarter, and the gestures of the Travellers' dances, expected tedium. The theatre was lit, in the traditional manner, with flares which cast a ruddy glow over the stage and the nearest ranks of the audience where he and Magon sat. A group of musicians, flautists and drummers, awaited the dancers.

The last of the audience arrived, bejewelled women, diplomats and emissaries from afar, judges from the courts below. He felt the hair stand up on his neck. A tall woman walked across the stage to her seat in the front row and he recognised Magon in her: the same dark hair, in her case a length of it pulled back into an unruly plait, the same eyes. Besides, her picture hung in the study. He touched Magon's hand. 'Crinon is my sister,' the Archivist said, smiling at his revelation. 'I collect, she makes. And she is Xharam'un'.' She was a secret person, a woman whose style revealed nothing: well-dressed, short hair, the correct flower pinned to her jacket. They were the last to come.

Cal looked at the stage and wondered if the little Dancer would appear. She was the first. She danced in the centre of the stage, her movement intricate and sensuous at once and he recognised the horten, refined of its crudities but unaltered in its passion. Too soon, the rest joined her and she was lost to him, every Dancer a sister, so alike in stature and appearance, costume, every one with a red maral, every one belled. The rhythm of the dance changed and she tumbled across the stage, her long plaits whirling, the scarlet silk hardly disturbed, so rapid was her movement. He saw her legs and slender feet. Again, he touched Magon. 'Mahuntal,' he said. 'She is the first among the Dancers.'

The dance ended; she did not appear again and he sat through the long performance growing dispirited. Fireflies moved on the air above the dancing floor.

'She's not a popular actress giving a performance.' Magon told him. 'She dances for Mahun.'

The dance was not applauded, but everyone stood to pray; then there was wine and conversation. He found himself moving amongst judges and Lectors, talking of his book.

Next morning, when he left his room, he was amazed to find the little Dancer in the hall. Magon, bending low over her, was saying a farewell. Cal stood still, the Talong bow in his hand, and watched the door close behind her. Magon forestalled his question.

'She came for information I have for her, concerning her son. I told you that anything, everything, apart from my duties to Annalat and in the Octagon, is relegated to the time left over.

'It was the custom among Temple Dancers to exchange any boy children born to them for a kinswoman's or a friend's daughter – in order to maintain a stock of Dancers. These children were and are marked with the lily; the boys are brought up in the trade of their adoptive mothers and marked accordingly. In 2307 the custom was codified by the Gynarchy and latterly it became the practice to purchase the girl child and the adoptive placing; it is no longer an act of freedom and goodwill. The girls are carefully chosen for what must have once been a racial characteristic, for their ancestry and likely lack of stature. Certain families expect to be invited to take part in an exchange.

'M'untal is one of those who object to the practice. Her son was taken three years ago and placed with a family of silkweavers in Far Maralis. I am about to reverse the Wheel and bring him back.'

Cal, seated on the hall chair, listened in silence. He was appalled to hear that the little Dancer had a son and pictured him as a huge white baby, like a leech, like the infant in Magon's icon from Gaia.

'She's married then,' he said.

'No. She divorced her husband two years ago. Temple Dancers expect to marry several times. Once the heritage is ensured and a Dancer has borne daughters, she goes her own way. In M'untal's case, her own way is without precedent. . . .'

The knowledge did not comfort him, nor improve his temper. He went with Magon to the butts; unable to abandon his thoughts, he could not draw the bow. His hands were unsteady, he loosed no arrows. The porcelain had been broken.

Cal looked at the money lying in the drawer. Mentally, he spent some of it. He drank and bought good husk; he saw himself entering the shops in the Glass Mall and emerging resplendent in clothes of his own choosing to walk towards the Quarter. Cudbeer's plight returned to him.

'I'm going down to the City. Can I take Cudbeer?' he asked Magon.

'I can't stop you,' said Magon irritably. He turned away and picked up his pen. Cal watched him write. Magon, he judged, thought it politic to keep his leash loose.

At night, they rode down to the City, two partygoers dancing across the suspended bridge which led from the gardens to the Old Citadel. The wireway left from a high platform at the edge of the citadel, the first stronghold, and they stood by broken towers and creepers, watching a car approach. The lights of the City below were reflected in its smooth silver belly as it slid upward depending, like a huge pearl, from its wire.

A veiled couple left the car and hurried away into the gardens. Cal and Cudbeer entered the suspended bubble. The front part of the car was a cockpit of glass, a viewing platform, and Cal went there to stand on the transparent floor, high above the dark jumble of rock and tree ferns at the base of the precipice; but Cudbeer sat in the lighted section, his eyes on his feet and his hands clasped tightly around his knees. Bats and a night hawk pursuing them flew beneath Cal. The descent was slow and the lights below approached in shoals.

They left the car at the terminus in the Glass Mall and passed through the first set of barriers, where an official glanced at their passes. The second check was more thorough; separately they entered a glass booth where an overseer wrote down their names and business in the City, and examined their Marks. Her manner was deferential and she bade them a pleasant evening.

They followed the illuminated signs which pointed the way to the central plaza. The shop windows were filled with glittering jewels, with gowns, with imported kinetic luxuries, with Zalcasian furs and snakeskin shoes. In the centre of the plaza the statue of a naked man on a rock depicted the virtues of commerce. He held a trumpet lily in his outstretched right hand. Smaller figures were carved on the basal rock, artisans hammering, weaving, and digging, and Mahun's cat twined about his ankles. They passed the statue on a high walkway, level with its flat stomach.

'She used him a lot,' said Cudbeer. 'Amalia the sculptor I mean, as a model. He got very fat. He lived in the Garden House when my grandmother worked in the Archive.'

Transparent stairs mounted up to meet them. They descended to Citadel Street. A uniformed woman stood outside Hotel Z, but she was only a porter. Cal grinned. For a moment he had slipped inside his old skin. The woman saluted them as they passed her.

'We could have a drink in the hotel,' said Cal, speaking like an astronomer who has discovered a new constellation. He looked at Cudbeer: his spectacles were crooked and they did not conceal the excitement in his eyes. Cal had put on the white clothes, Dayamit's rose-patterned sweater and flagrant slacks. In the window of the jeweller's opposite he saw Dayamit's reflection.

They went into the hotel and found a circular bar on the second floor. It was full of socialites and businesswomen. The men were as fashionably dressed as their escorts. Cal did not ask for rahi. Imitating Cudbeer, he ordered a double measure of golden ichor, blood of Mahun. It was strong and good. He ordered again. Reflected in the numerous mirrors he saw at least a dozen women watching him. They left Hotel Z on a raft of well-being and good humour.

They came to the Lily Exchange, where Cal paused to inhale the combined perfumes of husk and dust floating from the packing shops behind it. I shall have not Ala, not Zalcissa, but Niska, he thought, and ran up and down the marble steps like a child. Cudbeer, watching him, laughed. The alcohol had given him new assurance. He took his spectacles off and put them in his pocket.

They turned into the narrow streets at the Quarter's edge and crossed na Hinoor Circus. The streets of the Quarter spread out to the south and the west. Cal led Cudbeer up the Heavenly Way. Zalcissa's pavilion was sunrise gold. They both went in.

The pavilion of the droll Pulchrinella was painted with naked incubi; the flare burned outside. Cal pulled aside the door curtain, disturbing the rampant couple painted there. Dork sat on a chair painting his toenails with red varnish, his discarded wig on the floor beside him, his slender woman's shadow huge on the canvas. He looked up, and started. Cal heard him whisper, 'Mahun!'

'Did I come back the other night?' he said. 'There's a lot of grit gone from the box.'

He watched Dork regain his composure. Carefully he stoppered the bottle, and put it with the rest of his paint.

'Rafe!' he said. 'I'm sorry; I thought I had seen a ghost.

'Come here. What an improvement! Which hairdresser did it? You look absolutely different.'

Cal, wanting to say, 'I am, you stupid bastard. It's me, Cal,' smiled instead and spoke of his decision to stay in the City.

'I'll see you again then. Tonight?'

'Maybe next week,' (but how and when, he thought). 'I'm showing someone the sights tonight.'

Dork sighed and picked up his wig. He pulled it on and slumped in the chair, a pantomime of disappointed desire.

'Would you mind leaving then? You might be depriving me of the rent.'

Cal withdrew into the street and walked amongst the booths and pavilions until he came to Cloud Nine. He could not experience the place like a tourist: he was aware of every scrap of flaking paint, of the inadequate water supply and the uncollected litter, of the reality under the raucous music and the gaudy tinsel. Yet Niska's pavilion was draped in white silk, a blatant advertisement of her earning power. She preferred to entertain tourists; the number of wealthy men in Mahun's City was naturally limited. She excelled in parodies of the Temple Dances and could have been a Temple Dancer herself, had she not been the daughter of a whore. She was standing on her hands outside her pavilion, enjoying the inverted view. The first she saw of Cal was the expensive leather of his shoes.

'I like what I see. So far,' she said, somersaulting to her feet. 'Aren't you the Vernian lily trader, Rann – no, Rafe Dayamit? I thought you were of the other persuasion?'

He had forgotten what Cal knew; that Niska was Dork's cousin.

'So what?' he said.

She smiled and held out her hand for his money.

The bohea hall which stood at the western end of Paradise Street was the best in the Quarter. They sat in the best seats to watch the dancers and a woman brought them laced bohea. Cal drank steadily but Cudbeer was permitted a small glass only.

'Save your strength,' said Cal. 'You're not used to it.'

The pleasant hour passed and he took Cudbeer to Niska. He loitered in the street outside watching the to and fro of the crowd. A couple of matrician women passed. They were veiled, but he knew them now by their accents. Two bodyguards walked close behind them. He saw Dile the Fister go whistling by and he saw the Rosy, Aurora, walk with another woman into the shadows behind a pavilion. Aurora was the most vicious of the tribe.

A humming began in his ears and he shook his head violently, wondering what raw spirit had been added to his bohea. The noise continued; he saw again the tiled prison corridors, heard the sub-sonic control and the screams of the tortured man. And then, as the night was rent above, he knew the sound. Fighters! Aircraft! He had heard it once before with Swan. He looked up: Mahun's Branch drifted alone in the sea of stars, so quickly had they passed.

He realised that a crowd had gathered, women and men disturbed from their pleasures. Cudbeer stood near him, Niska's feathered cloak clutched to his stomach. Niska herself was clad in a sheet. They stared into the skies.

A second wave of fighters fled over, ripping the quiet apart.

'They're X-wings,' said a middle-aged man nearby. 'Must be from Hayna. What's it mean?'

'Off course? Practice? War?' The crowd speculated. The third wave passed over, black and threatening against the stars. There were no more and the City's night sounds crept (see breezes into a still afternoon) into the vacuum. Music came from high on Citadel Street where the Hill tigers were dancing, a prowldog howled his lust and various bitches answered him from every corner of the Quarter; the rattle of carriages and shays over the setts began again. There should have been uproar, but Hayla of Hayna had vouchsafed her vision only to the people of the night, to wealthy strollers incognito in cymar and veil, to whores and studs, beggars and invisible thieves; respectable citizens were no doubt cowering under their bedsheets or blind and deaf to the world in theatres from which they would be conveyed by carriage at the appointed hour. The crowd soon cleared; the show must go on, as Niska said, rearranging her silken sheet in more becoming style and turning back to her pavilion. The uproar beat on Cudbeer's eardrums, but it assailed Cal's soul, perturbed by the aerial visitation from beyond the mountains, the second alien invasion of his private space.

'Fifteen X-wings over the City. What's it mean?' said Cudbeer as they walked arm-in-arm from the Quarter. 'Fifteen of Hayla's fighters over a city declared inviolable by international treaty.'

'Change?' suggested Cal, recalling Tarla's sybillic mutterings.

'You can't change the Gynarchy,' said Cudbeer impatiently. 'What does it mean?'

'Things might be different if the Gynarchy wasn't there, if the Matriarchy was less corrupt.'

Cudbeer pressed his arm.

'You're just parroting the Archivist. The X-wings have gone, over Hayna now, landing. Look there!'

It was hard to follow his pointing finger beyond the buildings, beyond the City, high among the stars: left of Eshtur and 'Nyon, a bright and moving star, an intense point of light.

'I'm bad at stars. What is it, another false star?'

'You know it's not a star, nor a satellite. It's the ship from Sinein. Come home.'

'Out of orbit. On her beacons. Mahun!'

The light moved imperceptibly as they watched; they measured the ship's progress by her changing position against the constellations. She, a noiseless invader, brought visions of a different kind from beyond the stars, not violence but felicity, not international strife but universal concord, so silent she might be a star herself or a new *Daystar* returned.

'I wonder what cargoes she carries,' said Cudbeer. 'I wonder what she has seen?'

They peered at the sky until they could see her no more; then, blinking as their vision adjusted to the dim street, they walked on. Cal, leaning against Cudbeer and carrying the weight of the Archivist's arm across his shoulders in the easy friendship alcohol and a successful night in the Quarter conjure from the most fainthearted, watched the starship sail about his mind with a cargo of husk and dust, a crew of cryomorphs, and a persistent yaw which defied reason and physics; and all without a grain of grit, he reflected, smiling into the darkness.

They had wandered as far as the edge of the Beggars' Reserve. Again, he had forgotten he was Rafe Dayamit. In their fine clothes, he and Cudbeer were rare birds. He swore in Deep, and Cudbeer stared at him. A child tugged at his sleeve. He looked around and saw the pavement children, his brothers and sisters, clamour in the starlight for bread.

'Listen to me,' he said, in the speech of the Depths. The children stopped whining and looked at the rich man who could speak like them. 'I can only give you money now.'

The children clamoured, tugging at Cudbeer's suit; some of them jeered and made cat-calls. He picked out a boy whose oval eyes were like a doe's and a girl older than the rest. He told them to follow these leaders to the hospice in the morning.

'Silvanor.' Cudbeer emptied his purse into Cal's hand, Dayamit's wallet was stripped.

'That's all I have here,' he said. 'Now go.'

Like a bundle of leaves blown by the wind the children ran off towards the bright lights and the food stalls of the Quarter.

'Where are their mothers?' asked Cudbeer in horror.

Cal laughed.

'The City is their mother,' he said. He stood beside Cudbeer in the broken, dusty street. Cudbeer, looking back at the Quarter and around him, became aware of shifting bundles of rags in the doorways, Mahun's destitutes.

'I'm sorry,' said Cal, observing his distress. 'It's an accident that I've brought you here. Let's go.'

'No,' said Cudbeer. 'Can't we do something?'

'Do what? You Hill people make me puke.'

'Give them money, food – as you have just done. Set up a refuge?' Cudbeer persisted.

'What would that do? Prolong their hopeless lives. Make them even more dependent on charity.'

'We could start a workshop.'

'A workshop? Making what? Backscratchers? Listen. People like you are shit on the blanket. I refuse to stand in this filthy place discussing ethics with an archivist. Let's go.'

Cudbeer was silent. They turned back. Suddenly a dog howled in a deserted garden and a distant pack of prowldogs answered it. Cal swore again. A whistle shrilled, a camel whistle. The Beggars in the ruined doorways, on the ground, and in the gutter got up and began to move swiftly in every direction.

'Get in here,' said Cal, shoving Cudbeer into the shelter of a bricked-up archway. They heard the thunder of staves on shields and a running and stumbling crowd filled the street. Across the way a woman screamed. Cal took his knife from its sheath on Rafe Dayamit's belt.

'Don't be a bloody fool. Put it away.' Cudbeer shouted at him. 'I know who you are; you don't want to be found out do you, Cal?'

Cal looked at him and at the knife. He remembered Luce's blood. He was not surprised at Cudbeer's revelation; the quiet scholar was only another character in Magon's play.

'Hyason,' he said. 'She put me in prison. I'll kill her.'

'She won't be here. She's the First Officer. They keep her for special tasks.'

The security corps swept the crowd along before them with stave and lamp. The chaser dogs were leashed but ready. Cal and Cudbeer were still arguing when the nearest trooper reached their place of conceal-ment, but Cal had been persuaded to put away the knife. The camel gestured at them.

'Come on,' said Cudbeer, dragging Cal forward. They were swept along in the crowd.

Na Hinoor Circus filled with the turbulent crowd; a ring of troopers surrounded it. Troopers and stavemen began to penetrate the crowd. Their lamps lit up terrified faces, open screaming mouths, raised sticks. Cal saw a woman fall to the ground and disappear underfoot; a trooper brought his baton down upon the head of a child.

'If I see her, I'll kill her,' he yelled wildly at Cudbeer.

The people on the fringe of the mass began hurling stones at the troopers. Cudbeer fought to keep his hold on Cal as they were pressed by the crowd. Their involvement was quickly over; they were herded to a checkpoint where an overseer examined them.

'He's drunk,' said Cudbeer, retaining his hold. 'Raving drunk. Here, right arm. He's a visitor.'

The overseer eyed Cal with distaste. She spoke to Cudbeer.

'Sorry sir. Necessary. President Chacma's visit. Hope we haven't spoiled your evening.'

Cudbeer dragged Cal away.

They walked along Broadwalk towards the Glass Mal, Cal silent. The Temple on the hill behind them was lit and they heard the third hour trumpet; on Paradise Hill only the security lights of the Octagon showed, ablaze. Slowly the silver cars floated upward.

They passed the two barriers and sat wearily down in a car, Cal's anger beaten down and transmuted into a frustration which made him bite his knuckles. Cudbeer was the nervous archivist once more, his holiday over. The car bore them upward, rising above the troubled City. They looked at each other and began to laugh, in slow individual bursts which accelerated into a hysterical male howl of derision.

Cal took three hours' sleep and woke before his bedside clock summoned him. He took Rafe Dayamit's papers from the top drawer and read the printed rules of Citybank. But the bank did not open until ten. He took the wafers and the cash account record; possibly the hospice would accept a credit.

In the kitchen Slake was soft-footedly preparing breakfast and mist curtained the windows; of Magon there was no sign yet, but Slake had taken his porcelain cup and saucer from the cupboard. Cal drank the bohea Slake poured him and went out. Pausing at Cudbeer's desk on Level 13 he scribbled a note on the blotter: 'Better tell him where I am.'

He descended again by the wireway. The mist, from which the blue and black towers stood up, lay low on the City. Even the Mamelon was veiled. He thought of the Beggars, of the Travs and Strays, locked in their pound and unable even to beg. He wondered how many of the children had escaped the net; they were masters of concealment, fitting their starved bodies into pipes and drains and under baskets. After Swan's death when such a round-up had occurred, he had been able to curl into a husk carton and so escape detection. And if some of the boy's group were still free, how many would they collect from other parts of the City and bring to the hospice?

He had no appointment, but he knew that the mother would see him. The sisters turned away no one in need and no one whose money could help to relieve that need.

He came to the house. It lay in the angle of land between the Uynal and the Bania. He remembered playing in its garden after an attack of sewer fever which had nearly killed him, and he walked through the arched gateway which pierced the former warehouse. A high wall protected the children from the dangers of the Bania but not from its odours; there was no such wall at the end of the garden where a terrace overlooked a long slope of masonry and the river below, clouded and racing, at high tide. The sisters had a strict rule which forbade unsupervised play on the terrace. He remembered standing there in a crowd of pavement children like himself. They were singing and they all held the strings of red balloons. The sisters had declared the last but one day in Alcuon to be his birthday.

He remembered also his sorrow and tears when, recovered, he was sent back to the streets.

He stood in the garden and watched the mist dissolve from the Quarter and the derelict factories across the river. His clocktower stood up above the blackened roofs, the glowing golden ball, as ever, balanced miraculously on the finial of its tiled roof. He thought it was too high to take another tenant kindly.

The same worn swings and battered slide were in the garden. The wooden donkey had lost his other eye but his smile was in place. He had ridden the donkey a long way into the gardens of his imagination. The grass was scuffed and dusty, worn by many scampering feet. He heard the children at their meal inside the hospice; he heard them begin the closing grace: 'O Mother M'un take thou our thanks.' A sister came into the garden and looked questioningly at him.

'I'm Rafe Dayamit,' he said. 'I want to pay for some meals for the pavement children from Daid's Ground below the Quarter. I met some of them last night and told them to come to you.'

She smiled. 'They arrived at five this morning,' she said. 'We didn't know what to do, so we're giving them breakfast. There's an older girl with them; she said a Hill tiger had promised them food.'

'How many? A boy with huge brown eyes?'

'No boy; fourteen, no – fifteen including the girl.'

'No.' He put a hand to his forehead in a gesture of despair. 'There must have been thirty or forty of them.'

'I'm afraid they will have been caught in last night's round-up: the usual policy before a state visit. This time it's Chacma.' She laid a comforting hand on his sleeve. 'Don't worry. At least the government will feed and delouse them.'

'But they are locked in a pound like dogs.'

'I know,' she said. 'The way of the City is cruel; but Mahun will feed and bless them on the final day.'

He followed her to the office of the mother where he sat in the visitor's chair and drank the bohea the calm sister brought him. He arranged with Mother Serilla to pay for one meal a day for a year for thirty children, and for their medicines and clothing. The hospice could not accept his credit because the sisters could not afford to pay for an account of their own. He walked the mile to Citybank, waited until it opened, and drew a hundred and thirty bars from Rafe Dayamit's cash account. Returning, he laid the envelopes of money on the desk before Mother Serilla.

'Thank you,' she said. 'You have been generous.'

'I could do more,' he said, ashamed of his complicity in Magon's crime. 'I. . . .' He broke off; he had almost begun to confess to the nun.

'Come back in a year and see then how you feel. If you give us more now we might waste it.'

He took out Dayamit's wallet and drew a 20 frag note from it.

'Would you see that every child in the hospice has a red balloon on the 39th of Isk?' he said.

Mother Serilla smiled.

'How mysterious – and marvellous – She is. We used to give the children balloons when one of them had a birthday; we can't afford them now. Thank you. Did you like balloons as a child?'

'Yes,' he said. 'I liked red ones best.'

He left the quiet place and went out again into the noisy city. He was ashamed of his sentimentality; it was a weakness. He looked about him. The streetcleaners, their early tasks finished, had been given extra work and were hanging garlands between the lamp-posts on Broadwalk. Across the wide road the House of the Archivist, where Magon had been born, was bright with flowers in baskets. He felt a pain that was obscurely physical, a tightening of muscle and soul, of desire and despair together. He had come to the Glass Mall and he went into the first shop he saw and bought clothes with the assurance and the money of Rafe Dayamit.

Light entered his room warily in the mornings. He saw the outline of the high windows and the painted cupboard and, turning his head, the long painting of the City. The door was open and Magon stood there, his black cymar belted over his street clothes, the high collar of his dark shirt visible above the neck of the robe. Clearly it was late, and he had missed the rite; the arrows were loosed.

'You let me sleep!' he said, accusing.

'I wanted to go alone.' Magon made no apology. He came forward and stood in front of his sister's painting. 'Chacma arrives at ten. There is a service, a procession, lunch, a council session, a reception.'

'I shall survive without you. I'll be in the Library.'

'But you are to attend. Some events at least. And you should visit your aunt – the procession passes her house. If you want to hear Chacma, three in the Chamber.

'This is an invitation for this evening.'

The white envelope skimmed on to the bed. Cal picked it up, but he did not open it. The question of the X-wings returned to him.

'Did you see the fighters?'

'I heard them. Hayla chose the wrong day for her demonstration to Chacma, unless it was meant for us.'

'A display of strength? A provocation? A warning? I saw them fly over when I was with Swan; people were afraid then.'

'It's nothing. They will say it was a training flight, and it is. They frightened me, ah, twenty-eight years ago: Crinon comforted me with candies.'

'Why do they use such old craft?'

'Does it matter if they kill a few trainees? They are training the girls to fly sub-space: the best survive.'

'We saw a starship. Would that be the longhauler which left Sinein in 353?'

'Mm. Probably. They excite your ambition?'

'I suppose so. Real flight, higher and further than any bird.' He stretched, his arms making wings against the pillow.

'And the pavement children excite your pity – yet you would not return there. The Law says that Mahun will bless them all and take them in Her arms.'

'I know. A hospice sister told me.'

'Because,' Magon came close and touched his altered hair, 'pity is a dangerous emotion. Starsailors would have none.'

'Nor cold cryomorphs. Don't worry. Pity is not one of my familiars.'

'Then I shall go and smile at Chacma.'

From women piloting fighters, from an intergalaxial starship to a white pasteboard invitation was a long descent; when Magon had gone, Cal stretched out and let his consciousness come down from the stars.

The invitation was not a formal communication from the Matriarchy to the lily trader. In an upright and delicate script, Mahuntal Kiden M'una begged Rafe Dayamit to accept; she would attend him on the Long Verandah at nine in the evening. He lay back to consider her, the porcelain mother, the intricate mistress of the Dance. He remembered Niska and her silks, the ten bars. And he had spent it as if it were a bit he had found in the gutter. Pulchrinella cost eight bars; this was how Rafe had lived. Achille. He guessed at a likely sum. This was how Magon had lived before his advent, maybe still. But the Dancer sought him, cost nothing, not even the effort of emotion since he spent that wildly in another shop. He looked at the suit Slake had selected for the day. It hung beside the tall cupboard, tawny linen; the subtlety of the shirt colour was too nice for him but he knew that Slake, with his craftsman's eye, had chosen correctly. His polished shoes stood together, toe to toe, heel to heel.

Cal flung back the bedcover and examined his feet. The soles were softening from his new habit of wearing shoes. He saw from his reflection in the mirror opposite that his lean body had acquired the polish of well-being, that the archery which was supposed to be an effort of the soul had improved the muscle of his shoulders and back.

The clock in the hall began to strike: nine glasslike chimes. He jumped from the bed and went singing to his bath.

Ignoring the covered breakfast Slake had left him, he read the note on the table.

> Rafe. I have taken the liberty of providing you with a document case which I hope you will find useful, even luxurious! We of the City pride ourselves on the excellence of our tanneries. Please apologise to your Aunt on my behalf and blame me for detaining you beyond the allotted time – I imagine you will tell her of your decision to remain in the City to write.
>
> Regards, MN

Refusing to play, he took a pencil from his pocket and scrawled 'Thanks, Cal' across the note. He laid it on Magon's blotter.

The corner of the document case was discreetly marked with a gilt octagon. Inside he found price lists and more market reports in the untidy handwriting, so similar to his own, of Rafe Dayamit. An unsealed envelope addressed to Lissa Dayamit M'unah contained a small sheet of paper on which rows of strange characters were embossed. He carried the paper to the window but could make nothing of them. He took a handful of Vikkutrian raisins from the bowl on the table, and went out.

The house on Mayalon Street was an old Craft Revival dwelling dating from the Huyatt period; its plastered walls were painted white, carved posts supported both the verandah a little above street level and the roofed balcony on the first floor. He had passed it many times before. A small blue plaque in the shape of Mahun's cat was fixed to the wall by the front door and the lettering on it declared 'City of Mahun. Preserved building'. He knocked on the door.

The girl who opened the door had hair like flames. She was white, her pale skin dappled with freckles. He looked at her, remembering that the silkweavers, carrying with them the caterpillars which were their fortune, had travelled from Sinein to the City in the first millennium; the ancestry of the Dayamits was surely complex.

The girl smiled a welcome. 'Rafe! Where have you been hiding?'

He ran lightly up the steps and embraced her. He wondered which cousin she was.

'Cuddling a girl.' She laughed at him. 'You've shaved off your beard. You look quite different: much more handsome. And you've been to an expensive hairdresser, I can tell!'

'Have I changed so much in a year?'

She stepped back to consider him and while she stood, her hand to her chin, a sharp voice called from within.

'Lota! Who is there?'

'It's Rafe, Mother. At last.'

Lissa Dayamit stood in the shadows of the hall and stared at her sister's son. She was a short and formidable woman, pale, with grey hair tied behind her head. She stepped forward and put a hand to his face. Her fingers explored his face and he, enduring her touch, realised that she was blind.

'Where's your beard, boy?' she barked.

'Clippings, rubbish down the drain. They are not in fashion any longer.'

'You are late,' she said in softer tones.

'I'm sorry, Aunt. I've been staying with the Archivist. He told me to offer you his apologies. And' – he took the envelope from his pocket – 'this is for you.'

She took the sheet of paper from the envelope; her fingers moved swiftly over the raised characters.

' "–greetings–love–expect a good harvest–girls well–Hysan is to marry next year–she wants a bolt of yellow silk"–now, which yellow does she mean? No doubt it is for Hys.

'Who will she marry, Rafe?'

He had the answer ready.

'Cheon Ammist – he is our neighbour's son.'

'I know. A dark boy, solid, sturdy, altogether reliable: a good choice. You left your mother in good health?'

'Never better.'

'I suppose I must excuse a young man,' said Lissa Dayamit. 'Haven't you a kiss for your aunt?'

He kissed her in the formal Vernian fashion, twice on each cheek, then pulled her close and hugged her.

Lissa Dayamit moved easily about her house. They went into the drawing room, and a serving man brought in bohea and hot cakes. The room was furnished for comfort, but with style, antique polished pieces prominent amongst the modern couches; the hangings and curtains were the best the Dayamit factories could produce. Opposite the window hung a small cityscape by Crinon M'una.

Lota sat near Cal. Her brothers, three huge men, came into the room and greeted him. Their sleeves were rolled back, their fingers calloused and oily, the brown shuttles on their left wrists the indicators of their constant industry. Cal read their thoughts: his hair is dyed, lily trading's a soft option, can you see him with dirty hands? Nila, the elder daughter, sat by her mother; in her, the brilliance of the hair was subdued, sandy, and her eyes were quiet; she sat still and spoke little. He listened to their conversation, joining in where he could. He talked of his horses (for he had read the diaries more closely and, in the Archive, consulted the bloodstock register). As he listened and watched, his mind was busy, putting together his incomplete image of the family; he saw that, like true friends, they did not need to speak to each other in order to communicate. The brothers, so big, were not indistinguishable: Fleish was the oldest. He was the engineer. Welch was an expert in weaving techniques, and Lifad, the middle one, oversaw the workers. Nila wove bright stuffs, while the volatile Lota specialised in the dull-hued slubs which were used as corse-cloths in the Temple. They were good people, careful citizens; they went to the Temple each Triple Mahun and Lissa and Nila attended the early service every day. They worked hard and prospered.

'You are very quiet, Rafe,' Lota teased him. 'Too many nights on the town?'

'I've been working hard,' he said. 'As well as the planting, I've been studying Huyatt again and writing, another book I'm afraid. . . .'

'No!' they cried in unison and in turn. 'No! When can we read it? Have you found a publisher?'

'It will be finished next year,' he replied confidently. 'The Study Committee is going to publish it, I believe, but that is arranged through the Archive: out of my control.'

'I shall enjoy reading it,' said Lissa Dayamit. 'Though I hope your conclusions are not as unlikely and as unnatural as before. . . .

'How can you write and work on the farm at the same time, my boy?'

'I'm staying in the City for a while, at least until next Alcuon. I have permission to work in the Octagon, and I will be staying with the Archivist.'

'Moving in elevated circles,' said Fleish.

Lota giggled. 'Living with him? Better take care!'

'Lota!'

'It must be nearly time for the procession,' Nila said softly, tactful. 'Are you coming out, Mother?'

'Yes. I love the smell of the Cat, the sounds – the hooves, the drums and trumpets. I can see it all in my mind.'

Lissa Dayamit sat on a chair on the balcony upstairs and her children grouped themselves about her. Her counterfeit nephew, on the edge of the group, near the balcony rail, looked down into the street. There were no Beggars, not a single pavement child: they had rounded up the lot. The workers from the weaving sheds formed a press on the opposite pavement; directly below him stood a group of forewomen and traders from the nearby shops; other families were gathered on neighbouring balconies. He heard the Temple trumpets squawk and then, like dry sticks in the wind, the rattle of staves, as stavemen came running down the street, clattering their weapons against the setts; but the street was already clear. They formed a close group at the exit to Broadwalk and waited for the procession.

A company of the Wall Guard led, sweating in their fatigues. He knew they were all trained in unarmed combat and the bow. They were fit and lean, seeming impatient at the slow pace they must maintain; the men among them looked as though they had been selected for their musculature alone. Three of them carried the City Banner, its blue length falling about their green shoulders, its golden lilies distorted in the folds.

The mounted security corps followed, the officers among them reining back their chargers till the necks of the horses were forced into a curve.

He saw Hyason Sarin. She was beautiful. She sat her white stallion strongly, subduing him with a cruel bit; her hands in white gloves were steady on the reins, her white uniform restrained the curves which should promise pleasure and her golden buttons were obscene nipples. His heart beat with the drums. How easy it would be to kill her from the shadows with a bow, not with the lovely recurving Talong bow, but with a crossbow, swift and sure. One of Chacma's remote kill weapons would be even better. He sweated. He heard one of the brothers exclaim at her regal presence. He could have spat on the white peak of her cap.

A body of stavemen and overseers followed her with three drummers and a sinister symbol, the pointed tricolour of the Security Corps.

The carriage wheels rattled on the setts. In the first, the Gynarch sat alone, her blue robes folded about her, the hood and veil of her golden cymar drawn across her face. Her hands lay in her lap and the three consecrated rings shone on her fingers. The second carriage was full: Annalat M'una sat beside Chacma, her tailored suit visible under her open cymar, her greying hair covered by her scholar's cap. She pointed out the sights of the City to the President and he, bending towards her, followed her gesturing hand. His huge hands were spread on his knees, his neck was a thick column and, above the dark red military uniform with its medals and braid, the coiled plaits of his tribal hairstyle were a splendid incongruity. Magon sat opposite them, altered by the occasion, soberly robed in indigo, the silks of his degrees cascading down his back. As the carriage passed beneath, he glanced up, finding Cal's eye. Lota and Lifad exchanged a look.

The third carriage was empty and represented the She. Beside this carriage walked Temple archers and the tall Temple guards with their braids and catskins. But women of the security corps walked with the first two carriages and among them was the president's own guard, in threatening black battledress. Expediency had prevailed over the custom of the City: they carried rkws. He heard Fleish exclaim at the sight.

He was glad that the camels had passed and that Magon too had been borne away with the ceremony.

The Gynarchs shuffled past in their slipshod sandals, the varying blues of their robes indicating their rank in the order. Sweet smoke floated up to him. Insistent in the din of shouts and wheels, he heard the plangent bells of the Dancers and their orchestra of flutes and gongs. They did not attempt to march or walk sedately, but spun or leapt as they pleased, their bright skirts whirling. The group on the next balcony dropped flowers on them. He looked for M'untal, and felt Nila move to stand beside him.

'There!' she said. 'That's our best Dancer, Mahuntal. Isn't she dainty? You wouldn't guess she has been married and divorced and has a little girl of three.'

'I wouldn't,' he said. She danced on the edge of the group as if she were too fine to be hidden in the company and must be displayed. He hung over the rail, and watched her cartwheel underneath. Nila, leaning on the rail beside him, admired her.

'I wish I wasn't so big and pale and clumsy,' she said.

He looked at her. She was nearly as tiny as M'untal, her cloud of hair an aureole. He gave her an amused smile.

'You look to be about the same size as the Dancer,' he said.

'But she's a Dancer!'

'I believe they have to sacrifice a lot,' he said, recalling Magon's exposition in the hall. 'Personal life, time, their dearest wishes. . . .'

'So do I! I'll show you my loom later. You can have some of my silk: one length represents three deks.'

M'untal danced away down the street, her small bare feet light on the granite; she had not looked up, though he had wished for flowers to shower on her. More shuffling Gynarchs followed the Dancers.

Among these, a crowd of tall and muscular women bore the image of Mahun. For a deity, she wore today frivolous costume, a red maral to represent joy. Her fringed sash was tightly tied in the intricate celebration knot, silver like her cymar. The hair of the image was plaited and laced with coloured cords and stuck with flowers; her black eyes stared blankly up the street.

'She is kept for days like today,' whispered Nila. 'For secular processions. I hate that dress.'

'She means she hates it because it looks like a whore's dress,' said Lota.

'I like it,' he said. The red of Mahun's joy was the red of the Dancer's silks.

Some among the Gynarchs carried the cats and most of the animals were content to loll comfortably across an arm. One escaped and went leaping and spitting up the carved balcony post next door, havoc amongst the delicate petals of a lily-flowered hibiscus; it was caught and passed down.

'I can smell her,' cried Lissa, sitting straight in her chair. 'Is she behaving?'

The black leopard had two keepers, massive women; each one held an end of the steel chain which was locked to her collar. She had her own guards, armed with staves and armoured in leather, lest she should misbehave and lash out. She stalked and swished her long tail; the bright sunlight revealed her spots, dark in her dark coat.

'She's putting up with it,' said Lota.

'Good. Remind me to send that goat carcase up tomorrow. They may be glad of it, and I like to think of her feeding on meat from our land.'

He looked down at the broad collar and the chain; they were secure, but he was glad to be above the cat and close to the house windows. The striped cat had run up the post like lightning.

The trumpets cried brazenly out. The cat ignored them and went her way, indifferent to her tormentors.

He saw the Temple Prostitutes, a shifting crowd of gold and white drapery.

'Let us go in,' said Lissa. 'The Cat comes last.'

'The Holies are here, Mother,' Lota protested, 'and you know there's lots more.'

'Nothing I wish to witness.' Lissa retreated, and Nila, a dutiful daughter, followed her.

The unofficial anti-procession surged past, some riding on donkeys. An organ grinder, wearing a monkey in place of a hat, provided its music. Tarla leaned on the Bitch's arm and Dog was drinking from a rahi bottle and laughing with his followers. The Ironmen marched amongst the Faces, hostilities confined for the day to inventive jeers. Stoker leaned heavily on Bale, already in flight: there was no need to draw back into the shadows – besides, he was Rafe Dayamit and the Archivist was his friend and protector. Magon loved him. He could view the quarrels and seductions of the gutter from above. Zalcissa sat with Ala in a shay, her hands busy at her crocheted lace. Pulchrinella stopped underneath the balcony and curtsied. She was as slender as a girl, unnaturally real, a painted mask.

'Come down and join in the real procession,' she said to Lota. 'We're all girls here.' Dork's alto voice was sarcastic.

She leered at Cal and winked with one of her black-rimmed eyes. Since he was Rafe, he bowed extravagantly and kissed his hand to her. He thought that if ever he encountered Dork again, if ever he was himself again, he would bruise those wide eyes and then he would laugh and grind the pretty face into the dust. After a fight in childhood, they would buy or beg a sugar cake and, sitting on the wall above the wide tidal reach of the Uynal, divide it equally down its sticky centre line, where the crystals formed a mountain range.

Dork grew tired of flirting with him and tripped off after the other drolls, his high heels catching on the stones.

'Who was that?' Lota stared.

'Some poor devil from the Quarter,' he said. 'Probably earns as much as you.'

'But how? Is she an actress?'

'You could say so,' he said but Lifad, interrupting him, said, 'If Mother hears you teasing our cousin, she'll have one of her fits and then you won't be allowed out for deks.'

'I'm not teasing him. I want to know.'

'That was a droll. A Grade B1, a transsexual who can't afford the operation.'

'What operation?'

'He wants to be a woman.' Lifad went into the house, leaving his sister staring after him. Eventually, she turned back to her strange and beautiful cousin.

'Come on. I'd better take you round the sheds.'

He watched the shuddering looms swallow thread and spew cloth. Beyond the engine-house were the stables. He had to admire the horses, standing on the brick floor of the passage behind the stalls, too close to their iron heels, forcing himself to stay when the unrealiable animals suddenly moved. He listened to Lota enthusing and pretended he understood.

Lota led him into a smaller shed, and there Nila was, working hard at her loom. She rested her busy feet and laid the shuttle down.

'Hello,' she said, and smiled at him. Lota left them and he was easy again, admiring her, touching the silk. It was as blue as a halcyon's wing.

'You can have this piece,' said Nila. 'My gift.'

'What would I do with a piece of silk?' He heard Cal speak.

'How beautiful it would look,' said Nila. 'Blue and gold: the spirits of Paradise wear such colours. A vision in a wonderland.' He listened to her dream and Lissa's step, soft in the dust, startled them both.

'Lunch before you go?'

He declined. It was still early, not midday. The sun shone in the yard.

'You'll take a glass of wine with me.' This was a command. He followed Lissa into the house and she led him to a square room on the lower floor, her office, the centre of her empire. The walls were lined with ledgers and sample books; on the desk a swatch of silks lay like oil spilled on water. He watched Lissa lift a bottle from a bucket of ice, uncork it, and pour as if she could see the two glasses as clearly as himself. The chill had enhanced the taste of the wine and sharpened it. He wrinkled his nose at the bubbles. She listened, her head tilted, intent, to hear him drink.

'I fear you are a rahi drinker like your mother,' she said. 'It's a pity your father doesn't return more frequently. He would teach you to appreciate good wine.'

'Oh, I like Ceremana,' he said.

109

'My Lady! We can only afford that on Feast Day.'

She pulled up a chair for him and sat down at her desk. He saw from her stiff posture that she was about to deliver a lecture.

'Now, my boy, you are young and the young are easily infatuated. I'll say what your mother won't: we all want to see you settled. You are twenty-three, time to think seriously.

'Don't throw your inheritance away. Great men are so rare that they cast a shadow, a wake which drowns true innocence. This is not our way. Those are Sineinian customs. You understand me?'

'Yes Aunt.' Had Rafe been as subdued as he was by her presence and her values?

'My husband was a good worker. He gave himself to the business and the family. Men are dirty beasts but he never inflicted himself on me. If he visited the Quarter, I never knew it.'

He listened as she expounded her creed, bracing himself against her righteous flow of words. At last she paused, and he said, deferentially, 'I must go soon, Aunt. I am supposed to go into the Council at three to hear President Chacma.'

'Hm. That barbarian. Make sure you stay and hear our Matriarch as well.'

'Of course. The meeting marks the start of a Long Assembly.'

'Well then, give me a kiss, and don't leave it so long before you visit us again.'

Released, he fled into the street. It was hot, so hot; he had been indifferent to it but now that he was a wealthy and respected man, with money to spend, he felt it. He walked into the glass atrium of Hotel Z and ordered ice, water, and rahi.

The apartment was cool, the welfare of the paintings paramount. He stood naked in his shadowy room and shouted for Slake.

'I felt hot,' he said. 'I've never felt the heat before.'

Slake was sympathetic. 'It's the effect of the cool air in here: you don't expect Him to care more for us than for His paintings?'

'What should I wear to the Council meeting? I haven't a clue. And what should I wear this evening? Will it be very grand?'

The New Citadel, which was four hundred years old, stood on a platform of floodlit lawn and lights burned in every one of its windows. Cal walked towards the steps. Slake had dressed him formally in black: he felt confined by it. He went up the steps reluctantly, solitary amongst the other guests; as he bared his arm for the overseer he watched the jewels and glitter of the women. The first hall was walled with pale stone, honed to a marblelike gloss and patterned with embedded fossils. A glass rotunda hung in the centre of this hall and within it, people were dancing in the Sineinian manner, cheek to cheek. The music was foreign too. He passed some statuary and urns full of flowers. Here, beside a tank of water in which carp circulated, was a buffet and the waiters were running with piles of plates and great dishes of cold fish and fowl. He accepted a glass of sparkling wine and drank it, standing still in the ante-room, while the guests passed him by.

The second hall had pillars of glass and at the far side of it he saw Magon's sister in the centre of an excited group: they were all looking at a painting and gesticulating wildly. He idled, watching them, but no one noticed him and his memory of the little Dancer's sensuous arabesques and the teasing glimpse in the round dance of her fawn and certainly warm and female legs pressed him to make the pasteboard assignation in his pocket flesh. He set down his empty glass on a table nearby; there were other objects on the table, carvings. He felt compelled by their presence to move the glass away and then forgot it in his contemplation of the tight array of grotesque shapes. They stood close together like a laughing group of men surprised by the sudden and accusative entrance of a woman. He was sure they represented men for they carried burdens on their backs, or in the places where their backs would be if they were not so much like trees or rocks, natural objects threatened by an elemental force. A pother of straw and dust lay over and around them: if he flicked it away the figures would gleam with the innate polish of smooth wood. He touched the nearest and found that the grime was stuck on, somehow part of the figure, intricately carved or etched.

He was no longer alone in this crowd of strangers. A beautiful woman had silently taken hold of his arm. She wore a low-cut gown. Her perfume, civet orchid, overwhelmed him. But she had only come to talk Art.

'Enchanting, isn't it? A lot of people find it difficult – and I've met at least three who felt insulted by it. You're a man: what do you think?'

He pretended to understand her rapid words and implied opinion.

'I think it has promise,' he said. Were these the proper words to use?

'Of course, Chenodor would prefer it if there was only one use for a woman,' she remarked, and was gone.

In a frame on the wall, he found a further comment on the work:

Raist Chenodor: Possession, 499AR. Wood, plaster and string.
The sculptor has made the claim that true worth cannot be eroded.

That a man, his fellow, had made something good enough to put on public display in this citadel of women pleased him, heat as fiery as rafi in his belly, and he wondered if Magon had seen it. He walked on and entered a third hall, dim, hot, close – and gasped, as did every new visitor. The glass wall which made one side of it was etched and faceted, prismatic, polycoloured, reflecting the lights directed on to it. The floor

111

and the other walls, the furnishings, were all dark; the gems on the women and the beads on their gowns borrowed light from the glass wall, glowing points in the blackness. An open door in one of the dark walls framed the outer darkness and the stars in the sky. He went to it; this was the way to the Long Verandah. Slake had instructed him well.

This side of the building was in shadow. Before him the night-haunted gardens, perfumed and mysterious, stretched for miles. Somewhere out there lay the butts. Far below, to his right, where the dark land sloped downward, was the sea where illuminated ships sailed and the two lighthouses threw out their regular ribbons. Eshlon and Mahun's Branch pulsed steadily, their constant light interrupted by the years. The Long Verandah stretched right and left, a landlocked jetty from which pleasure craft might put out. Under its roof, the round lamps floated, pearls. He stepped on to it.

Chairs and tables had been placed amongst the shrubs, chairs inhabited by small intimate groups, tables on which the trappings of wealth were carelessly scattered: jewelled spectacles, coins, silver purses, glasses of wine, miniature caskets filled with dust which, in the Quarter, would be tins of husk. Scraps of conversation came to him as he walked, demonstrating hs own new insouciance with Rafe's silver cigarette case and lighter.

'I think they should be freely admitted.'

'A mercenary does not require a university education.'

'The Archivist. . . .'

'What a waste of money and resources!'

'But Magon told me. . . .'

'There will always be the exception. I don't object to that.'

'Maja Hinoor married a man who was her intellectual equal. . . .'

'Who is that?'

'I see!'

He had reached the far end of the verandah, where a glass moon hung from the angle of the roof. He looked at Dayamit's watch. He was early. He was nervous. The seductive art critic had begun it, sapping his confidence, nibbling at his will; the Dancer with the red maral would finish him off. He wished himself elsewhere, anywhere, at the top of his tower or in the foetid darkness of the sewers, walking in the Quarter where money ensured a transaction free of involvement, walking on the beach where the nightdark sea would be calm. Chacma had the right idea. The two wives he had brought with him from Cheron had attended him to the Council chamber and retired gracefully after the welcoming ceremony. The president of the Independent Republic of Cheron had spoken well. He had spoken in his own language, using his strong voice and the emphatic vowels effectively. The vocatives rolled around the oval chamber. Filka, solemn in a grey cymar, translated.

Chacma had spoken of the Treaty. Forcefully, he had delineated his objectives. He did not refer to Hayna nor her hereditary rulers, but spoke of the unity of peace. He proposed the formation of two new peace committees, one in Roakn and one in the City, whose task would be to prepare an agenda for preliminary negotiations. These negotiations would lead to a meeting. His intricate transparencies had continued for an hour.

When he sat down, one of his ministers leaned towards him and whispered in his ear. The grey-haired officer on his left consulted a paper and Cal recognised the original of the dining room portrait.

Annalat Abayon, the Matriarch, stood up to answer him, first scanning with her keen eyes her rows of councillors. She opened the folder which contained her speech, but never referred to it.

'Most Honoured President, Lion of Cheron.' She addressed him in his own language, made her speech in it while Filka interpreted. She said that the President was no doubt correct to assume but that she, and she did not, could not, in the name of her people, she would not agree, but she did suggest, indeed she insisted. . . . She thanked the president for the great honour he did Mahun and her City, her citizens and herself. She sat down and the Archivist spoke to her. Cal watched Magon's lips silently move, and heard the measured voice absent from his ear; he listened to the fencing and parrying of the two principals and marvelled at the lack of subtlety and the evasions. Translated from their sonorous syllables, Chacma's words were hollow. Annalat preened and bowed to him while she spoke her denials; and the two Nonpareils, father and son, sat in opposite camps. They had not acknowledged one another in any way. He saw Magon impatiently tapping one finger on another during Chacma's speech; during Annalat's, he folded his hands together.

When the trumpet sounded the end of the session, Cal had hurried out, back to the Octagon to wait for Magon and an interpretation. But Magon, rushing in at five minutes after eight, had gone straight to the bathroom with nothing to offer but a few empty remarks. Cal had left him shouting orders at Slake.

Here she was. He dropped the weed into the garden behind him. Child-sized, miniaturised still further by the distance and the parallel perspective, she had begun the long walk towards him. She walked lightly in jewelled slippers. Like the other women she wore a gown, a dark blue gown which glittered; her long black hair had been made into some sort of crown on the top of her head. The bells of her Dancers' costume had been reduced to a single chime, the pendant terminals of a zone. Increased by the hair, the top of her head now reached his lower lip. She greeted him formally, with the triple kiss, standing on tiptoe to reach his cheek.

'I hope you haven't waited long,' she said and then, quietly, 'My sister is near. Shall we move?'

She took his arm and they returned to the darkness by the citadel wall. Here, beside a potted orange tree, she stood on tiptoe again and kissed him briefly on the lips. At once, she relapsed into formality.

'I don't know if you have been to one of our receptions before, Mr Dayamit. There is usually a period of time for meetings and greetings, supper at about eleven and then an entertainment. Jugglers tonight, I think, some circus act; and the Zalcasian dance troupe.'

'Rafe,' he said. 'My name is Rafe. It means rock and is similar to another Vernian word – raef, ar ay ee ef, are tree squirrels. The girls keep them as pets.'

'I'm sorry,' she said. 'I am M'untal.'

'You're famous. I heard some people praise you today.'

'Perhaps.' She smiled. 'I have danced all my life.' She smiled again, with the candour of a small child. 'I don't know how to treat you, I don't know anything about you.'

'There is little to know, and what there is is very dull,' he lied. 'A provincial trader with a good income and an interest in old books.'

'I'm sure you're not dull! You're the friend of the Archivist.'

Even here. Which scene was this?

'Do you know Magon well?' he asked.

'No. A little. Better than I used to,' she said. 'And I know his sister, the painter of the City – '

'Did Magon ask you to invite me here?'

'No. Of course not!' Now he had offended her. She laughed. 'I did ask him if it was all right to invite you.'

He turned and looked into the dark hall where the marvellous windows still shone.

'Tell me the history of those windows,' he said. 'And take me to meet some of these people. I want to forget Magon for a while.'

'You would have to ask Him about the window,' she said, emphasising the pronoun exactly as Slake did. 'He knows everything.' It was not spoken cynically. She took his arm again and they went on, into the building. The close darkness surrounded them, anonymous couples and a cocktail of perfumes. The glass waterfall shimmered. He moved his arm away from hers so that he could touch the back of her neck. She shivered. She was not like Glaver; she was an innocent. It made no difference. He touched one of her breasts. She did not move, one way or the other. She spoke, very quietly.

'No,' she said. 'You must wait. You're not on Paradise Street now.'

'What d'you mean?' His Depthside accent was returning, he had nearly sworn at her.

'Nothing. Lots of people visit the Quarter; I merely supposed you were one of them.'

'But why Paradise Street?'

'Why not? It's one of the streets there, isn't it? Come along; we were going to meet people.'

He was introduced to women and men until he grew tired of it. He met dancers, councillors, doctors, lectors, and the huge ego to which M'untal had once been married. A heavy, bearded man stood alone, cradling a glass of spirits in one of his vast hands. 'That's Chenodor,' said M'untal in a piercing whisper. 'The sculptor. He made the carvings on that table.' Those boatbuilder's hands, roadmender's fingers, delicately prising away wood in flakes . . . how? He wanted an explanation, an introduction, but M'untal propelled him onward, her tiny hand as fast on his arm as a leech. They passed near Chacma and his wives; near the Matriarch and her family, her two schoolboy sons neat in silk suits and solemn with the occasion; they saw Destorio Nonpareil with a beautiful woman. Cal took M'untal's hand in his and led her from the room.

'She's not his wife,' said M'untal. 'He is the complete Cheronian.'

'And Magon?'

'Lots of people have mixed parentage,' she said. 'And lots more lose their fathers to Cheron and Chacma. My father is one of his commanders.'

'No,' he said. 'I want to know what you think of the Archivist.'

'I thought you wanted to forget him. It wouldn't be sensible to discuss him here, would it? He's just over there. Now we shall have to speak to him.'

Magon was talking quietly with his sister; he smiled gently at them as they approached. Cal saw that he was wearing the face of the Archivist. But Crinon stepped forward and kissed M'untal before she turned her gaze on him.

'So,' she said. 'Rafe Dayamit. Very presentable.'

She spoke to him. 'I paint: they let me make eccentric remarks. Magon has told me a lot about you.'

'He hasn't told me anything about you.'

She laughed. 'I am his big sister. What do you want to know?'

'That's easy. How you mix light with your oils.'

'Oh, prettily put! You will have to come to the Garden House and see how I do it.'

He asked her what painting she was working on.

'The Cape – early morning. The blues are being troublesome. I want to try a portrait but Xhara' tells me I shouldn't attempt it; I daresay she is right. There is Xhara', I must go. She has to play for the Beast in half an hour: he won't appreciate her.'

Crinon could move with stately haste, and the crowd parted and melted away before her.

'She is usually calm.' Magon spoke to him. 'She's worried about

Xharam'un's recital, and she dislikes the President – a great deal.

'Now M'untal, look after him. I must go and present my compliments to my father.'

He sat close to her on one of the couches in the rotunda. She tapped her heels together, her legs hanging stiffly over the edge of the couch like a child's. Beneath her sparkling slippers and the glass floor he saw the coiffed hair of the women and the curled heads of the young men who accompanied them. It was noisy; the harmony was discord to his ear. He watched the couples move: most of them danced badly, whatever the mix. The boys were the best, dancing rhythmically together, but the embracing women were obviously and extravagantly sensual.

'You should show them how,' he said.

'A Temple Dance in here!'

'The first one you danced in the theatre was an altered horten.'

'You're right! That's very clever; most people can't see the connection between our dances and those of the City. An horten would be out of place here too.'

'Let us try one of these Sineinian dances.'

She took the hand he proffered.

'When I was a child,' said M'untal, 'I used to think that men couldn't dance; not only that they were forbidden to because of the Law but that they were physically unable.'

The movements were simple. Here, in the brightly lit glass bubble, he was permitted to touch her and her body pressed against his. He revised his opinion of her, not innocent, but possessed of integrity; she could live in this hierarchy and still tell right from wrong.

'I've seen you before,' she said.

'I've seen you before.'

'Not at the Display!'

'In the Octagon and – '

'No. None of those occasions. I saw you in Court; when you train for the Gynarchy, they take you into the Central Court.'

'So?'

'I saw you on the Chair. You looked very different then, pale and ill; and your hair was darker.' She touched it.

'I must talk to you,' she said. 'There is a lot to say and much I don't understand.'

'Neither do I. But, as you say, Magon knows everything.'

'Let us go now.'

To talk, to unravel the Archivist's web?

'Now?' he protested. 'I'm hungry. I haven't eaten since this morning.'

'Alna will find you something.'

They walked quickly through the dark courtyards, where he would have lingered to taste her, slowly, eyes by lips, breasts by belly, and then. . . . They entered one of the towers, but they did not climb it. Her apartments were in a wide wing of the building. Her maid opened the door.

'This is Mr Dayamit, Alna. He's hungry.'

'I dare say he is. And for what?' The woman smiled at him. 'Quietly now! Fiora is fast asleep.'

He saw silks, hangings, embroideries, flowers, pottery from faraway places, books; in a corner a bag from which protruded the hem of a yellow maral, toys, a child's chair. A dark brown cat got up from one of the embroidered cushions, stretched, and wailed. M'untal picked it up.

'This is Plama. Say good evening to Mr Mystery, Plama.

'She is named after the big Cat, the leopard you know?'

'I saw her this morning – I saw you this morning! Lissa Dayamit talked of sending her a goat.'

'Yes. She eats one a day. And she has cousins in Zalcasia, doesn't she, little Plama? There's one of them – across that couch. My father shot her.'

Shot her! He stroked the pelt, moved his fingers gently over the dark blots in the creamy fur.

'With an rkw. You can't shoot snow leopards with a bow.'

'Magon could.'

'I doubt it. They move too fast. The bow is obsolete anyway.'

'Like Temple Dances and oracles?'

'They are sacred!'

'Perhaps Magon will give up the Talong when you give up the Dance.' He sat on the leopardskin.

'Take off your jacket. You look like a puppet.'

'I am a puppet,' he said, but she laughed at him and watched him remove the jacket.

Alna brought him a tray like a painting. The tall glass held a wine which was almost green, except that the lamplight made it glow like lemons in a tree. On a white plate three slices of meat lay beside an arrangement of curly green leaves, black grapes and oranges cut thin as paper.

When he had eaten the sparse and decorative meal he asked the way to the kitchen, carried the tray there and put it beside the sink. Alna sat on a stool, polishing a chain of silver bells which chimed as she rubbed them.

'Take care of her,' she said, without arresting the steady movement of the cloth against the metal. 'She's had a rough ride; Dancers often do but they don't all, thank Mahun, have mothers like hers. I've nursed her since she was an hour old.'

She spoke the traditional lines as though she were the traditional crone; in fact she was probably no older than Magon.

'I won't harm her,' he said stiffly. 'I wouldn't be here at all if she had not invited me.'

'I wonder. . . .' Alna mused. 'She's bad at choices; the blackness of the Mamelon sometimes seems to spread up here. I doubt if she could make up a dance of her own.'

M'untal had moved; she was curled up against the leopardskin, her hair exactly the colour of its spots. He sat down beside her and she straightened her neck and looked at him.

'Who are you?' she said.

'I am a City child, born, I suppose, on the pavement somewhere. Magon saw me twice: once at Space Park, once – elsewhere – and when they arrested me for having no Mark – see? – he arranged a Surrogation. Rafe Dayamit was given the milk instead of me.'

'How horrible!'

'It wasn't too good for him.'

'Don't jest. Did he deserve to die?'

'Not really. He was no better, and no worse, than a thief; but he was in Magon's way. You must know their system; and Magon is a great manipulator. You understand why I called myself a puppet?'

'Yes; but you must be better off than you were, whatever happens.'

'Perhaps.' He was reluctant to say more, but she probed. Questions were her chief mode of expression in conversation.

'Is it difficult being someone else?'

'At first; not now. I've read a lot about him. I visited his – my – aunt this morning.'

'In the City – what did you do?'

'What thousands do: scratch for a living. You don't have time, in the Depths, to reflect and pursue abstracts; you are too busy finding food. You've seen the Beggars.'

'No. I only go into the City when there is a procession.'

He laughed. Her innocence was ignorance. He would spare her the children and their public agony.

'So how did you live?'

'On my wits. By carrying parcels; by finding the things rich people throw away and selling them to a dealer. Besides, I can read and write; lots of people want writing done for them.'

He did not want to tell her how many purses he had stolen.

She looked all the time at his face, her forehead creased.

'What is your real name?'

'Cal.'

'Cal what?'

'Just Cal.' He told her how he had come by it. 'I've no family; no mother.'

'I have a little boy. He lives in Far Maralis. I haven't seen him since he

118

was a dek old; Magon brings me reports of him. . . .'

'What about the girl?'

'She is my trust. Because of Magon, I am the first Dancer even to know that. Would you like to see her?'

In the cot, the sleeping child stirred and clutched the toy monkey she held. She might well have been M'untal's own, so precisely did their features match. Such intimate domesticity was foreign to him; the room smelled of soap and of the warm body of the child. He put his arm round M'untal only because he wanted to bring her away from the altar. She leaned against him and cried a little; when they were again in the main room he said anxiously, 'I can't help you.'

'I know.'

They sat on the couch, dolls arranged by circumstance.

'Magon helps me.'

'Ssh.' He began to kiss her, though she was stiff and the stones about the neck of her gown rough under his hands. The crown of hair unpinned itself and coiled on to her shoulders. She sat up and removed all the pins, shaking out her hair. It uncoiled slowly and she stood up and swept it all to her back, so that he could see the length of it. It almost reached her tiny feet. She stood still, proud of it, and then she came back to him and lay down.

'The skin is pulling at my dress.'

'Take it off. I'll take it off.'

'No.' She moved away from him and looked at him with sad eyes. They were full of tears again.

'I'm sorry,' she said.

'So am I. I'll go.'

'Don't go. Hold my hand.'

She went to sleep as swiftly as if she had tired after lovemaking; he covered her up with one of the embroideries and left her, angry, frustrated, suspicious of them all.

At this hour the great garden was his, the parkland and the massive granite rocks. He explored like a traveller seeking refreshment, finding first the places which had become familiar favourites, the long canal, the marble fountains, the statue of the running boy. He passed the empty theatre where M'untal had danced, his reaction physical, painful, bruised. He passed the Garden House, silent among birdcalls, and began the climb towards the chasm. Before him the planting of Zalcasian pines flourished in the warm air as in their native snows. Beyond the pines and near the hilltop, Shekarah's towers twisted skyward.

In the glades the deer stood still and looked at him and a purple jayquin hanging from its branch quizzed him with a crooked stare. Underfoot the soil was dark, dense, and loamy where he scuffed it, overlaid with pine needles. The scent of the pines filled his lungs, his mouth and nose, an antiseptic cleansing draught. He paused at the first lookout to listen to the sea running inland. The chasm sides were damp with spray. He followed the path up, towards the folly. Here, the pine trees grew close and straight, and the path made many turns among them. He heard first the thud of feet on the soil and then his breathing, the deep inspirations of a runner. There was no time to shout or lift a hand in greeting. Magon came straight down the terraces, avoiding the path, and stopped his progress with a hand to a branch. His feet made furrows in the soil.

'Good morning, Cal,' he said. The urbanity was gone; the cultured voice had a perceptible edge.

Cal stepped back. A branch pressed him and he ducked under it, putting wood between them.

'What in Aash is the matter with you?' Magon's anger made his lips tremble.

'You're troubled. Hurt, possibly.' Cal would have rolled in the dirt to appease him.

'Possibly.'

Magon took a handkerchief from his pocket and wiped the sweat from his chest. He pushed the damp curls from his eyes. They walked on down the path, Cal warily, Magon pausing at times to look up at the trees. Neither spoke. Lines from a Trav song came into Cal's mind.

What is longer than the way,
What is deeper than the sea?
What is louder than the horn,
What is sharper than the thorn?
What is greener than the grass,
What is worse than hunger was?

It was a ballad of blood and culpability. 'Love is.' He felt Magon's hand on his arm, an ambiguous grip, and let the arm swing. The grip tightened.

'You could kill me if you wanted,' he said, looking into Magon's face.

'Yes, I could. Damn you,' said Magon, and let go.

'She cried. Nothing happened.'

He watched Magon's retreating back for a sign; none came. He had to run or be left behind.

Together they walked the paths of the formal garden, striding over the ornately patterned tiles; the flowers were stiff and heraldic but the statues against the brick walls had lissom limbs and inviting smiles. On the promontory the cropped turf appeared natural, not of gardener's art, a transplant from a temperate clime; at this hour it was studded with white-eyed dawnflowers which closed and died under the sun. They took the further path to the shore and, stripping on the summit of an inclined boulder, dived from it into the sea to cleave the breakers which thundered inshore. He was a fish, cold and streamlined, his warm flesh green like the water. He held Magon's feet and let himself be towed under.

Level 15 was dim after the sunlight. He was glad to leave Magon and the garden, simmering now in the morning sun. He immersed himself in Huyatt's clear prose.

At two Filka, touching his shoulder, brought him back. In the dining hall he ate swiftly, hungrily; sleep and his dreams claimed him. Reading his notes on Level 15 two hours later he saw that many phrases were questions. He fetched Glisa's inadequate maps and began to plan his journey to the east. At seven Filka, touching his arm, bade him goodnight. He switched on the reading lamp and began to read *Ethos*. 'Men,' said Huyatt, 'are houses of power. Woman is ultimate.' He flicked through the book, finding a footnote which read, 'Despite his apparent piety, Huyatt was an atheist.' He opened Verelustra Tain's commentary; she maintained that Huyatt had worshipped Mahun. He considered the likelihood of censorship and substituted Monos for Mahun; after that the commentary made sense and *Ethos* became a handbook of self-government. This reading bored him. He cleared his head of allegory, of metaphor and simile and read the prose for itself; the language was obscure, full of archaisms and literary references, but it had an inner music whose repetitions and lost fragrances delighted him. He forgot everything beyond the page.

His head ached. He sat alone in the silence of the Library and heard the clock strike eleven. He left his books and took the lift.

The apartment was silent. Magon's empty glass stood on his desk. A drop of Ceremana sullied the clear crystal. Cal fetched a glass for himself and, finding the half empty bottle in the kitchen, carried it with him to the study. He sat in Magon's chair drinking slowly until the last of the wine was gone. He went to bed.

The cry that woke him was that of a man going under. Reacting slowly, sleepily, he got up from the bed and stood still to listen. The red door, the chequerboard: in Magon's room a lamp illuminated the ancient painting of martyrdom. Magon was asleep, his face contorted, his rigid arms stretched out. He watched the frantic movements, listened to a torrent of words in which he heard the name of the Archivist's dark sister and, many times, his own. He knew you should not wake a dreamer. Someone awoken from a nightmare might go mad. Tarla could interpret dreams. Perhaps she would deal the cards for Magon.

For a time, he crouched beside the bed, covering one of Magon's hands with his own. The martyr on the wall looked bleakly up into paradise and Cal, for the first time, noticed the seedling fig tree which struggled amongst the painted stones. He recited the third Apology and, remembering that the heretical book lay open in the room, spoke a prayer of recantation on Magon's behalf. The hot hand moved, gripped his. Magon was awake.

'I woke you,' he said. 'I'm sorry. It was a dream, an old recurrent dream. Crinon is drowning off the Point and I can't reach her.'

'You were calling for me.'

'Was I? That's good. Rafe was able to soothe my distempers. A quarter fold of husk and a kiss – that's all it takes. Is there any left?'

'A little. Enough for a kitten, or a novice.'

He fetched the jewelled casket. His bare feet marched in time with his thoughts. This-is-it-this-is-it-THIS-IS-IT. He's the master; he pays me well. I'm the servant: who am I to resist? He measured the husk roughly, rule of thumb. Magon opened his mouth. The powder fell in a fine jet downward, past even white teeth, tongue laid flat. I'm the physician. Magon closed his mouth, swallowed. I minister, he administers. 'Ah,' said Magon. 'It bites.'

Cal sniffed at the powder that remained, delicately, wrinkling his nose as the powder pervaded, invaded. It darkened the crease in the folded paper, an infinitesimal, tranquilising, dose. He leaned back so that the line of this throat and jaw made a fine, firm, curve and showed Magon how it was done, tapping the fold gently, a veteran from the Depths.

It was very good husk. It went instantly to his head. The room swelled to accommodate him, hollow as a clapperless bell. The martyr moved his beautiful, pained face and smiled. He was the clapper and the tocsin sounded within and without. He was the bell; Magon and the drug took hold of him together.

Crinon put down her brush. The painting was finished. A dark mass of trees gave way to the steep, bald, steps of the Domes; the vultures and the small figures of distant Dismemberers went about their grisly business. Xhara' called the painting *Dreams of Death*. . . . The northern verandah where she worked in the mornings was cool, shady; in the water garden the same relative coolness came from the mental association between water and refreshment. They both, she and Xhara', loved the water garden but now Xhara' had gone, retreating as she did every Vern to Evanul, where she found a different peace beside the sea. Her holiday would bring fresh colours to her brush and new notes to her flute. Yet this year the peace was illusory, the holiday a short break in the continuity of intrigue which surrounded them. Xhara', on her return, would have the same adjustments to make. She must write, comforting endearments, while she wondered how Xhara' would cope with the intrusion: the silkweaver and her child, the sturdy boy who was little M'untal's son. Lorilla and Ister, or should she call him Luth? A housekeeper indeed – a keeper of Magon's secrets. And Rafe – Cal – whose graceful body made her painting fingers itch to begin, to stalk him, to capture, to pin his golden gestures down. He was deprived, disturbed; Xhara' would love him, as she loved anything which had been abused, a dog, a Beggar child. . . .

She rubbed her eyes to clear away the picture of Xhara' walking on the beach and deposited blue pigment on her lids. She stared at her painting seeing only the colour, half aware, as she remembered each brushstroke, of the birdsong in the garden. The house was very old. She looked into it: darkness, peace. It had always been a house of makers. Shelda had lived here, Lys Hinoor, Shekarah building her folly, Sinon growing fat amongst his brood. In such tranquillity who but Magon could imagine war?

The house had decayed with Sinon, falling vacant at his death. For twenty years it had stood empty while the garden encroached. Then, out walking, she had come upon it. The main beam had fallen, the verandahs were choked with thornweed and poison apple, and a coral snake had slithered under the house as she approached. Under her hand, the house had rediscovered its sense of peace and isolation though it stood only a mile from the Octagon. It had lacked a studio and this she had built, matching the woods carefully so that it seemed an old part of the old house.

She, Crinon, had made the garden out of an acreage of weeds and rioting trees. She had made the ponds and streams, the secrecy and calm. As if it understood her, the garden had responded. The lilies flourished, the scented climbers, the specimen plants . . . and the birds had come because they knew she hated cats. Mama, the great python, had come to lie beneath the house, sanctifying it and driving out the poisonous corals. Xharam'un' had come.

The birds were silent. Heat lay on the garden and stilled it; the boy would soon be here. She had not breakfasted, she had not lunched; like the times, her thoughts were in disarray.

Cal put his hand on the gate and unlatched it. He looked into Crinon's enchanted enclosure. Red and yellow parakeets hung like ripe fruit in the trees. He opened the gate and went in.

A stream flowed by the path, wearing its way into the litter under the trees. He saw his face in one of its deep pools and leaned over the dark water seeing his reflection gaze up at him, pale as a ghost. A white petal fell, shattering the image, and he watched it reform.

He remembered his headache, but it was receding. Ten minutes and it would be gone. Magon had taken dust with his morning bohea, as an analgesic . . . the memory of his touch was fresh, hot. He was clothed and felt naked. He had not taken a bath.

The house was shadowy and silent. Perhaps Crinon slept. He walked

123

on the verandah noticing wooden statues, plants in pots. An old dolls' house stood against one wall, a forlorn reminder of childhood. Crinon emerged suddenly from the house, a piece of bread in her hand.

'Good afternoon?' It was a question.

'Yes, I think so. My head was aching.'

She had been told of his pleasures.

'Husk head?' she said. 'You must be mad. Rafe used dust.'

'He used husk. I took the last of it.'

'And Magon?' She had dropped the stone, not he. He chose to ignore the dark stone plummeting downwards and studied the ripples.

'He had some.'

'No. I won't make vicarious excursions into his private life. I'm asking you how he is today. It is less than three deks since Rafe died.'

'He's all right. Null, I'd have said not long ago, before I was taught to speak properly. He talks too much.'

'That's a bad sign. Magon chattering. . . . Now, do you mind a life class for two? Just you and me.'

He grinned at her. 'Whatever you say.'

'By the water then. I'm interested in reflections. This way.'

He followed her. The pool she led him to, the first and highest of three connected by runnels and infant cascades down which the water trickled with a sound which was the spirit of tranquillity, was as still and as calm as Crinon's heart. These thoughts, emerging in his mind as he stood on the margin of the pool, were new; not the rapid decisions of yesterday's destitute. Another sort of her lilies floated on the water, white and gold discs, and their flat leaves made islands against which the water jacks rested before they set out again on the eternal search for food, their paddle-footed legs making sets of miniature ripples, like his own reflections manifold. . . . And his own reflection hung there among the lilies as elegant and as confident as a Hill tiger's. He doubted, looking at Crinon bending over her inks and paper and already withdrawn into her private world of shapes and line, whether she had ever made time for Rafe Dayamit.

She watched him undress and arrange his golden limbs for her. In shadow his skin was the colour of cinnamon bark or husk; in sunlight it gleamed like a newly opened trumpet lily. She recalled that topazes too change their colour in the heat of the sun. He moved confidently. He has overcome something, she thought: his fear, his ego. He has made a discovery.

'Can I work?' he asked, pulling a bundle of papers from amongst his clothing.

'Why not? A thinking nude,' she said, already absorbed in the marks she was making. She sat cross-legged, the pad of paper across her knees, a straw hat squashed on to her mass of black hair.

124

'What is it?' she said presently. 'The work?'

'It's Huyatt.'

'That old dreamer!'

'No. It's not a traveller's tall tale. It's an allegory. The journey to the east, or west in his case. There's literary precedent for that too.'

'Gildo will be interested. He's a writer. Coming to supper.'

They worked on. The bamboo thicket cast slender shadows across his legs and she grew impatient at the inadequacy of her line. She began to draw his head and found a grove of bronze and golden line in his hair.

'Surely Huyatt came to the City?'

'He may have done. It doesn't matter. He meant his readers to explore his meaning not his fancy. To follow his path.'

'Do we all have to make a journey?'

'Aren't you beginning a new one? You used to paint the City.'

'A body is a landscape.'

The bamboo's shadow had retreated. He lay full in the sun. She gave him her hat. The reed had learned the shape of his body, her line flowed. She drew his reflection, a twin afloat among the water lilies.

'Magon makes a journey,' she said after a time. 'With you – with us all.'

He sat up, destroying the pose, and pushed back the hat to look at her.

'Perhaps he has shown you the map,' he said.

'Yes, yes,' she said with irritation. 'The line has come. Please!'

'As long as you can paint you'll go anywhere with him.'

'That's about it. A similar motive to your own.'

He shifted irritably. He wanted to question her, to make her lay down the pen and put aside the drawing that made a barrier between them. The ink was drying on her pen. She dipped it again. He lay down and looked at the water, hearing the whisper of the reed as she made her marks. Between gazing at the lilies on the water and the circling fish, he dozed, the hat over his face.

'Sinon lived here once,' she murmured, just louder than the insects' hum.

'You want me to grow fat like him?' he said sleepily. 'Dozens of children?'

He listened to the garden and felt the heat of the sun. A rose dove crooned.

'What an idyll!'

The man who peered over the bushes was grey-haired and fleshed with good living. He carried a small parasol of plaited straw which he tilted to shade his bald crown. So this was Magon's creature. He did not look like a base thief from the Depths. Nor did he look like his *alter ego*, the lily trader Dayamit. He was the genius of the garden, exhausted by a long afternoon's creation. A pile of papers, weighted with a pebble from the pool, lay beside him. Gildo could easily read the sprawling writing. 'Huyatt,' the bold strokes declared, 'was no dreamer – ' Interesting!

The real creator of the garden looked up. She smiled at Gildo.

'Come! See! Won't Xhara' be jealous?'

He descended the short flight of steps and squatted beside her on the staging, while she displayed her work. He was amazed. He had believed her a pure landscapist but here were figure drawings which surpassed everything she had done before.

'You've surprised yourself – and me,' he said.

The boy woke. He joined them, looking at the drawings in silence, as if totally aware of his own contribution. He eyed the plump Gildo and held out his hand.

'Perhaps you should introduce us,' the writer said to Crinon. 'I know who he is but I don't know what to call him.'

'You had better call him Dayamit.'

'I'm Rafe,' Cal said, shaking Gildo firmly by the hand.

Gildo was amused. As if from a fourth dimension he saw himself, fat and balding, exchange this most formal of greetings with a stark naked boy in a garden full of green shade and secret glades. He broke into loud laughter.

The table on the verandah was in shadow; red pottery gleamed dully. Around the table the empty chairs waited. Crinon's birds perched on the verandah rail and a silktail monkey, descendant of Tsiksik, chattered impatiently there.

The sculptor Chenodor offered them grapes. The green parrot would take the fruits from his lips, but the jayquins were shy and only accepted them from his hand. A patterned macaw sat on his shoulder nibbling at his beard. Amarant and Faya, side by side on the couch, had eyes only for Magon's boy. In her belly Amarant felt the spasm which heralded an infatuation, while Faya once more regretted her vow.

Chenodor, turning from the birds, saw a slight boy stand aside, one among the group of primitive wooden figures by the open door, to let his hostess pass. He wore the slops of a City Artisan, but in white, and a singlet of brilliant cinnabar. A shaft of light from the dying sun illuminated the left side of his face. And this, Chenodor thought, is the chief diversion of our would-be leader. Mahun aid us – or, as he would have it, Monos; needs must. The boy seemed intelligent enough. Indeed, he no longer looked like a Depther; the last shreds of awkwardness which had impeded him amongst the discriminating crowds in the New Citadel had been sloughed off. He stepped forward and stooped to shake hands with and confront the renegade who, as Crinon had informed him in one of her handwritten proclamations, admired and understood 'Possession'.

126

Cal took a seat in the eye of the group. The table was laden: spiced fish, shellfish from the bay, roundels of white cheese. The breadrings were warm and piled in a basket; another basket held multicoloured fruit; a third, salad. 'We had better begin,' said Crinon, 'before the moths descend.' She lit the lamp. Only one chair remained untenanted, one plate unsullied. Cal sat between Amarant and Faya, being himself, knowing they all knew the truth, trying to live all the lies. Crinon used his own name but Faya and Amarant called him Rafe, while the two men addressed him as Dayamit. He listened to the bitchy gossip they exchanged with relish.

The divertive novelist, Faya, whose romances were popular in the City and the East, looked after him. She filled his plate and glass. She was thin and incredibly tall, but her long fingers, moving now to break off a grape, were beautiful. Rings covered them, a soft gleaming pearl, peridots, opals, topazes. Crinon made her hold the biggest topaz close to his left eye and the company smiled and laughed. Amarant's hands were small and neat, bearing no sign of her skill with large rocks: she was a monumental sculptor whose most famous work, the hundred-foot statue of Mahun, commanded the lower headland and could be seen many miles out at sea. She had edged her chair close to his, closer than was necessary or correct. He realised, not for the first time, that his beauty might be an encumbrance.

Amarant sat still, enjoying his proximity, her hands busy tearing bread. She conversed with her lust. If only the others had gone, but not here. Under the vines. It wouldn't take long, you're accomplished. I can't wait; I want him now. Her fingers massaged the bread. You'll have to wait, you fool. But it will be; he will succumb. Clearly he has no conscience, a cat like Achille.

Sipping the fourth – fifth? – glass of wine, Cal, moving his leg warily, waiting to see what she would do, pondered new enigmas. What place had these makers of luxuries in the many worlds of the City? What were they to Magon? Why did they know his true name and identity? How?

'It must be a shit of a life, being a Surrogate,' said Gildo, recalling him from his reverie.

'Depends what he has to sublimate,' said Amarant acidly, but they ignored her and the writer continued to speak.

'How do you come to be working on Huyatt? If you'll forgive me, how could you, in the circumstances, learn to read at all?'

'Rafe,' said Cal. 'If you mean him, has a good degree from CU.'
They laughed.

'But I, I have my wits and I am lucky,' he said. 'Lucky at cards, lucky at life.' He told them the story of Magon's red Huyatt, fallen in the gutter; he told them how Verelustra Tain had coached him beside the bohea stall in Matriarch Square; of his studies in the Depths and the ways in which

127

he had stolen knowledge in the City libraries. When he was silent, Gildo began to question him again.

'What have you found in Huyatt?'

'Allegory.'

'Not a new idea.'

'Rafe – there's a manuscript – says the whole thing is an extended metaphor of Huyatt's search for the perfect lover who should be a boy aged sixteen to eighteen with narrow hips, black hair and a white skin, and a voice like ice dropped into water. He calls Balkiss a symbol.'

'Dear boy! Rafe was always fond of the subjective. Hot nights in Odalion, you know – they infect the mind. . . .'

His voice died. For an instant a compensating chatter rose from the others, and died too. Only Faya's brittle voice lingered: 'More than a toy. An object lesson – '

Magon stepped on to the verandah, depriving them of the starlight. His shadow climbed to the roof. Crinon broke the spell.

'You're late, Magon,' she said. 'Sit down. Gildo, pour him some wine. No, the fresh bottle.'

No one else spoke. They watched the Archivist taste the wine.

'488?' he said to Gildo.

'Indeed.'

Magon looked carefully at each lamplit face except Cal's. Only Amarant returned his level gaze, her lips compressed.

'Have you met Lorilla and the child?' he said. 'No?'

'She will bring in the tea,' said Crinon. 'You engaged her as a servant, remember? Luth is not in bed yet: they can see him too.'

Like the conversation, familiarity had died and communication had become a series of terse asides. Cal felt that everyone had donned a mask; the yellow lamplight smoothed out creases and made each face glow in bland parallel.

'Faya,' said Magon, and gave her his professional smile.

The reports were oral, conned and memorised so that there was no evidence. Magon summarised them: this season, consolidation. Faya's workers spread the word throughout the leisured classes where disaffection from this Matriarchy was rife; Amarant's cell in the Quarter met every month and (here Magon's voice developed an ironic ring) contact with Achille had been made. Gildo kept the record in code and it was hidden – where, no matter, it was well concealed. When the rainy season had passed, then action (for some) would begin. Chenodor and Oyno met a month ago. The City-born mercenaries were being readied in Cheron. He spoke urgently, 'I discussed the situation with Chacma and my father. Keep these matters in your heart of hearts. . . . My journey will have a twofold purpose and, when I reach Zalcasia, Oyno will be there with the corundum gun. The permit defines my journey as "vocational".

I urge you all to be diligent and watchful. Chenodor will take the reins when I am gone.'

As he spoke, he let his mask fall. Once, he looked in Cal's direction and allowed a slight movement of one eyebrow to acknowledge his presence. It was clear that he enjoyed this role, the revelation to his lover of the absolute nature of his power.

'Any questions?'

Amarant was the only person disinterested enough to speak and she spoke directly, pitching her question on a personal level.

'What about him? His resemblance to the late lamented must be a liability.'

'I've dealt with that,' said Magon curtly. 'His languages qualify him. His IR is two points greater than Rafe's and his ability to absorb word-patterns so far up the scale, it was judged abnormal – and he knows a great many more Depthers than you do, Amarant.'

She inhaled, as though she wanted to say something else. You Cheronese bastard, she thought, I don't need your bum-boy to remind me of my duty. She whispered in Faya's ear. Faya laughed.

'How do we know we can trust him?' she asked.

From his obscure corner, Cal looked at her flushed, excited, face. A deep frown divided Amarant's brow. She, he felt, knew fear. In the Depths, in the bland and fatal lazar house of the Block, confronted by Magon's secular passion for him, to know everything he was and had been, he had been full of courage. Yet safe at last in Crinon's garden, beneath Magon's radiant influence, he was afraid. Faya threatened him.

'She means,' said Amarant, smiling at him, 'what credentials, apart from your beautiful body and obviously excellent, if untrained, mind, did you bring from the Depths? Have you a good character from your old friends and employers, thieves perhaps, beggars, whores?'

'I – ' he stammered, 'I – '

Magon answered for him.

'I assume that I can trust you, Faya – that I can trust all of you. Without that assumption I may as well kneel before Annalat and confess.'

The bohea which the new servant, Lorilla, carried in brought relief. Its sparse scent drifted from the gilded pot she lifted in one hand to pour. The little boy watched the hot liquid stream and sniffed and rubbed his nose. His upper lip trembled exactly as M'untal's did when she was unsure.

They had gone, trailing across the garden in an untidy line. He, Magon and Crinon remained. Lorilla, somewhere in the house, sang to M'untal's son. Beyond the railing the garden was a mystery and the lamp on the table was a magnet for moths. One had settled on the last of the grapes, its dark wings trembling. Amarant had trembled when she kissed

129

him goodbye. 'Why trouble your pretty head?' she had whispered. 'Maybe old Huyatt's a forgery like you,' and she had pinched him on the right buttock, sliding her hand softly down to reach. The translucent tea bowls were empty and cold. Doos Gildo had taken the rainbow cup, scattered with silver imps as mischievous as his thoughts, Raist Chenodor the malachite green, Faya the turquoise which glowed like a jewel, and Amarant the purple, bleeding darker striations into itself like murex in a dyepit. They had given him the golden cup, which left the crimson one for Magon and the pure white for Crinon Hinoor.

Magon's sister lit a cigarette.

'My mother,' she said, 'was a wonderful woman, a fine scholar. She loved us dearly and she never excluded us. Distinguished guests grew used to us climbing on their laps – but I think she forgot we *were* children. I remember hearing, when I was perhaps nine, the most gruesome details of Annon's uprising. I was playing with my dolls' house and Magon was cutting out paper horses on the floor. They castrated all the men, branded them and turned them into the Burnt Lands. Maybe Magon will tell you what Chacma's torturers did to the women – I can't.'

'You saw Chacma – and Father. Mother married him at a Cheronese civil ceremony; she didn't insist on the Temple. She knew the truth and she always lived alone. We saw Father every eighteen months; sometimes he came with us to Evanul to bathe.'

'He taught me to swim,' said Magon.

'And to contrive and connive and lie.' Crinon smiled at him.

'And steal. You forgot that.'

'Oh, I'm not party to every one of your crimes.'

They were both smiling. Cal studied Crinon's mobile, expressive face with its echoes of Magon's. They were not obverse and reverse of a coin. She was honest, yes, frank; she was also proud and quite certain that she deserved the privileges she had been born with.

'I met Xhara' when I was twenty,' she said, 'when she came up from Odalion to study the flute. Soon after, we bought a house – one of those on na Hinoor, on the edge of the Quarter. The tall houses. They're derelict now.'

He nodded. Their blank windows had overlooked the recent round-up. Three years ago he had roosted in one of their empty attics while on the floors below a family of Beggars quarrelled.

'You deserted me.' said Magon. 'For almost two years. I was alone throughout Mother's last illness while you played with Xhara'.'

'It was a long time ago.' Crinon spoke soothingly. 'Things have fallen into place since then. You were glad enough to claim me when they chose you as Archivist – Mother certainly did her groundwork well.'

Her cigarette had burned out. She crushed it into the dregs of her wine. The fluttering moth had scorched its wings on the lamp glass and she looked at it and shuddered.

'Magon. Kill that thing.'

He ground out the last of its life under a glass, reached across the table and touched Cal's face.

'We should go. It's late. The owls are stirring.'

He stood up, stretched, and stepped down into the dark garden without a formal goodbye or another glance at his sister, expecting Cal to rise at once and follow. Crinon detained Cal, a comforting arm about his shoulders. His head rested for a moment against her breasts and her aura of turpentine, her unique signature, enfolded him. After this, he thought, I shall not fear them.

'Take care,' she said. 'He appears so confident and strong – but he has his own personal hell. I hope you never see it. I am afraid he has collected you just as he has collected the sculptures and paintings, the little carvings. If he finds you wanting – once he found a piece of amber on the beach. He was still half a child and he believed it had been carried all the way from Noiro in the Shaklian current. The amber was tested and found to be copal. He destroyed it. He burned it and while it burned he held his left hand in the flame to teach himself, he said, to see clearly.'

'Go now. M'untal will be here tomorrow.'

He kissed her and ran after Magon. Her last statement had brought him no joy, none of the lust he would have felt a dek ago. He was tired, confused by the undercurrents within the group, amazed to see Magon a pitiless leader. The rift in his own soul seemed to be public property. He remembered M'untal's fear, her rigid limbs, her tears. Holding his papers close he walked by the cascades in Magon's wake and up the hill.

The Octagon had also lost its peace. They carried their discontent about with them like luggage; but he could easily set his burden down.

'I'm going to bed,' he announced, 'to sleep.'

Magon grunted. It was an ugly sound to come from such a mouth.

'Goodnight then,' he said. 'I shall wake alone.'

The bedside clock said eleven-ten. He scattered his clothes on the floor as he walked towards his bed; the mattress was soft and yielded under him, the sheets were cool. He was in it now, possessed of their secret, allocated a role. He tumbled into a deep well of sleep.

When he woke it was as if he rushed upwards from an abyss beneath the sea. Underwater, sound was distorted. He surfaced. The clock said four. It was pitch dark and the world was full of fury. In the next room Magon was weeping. The time for guilt had come.

The scourge lay beside the prayer desk on the floor. Magon, fallen across the bed, held one of the great corner posts, his back a mess of bloody lacerations. The convulsive grip was hard to break, the pillow a soft unyielding weight, Magon as heavy as the world. He groaned.

'Don't fetch help.'

His voice was muffled by the pillow.

'I shall be gone less than five minutes.'

In the kitchen he boiled water. There was dust in a bathroom cabinet, a brown bottle with a pharmacist's label. He made an infusion of the yellow powder, a double dose. He fetched a facecloth and cold water. Magon's eyes were closed now; inside the red darkness under the lids he might find quiet. He could do nothing about the stripes but count them and swear. He drew the sheet up to Magon's waist and bathed his face. When the infusion was cool and the brown eyes open again he gave him half. Magon went under slowly, his fingers relaxing first, his eyes filling with otherworld visions. Cal sat on the bed and held one of the fine hands.

The martyr on the wall was a hideous mockery. He glared at the painting. How many casualties of spirit and body littered the road of the religious? He thought of Crinon with her inner peace. He thought of Rafe Dayamit. As for himself, he feared nothing now that Magon had made his strange demonstration of love.

Anger overtook him. He got up and threw the scourge into the corridor, handling it with superstitious distaste as he had the dead monkey by the river. He felt he should soon vomit. The holy book was open. As he picked it up he read the Rules on the open pages, each definition preceded in scarlet letters by the word sin. He flung the book at the martyr, but it bounced against the painting and fell impotently to the floor. The dehumidifier began to whir and he crossed to the window and opened the only louvre, hoping that the damp air would destroy the painting overnight. He sat again beside Magon and watched his sleeping face.

Soon after first light, when the soft closing of the outer door announced Slake's arrival, he sent for Cudbeer. To Slake he said merely, 'The Archivist is ill. He won't require breakfast.'

Cudbeer was sleepy and irritable. 'It's six-thirty,' he complained.

'I've been up since four. So think yourself lucky,' said Cal. 'How well do you know the Archivist?'

'Not very. I know about him of course. Certain things, but not from him.'

'Yes?'

'Certain things – everyone knows. I suppose I know a bit more.'

'Do you know of his journey?'

'That's most of the bit more.'

'The Desert Fathers? Oyno? Nonpareil?'

'I'm known for my discretion: the Slake of the Archive,' said Cudbeer, shedding his diffidence and his spectacles. 'You're indiscreet. You're a liability. What if I were of Annalat's camp?'

'Lucky for you I'm not. Relax. I'm part of his scheme. Has he changed his plans?'

'No. This has nothing to do with the scheme. How much do you know of his personal life?'

'No details.'

'Then you don't know that he's a heretic.'

'Of course I do.'

'The Desert Fathers believe in guilt and penitence. . . .' It was hard to speak of it. He felt sick again. Cudbeer went whiter with every stumbling word.

'He is ill with a fever of course. No visitors. I've given him two sleeping draughts. He won't wake for several hours. Can you sit with him while I fetch Crinon?'

Cudbeer nodded. In Magon's bedroom he looked about with mute astonishment. Cal had drawn down the blinds but the injuries were evident, brown shells of dry blood, long, unwavering corrugations. Cudbeer sat on the edge of a chair brought in from the hall.

'He's had his day. He's going.' Cal said roughly, gesturing at the martyr.

This time, he took the lift. In the garden he paused by one of the lead cisterns and put his face in the cool water.

The Garden House looked closed, asleep, but on the shady verandah all the pots and baskets of flowers were freshly watered. She was breakfasting in the kitchen. The bread smelled like a love charm. Chopped meat and garlic lay on a board near a recipe book and the room smelled richly of coriander and cumin.

She smiled, a slight frown of puzzlement wrinkling her brow.

'If I have to cook, I do it while it's cool,' she said. 'It's far too early to draw.'

He stood on the far side of the table, not knowing what to say. Various forms of words passed through his mind.

'What is it?' she said. 'What's the matter? It's Magon.'

There were tears in her eyes. He nodded.

'It's all right,' he said. 'He's not dead or anything.'

'Cal, oh Cal.' She blew her nose on a kitchen cloth and sat up straight. 'I know what has happened. It has happened twice before. I should have warned you. The last time was about four years ago. Didn't you see the scars?'

'He said Arkite threw him. Against a tree.'

'How stupid. It's guilt – you know that – he cannot love without guilt, and this time he has compounded it with remorse. That execution, the Surrogation, that damned all-male religion; and you – you're a Dayamit reborn and enhanced.'

Crinon got up and shouted to Lorilla; she moved forward and saw his face.

'Oh my Lady, not you as well. It's not your fault. It's his. He's an idiot. So intelligent, such a fool.'

She left the house at a run, and he followed her. The flowers in the garden were livid-hued, bursting with nectar; the birds shouted.

Cudbeer was glad to go. After rehearsing him in the fictitious version of Magon's illness, Crinon sent him away. Without tears she looked at her brother's wounds. She took his pulse and set as much as she could of his bed in order without moving him. She demanded to see the scourge, and Cal brought it to her wrapped in the towel with which he had sought to conceal it.

'Hideous thing,' she said, touching the thongs. 'It comes from Diridion – see the silversmith's mark on the handle?'

'I thought he had bought it in the Quarter.'

'Ah no! The religious take an exquisite pleasure in discipline. No cheap trash for them. Whatever the vices of the Quarter, whatever peculiarities of behaviour exist there, the religious can outdo every one.

'Tell Slake to destroy it. It's all right! He's seen it all. He's safe.'

Together they lifted the apprentice saint from the wall.

'Careful,' said Crinon. 'It really is without price, although it is a copy. The original was destroyed in a war. This one is more than two thousand years old: that kind of lineage doesn't bear contemplation.'

Magon spoke from the bed, his voice so normal that they both turned to look at him.

'It came from Gaia,' he said. 'It came in a starship across the galaxy. In Daystar.'

He saw Cal smile and knew that he had enhanced Cal's dream. Unaware of doing so, he sharply drew in his breath; the action of turning his head to look at Cal had parted the drying tissues of his back.

'You'll have to put up with it,' Crinon snapped, struggling with the canvas. 'You've had as much dope as you can take.'

In Cal's room, they propped the painting face against the wall. In its empty place they hung Crinon's clear Cityscape; behind the coloured towers Mount Bai soared, cloud-capped, gorgeous.

When Magon woke again, Crinon was sitting near him, drawing.

'Me?' he asked.

'You. I've left out the damage. Silly brother.'

She abandoned her work and, coming to him, bent and kissed him.

'Silly boy, stupid king,' she said. She began to tell him the story he had loved as a child.

'Once, in a kingdom by the sea. . . .'

Cal went to bed and slept for eighteen hours. Discreetly, next day, Slake awoke him with a tray of breakfast.

134

'She's still here,' he said. 'And I heard the Archivist laugh.'

Tucked beneath the beaker was an envelope addressed to Rafe Dayamit. He recognised the handwriting and tore it open.

'I was sorry to miss you at Crinon's,' she had written. 'And sorry the Archivist is ill. Can I see him?'

Eventually, he found the right words.

'Come tomorrow, but don't be surprised at anything you see,' he wrote.

He signed it with his own name, and addressed the crisp white envelope correctly to Her Excellency Mahuntal Kiden M'una.

Slake called him from the room. She stood in the hall, timid and fragile as she looked up at him. Because she was so different (he had half forgotten), a mute conspirator who had scorned his frantic body, he hesitated. She carried flowers, pale green fronds of kyani and several stems of nias, their scarlet flowers bright in the shadowy hall. The same flower was tucked into her long plait of hair. She had on her Temple costume and the bells chimed. He stared at her, wordless.

'Clod,' she said. 'What are you dreaming of?'

He was conscious of the open bedroom door.

'Crinon is here,' he whispered. 'Remember what I told you?'

'I remember. No amazement.' Her voice was like her bells, she had summoned him again. In the red maral, pleated and folded, she looked as though she might soar to dance with Shelda and Eshtur. He, winging with her, might take her hand, take her, as they flew.

'I begin my Temple servitude next dektron,' she said. 'Then I must dress like this all the time.'

'You are going away?'

'Only for two deks!'

He led her into Magon's room and around the bed, so that she faced him. He did not see her stare or start. Smiling, she laid her flowers on the bed. She bent down and kissed Magon on the cheek, glad, he thought, of the opportunity. She kissed him twice more. The familiar formality distressed Cal. He shuffled and scowled. He had forgotten, too, that she had asked his permission to see Magon.

'I am sorry you are ill,' she said.

Magon looked steadily at her.

'You find me at a disadvantage, M'untal,' he said, extending an arm. He took her hand. 'Come, sit. Cal.'

They sat on the bed, side by side.

'Smile at me, Cal. Where's your winning smile?'

He looked past M'untal's nose into the brown wells and encountered flint, ice, obsidian, adamant; and then the lines about his eyes appeared and Magon smiled. He smiled back.

'This is a bad time for pleasantries,' said Magon. His hand eclipsed her neatly painted nails and her rings. 'But I must know if the boy is well?'

'Oh yes!'

'You see I did not desert you. Perhaps Mahun heard your prayers.'

'Undoubtedly.' Crinon spoke, entering the room with clean linen piled in her arms.

'Even Archivists and maniacs need clean sheets,' she said, dumping her burden on the floor.

'But I can't move! And M'untal and Cal are here.'

'You can move. You have moved. And so can they. I'm a painter, Magon, not a sister of charity.'

'You don't love me?'

'Fool! I hate this, all this drudgery – fiddling and messing with household tasks.'

'Tell Slake to do it,' said Magon.

'She frets, because she has left her children at home – her canvases and her dreams. Painter, look what you have done to my perfect room with your sheets and extra chairs and drawings everywhere.'

'Better a disordered room than a disordered spirit.'

'Come here.'

Unexpectedly Crinon obeyed him. She pulled a chair close to the bed and sat down, her hands calm and folded in her lap; and his hand, it was back, returned to him, and folded in its fellow.

'I shall tell you a story,' said Magon.

'Once upon a time there was a king who ruled his subjects with a rod of iron. He would not allow them to dance in the streets, nor read books, nor look at pictures; and the birds of the city were forbidden to sing. Anyone caught enjoying one of the forbidden pleasures was brought before the king who beat him with the rod of iron until he died. Many great and good people were killed in this way. Yet most of the king's subjects were content because their city was kept tidy, the streets were swept and the windows of the houses were always clean.

'One day a scholar came to the city. He had journeyed through the forests where the birds sang all day and all night, from a country where books and pictures were given to the people every day by their ruler and where dancing was the way of life. In the king's library (for naturally the king himself had plenty of books, and pictures, and he liked to dance in his palace) the scholar read the Book of Days. He read that the king's time had come.

'A white bird flew into the library and perched on the scholar's shoulder. She chirruped in his ear. The scholar sent her into the city and she gathered all the children together; and the scholar, coming out to the market place, met the children there. Then the children gave the scholar their dolls and toy carts and kites and he took all the strings from the toys and gave them to the white bird and her friends.

'The birds flew to the palace, all together in a shower of wings. They bound the king and lifted him high. They flew with him out of the palace, over the city, and way into the mountains. And there the eagle bit through the strings that bound the king and he fell to his death on the rocks.

'After that the people of the city danced when they liked, read books when they liked and painted many pictures. The birds sang all the time. Joyously.'

'And the scholar ruled over the city,' whispered Crinon.

'It's a children's story,' said Cal.

'It is a folk tale, not a children's story. From the Zalcasians.'

'Mother used to tell it,' said Crinon.

'I know it too,' said M'untal. 'It is in one of my old books. I always thought that the scholar was no better than the king. Using children like that! And birds, the symbols of freedom. If he had pardoned him, or set him free – '

'He would have been a noble idiot. Come – ' Magon smiled as he spoke to her. 'It is a fable. Would you wish it to be true?'

'I wish many things – as you know. But unless someone finds Huyatt's magic ring, they will never come true.'

'What if the ring were found? If it were in this room?'

'If! Next dektron I must dance for Mahun. And I wish to. I must serve the She. And I wish to.'

'Yet Mahun took your son away.'

'Not Mahun. The Gynarchs, the Matriarchy. I love Mahun.'

'So does Cal,' he said. 'But it doesn't blind him.'

'It was easy for you to abuse your privilege and spy in the Archive.'

'No. I keep the Register, but the Gynarchy watches over Exchanges. I am not permitted to see the Temple records. To read them I would have to break down a door.'

'Crinon then.'

'Crinon has no key. She is no longer one of the soronai.'

'Someone found out for you. Just as someone exchanged Rafe Dayamit for Cal. Just as the scholar employed the birds.'

'You think I keep birds?'

'Yes. A flock.'

Cal, excited by the double-talk, said, 'I know them. One of them has cool hands with silver-tipped nails, another keeps her hands wrapped in her cymar; another works in City University. Several work in the Octagon. Several are artists and writers. Three of them are here. Rafe Dayamit was not one of them, but I am.'

'To entrap Annalat, you would have to use Chacma,' said Crinon openly. 'And what of the people?'

137

'Bread and circuses,' replied Magon. 'Clean streets and sparkling windows; husk.'

'You must still collude with Chacma.'

'And what of Mahun?' said M'untal. 'What then of the golden Mamelon and the blue towers?'

Cal thought of the pacific image in the cellar.

'How could I destroy her, little crane?' said Magon. 'We would all be free.'

Cal walked with M'untal to the lift. She kissed him, soft, her lips brushing his, and he began to drown; he was wrong, all wrong. It was Cal and M'untal; Magon was far away, nor could he venture here. He got into the lift and travelled down with her. Together. They walked into the garden. Why not ask her?

'You won't be able to see Luth when you are Serving,' he said.

'Hush! You'll hurt me again. Twenty days is not long.'

'A long time for a little boy without a mother.'

'It's not like that. He has two mothers now. And Crinon and Xhara' when she returns.'

'I don't understand,' he said, dredging his memory for the ghost of M'nah, jealous of the child. 'You women are she-cats; you don't care which kitten you nurse.'

'Hush!' she said again. 'You insult Plama. You can go and see how he copes with his women.'

'Why does Magon call you a crane?'

'How should I know? He has several odd turns of speech; I don't find it unsettling.'

Without turning a hair, propped awkwardly on his pillows and his elbow, he had recited that tale. King, rod, scholar; Magon chastened, Magon victorious.

'He is a soul in torment,' she continued, when they came to the empty theatre. 'A heretic, lost. Does he know what they do to heretics?'

'He knows. It's the same for revolutionaries.'

'The same sin. To deny Mahun. And the Desert Fathers exact terrible punishments; we studied them in my novitiate – an exercise in mistaken faith. Where they weep and chastise the flesh, we dance.'

She moved across the grassy stage and began the movements of the Wheel. He watched her and said nothing, thinking her explanation simplistic. How calmly she accepted the complexity of Magon's demands, his convoluted nature. It could only be because she did not know him; to her he was still the Archivist. But then he remembered how he had held her and assigned her the role of integrity.

M'untal knelt, centre stage. The sun threw her fluid shadow across the circle and down its sloping bank.

'The circle cannot be broken,' she explained, drawing one with her right hand. 'It is complete, and has no end. We say it is the only perfect shape.'

They crossed the lawns and came to the edge of her private garden. The statue of the boy among the beds of nias and kyani was an impudence; he wondered who had bared his flesh for the sculptor, balancing on one leg while she captured his soul in stone.

'I must go back,' he said, omitting the two words which would complete the sentence: 'to Magon'.

'Don't look for me for the rest of the quarter. I am to be purified for the Service and instructed in my duties. I am not allowed to see any man.'

She ran up the long flight of steps to the terrace. She did not turn nor wave, though he stood still until she had gone.

By the afternoon, Crinon's litter of drawings had spread into the study. Cal, sifting through them, looked at the gall and bistre images of Magon, of himself; the rich man and the pauper, the Archivist and the pretender, the seducer and his victim. He laughed. Butterflies, he thought, were not more easily trapped. And she, dancing towards the net, paused sometimes to spread her wings and sun herself; unless the huge and clumsy net, falling backward, caught him in its green and obliterating folds. One day Crinon would make a likeness of M'untal.

On a low table, placed between the two upholstered chairs, a game of chess had been abandoned. The pieces Magon had played were black, it was obvious, while Chacma's were blood red. Each piece was an exquisite carving, but few of the pieces matched. He picked some of them up to examine. He did not know how to play, but he saw that the game was war made abstract. The largest pieces mimicked warrior queens; the smallest were their infantry, terrifying masked females armed with spears.

'Mother began the collection for him,' said Crinon. 'He was lucky to find another five from the same set; in an antique shop in Roakn I think. They're valuable, naturally; most of them were carved during the second millenium. If the pieces matched, they would be priceless.'

The red queen in his hand was a little like one of the Temple archers, in her grace and strength; but she was not of his City.

'Who is she?' he asked.

'Oh, that one. She is from Diold in Ineit; where my family came from – before the chessmen. I don't know who she is meant to be – perhaps no one, a generalised terror.'

He put the piece back on the board. It seemed to stand in a dominant position. He thought of Chacma sitting, bulky, warlike, in his chair and of the implications of calling the chair his own, with its suggestions of domesticity, of a settled life. He thought of Magon moving his black pieces, impatient for the alien president to be gone; of the Cheronese guards who must have been posted outside the door, outside the lifts, on the stairs, bringing weapons into the peaceful Octagon. There was a section in W on warfare: warfare from Foundation to Reformation, Gunaian weapons, Gaian weapons, the genocides and matricides of his planet, the infights and Triber shams of his own sub-world on the City streets. For Chacma, war was life; he scrapped with Hayla of Hayna and intrigued with the peaceful nations, intent upon his own game of chess.

Crinon put down her book and came to the table.

'Magon thought he was beaten,' she said, and moved three pieces. 'There now, Apeman, Crinon has done for you.'

She removed the pieces from the board, and folded it so that it became a box. She began to pack the women away.

'He was tired, that's all,' she said. 'Tired and desperate. And now – he got out of bed earlier. He can hardly stand. He moves like an old man.'

She slammed the lid of the box shut and flicked up the catch; if Magon had seen her expressing her distress so carelessly, Cal thought, he would have cried out.

They tidied the room, moving lazily amongst the sheets of paper, piling them in a corner. Crinon picked up her novel again, and Cal toured the bookshelves. Then Slake appeared, an unquiet Slake, carrying a duster with which he flicked irritably at the door handle.

'He's awake,' he said. 'And he's bored. Will you both take tea with him before he drives me crazy?'

Disturbed from their idleness, they looked at each other. Crinon smoothed her hair and Cal, squatting on the floor, retrieved his shoes and put them on.

'The Dancer,' said Crinon. The striking clock and Slake, exiting on the last chime, interrupted her.

'What about her?'

'Need you be so aggressive? I was about to give you a warning, that's all. Now I won't.'

'Please yourself.' He was bored too. He overtook her in the corridor; he would be the first. The smile was for him alone, such a brilliant burst of affection. He did not need to make the conventional enquiries. Two discarded books lay on the bed and marked Magon's restless state, but the Book of Monos was closed on its rest. Outside, the afternoon heat had stilled even the fish in their tank and the window glass had darkened. They heard Crinon moving china.

'What were you reading?'

'Oh, nothing. Some lists, records from the second millennium – a time when the starships were away.'

'Can't you get up?'

'I shall certainly get up tomorrow.'

'That would not be wise.' Crinon moved in with cups and plates.
'Perhaps for Ingemi.'

'You missed something quite remarkable at the Reception, Cal. I
looked for you, but they told me you had gone. Shiron, the knifethrower.
A pillar of fire in her scarlet gown. The knives were like flames too. A
double conflagration. I can't imagine where she got that gown. Sinein,
perhaps – '

'Roakn.'

'You know her?'

He had spoken out of turn. If they had been in a public place. . . .

'Once.' Magon was hunting. He could feel the predatory, possessive,
stare; unreasonably, it excited him.

'I wish you would introduce me.'

'Unfortunately.' The deliberation could only be assumed.
'Fortunately, Rafe Dayamit does not know her.'

'My lady, Magon, how I wish it was next year and all the lies done
with.'

'My God, Crinon, how I wish you were safely out of here and in your
own house.'

The quarrel took place a little way above his head. It wasn't his. He
sipped and watched them. As children, they would have punched and
kicked; adults, they assailed each other with words. Crinon was right; but
he was on Magon's side.

He gave his bed to Crinon. A sleeping mat of the type used by Artisans
was unrolled for him in the study and supplied with pillows. Before he
went to it he opened the door of Magon's room and stood in the dark
listening to his even breathing. He shared with Rafe the cause but not the
blame: the desolation was Magon's own. Now he felt affection, tender
solicitude; he had been flayed and parted from his tough exterior skin.
He had nothing to measure his love by; he supposed that M'untal felt so
towards her boy. His desire for her was not part of it and unconsciously
he twisted and shrugged like a fish on a hook.

Magon's voice surprised him.

'She is unique,' he said.

Cal did not reply, but closed the door and went to the study. He lay on
the mat, conscious of his loneliness, sinking towards sleep; but, even as the
tide rose up to take him, he started awake, seeing her eyes magnified by her
tears. He got up. The roomful of Magon's possessions now included
himself, and nothing of M'untal was there but the image in his mind. He
switched on the desk lamp and took a sheet of Magon's headed notepaper.

'If I had such paper and such a name,' he scribbled, 'what would I
write? That you are unique? He said so, ten minutes ago.

'Since I am not even Rafe Dayamit – ' He scratched out the line and
began again: 'I am Cal – ' He paused to read what he had written,

141

screwed up the paper and threw it across the room. He lay down.

Dayamit sat on the end of the sleeping mat, writing hard. As he filled a sheet, he tossed it to the floor and Cal picked it up. The paper had become thin and translucent, but the words were solid, brittle, and black on the paper, like burnt grease. Cal ate the sheets of paper, consuming them with the hunger of a starving man. In his mouth they turned to flesh; they tasted of blood and semen.

Dayamit looked up. His face had altered. Clearly, the conditions in hell were not to his liking. His face was pale, bony; the golden eyes had swelled and were covered with green veins, like those of the Cat. He blinked slowly.

Her letter arrived in the morning. Characteristically, it began with a plea.

> All is well again, is it not? I cried when you left, but after my failure I had no right to keep you. Let us –

He thought, she has written to Magon as well; what has she written? He rushed to the kitchen to confront Slake.

'How many letters came this morning?'

'One,' said the agamite, continuing to remove bread from the oven.

But Slake would protect Magon. He returned to the study and sat on his disordered bed to finish M'untal's letter.

> Let us make a fresh beginning. I have consulted the cards and I will meet you on Mahun's Day. It is the traditional day for new bonds.
> Don't reply. No man, remember!

Defensively, she had signed her full name. He studied the ink, the penstrokes; he saw her body moving in the Dance in praise of Mahun. Crinon had put flowers in the room, great jugs of horned lilies, the red of M'untal's skirts. But M'untal's red flowers were for Magon. He reread her instruction. No man. Neither himself, nor Magon. And she had made a pact; absurd to think of Magon as a rival.

He spread his books on the table and took a clean sheet of paper.

'She'll have to tidy this up,' said Slake gloomily. 'Their father's coming this afternoon. I don't see how she can work like it. You're as bad.'

He picked up three of the drawings, spread again, a contagious plague of paper, and examined them with a professional eye and a face filled with despair. Cal thought Crinon insensitive for leaving them where the eunuch could see them. Hard shit, Amskiri. At least we didn't give you the milk.

Cal worked, filling page after page with notes. The hours passed. All at once the clocks struck three and voices filled the hall. He bent over his books hearing Destorio Nonpareil speaking in Maralay, commonplaces, Crinon's joyful greeting, and the door of Magon's room closing. He laid his head on *The City in the Cleft* and slept.

Crinon was in the room, a blend of linseed and lemon, of flowers and turpentine; he opened his eyes. Her gentle hands were touching his.

'Father would like to meet you,' she said.

'Me? Or Dayamit?'

'You, stupid.'

Once more, he was on trial; the ordeal was by confrontation, another performance. Destorio Nonpareil held out his right hand. He shook the hand as if he had all the confidence of Rafe Dayamit. Nonpareil's eyes were brown too, deep lines about them; the black remained as a shadow in his grey hair, but it curled, still thick, still vigorous. He thought he knew what the man was thinking; the way his feet, in their laced shoes, were firm on the floor, the way his legs, muscular under the grey cloth, were set, told him. His hand was released.

'I won't say I'm pleased to meet you,' said Nonpareil. 'The only other Surrogate I have met is Annalat; in Maralis Surrogation seems to be a way to the stars, an original way of refreshing a stale environment. New blood in Cheron comes by promotion from the ranks.

'Tattooing the entire nation was always a folly.'

Magon stood behind his father. A patterned shawl of Crinon's covered his shoulders and he needed to shave; he looked like a brigand.

'It was originally a mark of grace,' he said. 'A visible sign of Mahun's choice.'

'So he is now one of her Vern communicants? What will you do if there is a delay in your plans – send him home to his mother?'

'No. His death certificate has already been signed. He will die in a contained cholera outbreak in early Vern next year; frequent visitors to the Quarter expose themselves to such risks. We shall be gone. Cal can be himself once we have crossed the Odal.'

'You are too confident, Magon.'

'You are overcautious, Father.'

'I suppose you have remembered to reserve a suitable cadaver.'

'Naturally.'

Cal stood quietly beside them, listening as they discussed the fate of Rafe Dayamit, the morbid arrangements for another version of his death.

'What can you do?' said Nonpareil suddenly.

'I don't know yet.'

'Honest, at least. A rare virtue in a thief.'

He let himself be insulted, reflecting as he stood there in the Archivist's study, amongst the symbols and the rewards of power, that, since he was dead, he had nothing now to lose.

* * *

143

A day passed. A servant delivered a parcel of blue silk addressed to Rafe Dayamit M'unor. Cal sat at Magon's desk and penned a note of thanks to Nila. Perhaps he would give the silk to M'untal. Two days passed. He drank Ceremana late at night and slept badly.

'You should go to the Quarter,' said Magon callously on the third night.

The fourth day passed. In the late afternoon he went to the greenhouses and asked Nan the gardener to send M'untal the most exquisite flowers he had.

'These?' said Nan, leading him past fleshy orchids fattened on mist. 'This?' The pendulous flower had scarlet stamens and white wings like handkerchiefs or doves.

In the temperate house, she showed him the pale flowers of the north, as like M'untal in delicacy as the red nias were symbolic of her will. She showed him the beauty of weeds, Vern and Maralis's own dense chokeweed, harbinger of a good lily crop, thornweeds, and the invaders, briars, thistles, and dandelions, the traders' gift. He saw his first roses and the little flowers which, in Sinein, starred the meadows. He chose sweet-scented flowers, the white and nodding heads of snowdrops from the northern winter, and honey-hearted violets.

The tenth day came, the twentieth of Kriy, Ingemi. In the study, Slake handed him a letter. 'Hurry,' she had written, 'Minutes, and don't expect to see *me*.' Puzzling over the final sentence, he hurried to the lifts.

Alna let him in. The white door of the bedroom was open but, inside, he came face to face with a mirror. He saw his own tense face and body. Behind him, Alna adjusted a painted screen and he saw her wane and M'untal appear. Her image inhabited the wide mirror. She sat facing a triple mirror and the glass on the wall behind her, his window, reflected the triptych. Plump children cavorted around the triune mirror, black as the wood they were carved from. Some of the figures looked out into the room and others the opposite way, into the mirrors and so, onward, into an eternity of infinite reflection. The figures on the screen which shielded M'untal were those he had smiled at on his way into the coloured world of the Shack, Garissa, Tycee, and Shailsh, her posture telling him what M'untal would not.

The carved stool she sat on was no throne, but a narrow ship of satinwood, which supported her body as if it were fine gold and she a faceted gem.

She, with a golden face and stiffly braided hair, had become like one of the statues which bowed and danced before the wind and the rain in the arcades outside the Temple. Her lips were red and lustrous, her eyes lidded and rimmed in dark green. The eyes of the deer had become the eyes of the panther. Gold, turquoise, amethyst, ruby, sapphire, carnelian, and sard hung from her ears, her wrists, her ankles; intricate

144

constructions, pierced bells and triple-linked chains, imprisoned her. Yet he saw more of her body than he had ever seen before, the short-cut bodice replaced by jewelled bands which her breasts pushed outwards, her naked back a smooth strait of brown flesh. None of it was for him. She was remote, the essence of the deity. A kind of reverence overtook him; he felt he should bow down. The perfume which flowed from her, choking him, was that of the trumpet lily.

On the table in front of her were the boxes and jars of colour with which she had altered her face and made a golden mask of it and, amongst the potions, a fading incongruity, his snowdrops and violets in a glass bowl.

A scarlet fan on which a prayer was written in the foaming letters of Crypto-Maralay was spread beside the jars; on the floor lay the blue parasol with which Alna would shield her when they rode in an open carriage through the streets.

She could not smile, covered as she was in the thick paste, but she lifted one gilded hand.

'M'untal?' he whispered. 'How can you move?'

For answer, she stood and turned in front of the mirrors. She began to sway and move her feet in tiny, exaggerated steps. Her hands fluttered in an ecstasy of confined motion. Then she was still.

'Au revoir, Cal,' she said, her voice escaping from the painted lips.

Her handmaiden propelled him from her presence.

He felt relieved and resolute when she was out of reach; somewhere beneath the golden dome, invisible from the study window, she carried on her separate life. Magon came into the room and rested a hand on his shoulder.

'I think I've taught you anxiety. I'm sorry.'

'There's no anxiety like having nothing to eat.'

'Then why the contemplation through the window glass? If I can tolerate her presence, surely you can bear her absence?'

Cal turned. Bloody liar. Dissembler. The large hand, and the small.

Magon was not dressed, but the wrapper he wore must drag at and rasp his wounds. He moved stiffly and there were deep shadows beneath his eyes.

'Life was simpler down there,' said Cal.

'Was it? Have you forgotten the terror already?'

They sat in the study, drinking the bottle of Ceremana with which it had become their custom to finish a day. Magon lay in his chair, a cushion in the small of his back keeping half the bruises from contact with the chair; Cal sat on the floor sorting half-heartedly through a pile of documents relating to the Tayaal.

'Came earlier,' said Magon abstractedly. 'Evening bag.'

The white paper, cast from the pile on his knees, floated to the floor. Cal, retrieving it, read:

To Magon Nonpareil, Archivist of the City of Mahun, from Mahuntal Kiden M'una in greeting and love: False Law XXii.

His jealousy returned hot foot, flushing his face; but the single line below was for him.

Cal my love, read the next verse. 3AiV is Mahun's Day.

Obviously this was a personal message; Magon's was cryptic and religious, a response to his testing of her faith.

Together they went out and down into the Library for the heavy volume of the False Law. Magon carried it into his office and they leaned over his desk in the light of the lamp, searching for the verses she had named. Domenikos's four-thousand-year-old ascetic knelt in the painting above them, remote in his struggle among the rocks.

Magon read his verse aloud, his voice strong and resonant, as if he spoke to a congregation.

Every man has his purpose. On the Wheel, none are outside my pattern. Beyond the Wheel is utter darkness, and there dwell the damned.

But Cal read inwardly:

He came to me in the garden and was blessed.

In silence, Magon closed the book and returned it to its place. The hands of the clock stood at one.

'This is my own time,' he said. 'There is another archive you must see. Come.'

The lift took them to the lowest level of the Archive, ten below ground. Pressing the panel, Magon sent it back to the top of the building. He took a key from the heavy ring on his belt, where two score keys jangled, weighing him down with the symbol and actuality of his office.

The door Magon unlocked bore a notice reading 'Auxiliary Generator #3' and the room beyond it contained the large machine, lettering on it confirming its origins in Cheron. Magon locked the door behind them. The second door was unmarked and led into a windowless cubbyhole, lit with a dim yellow lamp. Again, Magon locked the door behind them. The walls were painted dull green and a row of pipes ran down one of them.

'Beyond this room,' said Magon, 'are three more levels of the Archive. Look.'

He spread his palm against an area of wall at shoulder height. The wall slid silently aside.

'Knowledge can be buried and outlawed, but is seldom totally forgotten. This is called the Forbidden Archive.'

The room was vast and brightly lit, filled with rank upon rank of shelves containing reels of shiny black tape. The lowest shelves held clear domes containing stacks of discs like plates of glass piled one on the other.

'Those are useless. Old, worn out, unplayable. These can be read.'

He laid his hand on a different set of shelves. They were packed with transparent cubes containing smaller cubes of varying colours. He extracted a box from a stack and took a red cube from it.

'This is a complex cube; it can be printed with sounds, with words, or with moving pictures. I can make it give up the information stored on it.'

Cal looked at the tiny cube. Devices like this had enabled *Daystar* to voyage beyond time. In another age.

'How? You?'

The machine was as white and elegant as a piece of structuralist sculpture. Its glassy screen did not reflect their faces. In front of it stood a desk with a shiny top.

Magon dropped the cube into a slot: it disappeared inside the machine with a click. A group of letters and numbers appeared on the screen and the desktop became an illuminated plan, an esoteric pinball machine.

'Mahun,' said Cal.

Magon touched several of the coloured areas before him, his fingers deft.

'Get a chair. That's right, here. Sit down. Now touch the green.'

Cal obeyed.

'Touch the white.' Magon's voice, disembodied, issued from the machine and the same instruction appeared on the screen.

Cal obeyed the machine.

He saw *Daystar* erect beside her launching platform, her silver body reflecting the pattern of the clouds and the letters CITY clear on her nose.

The picture faded and letters flowed, writing themselves across the screen in Magon's distinctive hand:

For Cal, an exposition.

Daystar was waiting. Her crew wore white and every arm was marked with a star. A room full of chairs and couches, men and women patiently listening to a speech. He saw that the captain of the *Daystar* was a man. He saw a pair of lovers: the wax cryomorphs alive, Hero and Chiara. They kissed each other and bared their arms for the first injection. They too had the starmarks of sailors but his arm was also marked with a brush,

147

and hers with the pen of a writer. They lay in the body bays, stark and frozen. *Daystar* soared.

Another ship was readied for launch: *Evenstar.* He saw her engines fire, her flight arising and then the golden flower. The explosion ruptured the ship, but death's indecencies were veiled in white vapour. He felt tears on his cheeks and looked at Magon.

'After that came the Reformation,' said Magon.

'How could the knowledge be denied?'

'Fear? Of such a death? Of the implied order? Of such another failure?'

A blue planet filled the screen. The continents were unfamiliar, five great land masses. These were not the well-known outlines of Mahkrein, Sinein, and Ineit. The planet was Gaia. Her music entranced him, bright and ancient, a timeless fugue.

He looked on the City in the Silver Age. A great bank ran east through the suburbs and women were attacking it with picks and shovels, with passion. He saw the vehicles which had ridden it, ovoid and incandescent, white with the speed of their travel. He saw a place that was surely na Hinoor circus, but moving metal boxes choked it. Known territory was alien. In a series of intercut images the City was presented to him. Before and After. The Reformation had removed as much beauty as ugliness. Slowly, the glaring lights went out, the pace of the pedestrians slowed, quiet returned, and the place became recognisable, his beloved City. The people in the crowd looked prosperous, happy; he saw no Beggars, no pavement children; perhaps Huyatt himself walked there. A graph showed him that in that happy age the life expectancy of a woman was a hundred years and that of a man near it, at ninety-seven; a second graph showed him that M'untal might expect to live for seventy-five years; he would probably be dead before he was sixty.

Now a middle-aged man was preaching to a crowd of men in a public place, exhorting them with harsh words. The pictures jerked and went out of focus; he rubbed his eyes. Something flamed in the crowd and the preacher fell over. A crowd of men were driven along Broadwalk in chains; their handgrips were like the ones which had tormented him. A disembodied women's voice described the torture in clinical language. Remembering Crinon's words, he covered his eyes; but, looking too soon at the screen, he saw the mutilation, and it was as Crinon had told him. Magon watched, apparently impassive.

'That rebellion was in 401,' he said. 'There was another during my childhood.'

The screen was dark. Blank. He saw small points of light. The inside of the Mamelon. He wanted to look away. The She wore a golden mask, and the devotions were calm and ordered; this was not the female orgy of street legend.

'Recorded treasonably,' said Magon.

A celebration. The ancient Dancers were all like M'untal. The Temple cats, in a leafy garden, crouched to murder birds. Text appeared.

'My vanity,' Magon said. 'Several of my family were Archivists, the rest always writers or painters. It is a long tradition. The men, until myself and until Annalat's prohibition five years ago, were soldiers like so many – mercenaries of Cheron. There is little scope in Maralis for a military man, for any man – except as a semen manufactory.'

'Or a toy.' Now he had voiced his allegiance. Magon smiled.

The handwritten entry recorded the birth in 253 AR of a daughter to Lys Hinoor M'una, Archivist.

Suddenly, Chacma was grinning at him, Magon's father in the background. They were looking at a table on which lay a variety of remote kill weapons.

Something out of focus lurked in the bottom of a pit.

'The only pictorial record of the Burnt Lands.' Magon gripped Cal's hand. 'Worse, infinitely worse than anything in the Block, worse than – castration.'

The creature lifted a hand. Once, it had been a man.

'I dream of it,' said Magon.

Cal saw a man lying in a white hospital bed and supposed him to be a victim of the tortures and the unspent radiation, of the stew of chemicals from which the Burnt Lands got their name. He twitched incessantly. His skin was a jaundiced yellow, his mouth slack, his eyes on another world.

'Last days of a husker,' said Magon, his voice abraded by emotion.

'Shit, Magon! One in two thousand become addicted; I'm lucky at dice. And the lily is sacred. . . .'

The screen went blank. They leaned back in their chairs and made the slow return to the present. Magon looked at his watch.

'Two-thirty. I must sleep.'

He touched the magic desk. The red cube fell from the machine and Magon picked it up and cradled it in the palm of his hand.

'I will meet you on Mahun's Day.' The Dancer had made him a promise. A tented city had sprung up overnight in the gardens and he dragged Cudbeer towards it. There was no sign of Magon but he saw Annalat M'una drinking with a diplomat outside a silken tent. A carousel brimmed with Dancers, perched like birds on the coloured horses, and he stood below it looking for M'untal: she was not there. His passage through the fair became a search which Cudbeer hindered, darting here and there as the differing distractions claimed him. At the wild beast show Zalcasian dancers, flushed scarlet in their felt and furs, pressed

149

him and he saw a tiny Temple Dancer pinned in the throng; she turned her head, but she was not M'untal. Excited by the thought of Cudbeer's terror he allowed himself a ride on the whipwheel; Cudbeer clung shrinking while he laughed at the sensations, the fall and rebound.

The notice outside the yellow tent read 'Tarot by Tarla'. It invited the credulous, nor could he resist it. Pushing Cudbeer before him, he kept his face averted; once inside he sat in the shadows beyond the lamplight while she dealt the cards for Silvanor.

The seven crowded and renewing deks since his arrest, seventy days, had altered her. The flesh of her cheeks had fallen away and new chasms opened; a different cockatoo with a sulphur crest clacked its beak in the cage. But her hair was newly dyed and her carmined lips kept faith in paint with the seductive shape of their youth. She finished the star draw and told Cudbeer his prosaic fortune. He appeared content when she intoned, 'Wealth, marriage, women, a woman with a great deal of sense . . . sensuality', the habitual blush spreading over his features and crimsoning his neck.

Cal took his place. Softly, he put his hand on hers. 'Tarla,' he said, 'you have a new bird.'

She knocked over her chair in her haste to embrace him. Holding his head against her broad bosom, she stroked his hair.

'My sweet,' she crooned. 'My sweet.'

When she released him he told her his story. He told her his new name. He told her that certain of his new friends knew the truth.

'The camels came and questioned me,' she said. 'I told them I had sold you husk. They gave me a warning; they don't trouble an old woman. And the licence squad came and checked everyone. My papers are always in order but they fined Zalcissa and they took Dog and kept him for three days.'

'I feared for you. I sat in the Block and thought of you.'

'You thought of yourself,' she said. 'You confessed. Afraid of the Burn. Look.'

From a pocket she took a creased and soiled piece of paper. It was a cutting from an official news-sheet, the printed story illustrated with a badly foxed print of a man who resembled himself. He examined the picture closely. Dayamit's trim beard jutted at him.

'It isn't me. It's him.'

'My sight isn't what it was,' said Tarla. 'He's got your eyes.'

'Look again, Tarla dear.'

She looked, from his face to the grey print and back again.

'He might pass for you,' she said.

Cudbeer looked over his shoulder. 'No mark,' the caption announced in staccato phrases. 'Executed recently. An unhappy traitor. Examination showed him to be decadent and corrupt. A thief without religion or means. Arbiter Talamun Mahud spoke for him. The verdict was Guilty. Execution followed the same day. An order for burial in the Burnt Lands has been signed by the Archivist.' Cal looked at the photograph again. Rafe glared back at him. He thought of Magon with this flawed creature and crushed the paper in his fist, dropping it on the table where it lay, litter, on the painted cards.

Tarla looked at him, her eyes bright with the wisdom of age and with professional interest.

'So you are the pet of the Archivist,' she said. 'Mahun! But it's not a bad fate. Perhaps my reading was pied that day, for the cards didn't show it.'

'Tarla – ' He wanted to reveal more to her, to explain the Scheme, but Cudbeer's hand, tightening on his shoulder, silenced him.

'You'll see me again,' he said, turned swiftly and pushed aside the tent flap, emerging diminished into the brilliant sun. Cudbeer came after him.

'I paid her,' he said. 'Over the top. Who is she?'

'A figure from the past,' Cal said shortly. The gaudy delights of the fair now depressed him; Cudbeer trailing, he walked to the Long Lake and flung himself down on the shore by the cruising waterfowl. Cudbeer looked down at him and watched him pout and frown.

The red-eyed drake was harassed. Like a little steamer he scurried up and down, pausing to bow and flutter at his mate. If another drake approached, he lowered his head and drove him off.

'Stupid bastard,' said Cal, laughing and chirruping at the drake.

'Will she tell?' Cudbeer, ignoring the antics of the ducks, was ready with his question.

'How do I know? She's an honest gossip. She's probably afraid.'

Cudbeer pulled him to his feet. 'I'm thirsty,' he said, removing his spectacles.

Why spoil the day? Last night, Magon had told him that the fountains would run with wine; he had laughed and, turning on the great bed, stretched out and slept again. Cudbeer received his report with an incredulous laugh and they went to see if it were true.

A boy and girl stood in the bowl of the Merman Fountain, soaked and laughing, catching showers of Baialt in gaping mouths. The flowery scent was overpowering.

'He didn't lie!' Cal said in amazement.

'This is new. Where's the Ceremana?' Cudbeer looked about him.

'Too good for fountains; this'll do.' Discarding his shirt, Cal joined the couple in the pool.

But wine by the fountainful is untenable as a concept and in reality; it sickens, the delight of the bouquet gone, the smooth kiss of crystal on the lip removed, the fragrance ruined, the first sip a torrent. Cal drank, splashed the girl, and left the fountain. Cudbeer, dipping his hand, was content to drink from its cup.

They came upon an animated group which picnicked beside the sweeping trails of a bell vine. Crinon raised her hand and called for them to join the party, Amarant poured bubbly, Faya overloaded plates. Chenodor and Gildo, their wives and children, Luth sturdy amongst them, Lorilla and Alna: they were all carefree. Chenodor's head was bent over a fragment of pale wood and the tiny knife with which he scored and scraped it was eclipsed by his great hand. Near him, on the grass, lay an open ivory case full of the knife's fellows: miniature chisels, diminutive gouges, like the tools of a surgeon. He did not look up when Amarant offered him wine, nor when the shrieking children pursued Fiora's kitten, escaped once more from the tight prison of her arms. Crinon eyed the cat with unconcealed distaste.

'If they were not consecrated animals,' whispered Faya mischievously, 'Crinon would poison them all.'

'Cats,' said Crinon, lowering her glass, 'should be the creatures of Aash. They come out at night to kill and maim; they sleep by day and their dreams are full of blood.'

'As their bodies are full of grace,' protested Gildo, smiling.

'Maybe. But the boldest leap of a big cat cannot compare with the flight of the commonest bird.'

'Or a starship,' said Cal.

Everyone looked at him, waiting to be amused.

'He's obsessed,' said Amarant on cue, folding her arms about him. 'Poor boy. Won't you have a used sculptor today?'

Cal laid his head in Amarant's lap and let her feed him titbits from a cold fowl. She tilted her glass against his lips and he drank her wine. She wiped his lips with her handkerchief and watched him fall asleep.

'Spoiled boy,' said Crinon later, slapping him. He started awake. Amarant's lap was soft and warm; he had dreamed of the deep reaches of space, the shoals of time.

'The Dance!' He heard indulgent laughter as he sped.

The Dancers, processing with garlands, weaved a sinuous web on the hill. No sacred dance this. It was a celebration of freedom, the day when Mahun had created herself. And there was a difference of costume: the Dancers' dark blue marals were open from the knee and printed with scarlet lips. They showered the crowds with luck, localised duststorms of rose and gold pigment. He located M'untal and she acknowledged him at last, a graceful dip and bow which might have been part of the Dance. She was herself no longer a stiff votary, but supple and lithe, the best of the Dancers yet one of them. She disappeared as the throng pushed him aside and the Dance went on down the hill.

Left alone, he sighed and walked to the lake shore; he sat down near the place where his sulks had concerned Cudbeer. He was sticky with sweat and wine, streaked with the Dancers' fortune dust. The yellow gum trees dripped their resin in the lake where it floated, iridescent on the surface, before mingling with the water. A boat was tied to the nearer island; he heard laughter and the cry of a woman in ecstasy.

Turning his head, he saw the crowds strewn like multicoloured flowers across the slopes below the ivory towers, the tents and fairground engines. Lights sprang up, greater clusters of bloom; music called him. Ignoring it, he walked by the shore.

He thought of Magon and the Forbidden Archive, of his own divided self; of the City, and Glaver left there untasted; of husk and the greater delusion of dreams. He wanted M'untal. She had teased him long enough. He did not know where to look for her, where to seek the promised blessing. Magon, too, had hidden himself; ah, Magon. Last night, he had read the legend of Inana aloud from Lys Hinoor's version, the subtle transcription making the demiurge's every passion a stately banquet of words. Later, Magon left the bed. In the borderland between sleep and dreaming, Cal heard him move about the room, the clink of his keys as he dressed. He was no longer in the room. Perhaps he was buried now, thirty-nine levels below, burrowing in the forbidden records. He dreamed, sliding in the yellow mud, a worm between the layers of red soil and lily roots, turning in the cool room; outside, the hot night. His breathing became even, soft as the name of the month. He saw M'untal, but she had Magon's face and then Magon himself appeared amongst the stars, tall as *Daystar*, a black magician. Golddust spilled from his hands; he lifted them and the constellations trembled.

Cal got up and walked on the shore. The shadows of the tall Zalcasian pines combined with the swift dusk. The scent of the pines, coming to him, was a solace. He reached them and followed the path. Here, Magon had confronted him. Shekarah's folly twisted on the hilltop, higher than the trees.

She was sitting on the lowest step of the Stairway to Nowhere; she came to him and kissed his hands. Laughing, she flitted up the first four steps of the spiral, inviting him to follow, in her dark dress a silhouette against the deeper colour of the sky. He went after her but, on the steps, she was as nimble as he and she dared him higher on the crazy spiral till they reached the giddy top. Here he caught her – there was no escape – but, leaning against him, she began to name the emergent stars and to show him the pulsing lighthouses up and down the coast.

'When – ', he began.

'Ssh,' she said. 'Listen. Now we must descend.'

The resonant salute of the waves pushing deep into the chasm below them, the kiss of the warm air, enchanted him; but, impatient counter-point to these, he heard Magon's footfall on the stone.

'Look.'

He was waiting for them in a room without walls, a room higher than the treetops whose only limits were the starry sky itself; he was naked, open, without guile and without his subtle and persuasive words. Without the props of the Archivist's cymar and keys he was a newborn entity, so that Cal's first thought was not of the blessing M'untal had promised him, joyous and unrestrained sex on this festive night, but of the future when all men would be as perfect as Magon, powerful, intelligent, and virile, leaders, judges, and teachers; no longer playthings and ornaments like Achille, and himself, drones bred of a civilisation which had lost its way. Sure enough, the wine, the heat, the noisy blend of Sineinian and City music and the licensed misrule of the sacred day had clouded his reason; but what of it? He did not care if he was drunk, deluded or led by the nose. For the moment he did not care what outrageous combination of male and female might occur, nor what might come from this wild rut at which M'untal and Magon would both dance: they would both be his.

Every tower and limb of Shekarah's Folly had been built aslant and askew, a palace conceived and built by a madwoman, but the way up was plain, a bare and riserless staircase, which mounted not to the illusions of nowhere but to visions of a wonderful future; and M'untal's hold on his hand as she led him there was tighter than the hellwrought grips themselves. She kissed him first, quite expertly, and then she got hold of Magon. To manage this double seduction and free herself of her net of inhibitions and questions she must have used one of the sublime trio: alcohol, dust, or husk. He hoped it was husk because it made her more like him. This was what she sought: he had felt her trembling in his arms. She stood back and watched him approach Magon, watched his lips travel across Magon's chest, over smooth skin and rougher hair, to find his compliant mouth. Amarant's pale face rose slowly in his mind. She was laughing. He began to laugh incontinently, as if he was flying high, wheeling above the City with the marvellous swifts. He could have screamed himself like a swift rejoicing, or crowed; instead, he reached out and brought M'untal into the centre of the vehement embrace.

'Dogs sleep like this,' thought Cal, waking in the dark. 'One heaped on the other, heedless, limbs careless, abandoned and disposed where they fell. He has enjoyed her, I have enjoyed her, she has enjoyed us both.' His unfashionable use of the verb fixed the deed and set it in the past, a precious memory already four hours old. 'What are we but clever dogs, beasts which walk on two legs, animals with pretensions?'

He extracted his arm from beneath Magon's neck, a leg from M'untal's waist, and rose, softly padding the dust of the enchanted place. He stretched and yawned. Nothing, no creature, was awake but him.

154

Magon and M'untal, stirring, shifted and slept on. He searched his clothes and Magon's and, finding a handful of almonds, chewed on them. Then the sun rose, Shelda in her realm, her long fingers reaching out of Vern. A lone stag crossed the open space below the towers and went into the wood.

'Hungry.'

Magon, awake, leaned on his elbow. They watched M'untal asleep. Now that they had left her, she curled her body into a ball, her breathing even, her long hair a disordered veil. Cal covered her with her celebration maral and they sat in silence to wait until she should wake. All three were still marked with the rose and gold powder, the largesse of the Dancers. The sun gilded Cal and the lily on Magon's arm; the weals across his back still glowed an angry red and M'untal, touching them in the dark, had whispered tenderly of his stupidity and kissed them all.

The City clocks began, and time began. M'untal sat up. No one spoke. The chiming bells became prosaic intrusion, markers, and the enchantment was broken. When her hair and her body were confined in ribbons and cloth, Magon picked M'untal up and carried her down the stairs and beneath the pines until he saw the door of the Octagon; and Cal, a pace behind, attended them.

Cal went uneasily to Amarant's studio in the east wing of the New Citadel. In public he had teased and flirted with her; in private he feared her voracity.

It was plain that she was a celebrated sculptor. The studio was vast with long roof lights, with chains and tackle for moving and lifting huge blocks of stone, with scaffolds and ladders and giant doors through which the stone could be brought. The stage was empty, the arena swept clean; but two subsidiaries, sheeted, waited in the wings: the lesser figures for her latest commission, a memorial to the great Arbiter, Shuma M'una, depicting Justice subduing her subjects, Mind, Body, and Soul. The work, when complete, was to be erected before the Courts of the Nines.

Amarant unsheeted the first figure, and he saw Magon in granite, pensive but powerful, wearing the cymar of his office, gripping books and a pen. Amarant smiled at him; he expected, so spellbound was he, to see M'untal as the soul, and the figure when uncovered was female, yes, but shrouded and draped in linen, a pillar of white marble folds.

The lower studio, more intimate, was crowded with clay figures and with framed and unframed drawings. Amarant poured white wine for him and spoke of the commission.

'The stone is in Baia,' she said. 'It is golden too. I hope I can work it – sometimes these tinted limestones have a great stain inside.'

She looked at him. It was clear that she was excited by the prospect of the task and by his presence in her studio. He thought of Mahun's Day,

155

and wished he had not responded to her jest. Unlike Crinon at work, Amarant was carefully dressed and wore a row of smoky stones, petrified opalescent pigeon's eggs, about her neck. He undressed behind a screen and stood on the dais.

'Crouch. More fear,' she said. 'You can move if you get tired but please return to the pose.'

She watched him move. Again he regretted this involuntary ability of his, of his flesh, to attract women like bees. She had put on a clean white smock and tied back her hair. She began swiftly to throw the red clay into a heap, a tower; he was relieved to see her dirty her hands with it, to stain the front of her smock and her face where she pushed back wisps of hair. Now she resembled Crinon, absent in her art. The figure began to resemble him. Unlike Crinon, she was silent as she worked. Suddenly, she left the clay and approached him. Coming close, she ran a finger across the muscle of his upper arm and moved his left hand closer to his body. She left a trail of clay on his skin and instinctively he shrank from her.

'For heaven's sake! Perhaps I should get a professional model,' she said crossly.

She continued her work, moulding the clay swiftly as if she feared it would dry before she had captured his perfect youth, moulding it fiercely with, it seemed, whatever came to hand, a variety of wooden tools, her fingers, her nails. He watched her, thinking she would use her teeth if it helped. The cool of the studio, the damp clay and wet cloths chilled him, though he knew that outside the midday sun burned. He shivered.

'All right,' said Amarant. 'You can dress.'

Clothed, he felt secure and went to look at his clay self. This woman too had caught in the redbrown plastic clay his outside. The crouching boy looked as though he regretted nothing, the rough texture of the daubed and striated clay giving him life: he might have stood and fled from her hands. The sculptor looked up from cleaning her nails.

'It's no good,' she said. 'Too compact. You'll have to come back – twice at least. Lunch?'

He hesitated. He had intended to leave at once, to go into the Library and work until the evening. Until Magon. He yawned. Immobility was tiring. Amarant was friendly, soft almost; when she smiled she was even desirable, except that he did not desire her. She had beautiful grey eyes.

'Come on. You're acting like a virgin,' she said. 'I'm inviting you to lunch.'

'All right.' He followed her from the studio.

Her rooms too were spacious, filled with sculptures and images, with primitive forest women of wood, clay, and feathers, with cones and cylinders of stone arranged in groups, with copies of ancient Gaian work, smooth, concerned with space and the lack of it, with holes and slippery solids. A pretty boy was being roughly footed by a magnificent eagle; next to the detail and precision of this impossible rape lay a group of the half-animate clods he recognised as Chenodor's.

'That's Dispossession,' said Amarant. 'The counter to the piece in the Citadel. You said you liked Chenodor's work.'

'Magon doesn't. He says it's crude, obvious, and typical of an aggressive heterosexual.'

Half-a-dozen of the clay stones had been formed into an orderly queue before a screen of torn paper; on the far side of it a pair of them were bound together with a length of rusty wire.

'You have a mind of your own.'

'Rafe hadn't – his opinions and his clothes are tigers' fashion and Slake says he had no natural authority.'

'He did, you know, but he knew when to keep quiet. He would soon have become a hindrance: he was a natural conservative – nothing to gain by upsetting the applecart.

'He came here once when I was modelling Achille; he did nothing but complain about Magon.'

'What did he say?' He had an intense desire for the opinions of others on Magon Nonpareil, a need to determine how and where the man fitted in the lives of his peers and inferiors when he had doffed his cymar and his title.

'I can't remember: it was at least two years ago. What does it matter? He can't trouble you – or have you seen his ghost in the Octagon's shadows? Under Magon's bed perhaps?'

He was still not master of his face: his expression must have recalled his fear of the malign sprite which had invaded his dream. She laughed, as Magon had done.

'Still the credulous Depther?'

In a corner of the room stood Hero, an unremarkable sculpture, dull even, but dynamic with legend.

'He was the first to sign for *Daystar*'s last flight,' said Amarant. 'His wife died on the voyage – a calculated risk for a cryo volunteer. He wrote a memorial to her; it's in the Library, alongside her poems. There are wax figures of them both in *Daystar*. Hideous things.'

'I like them,' he said enthusiastically. 'Hero dreams of an impossible union.'

Amarant looked at him with raised eyebrows.

'I mean,' he said, 'with space, in flight, with the stars and the emptiness.'

'I see. Where you would like to go? If we lived in another land, another time. . . .'

She brought him a waisted glass filled with a clear amber liquid.

'Go on, it's not poison.'

He drank, tasting the pine forest; pungent resinous fumes filled his nostrils.

In the dining room a circular table was set for two. Amarant gave him a challenging smile and poured wine with a steady hand. She sighed.

'If you were mine,' she said, 'I wouldn't let you out of my sight.'

Cal spilled his wine.

'You all want to own me,' he said angrily. 'In the Depths life is simpler. Sometimes there's a willing partner; if not, hard shit. Money buys it, but who has money all the time?'

Amarant was unsympathetic. 'He pays you well. Poor boy, enjoy it while you can.'

He wondered if she referred to the coming cataclysm, or was merely being provocative. He ignored her remark and ate.

'There is no compulsion to work,' he said. 'No need to look for the next meal. Up here you only toil if you feel like it. I should be in the Octagon now.'

'That's not true!' Amarant's protest was shrill. 'I am not working now because you hinder me. Distract me.'

'You invited me. And now I shall exercise a guest's privilege and go.'

'Back to Magon?'

'Yes.' He pushed back his chair and retreated. She followed him. In the salon the sculptures crowded them.

'I really wish I had hired a professional,' she said, and grasped his arm. 'How professional are you? Are your kisses as fine as that beautiful mouth?'

He gave in. It was easy. Enjoy yourself.

'I hate him,' she said. 'Hate and admire him. He has taken my mind with his damned Scheme – his just revolution – but he shan't have my soul. I despise him. That's why I steal his boys.' She talked too much. He kissed her until her head declined and her back arched; she rested against the marble feet of Ganymede. He spent himself and died in her.

'That's enough,' he said. 'No more.'

'Until next time.'

'No next time. You should learn to keep your hands for the clay and your taunts for the Matriarchy.'

He left her smoothing her skirts and her hair and went out into the afternoon. Walking swiftly, he crossed the sunlit spaces of the deserted garden and took refuge in the Octagon.

Time and the place took hold of Cal. He was conquered. He never saw M'untal, except in company; her full belly was not noticeable until midway through Verrun but Taressa and her friend Parstrie had taken him aside before the end of Ah and asked awkward questions. Taressa's gaze was as intelligent and direct as M'untal's was shy and defensive. He

158

did not deny his involvement nor affirm it and M'untal's sister went away unsatisfied. Slake told him how she complained to all and sundry of the iniquities of lily farmers' sons. Sometimes he saw M'untal dancing: she moved about the growing centre of herself and was motherhood; sometimes he sent her flowers and she replied on pink cards in nostalgic phrases as faded as old photographs. His memory of the golden episode altered until he remembered only the delirious possibilities and none of the facts. To aid the deliberate obliteration, he let Amarant toy with him.

The sculptor began to recreate his body from a seven-foot cube of limestone. He crawled out of the rock, a crouched and suppliant figure whose face showed no fear. He was present when the stone arrived and silently watched the haulage, block and tackle, easier with the dangling tons of petrified seafloor than with the shifting team of horses which had dragged it up the Hill. Amarant stood in front of the stone, her neat fingers already greedy; she touched the stone and rubbed its rough excrescences between her finger-ends. When she found the stone in Baia, she told him, she had been visiting an old friend. Dayamit's father, Siamon Hennist, tended his vines in Baia, he thought and half expected her to confide a connection, one of her sharp tilts at Magon, there. 'The Justice and I,' she said. (She was the niece of the despoiled and incarcerated Mazh Abayon; winegrowers were her servants.) 'She likes to escape, a few hours out of town. We took a bottle of muscadel and some fruit up to the quarry. It was embedded then, part of the Hill. But I could think of no figure for it and it lay in the yard for two years. Then you happened, that amazing flexible tension amongst the stuffed intellects at Crinon's, all wonder, innocence and thrusting boy. You look innocent, you know?' She kissed him, lingering on his lips in the stone dust, the shafts of light from the open doors and the workwomen's rustic humour. 'Now get out. I can't concentrate with you around.'

They told each other trivial secrets. Forgetting Glaver and M'untal, but never Magon, he became infatuated with her; her edgy humour and her eyes with their subtle mockery made her the antidote to Magon's serious devotion. Amarant, Amita; she brought back the ghost of his lost love. Sex, she told him, was the water of her life, the sweet conserve on the bread; its temporary nature inspired her. For a time, he believed her the most accomplished, the best of them all. The small ivory of Achille which she kept beside her bed testified to her taste. Greedy, like me, she said, kindred spirits. He visited her on Fiorin and Aash, twice each dek. They complained to each other and spun tales of fancy and ambition, Huyatt and the Tayaal, her crazy desire to knock down the sombre pile of Citybank and build a pleasure palace there, pillars of glass and soft beds, low couches and young men in an indoor garden, right on Broadwalk in sight of the Nines. But seriously, Amarant told him, they invest everything in the future, those snow cats, mothering the seeds of genius. Look at yourself: an IR of five hundred off the streets. They waste themselves, and give birth to drones. I tried it once, the cold syringe. It was dead. Nine months of nothing. It came away in pieces. I chose a Hinoor would you believe? Seduced, he whispered of M'untal and her embarrassing pregnancy. 'What a puppet master he is. The mind of a monk and the prick of a mule,' she cried. 'I wouldn't take him as a gift.'

Ah hushed the garden and in the intense heat, the broad leaves hung down and the flowers lasted hours not days; in Crinon's garden every plant grew tall, a Vern tangle smelling hot and wet, sweet like his afternoons with the sculptor. Xharam'un', returned from her holiday, befriended him; she taught him the sparse notes of the flute and he pretended to play it, sliding his wind up and down the scale and picking out old tunes. Far away and long ago, said Xhara', listening, you could play properly if you wanted. There isn't time, he said, not even in this garden. I'll come for lessons in my next life.

The rains came, the first great drops throwing up jets of dust, no showers these but torrents. The rains loaded the watercourses and overflowed from the fountains, filled the tanks and cisterns to the brim, raised every day a thick mist in which trees floated. At night the rain ceased and a wonderful aftermath, the refreshed essence of wood, flower, and soil, filled the gardens; puddles made an obstacle course which some of the women assaulted boldly; others, balancing on their high heels, used their folded umbrellas as probes and skirted the waters with silks withdrawn and ankles exposed. At two every afternoon, the rain began again, subduing the colour; every surface gleamed, every leaf had a coat of water.

Amarant dropped him. There was no warning and no goodbye. His stone self was half out, a crawling figure, emerging from the stone. He saw her close under an umbrella with a new boy. Not someone he knew. One of the boys, Hill tigers, glitterati.

One dismal afternoon in Verrun, the rain outside the windows silent confirmation of his dull thoughts, he walked in the Octagon's galleries. He passed yet another statue of yet another Archivist, looked up and saw a woman he knew to be Verelustra Tain, his Lector and unknowing mentor, at the far end of the room. She stooped over a figure hidden from him by her blue gown; she moved, underlining some point she made with a flourish of one of her blue wings, and he saw M'untal, her mouth serious and her eyes wide as she listened to the words he could not hear. She wore a striped maral, red and gold; stripes, he knew, were considered becoming on a pregnant woman, and the fashions of City and Hill were the same. He stood still, protected by the shadow of the ancient Archivist, and considered her shape: she was rounder, and her neat breasts had become full. He thought of the pink interior of a pomegranate and its crimson seeds nestling there; he became excited and hopeful, fervently praying that the discreet bulge below her breasts had begun in him. Unconsciously, he moved forward, stalking the women; from the concealment of another statue's skirts, he heard the brisk tones of Lector Tain. His shoes made him awkward. As he crept down the long room, he saw her retreating and M'untal turning to leave by the stair. The presence of both had prevented him from speaking to Verelustra Tain and idly repeating some of her old lesson to see if she had an inkling of his true identity; now he would be denied M'untal as well. But she had feminine concerns. The blue-gowned back continued to retreat while M'untal took a mirror from the folds of her girdle, peered into it, and smoothed the shapely' arches of her eyebrows with a dampened fingertip. Thus, he surprised her.

'Rafe!'

'That's not my name.' There was no one else about and he was surprised at her deviousness. Perhaps it was learned in private lessons from Magon.

'Why do you never come and see me?' he said, the desolation he felt expressing itself in truculence and a return of his City accent.

'I. . . .' At least, she had no ready answer. 'It wouldn't help matters.'

'It would help me.'

'You're all right: grazing a lily pasture, I hear.' This was the only time she looked directly at him throughout the conversation.

'No longer. Tressa's news is out of date.'

She looked at the shiny floor. She seemed to be studying the reflection of her small feet. At last she looked up and laid one hand on her stomach.

'This,' she said, 'impedes me. I can't think about anything else.'

'You were careless. A Hill queen doesn't need to ride bareback.'

'No.' Her smile was private: she was looking inward at a memory he could not share. 'I knew what I was doing. The only mistake I made was in believing I could somehow have, and keep – what folly! – both of you.'

He, the child of the streets, was shocked, rebuffed both by her understanding and her brazen reply when he had supposed, known, her to be innocence and integrity. He had corrupted her. He adopted a new position, a moral stance so far from his own irregular index of old homilies and City saws that, as he spoke, he heard the falsehood in his voice.

'Don't you care what your sister and friends think? What about the Dance and the Gynarchs? How will you conduct yourself without a husband to show them?

'Don't you care who fathered it?'

She answered boldly, smiling wide (at last) and sympathetically as she resumed her interrupted course towards the staircase.

'It doesn't matter which,' she said. 'We both know who will claim him.'

161

He stared after her, noting in the midst of his abstraction how each one of her straight and tiny feet, visible in sandals with narrow gold straps, flexed at the toes and mounted up in a direct line, one after the other. He supposed that she would take the lift from the floor above and ride until it stopped on the thirteenth floor where Magon's office was. The curtained watercolours on the walls emphasised his separation from everything that was coloured and alive. He walked over to a window and watched the rain falling into the fish tank, dropping steadily like the episodes of his betrayal. He wished he had made a vow like Faya's and needed no intimate contact with the opposite sex.

When he stood by the wall of windows in Magon's room he saw rivers of rain wash the glass and sluice away the last of the red sand, forming deeper runnels where centuries of the Wind had made striations. The glass, in the diminished light, was clear. Hard exercise filled Amarant's place and made him tired enough to forget M'untal. They prepared for the great journey; he worked at his languages; covertly, Magon prepared his papers. In the gymnasium, he began to study combat and entered the lowest rank, a pretender to an apprenticeship in I-tan. He agreed with Magon. The unarmed combat of the warrior queens became a male body. Once, he threw Magon. His teacher rebuked him. I-tan, she said, is not violent; it is a gentle and precise art.

The Ayal overflowed for the second time and the Uynal, rising above the highest notch on the board at Judges' Bridge, flooded the centre of the City. Wet if he chose, or dry and snug in the Library, he drank words: Huyatt and the universe by day, Magon's brown eyes and liquid voice by night. Udan drew near its close. The rain stopped.

He had written a long letter to Rafe's mother, amusements, study, and would she please come up and visit him, collect Hys's wedding present, in early Vern? – but by then, Rafe would be dead. He had a new task to master, one which would have made Rafe laugh: he must learn to ride.

His fear of horses was irrational and derived from their spectacular size and mindless movements. He did not understand why Magon classed them with poetry, painting, and the Dance.

Magon took him to the stables: vast marble halls, dozens of horses, all with muscular quarters and hard hind feet towards him. Magon slapped Arkite and the great horse moved over, turning his head to look at his master, blowing a greeting – not quite fire – from cavernous nostrils. Wisps of hay hung from his lips; he looked as though he could eat a mountain. Next to Arkite stood another bay horse, not so big; but it had as much muscle and its ears were laid back. He recognised it as Dayamit's, and quailed.

'That's his,' said Magon. 'Come here.'

Her name was Choru and she was the copy of Huyatt's white mare

Alna, a barbon from the Tayaal. A lamp ignited: he understood. She was perfection, grace by the strength of the huge bay stallion, her narrow head a concept in bone, her eyes friendly, intelligent – if you could use such a word of a horse. She held up her long tail with pride.

'I enjoyed the hunt,' said Magon, grinning broadly at his sudden conversion. 'Though it had to be by proxy. One of the principal couriers found her, eating her head off in Dinoord.

'She's a matron, Cal, but only six years old. She's had three foals already: they work females hard on stud farms. I wonder what we'd get if we let Arkite cover her?'

'A brown and white horse?'

'Skewbald. It doesn't work like that. Rafe knew better.'

Within the dek – just – he could ride her. He began with a stolid mount, a young gelding which Magon called Slake although the name written over the horse's stall was 'Nzir. Magon was a hard master who laughed when he fell off. He absorbed the jargon easily, as he absorbed other languages, and found that his unique sense of balance served him well. He had the kind of strength the mare needed and light hands; he learned the wordless language of the horse, a grammar of bodily gesture; the set of Choru's ears discovered her mood. In addition, Magon taught him the practicalities of feeding, grooming, tack, leather, oil, and elementary veterinary procedures. For his diversion south into Vern, to Odalion and Evanul, to the house of Balkiss, he would be alone with the horse.

Sometimes Magon mocked him, teasing out the last of his incivilities. He learned to speak without a whine and forgot, for days together, how to swear.

Early in Alcuon, in the New Year, 501 after the Reformation and how many months – he wondered – before the Revolution, Crinon finished her painting. It was peerless, the culmination of everything she had so far made. If, in her Cityscapes, she had invented a new way of looking at buildings and the intimate inscapes of streets and gardens, in this she gave him to the world, preserving (as long as the canvas lasted), his unsullied beauty and the colours of his skin and hair, his eyes and her wondrous garden beside a mocking likeness of Doos Gildo, the sly observer, the old man in paradise. Whether the painting was a comment on youth and age, on regret and blinkered youth; whether it told a story, man and boy, or illustrated a fable of greed and ingenuousness, no one could tell. As always, Crinon had refused a title; even Xhara' said that the painting must speak for itself: what was it but pigment and poppy oil, a touch of pure turpentine? In the New Citadel, standing a little way away from the painting, he watched the *cognoscenti* discuss it. Their opinions, loud and confident, might have been noted down and made into a comedy.

The Matriarch approached him, her sons to heel. Ishkal looked nervously at him. He smiled. Ishkal was a child. The contents of his pockets would certainly show it: full of toys, an odd-shaped stone which had caught his eye, the grubby rag he called a handkerchief, a handful of toffees. Harendi, on the brink, had the new concerns of puberty, the cut of his hair, the best way to wear his collar, yellow kyani in his buttonhole. He stared hotly at the Archivist's prodigy.

'She has captured you exactly,' said Annalat. 'Insolent grace.' He was not sure whether she complimented or mocked him. He turned his smile on her and found that she, the prime councillor, the head of state, even she could be flattered. She had the eyes of a sadist and the scarlet lips of a seductress. He could not read her mind, but her reputation was for deviousness disguised as single-mindedness.

'Thank you,' he said.

'Let me offer you a drink.'

She abandoned her sons, took his arm and led him away. The white tablecloth was covered with glasses, hollow orbs and scoops of clear crystal, tall flutes; the waiter handled his corkscrew like a weapon, opening fresh bottles for her. She drank a modest cooler and he, with his new ripe social sense, did not ask for rahi, ichor, or costly Ceremana, but for a flute of the same chaste liquid. He raised it and drank. There was no one near but the waiter.

'You and I have more than a little in common,' she said, looking down at him, the stem of the glass between her fingers a micrometer to measure the extent of the subterfuge. She swirled the wine in the glass.

'Have we?' Cal did not exist; Rafe knew nothing and his intimate relationship with the Archivist was a casual infatuation.

'Ask Magon some time. Tell him Annalat is curious and refers him to AMS/Z.' She sipped her wine. 'What are your aspirations, Mr Dayamit? Merely to continue to write and to serve Mahun in the Archive?'

'To write well.'

'Excellent. A laudable aim.' Her attention had gone and the brief assessment was over. She bowed and left him to his own devices. The waiter had already poured him a second glass.

Magon worked late and did not come to meals. Then, when the last of the luggage was sealed and its bonds impressed with the Archivist's seal, Cal found him at home. He had turned the key quietly and closed the door without a sound, Swan's precepts on the surface of his mind. On the stairs and in the lift he had played a game of silence and shadows. The woman's voice was that of Nan, the gardener. He advanced into the study and surprised Magon and the gardener crouching in a cut and potted garden of flowers. Magon had a new expression of concerned responsibility. He, who had never allowed flowers, save during Crinon's solicitous tenure when he had no energy to protest, held a spray of white kyani. Flowers, he had maintained, should be left to grow; he hated to see them hang their heads and drop fading petals over his furniture. Now, looking up from the hollow blossoms, he smiled and said, 'This is not a conversion: I am choosing a gift.'

The garden had come to him and this was a variant of the custom Cal had observed, a gift of flowers. The question was there, without the need for speech, and Magon said, 'Madam Kiden gave birth to a twin, two hours ago.'

In front of a subordinate, the euphemisms of polite society; Nan studied her flowers and rearranged the pots.

'Good,' said Magon absently, adding a bright clutch of merythian to the flowers in his arms.

He returned almost three hours later – the hands of the little glass timepiece moved slowly and Cal waited for the chimes. He had been nothing more than a pimp, a procurer like Nadar. Magon had used him; the snorting Artisan had used him against the wall of Cut Alley; Tarla had used him, and Amarant. And M'untal was no longer blameless, sacrificing her integrity to her desire for Magon and her greed for impregnation, for a child – children, two of them: one each? Their unspoken conspiracy to get heirs, more for her, sons for him, was worse than betrayal, for his presence had made the union possible. Might marriage follow and he become a supernumerary, to be discarded and disposed of as Dayamit had been? His panic had made him forgetful. He looked round the room, stuffed as it was with the indicators of Magon's preference: the *trompe l'oeil* alcove with its naked declaration; the aboriginal aquatints, rough trade refined by delicate brown shadows; the indolent beauty of the swimmer on display in his romantic landscape; the bronze athlete which, despite the subtleties of finish and moulding lavished on him by the anonymous artist, was all muscle and meat. If he had been wrecked in an ingenious and original way, the athlete was dry land and he reached warily out and touched the statue's hand. He heard Magon lift the corkscrew and turn it until the soft wood squealed; when his glass was handed to him, the wine a great ruby glowing in his hand, he held it high for an instant before he drank his wages.

'What did you write?' This was why Cudbeer had unaccountably lurked with the Register in the corridor beyond the stairs.

'Leirion and Anyal, the children of Mahuntal Kiden and Magon Nonpareil. She chose the girl's name and I the boy's. This is the first incision and she will keep them both. She is already celebrated and, if God wills, need not give up the Dance.'

'May I see her?'

'She asked for you.'

'She can wait,' he said, the wine making him careless. 'They used to believe that velvet fruit bats drank blood and sucked away the souls of sleepers. That's how I feel.'

'You should give up reading folk tales after dark.'

Later, when the wine had gone and Magon had become the languid sensualist who was the reverse of the Archivist, he made his own contribution to the feast. Magon swallowed the powder as if it were a tonic and grimaced. Then they flew together amongst the grey swifts' wings, far out, away from the City in a damp cloud of droplets, the clouds of morning, until they came to the stars.

PART II

THE JOURNEY

Before I set out for Vern and the high peaks I packed my bag with the necessities I thought fitting for an arduous journey: my prayer beads, a virgin notebook and a new pen, a knife for robbers and scissors for my beard, a mirror in which to study myself and the landscape for, all men know, the reverse image one sees in a glass is true magic.
The Travels of Huyatt Tayal

Mirrors

They travelled the road, the old road, the once supreme highway where, in the Forbidden Archive, Cal had seen elongated vehicles career and pass each other like ribbons extended by a high wind. Tall grass interrupted the landscape, and the trodden pathway meandered about bushes growing at random and emergent clumps of specie lilies, green tassels pushing out of the earth. At intervals, the way was barred by thorns and clawthistles, thick Alcuon growth, so that they had to pause while Slake and the packhorsemen cut a path. Steep descents into jungles of weed, where bridges had once spanned minor roads and small ravines, hindered free passage. When the going was good, Cal gave the mare her head and Magon, calling after him, reminded him that there was a long way to go.

It took three days to reach the border and the parting of the ways.

Magon kissed him like a brother, on the cheek. For a moment they stood together on the plateau looking down across green Vern, and then he was gone, striding up the rampart of the ancient road where the men and horses waited for him. Cal saw Arkite plunge; saw him, mounted and mastered, lead the horsemen away.

He held Choru's rein tight, watching them dwindle in the vast landscape. The gardens had taught him space and order, the journey down the gorge and along the old road, of rocks and density of growth; here was a panorama into which he must ride to make vastness diminish. He looked towards the sea; it was many miles to Evanul. Closer, the valley of the Odal was marked by a darker band in the blanketing verdure; Odalion itself was buried in trees. Choru pulled against his hand; he stilled her and got into the saddle.

Chokeweed smothered the red earth of Vern. The tendrils of the plants crawled over each other, over the path and over the banks which bounded the fields; beneath the weed, two feet under the earth, the lily bulbs waited for the passage of the Red Wind. The seed pods of the chokeweed snapped as Choru's hooves brushed them. Once, a constrictor crossed the path, its length heaving under the weeds.

He came to the bridge. It was an ancient span, of metal and stone, wide enough for an army of horses. Its deck had decayed long ago and been replaced with massive timbers. A woman came out of the guardhouse. He showed her Rafe Dayamit's pass and the Mark on his arm.

He led Choru out on to the bridge.

The road climbed steeply up from the river; it was dry and rutted from the wheels of carts. At the top, he took Rafe Dayamit's papers from his pocket: the bank and credit cards and the universal pass. The litter under the roadside trees was rotting and damp; he scraped a hole and buried the lily trader as deep as he could.

His true identity lay in his pocket: the new pass, treasure, and his own money. His signature was reproduced upon the wafer and beneath it, a safeguard and sanction, Magon's signature, the guarantee of the Archivist of the Sacred City of Mahun.

'This is me, Cal,' he said to the horse. 'I'm Cal, from the City.'

Odalion was a pleasant town, on the north bank of the Odal. He wished Magon were there to walk with him in its leafy squares. His lodgings were comfortable and unremarkable, with a bookseller; the horse vanished with a groom and he was given a supper of Odalian lyfish and red onions. It was the house Magon stayed in when he came to take the census; the family was loyal and discreet. The head of the family gave him a printed guide to the antiquities of the town; he had free use of her bookshops and personal library. In two days the wind would blow; he went out early in the morning and secured his impressions of Huyatt's sojourn in Odalion. His mood was eager and enthusiastic; he wrote hard all evening.

The statues were covered, and the fronts of the public buildings shrouded. Boards screened the shop windows. He found a bar and sat alone with his drink, counting the hours. The work was behind him but he knew he had skimped it; he would have to go over it again. And there were two books in Kinas M'una's library that he should read. He felt like the statues, stifled, and he missed Magon's incisive words and the challenge of his body. The temperature, as always before the hot storm, had risen ten degrees; it was as hot as the latter days of Ah, that endless month named after one of the stars, a sigh of a name, like a limp soul wrung by the heat. He drank his rahi and thought of Magon riding north.

Behind him, the bartender was giving his counter a last polish before the seeping dust covered it for five days. A shutter banged. He looked at his watch. An hour.

This year, he thought, I am on the surface. Exposed. Last year, in the sewer, it was hotter than a kiln, but the dust stayed in the streets. Last year. Two days ago I was nineteen. I think. When he left. Left me for duty, no pleasure. Left me with the memory of his new concerns, the two small lives which might be mine.

Magon had given him one of the rough knitted sweaters which the seamen of Taimiss made in the rains, throwing it unceremoniously across the fire.

'Maybe T'or made it,' he said. 'You'll need it in Diridion.'

They had drunk to each other, to the Scheme, to the Revolution, to the Arts and the renaissance of Science, to the City, the Dance, the Horse, Love. . . . They had recalled the past year, and spoken of the new, of ancient pleasures and fresh discoveries, of a new *Travels*. No longer grateful nor disturbed by a sense of obligation, he believed that Magon had given him everything he possessed.

Magon had duties in Filesh, half way to Diridion, to collect together and collate a series of recently discovered documents; he could have assisted but Magon, resolute, told him the task was simple. 'After that, I must go alone to Diridion,' he said. 'My search requires solitude, a space for myself; and it is a time measured in deks rather than months. When you join me, we will take the census together.' He had not reminded Cal that the solitary journey through Vern was his own choice.

Cal bought himself another rahi. Fifty-seven minutes; he should return to the house. Someone came into the bar; he heard the suck and thud of the door and smelt the parched desert wind. Idly, he turned the pages of his guide; it said, 'Visitors require a secondary Mark, an indelible tertiary Mark, or a universal pass. Entrance to the museums is free.' He had shown his new pass and paraded his status; in Odalion, despite the statement in the guide, no one looked at Marks. The Mark of the Vernian was an ugly and private reminder when he took off his shirt at night. The drawing of Huyatt's lodging showed a tall, narrow house, carefully repaired and painted to appear unchanged since 247AR. He had been through it from kitchen to attic; it was the place where Huyatt had written his *Odalionsong* and a manuscript copy was preserved under glass.

Last year on his birthday, on the nameday created by the nuns, he had folded Dromio's husk. After the party; a Quarter party. The last time. Amarant, Amita. His mind, with the speed of careless free association, moved him to Glaver's balcony, the rigid bodyshield, the Shack, Luce impaled on his blade and her scarlet blood flowing, a river, over the brown arm. To rid himself of the memory, he looked round.

The bartender was deep in conversation with a boy, a Vernian of his own age, whose clothing was an exercise in disorder, the kind of studied disarray affected by the rich, the kind of clothing he wore himself. Like him, the boy had not shaved for several days. His striped cotton scarf was a Tlivoornese headcloth and it was tucked into the neck of a grey Artisan's shirt. He was drinking golden ichor neat. He drained his glass and put it down.

'Better get home, out of the wind,' he said. This time the door would not swing shut behind him; he must drag it against the pressure of the excited air. When he had gone, a red fan of dust lay on the floor.

Cal got up and put his glass on the counter.

'I'm closing,' said the barman morosely. 'Not worth keeping an empty bar open.'

'One for the road.' The rahi went down, sweet and cloying, the candy he had coveted as a child.

'Where can I find a bed for the night?' said Cal, using the polite City euphemism.

'This is Odalion, man, not the Holy City. Whores can't get passes.' He looked Cal up and down. 'I could get you an introduction. Some of the boys who pack the flowers. . . .'

'No thanks.'

He went out into the changed street. The light had gone and the sky had become a cauldron of red smoke. Yet, to the south, there was still a band of welkin blue. The elegant facades on the square were battened to withstand the siege. Anything that might shift, signs, lamps, flower-baskets, had been taken down or immobilised with sacking and twine. Twisted wreaths of sandy dust had been deposited on the coloured paviours. The branches of the zys whipped up and down; already their purple blossoms were broken and scattered.

He pulled a handkerchief from his pocket and held it to his face. The hot gusts moulded his clothes against him.

He was halfway down Tayal street when the storm began; he tried to lean against the Wind which shoved him forward. It was impossible. He held on to a post while he attempted to pull his shirt above his head. The sand stung. He could not see across the street, he could hardly see his hands for the whirling dust. Slowly, he moved by a wall; he had to close his eyes and feel his way.

Beyond the gatepost was nothing. He reached out and felt coarse twigs, a thicket of them. He clutched handfuls of wood. Underfoot was gravel, then grass. His foot slipped and he fell, tumbling down a bank.

He lay in a gully. Hands on his shoulders. They dragged him round a corner, into a small dank room which smelled of sweat, urine, and husk. An old man leaned against a pile of logs. The one who held him was younger, thin and dark.

The season's I-tan had prepared him; he kicked and twisted. The old man was a husker, shaky and weak, not worth attention. When he had the other secure, he said, 'I won't report you if you give me a fold.' He spoke in the dialect of Odalion and both the men stared blankly at him. He repeated his proposition in Citycommons.

'Let him go, then,' said the husker.

Cal looked at him. He was dressed in a long Baian shirt. The Beggar's Mark was visible on his left arm above a grubby cuff; a partly open cloth bundle lay beside him and an empty rahi bottle, a breadring, and a small pile of bruised apricots lay on the cloth. There would be a knife somewhere, perhaps two. He kept his hold.

172

'Who are you?' he said.

'He's Tash, I'm Bind. From the City.'

'Crap.'

'We got out three years ago. We crossed the Ayal,' said Tash, still and tense in his grip.

'How in Aash could you cross the fucking Ayal? What about the mudholes?' Unconsciously, he spoke Deep. He was mortified that others had done what he had only dreamed of.

Tash answered in Deep.

'We lived a long time in the scrubland above the Tlivoorn moorings. We saw how they cross the mud in the dry season; then we crossed ourselves.'

Cal sat back on his heels and the Beggar flexed his arms and moved away from him to sit beside his companion. The old husker stretched his hand towards his bundle.

'Don't touch it!'

'Just getting your husk.'

Cal stood up, watching him. He made Bind open the paper of husk before he relaxed sufficiently to examine it; the brown powder was full of barklike flakes.

'That's shit.'

Tash took an envelope out of his pocket.

'Here.'

The pinch of husk in the envelope corner was fine, smooth, velvet. The smoky smell of it lingered after he had put it in his own pocket.

'How,' said Cal, 'can you get husk out in the country?'

Bind laughed.

'Fields are full of it, aren't they?'

'But it has to be finished in the kilns.'

'No. In the old days they dried it over a fire. And if you can't do that – there's at least one whisperer in every town.

'Now tell us how a fine young Vernian like you comes so fluent in Deep.'

'I'm not from Vern,' he said. 'I'm a City boy. I'm Cal.' He showed them the green V on his arm. 'This is – '

'A counterfeit.'

'Not exactly.'

'Friend in high places?'

'Something like that. I was never marked; I never had a mother.'

'I knew an unmarked man,' said Bind. 'Thirty years ago. Came to a bad end. Cholera.'

Cal questioned him, feeling a bond with the dead. Bind was fifty-three; his remarkable health was due to the fact that he only folded husk on holy days. He had been born on the steps of the Lily Exchange, his

173

addiction was his destiny, his conversation all about it. Cal looked at Tash. He might be twenty-five. It was difficult to tell if he too had been mastered by the drug. The bent tree on his arm had an extra twist, the result of uneven growth. He had always been hungry.

Cal gave him a twenty-frag note.

'I don't know how you'll break it,' he said. 'Give him some.'

Tash did not thank him. He put the money in his pocket. After a time he said, 'If you'd been out in the Wind like we have, you'd know it doesn't blow continually. There might be a lull soon. You can get home.'

Cal left them. He crouched in the gully where the hot air smelled only of decaying leaves. Presently, as they had told him it would, the Wind dropped. He clambered up the slippery bank and stood on the gravelled path; the air was thick and choking but he could see a shadowy gateway and he went out of it and, turning left, ran skidding on the gritty pavement to the end of the street. The bleached wooden door of Kinas M'una's house was the entrance to a haven and he kept his hand on the bellpush until it was opened.

They were concerned and crowded round him. He told them he had fallen and been forced to wait for a lull. Kinas herself bathed the grazes she discovered on his hands; he was brought into the dining room and fed. Kinas's daughter poured his wine; her ten-year-old son wanted to hear of his adventures again and again.

'You might have been suffocated. You might have choked like our cat did on the fish bones. She coughed and was sick; Mother tried to get the bone out and Blackie bit her. Then she choked and died. She was all stiff when we buried her.'

'You'll go all stiff when you die,' he said, laughing at the child's discomfiture. 'I can look after myself.'

The magic powder lay in wait at the bottom of his pocket.

Reading did not help his headache. It was eight in the morning, day, but no birds would sing in the long night of the Wind; many would die. He went into the bathroom and stuck two fingers down his throat. When he had vomited, he felt better, and he lay on the bed listening to the Wind and trying to recall the visions of his husking. They had vanished. He turned on his side and slept, holding the pillow because he was alone.

The Red Wind sang to him, confined as he was in the house of Kinas M'una. It sang of the Tayaal, of dryness, desolation, and the deserts of all religions which turned from Mahun. In his dreams he saw Magon kneeling among rocks, half naked and scoured as the stones were, by the tempest in his soul.

He read Kinas's two books. One was a bound series of facsimile documents from Huyatt's time, interesting and irrelevant, ancient tariffs and laundry lists, inventories and land tax returns. The traveller's name occurred twice. The other was an anthology, prettily bound and charmingly illustrated with woodcuts, useless to all but dilettantes.

The Wind died. He went out and walked down the street; the paving stones were hidden by the dust and grains of it crept between the toes of his sandalled feet, a beach between the houses and the regularly spaced columns of the shrouded streetlamps. Every ledge and cranny on the steep housefronts bore its deposit of sand. He turned in at the gateway where he had lost his way and jumped down the bank. The cellar was empty except for the neat stacks of wood, the husk smell vanished. Perhaps the two huskers also travelled north. In the evening, he found an atlas on one of the library shelves, and made himself a rough map by which to trace his journey.

The fields of Vern were overlaid with the ruddy dust, every hollow a potential pitfall, every furrow a little dune, but the chokeweed had gone, torn up and cast away by the Wind. The leaves of the trees were tattered and he found dead birds in his path, pathetic in their miniature death, their claws uplifted and rigid, their wings twisted. Some field workers were dragging fallen branches from the roads and sawing them up for firewood, others shovelled the gritty deposits from the irrigation ditches which networked the fields, a pattern of essential arteries.

Letter from the Archivist's Convene to Melada Dayamit M'unah, Lily Farmer, of Erend Fields, Odalion

15 Lilb in Vern 501AR

Dear Madam,

We regret to inform you of the death on 14 Lilb in Vern, 501AR, of your son, Rafe Dayamit M'unor. The disposal certificate gives the cause of death as cholera. Your son was detained in Blessed Olva Hospital for only two days, during which he weakened quickly in spite of medication. Death occurred at 3 p.m., Standard Time.

In accordance with City regulations, his body and personal belongings, including all papers and clothing, have been incinerated. You are the chief beneficiary under your son's Will (Arch. Od/Day. 20); accordingly, B23, 501 has been credited to your account at Citybank, the residue of his personal estate after deductions for income tax, hospital fees, and death dues. The record of his recent lily sales may be seen at the Exchange. A bay Dinoordian bloodhorse is stabled at the New Citadel: we await your advice before any offer of sale is made.

A tablet to the memory of Rafe Dayamit M'unor has been erected in the Green Cenotaph; hours of opening are dawn to dusk excepting every Triple Mahun and during Verrun.

The City recognises Rafe Dayamit M'unor's contribution to her prosperity.

Annalat Abayon M'una, Matriarch
Magon Nonpareil, Archivist

Encl: Free Tempvis.
Disposal Cert.
CB Statement.
Condolences.

Letter (enclosed with the above) from Magon Nonpareil to Melada Dayamit

19 LiV 501

Dear Mm. Dayamit,
Death is always the occasion of sorrow: we may regret the passing of a relative but the demise of a friend is tribulation.

Rafe was a welcome guest. His conversation was always stimulating, his appetite for work an example. His uncompleted manuscript has been deposited in the Archive and I have arranged for a copy to be made for you. My staff and I will miss his habitual presence in the Octagon.

With deepest sympathy,
Magon Nonpareil

Cal woke refreshed from his long sleep. Evanul lay farther north than the City, further from Lutra, nearer the Zone with which geographers marked Guna's swollen waist; she was hot as the City in Ah. The village had no power and he had seen his way to bed by candlelight, but the unglazed windows through which the breeze came from the sea, the tank of water in the central garden, and the ingenious water-driven fans cooled the house. He found clean clothes laid out, and dressed. The housekeeper had been and gone; everywhere was neat and a breakfast set on the table in the living room. He read of Diridion as he ate.

Odalion had been full of women touting for hire as guides; in Evanul he saw only the villagers who glanced at him and away, recognising him as one of the wealthy from the City. Thus the site of Huyatt's obsessional passion was deserted, an old and decaying house on a hill beyond the village. A faded board outside it said, merely, 'The House of Balkiss'. Cal walked up the dusty drive.

The gardens had once been a pleasaunce, reaching as far as the river as it made its ageing way in loops and oxbows to the sea; it was all overgrown. Outside the entrance a false bohea sagged, broken by age and the Red Wind.

He walked into the courtyard. A bowl on a bench contained a few bits and he added two frags to the collection. An empty birdcage hung from one of the unpruned honey plums in the courtyard, but it had nothing to do with Balkiss or Huyatt for the feeder in it contained fresh seed and the label still tied to one of its bamboo bars read 'Origin: Upper Vern'. But perhaps it was the bird and not the cage which had come from Upper Vern and it had flown home.

With a shock of delight he saw that the first of the main rooms was panelled in coloured marble like the house below the City. Nothing in the empty house was identified or labelled for him and he went out again into the courtyard and, sitting on the bench, took out his notebook. Trying to imitate Crinon's penstrokes, he drew the face of the building, with its shadowy archway, in front of him. He thought his sketch was fussy and too delicate. The graphite in Rafe's gold pencil broke often and would not make a strong line like Crinon's reed. He drew himself seated on the bench drawing himself.

'Ho there! Hello!' He looked up, expecting to see a party of people with a guide, a strong cowherd or lily grower perhaps. An old man stood in the archway. He leaned on his stick and panted a little from the exertion of climbing up from the village. Cal smiled at him.

The old man came forward and peered over Cal's shoulder at the drawing.

'Charming, charming,' he said. 'Do you know Xharam'un's work? Abstract of course, but most remarkable.'

'A little,' said Cal.

'She comes down here for her holidays. You must be from Maralis too? From the City herself?'

'I am from the City.'

'I have it! You are the young man who has taken Cya's house. Now what did she say? You are staying for three deks and you are interested in Huyatt? Of course! That's why you are up here sketching Balkiss's front door.

'What is your name? She did tell me but I forget things that are less than a century old.'

'My name is – ' He hesitated. 'Cal.'

'And the name of your mother?' The old man gave him a strange smile.

'I had no mother, unless the City is my mother. M'nah the Beggar-woman cared for me, and Swan the king of thieves, and Tarla the whore.'

The old man looked at the gold pencil and the platinum ring.

'But you have found your fortune?'

'Mahun smiled on me.'

'She must have smiled wide.'

'So she did.'

'Do you like olives?' He pulled a blue paper package from one of the pockets in his cotton jacket. 'I have these sent specially from Ineit, but they have to finish the journey from Roakn by sea.' He opened the package, disclosing a glistening handful of the brown fruit. They ate together, spitting out the pits and dropping them on the stones that paved the courtyard of Balkiss's house.

'I am Herkel Galabrias,' the old man said. 'Once, I was a physician and now I am an antiquary. It is a suitable profession for an old man, a concern for stones and bones, ancient buildings and tombs.'

'You went to school?'

'In Ineit and then in Sinein. I was Chief Exemplar at Sollar Kein University in Sinein. Money buys most things, even an exit from the City and her Provinces.'

'When Huyatt travelled,' said Cal, 'he seemed able to move about quite freely. He never mentions passes or tertiary Marks. He wasn't marked himself.'

'Yes. Strange, isn't it? I daresay things were different in his day.'

'But it was two hundred years after the Reformation. The City was closed.'

'You will have to look more deeply into the Archive; no doubt there is a simple explanation. Huyatt also was a wealthy man.

'What do you hope to learn from this house?'

'There is a house like this in the City; at least, a house with a room like the first one, there. I suppose they are both of the Huyatt period.' He pointed to the room with the marble walls.

'Whereabouts in the City is this house?'

'Somewhere underneath Vern Street.'

'The workers have uncovered it, a sewer has burst?'

'You can get into it from one of the old cellars beneath the foundations of the Tiled Malls. I found it. No one else knows of it. One of the rooms in it has walls of coloured marble and in the cellars below it there is a spring and a statue of Mahun with a man.'

'Indeed? This is most interesting. What is she wearing?'

'A maral and a girdle tied in the triple knot.'

'Fringed ends?'

'No.'

'Ah, then it may be genuine. Could you show it me if I came up to the City?'

'I can't. I'm on my way to Diridion.'

'Of course you are! And after that there won't be time for antiquities. . . .

'Now, I must disappoint you – concerning this house. It is about the right date for Balkiss and Huyatt, but it belonged to the Odalian Lily 'change – still does. The custodians used it as a Vern retreat until the new house was built in Mais, outside Taimiss. In my opinion it was never a love-nest for the Traveller and his dream woman.

'The marble panels are very old; in the Silver Age, as you must know, antiques were in fashion. They will have been removed from a museum or ancient site and put up here. Your buried house will be a dealer's house of the first millennium: the land slopes under the Tiled Malls. It is steeper than it seems, part of the original city mound.

'The statue is more interesting than the house, possibly proto-historic; and the man is Tror.'

Cal repeated the name twice, but it meant nothing.

'Tror. He had become Tra even before the Reformation; the dedi-catee of the sixth day of the week and the second month of the year. Once, he was Her consort.'

'Mahun!'

'You do well to call on her name. She must miss him sorely. He was the father of Ingemi, the Twin.'

'None of this is in the Law.'

'Nor in the False Law. You have a great deal more to do than you suppose. The Tayal worship a demon with his name, I am told.'

'How can so much have been concealed? Until the Reformation everyone could read Maralay.'

'But not in the Archive, and not in the libraries of the liberated world. I am guilty of concealment myself,' Galabrias said. 'I'm your neighbour: the second house by the beach is mine.'

When night had come and the birds were silent, Cal sat against the outer wall of the house and looked at the sea. A surreal light emitted by swarming zoophytes, aimless wandering plankton, kindled the waves, plating each one as it reared and collapsed into the shallows. The sound of the breakers, loud close by, ran back along the beach like the echo of reality; Eshtur and her satellite stood above the sea. He broke the seal on the letter the courier had brought. The paper took the pallid light of the moon and the familiar handwriting was firm upon it, in the black ink he always used.

22 LiV 501

Dear Cal,

It is plain that the pillars of my city have fallen. Previous concepts lie in ruins.

God, but this is a desolate place, all rock and rain like piss every morning, the stench of goats everywhere. Later in the day it becomes as hot as the City in Ah. The Tayaal dominates, seen clearly from the tops of the watchtowers, red and black without structure, the colours of Aash. I would have preferred the sun and the vigour of Evanul, were it not for my task (were it not for my soul).

I have been ill. I am wretched, lonely, without even the silence of Slake who has returned with the horses to the City.

Arkos is my mentor and I get a catechising every day. Faith, like perfect love, is a hard road and I run it without progress. Any advance I seem to make is countered by his logic, the instinctive and unshakeable logic of a celibate priest. I run backwards, I dream of the sands, I search for a mirror, a looking glass which will reflect my soul. Arkos says that a layman cannot be given such a powerful weapon. Might you be such a reflector, a natural innocent on which I can fix my gaze? Guilt, he said, is its own reward, the inbuilt curse of pride, the wages of arrogance. We debated a long time. His statements do not bear analysis.

As for official duties, these were soon completed, and when you come we will count the miserable Diridians. Two months is a long time.

The Red Wind passed over us. Aash and her demons.

MN

He read the letter again. The hurried clauses, clouds before a hurricane, troubled him. The images that Magon sought to convey were clear in his mind and he too saw the multicoloured rock of Diridion and the supreme and distant Tayaal. Again, he saw Magon shivering among rocks, sick and alone; he saw the ancient priest who apportioned blame and served out more guilt to this most guilty of men; he saw that this Arkos would make him responsible when he wanted to be as free as he had been on the street. Magon's confession of loneliness made a desert of his own green solitude.

In the house, he put pen to paper but he could write nothing beside the cryptic line, 'I am the rat from the sewer, and I must feed.' After it he wrote the date, 34 LiV 501, so that Magon would know he had received and read his complaint. He sealed the paper together with the long letter he had written the night before, pressing the blade of his knife deep into the liquid wax. The rodent, self-pity, crept near him. He picked up the bottle of Ceremana, the ceremonial bottle Magon had handed him on the morning of his birthday, and uncorked it. In the morning the courier would return refreshed, no doubt, by a night with his wife. Bitterly, Cal catalogued the broken trail of his desires. He drank from the bottle, pouring the wine down his throat in a great gout. The package with Magon's name and the scab of red wax lay on the table. He put his thumb

180

under the seal, broke it in half and added another line: Mahun, Magon, what a fool you are.

Melting fresh wax, he resealed the letter and left it alone.

The wine did not make him carefree; he grew more depressed. What did Magon mean? He was confused, illogical, incoherent, drunk on prayer; he meant renunciation, he meant rejection.

When he had emptied the wine bottle, he found a fresh one in Cya's bins. When he was thoroughly drunk, he went to the beach and, lying on the sand, gazed up at the wheeling universe.

In the morning, he was still drunk. The courier, hammering at the outer door, woke him; the letters were carried away. Cal walked to the wine dealer and found he had no Ceremana; he bought four bottles of a rough and local red. As he returned to the house, a girl came up to him and smiled provocatively. He shook his head.

'But you want this,' she said, opening her hand. A tiny straw box lay there.

'Gold or brown?' he asked.

'Brown. You're a peeled husker if ever I saw one.'

'How much?'

She named a price which, in a licensed City store, would have bought enough to keep him on the wing for a month. He paid her price.

'Don't let anyone see you,' she said, and was gone.

He let himself into the empty house. It was midmorning and the days which his intellect were supposed to fill stretched like the long daylight hours before him. Tebora had been and gone: in the living room the chairs and couches had been set straight, the table cleared, the books pushed into line; in his bedroom, the quilt was rolled, the bedsheet smoothed and the pillows plumped. He drew the blind across the seaward window and set the four bottles in a row on the floor, the furthest against the outer door, the nearest by the bed. He drew the corks from the first two.

The straw box was filled to the brim with good husk, sepia powder like fine tilth. A section of lily leaf lined the box to prevent the powder spilling and, as he touched it, he felt the skin of his forefinger itch. He took Huyatt from the bedside table and, opening the cover of the book, tore out the flyleaf. Carefully and deliberately he folded the page and creased it with his thumbnail. He tore the paper along the fold and, taking the upper half, folded it into three. From the halfsheet, he made three papers, three nests for the dream powder, three cups to toast Mahun. He laid them in a row on the table and read the divided signature, Mago n Nonpa reil. He piled husk on each fold until all the letters were covered. The powder from the first fell easily to the back of his throat, each grain dissolving in peppery fire. The base of his tongue went numb and he

181

tipped red wine after the husk until he had to draw breath. He lay on the bed and waited to see what would happen.

Never before had he known such peace. The darkness was absolute and deep blue; he floated in it and waited to be reborn. Although it was so dark, so blue, so cold, although he could not move a muscle, he saw the stars pass by. Shelda warmed him: he could feel her burning from within his hands and feet; presently the surface of his body flowed away and he became liquid, a molten viscid mass which moved forward with such volition that he clutched his softened head and screamed. His nails dug deep into his brain. He looked back from his place in the sun and saw, on the white bench he had left, his convoluted brain and the full and rosy bag of his scrotum, lambs' fry on a butchers slab.

He sat up and lit the lamp, but the pain in his head made him douse the flame immediately. The stripes of moonlight gave enough light; to dull the ache he drank the wine that remained in the first bottle. He looked at the two folds on the table by the bed, took off his sweaty clothes and lay naked on the bed like the cryomorph he had been. Presently Eshtur and 'Nyon set and he felt his body absorb the second fold.

When he came down the second time, he remembered nothing of his visions, except a certainty that he had been in Diridion with Magon. It was dark. The heat in his limbs had subsided; he felt cold. He wrapped himself in the bedquilt and, as he did so, felt a new pain like wet rope across his back. He put his hand to it but there was nothing there except the smooth skin. He got up to finish the wine in the bottle; the bottle was empty and so was the second one. He opened the third and the fourth. He looked at the clock; the hands showed two but there was not, as there should have been, a moon. When he peered between the slats of the blind he saw the dark sea breaking on the white sand; he felt that the burning of his body must illuminate the shore. Thirst overcame him and he stumbled back to the wine, and to the husk. For a time he lay across the tumbled pillows and wept.

The room was bright and very white. He tried to focus his eyes on a glowing area of wall. A hand rested lightly on his wrist and he looked at it without coming to any conclusion about its owner. He tried the golden glow again; some letters swam across his field of vision and disappeared, leaving their images floating in the air. An H, a G, and an M. He closed his eyes.

The brass plate, which was partially obscured by his lashes, for he dare not open his eyes wide in the white prison room, said 'Herkel Galabrias M'unor, Physician & Soul Doctor'. The old man sat beside him, very still, entirely calm. Cal let his breath out in a long sigh.

'My place,' said Galabrias. 'My guest room.'

Cal opened his eyes properly. The room was neither bare nor white but hung with straw-coloured fabric; an area of clear plaster in line with the foot of the bed displayed a physician's door-plate and some framed certificates. A jug of flowers stood on a chest; there was a chair, a carafe of water and a glass beside the bed, and Galabrias himself, an old-fashioned electronic stethoscope about his tortoise neck.

Galabrias busied himself about his patient's body. Cal watched the gentle proceedings. He lifted up one of the arms of the bedbound patient and saw that his skin was white. The belly of the patient was sore, within and without, as if it had been kicked by an intemperate mule. Tentatively, he prodded the tenderness with his fingers and his stomach rumbled.

'I think I'm hungry,' he said.

The doctor gave a professional grunt, an enigmatic comment on the state of his patient.

'No food. Water only,' he said. Cal sat gingerly up, poured water and drank. His body was entirely covered in a white salve.

'Lucky not to lose more than the top layers,' commented Galabrias.

Cal examined his right hand; under the ointment, the skin was peeling. He stared at the hand; of itself, it began to shake.

'What's the matter with my hand?'

'Sthenics,' said the doctor. 'Seen 'em, haven't you? The old huskers in the metro. . . .'

'But I. . . .'

'Now you do.'

Cal was silent. He lay down and watched his hand moving on the bedcover, a leaf in the wind. Dr Galabrias finished his routine and sat on the bedside chair.

'You're well on the way to addiction, boy,' he said. 'If you take any more – one grain – of the stuff, you're finished. It's an unpleasant death and it usually takes more than a decade to achieve.

'Do you want a cure?'

'Dunno,' Cal shifted, sullen. 'And I'm not an addict. Yes, I fly, but I'm no addict; I'm a social user like everyone else. Only one in fifty thousand. . . .'

'That's you, boy; you are the one.'

'But I'm always lucky at dice.'

'Not so lucky at life, perhaps. That hand will stop trembling presently, and you'll sleep again. Know how much you had?'

'No. Quite a bit. And the wine.'

'The wine makes a marginal difference. I think you usually take three times the social dose; this time you had nearly six times your norm. Way over the party spirit.'

'What day is it?' Cal asked, when he woke again.

'The thirty-eighth – Aash, appropriate.'

Cal considered the lost days and though he could remember the substance of his hallucinations, he could not relate them to the missing hours. Magon's letter had arrived on the thirty-fourth; on the next day, dedicated to Fiorin, the tides, the moving waters, he had bought wine and been accosted by the thin girl.

'It was the thirty-fifth,' he said. 'It must have been Fiorin and. . . .'

'Now it is Aash, and you have lost some time? It is of little account; imagine you have been ill of a fever for three days.'

But Cal, lying back on the pillows, wrestled with the lost chronology. The doctor's mention of fever presently transported him to high Diridion and he lay still and watched Magon debating with the monks. The needlebite in the crook of his arm brought him back; he watched the glass cylinder fill with his blood.

'Blood is a good indicator,' said Galabrias. 'It gives up the body's secrets.'

Cal closed his eyes. He imagined, when Galabrias spoke, a vigorous man in his forties with black hair, perhaps, and a neat beard. His own incapacity had invigorated the old man and set him going. When he opened his eyes, Galabrias's bald pate gleamed at him as he scrabbled under the bed.

'Urinate, boy,' said the doctor. 'Sample for me. You'll have to manage with this: I didn't expect to be nursing a husker in my seventy-first year.'

Galabrias passed up a globular pot, decorated in the florid style of Lower Vern with swags of rose-coloured flowers and paradise birds.

His hand had stopped moving and was his own again. Every inch of him was covered in the white emollient, and it came off on his fingers. He sniffed at them. The ointment had the sweet odour of decaying lilies.

'Can I have some food now?' he asked Galabrias who, bearing the gross purple vessel, paused in the doorway.

'No. In two days' time perhaps. It depends what my tests discover.'

The door closed behind him with an emphatic click.

Cal lay like a child in the white bed and images of himself laid low by his excesses, of the child Cal sick of the sewer-fever in the hospice, and of the dying husker in the computer-generated picture came together and fused. A new emotion pierced him; it was not the absolute terror he had felt, pursued by the Marklice and their dogs, nor the panic which had overcome him when Magon pulled him from his perch in the chantry, but a small thing like the chill night air in Udan. He recognised fear of dying. In the Block he had gone from day to day without this fear, disbelieving every evidence, absorbed in his assessment and his anger. Now, in this peaceful house, he was afraid that Aash, when she came, would not softly lull him but would strike and rend his flesh. There would be pain. He let an invalid's indulgence possess him and thought of death.

184

He must have dozed. A bird trilled nearby, out in the warm afternoon light beyond the window. He scratched the dried ointment on his right forearm; perhaps Rafe's hideous green Mark would come away with it.

'I've washed his bedclothes,' Tebora's voice came from outside the window.

'I'm sorry you were put to the trouble. Not a pleasant task,' Galabrias replied.

'It's no trouble. I'm sure he's a good boy really.'

Galabrias laughed, as if to emphasise her pedestrian reply.

'If you could just tidy the room. I'm so sorry.'

'I've done it, sir. Except for the wine stains on the rug – lucky it wasn't one of the Zalcasian ones.'

'Bring that to me. I think I have a suitable solvent. Have you managed to air the room?'

Their voices faded. Cal watched night fill in the window space. Galabrias came in and applied a fresh coating of the salve. He lit the lamp and placed it on the chest; the shadows of the flowers there grew long and arched over the bed.

He was not ashamed to sit naked on the chair while Tebora put fresh sheets on the bed. She moved about the room like a hospice nun, absorbed in the exercise of her duties. When all was neat, she smiled at him.

'Shall I help you?'

'I can manage, thanks.' He returned her smile, and the white paste cracked across his cheeks.

She left him. He stood up and looked out of the window. Galabrias's courtyard was crowded with small trees, and pots full of flowering herbs; the greenery obscured the central pool. Some finches which hopped delicately in a cage were the source of yesterday's song. He drank a glass of water. Sitting on the edge of the bed, he cleared a small circle on his thigh of the white coating of ointment and dead cells. His golden skin glowed, a small sun. He walked across the room and studied the certificates that hung above the chest; they confirmed that Galabrias was what he said he was, a physician and an exemplar in disorders of the soul.

A large book and a pamphlet lay on the chest. He carried them with him back to the bed. The pamphlet was grubby and dog-eared, printed in Citycommons. Its title, brisk and, he thought, self-conscious, was *Your Life, Your Death*, and the author was Herkel Galabrias, Ph., E. Psych. It was intended for him so, diffidently at first, he began to read.

The Trumpet Lily (Fire Lily, Sun Lily, Mahun's Staff)

We are all familiar with the golden horn of the trumpet lily: it looms at us from the flags above the Temple gates, on the Courts of the Nine Judges, on the Octagon top, from official forms and stationery,

185

posters, notices, souvenirs, the very Marks of the Matriarchs and Gynarchs. Our culture has known it for more than four thousand years.

In the fields of Far Maralis and Vern, the lilies grow in their millions, –

So he was to have a botany lesson, and one in geography, history, philosophy and semiotics too. . . . He yawned. Galabrias preached, 'If you overdose you will certainly be very sick . . . your skin will itch and may also blister and peel . . . persistent overdosers will become addicts.' It finished like a classical tragedy with death and a moral: 'Severe addiction is incurable and ultimately fatal. A dedicated husker lives only to experience life after the fold. He loses all sense of balance regaining it only (he believes) after folding when (he insists) he can perform amazing feats unhindered by gravity. He is that pathetic bundle of rags on the metro; he is close to death.'

'Crap,' he said. It was the right word. Galabrias had obviously never tried husk himself, but relied for his account on the experience of others: his feeble phrase 'feel you are about to take flight' conveyed nothing of the reality. He knew: he had stooped and soared with the grey swifts.

He considered his state: he was in good hands and the doctor would attempt to cure him with fear; already he had called him an addict when this was only the third or fourth flight in more than a year. Besides, Rafe Dayamit had used husk. Magon used it – they used it together.

The book was bulky; he rested it on the mattress. It contained many diagrams and photographs, a medical text book of some kind. It was written in one of the languages of Sinein and he could not read it.

The picture of a trumpet lily guided him to the section Galabrias meant him to peruse. He looked at a photograph of a Beggar folding husk. A woman who demonstrated the more elegant method of folding dust, using a jewelled scoop, had a supercilious expression like a Gynarch. He turned the page. Some of the pictures were nauseating, an area of blistered skin for example and a close-up of a dilated pupil ringed narrowly with a startling blue iris. A dying husker was given full-page treatment, a Sineinese, possibly one of Galabrias's patients (like me, the thought came unbidden), caught by the camera in terminal rack. His spine arched, his face contorted; his fingers, stiff claws, scraped air. In many ways it was worse than the moving picture in the Archive: the stillness imposed on the twisting body by the camera allowed him to examine each digit, each member, each limb.

He turned the page and burst out laughing. That cold and mechanical voyeur, the camera, had been allowed the final intimacy: side by side, in explicit colour, two photographs of engorged organs on the extremity. The universal symbols for male and female in the bottom corner of each photograph were superfluous. He wished he could read the text beneath.

'You should know.' Galabrias had come into the room.

'Perhaps, but how can you?'

'Men of seventy-one know everything, Horatio.'

'Whose name is that?'

'Old words from Gaia. Take no notice.'

'Who is Horatio?'

'Who indeed? Magon Nonpareil perhaps. Horatio saw the prince die.

'The quotation I have in mind goes, "There are more things hidden in airless space, and many more secrets riding on shooting stars, Horatio, than are dreamt of in your philosophy." The speaker is a prince, the society one in which the men are dominant and the women suspects, wicked enchantresses or pitiful waifs; both men are scholars, friends. The play comes from Gaia, halfway through their second millennium.'

'Could I read it?'

'I don't think it has been translated into any of your languages. I read it in Sinein, years ago. I still carry many of its words in my head, simples against perplexing situations. The work would interest you: it is full of images from falconry, and they hunt with birds in the Tayaal, do they not?'

'Yes, and running dogs.'

' "Swifter than sunlight, more fleet than the deer, more deadly than the lion; footed like a hare, tailed like a monkey, the head a shallop of shadow and hollow bone." He was fond of obsolete words, the old spinner.

'Now, my boy. Your temperature, your pulse; the old routine. Have you read my little book?'

He stood in front of the bathroom mirror and saw his reflection reflected back into infinity by the other mirrors in the room. He wondered why the old man bathed in a room lined with mirrors, supposing, with the arrogance of his nineteen years, that older men did not care to study their appearance so intimately. Unless, like Magon's alcove, the room exposed the vanity of the soul within its mortal coat, a deathly conceit.

He was not the boy in Crinon's painting, the naked vigour Amarant had represented was gone; he resembled Meleager in his white paint, sad and thin. No bronze sambur fled over a forest of greened muscle; the shadows beneath his eyes replicated the greasepaint tears of the white-faced clown. He wiped the ointment from his mouth and saw that the curve of the lower lip and the clean line of the upper were intact. He looked into his yellow eyes and examined the flecks of green colour deep in each iris.

At nine in the evening on the fourth day of his fast, Tebora brought him an omelette the size of his hand. He ate it in two bites and felt as though he had feasted.

In the middle of the night, he woke up. The patch of sky in the window was brilliant with stars and Eshlon burned like a silver brand. His head was clear and the centre of his being still and calm. He thought of M'untal and saw her in her Dancer's clothes, scarlet, gold, and blue; he saw the two tiny brown babies with their newborn blue eyes and their small clenched fists. She had cradled them both in her arms and fed them both, one at each breast. He watched the sky and did not sleep again until the daystar rose in the rosy sky.

Breakfast was another feast: half a ring of bread spread with honey, a glass of bohea. Galabrias appeared with lint and a large bottle of oil which he shook and uncorked. The scent of bergamot filled the room. He tipped oil on the lint and began to wipe away the greying paste, dirt from a masterpiece.

Cal saw his golden skin again and the only stain on it was Dayamit's green Mark.

'Tell me about Magon Nonpareil,' said the physician conversationally, as he worked.

'He's the City Archivist. Rich, successful, handsome. He speaks several, no, many languages, three dozen at least, writes seventeen. Dialects too. He has a collection of rare paintings – some from Gaia – and sculptures too. He has a horse, Arkite, a big, deep bay – the colour of your chest over there – wilful, not easy to ride; but he obeys Magon. He's a good swimmer, and he runs; he used to follow other disciplines – javelin, I think – and I-tan still. He's a master archer: it's a passion with him. He goes to the butts every morning – first thing after getting up.' The words fell out in disarray.

'Dear me. He sounds like the hero of one of Faya's novellas. Now tell me about Magon.'

'He is religious.'

'Surely not unusual in the Sacred City? There, that's better. You haven't lost your looks, boy. A bit of cosseting and you'll do. You'll find your clothes in the bathroom.'

After lunch – each meal had assumed the significance of a ritual and he approached them as if they were milestones – he walked across to Cya's house, softly entering his bedroom by the outer door.

The room was in perfect order, as it had been on the evening of his arrival in Evanul. His possessions had been removed to the physician's house, all except the book. It lay where Tebora had left it on the bedside table. Beside it, a pathetic pile, lay half the flyleaf and the three folds he had made of Magon's name. He felt like a sorceror who has in error broken the image of his beloved. He carried the book and the scraps of paper into Cya's library; in her desk, he found scissors, paper, and paste.

When he had repaired the damage and pasted the leaf back into the book, he cleaned the page with a soft eraser which had an X scored on it in ink. The brown grime came away with fragments of rubber and he wrinkled his nose at the husk smell. He blew away the rubbish; he had taken care over his mending and the black script and his own beneath it were whole. He carried the book back with him and in Galabrias's courtyard picked a leaf of balm and laid it, smiling at the conceit, between the cover and the mended page. He put the book with his belongings.

Over supper, he met with Galabrias, smiling openly when the physician poured him half a glass of Ceremana. Galabrias raised his glass.

'Whom shall I toast?'

'Doctor Galabrias,' said Cal, drinking to him.

The old man smiled and sipped his wine.

'You are fond of Ceremana?'

'Magon drinks it.'

'I see. Flattery.'

'But I like it now. I used not to a year ago. I knew nothing then but rahi, rahi, and beer and husk.'

'Mahun! And women?'

'Women.'

'Men?'

'I was raped.'

He was a game bird. His entrails were slowly being drawn and read by the doctor of souls. He wondered why he trusted the man, this old neighbour of Xharam'un's sister.

'Did you ever sell yourself?'

'No. I just hoped to, and if I hadn't learned to read and write to sell my skills, it would have happened. I'd be cruising with the Ironmen today.'

Galabrias reached for his pipe and lit it.

'I have my vices too,' he said. 'It's curious, isn't it, that Herkel Galabrias, specialist in various addictions and the human psyche, was never licensed to practise in the City, the mother of the trumpet lily trade?

'I practised privately in Sollar for many years after I left the University. In 472 I went back to Ineit. It was almost twenty years before I felt the need to return home. Then the closest I came was Cheron and Chacma's vile regime; I worked in the prison hospital in Roakn for five years. It's age that has finally returned me to Evanul.

'You were telling me about your lover.'

'She had twins – a boy and a girl.'

The ghost of a smile visited Galabrias's eyes and mouth, gone before it was realised. He relit his pipe and puffed smoke at the ceiling. His eyes glittered.

'I do believe you are waking up this old antiquary,' he said. 'Go on. . . .'

'M'untal.' Cal spoke her name as if it were that of a butterfly and he the entomologist with net and killing bottle. 'Mahuntal. She is one of Mahun's Dancers. She looks exactly like those votive statues of Mayuna.'

'Why have you left her?'

'Magon and I. . . .' He stopped, on the hook. He tried another tack, rushing violently upstream of the man who played him. 'Crinon is taking care of her, of them.'

'Crinon Hinoor. A rare woman. The family used this house for their holidays during the long years when I was away. I returned one year, for a break myself. I well remember Crinon and her little brother picking up stones and shells on the beach. She was a delightful child but Magon – always polite and charming, and remote as if he knew more than the rest of us.'

Now that the extent of Galabrias's knowledge of them was revealed, Cal felt lost. He was the newcomer at this banquet of souls.

'Why do you ask me questions when you know all the answers?' he said.

Galabrias said nothing, but smoked his pipe and looked steadily at Cal.

'I told you before, Horatio. I know everything. It is for you to discover the answer to your own questions. I am merely the catalyst which provokes the reaction.

'Go to your bed now. Sweet dreams.'

In the morning, Galabrias began again.

'Let us take a turn in the garden.'

An archway in the far wall of the courtyard led into Galabrias's physic garden. A high wall of whitewashed clay enclosed it. They walked on narrow paths among the plants, and the herbs of three continents reached up to the sun and out over the path. Galabrias bruised leaves between his fingers as they walked, the scent flowing. Every plant had its crew of busy insects and some, idling beauties, rested with open wings. There was no Wind damage in this haven; like Crinon's enclosure it was a rare asylum, a sanctuary no storm would dare.

'It is an interest, no more. An antiquary's pleasure,' said the physician. 'These plants had their uses in ancient times and one or two are still used. For instance, I make up my own oils and sometimes a special salve to order for Cyrra in the City – perhaps you know her shop? In the uncivilised world beyond the City and the Five Provinces, medicine is an exact science. Such a jumble here of the old and the new: many people do better consulting a quack and trusting in her powers of suggestion. The chaos began in 3AR when they banned the use of unnatural magnifying devices; of course, they had forgotten that jewellers use an eyeglass and,

190

similarly, that the quality of sperm is discovered by the microscope. There were soon uneasy compromises. . . .

'Shall we sit here for a while?'

They had come to an arbour in the heart of the garden. A group of beehives stood amongst balms and spikenard and Cal sat on the iron seat beside the old man and watched the workers at the flowers.

'They are female too,' said Galabrias, and laughed. 'And they keep their drones on perpetual holiday. Isn't Magon's domain a prison for his fancy, total employment without purpose? And your life on the streets: where could it lead?'

Cal, feeling the sun on his legs and the warmth of his living body, began to speak about his childhood on the pavements, about the hospice, the towers, the sewers, Swan, the overseers and the camels. Here, in the quiet garden, was reality, and the teeming City seemed as insubstantial as a dream. Galabrias, leaning back in his corner, appeared to doze and Cal talked for a long time, the narrative pouring from him as if, in the peace of this other garden, he had found another of his selves. As he described Magon, poised and predatory before the cryomorphs, his panic in the chantry, and his emergence from Aash's shadow into Magon's room, his voice unconsciously rose until, aware of it, he stopped speaking. He looked at the old man: his eyes were closed and his breathing soft and regular. Cal stretched, moving quietly so that the old man would not stir; but Galabrias opened one glittering eye and looked at him.

'Strange name, Magon Nonpareil,' he said. 'Do you think he lives up to it?'

'It's his father's name. Destorio Nonpareil is a Cheronian, a chancellor in Chacma's government. Chenodor told me he is Chacma's closest advisor; Crinon says he is his brain.'

Galabrias sat up and searched in his pockets until he found his tobacco, his pipe, his knife and his matches.

'Do you know the meaning of the word "magon"?' he asked, as he commenced the ritual of pipecleaning. 'Consecrated, or dedicated; a word whose meaning has been forgotten. Maja named him of course. Magon Nonpareil – and Cal, whose name might be abbreviated from calamitous, calculating, calefactory, or even from serpentine kalamander – look, there is a sapling, overhanging the gate – but not, I must allow, from Caliban. No, don't interrupt. Names predispose. . . . Look at that. A bee-eater. Wretched bird!'

The yellow bird hopped among the green stems, picking off the bees as they worked inside the flowers. Galabrias clapped his hands; the bee-eater cocked its head and looked at him before flying away.

'I must get a bird scarer. I wonder if Tebora's boy would come up?'

'This garden is like Crinon's,' said Cal. 'A place apart.'

'A magic island? An enchanted forest? A haven? For me, its function is

191

that of the ambulatory; here one can walk with oneself, pause and meditate. It is a little like limbo, for I, and you too, are not purblind worshippers though we both acknowledge Her omnipotence.'

After the heat of the garden, the shady rooms were cold, and Galabrias followed him into the bedroom when he went to change before dinner. The physician lifted the Sinenian medical book from the chest and opened it.

'Here we are,' he said in the resolutely cheerful voice of his profession and Cal, coming to look over his shoulder, saw the photograph of a thin woman in a high head-dress who smiled from the page and who, like M'untal, suckled twins, one at each breast.

'A multiple birth, several fathers, one womb: dogs were once supposed to enjoy such a bizarre method of breeding. Any dictionary will tell you that superfecundation and superfoetation are the same: the conception of a second embryo during the gestation of the first. Here, the word means – I translate – the conception of a second embryo at the same time, or very shortly after, the first. This lady is one of the Vulyar, a hill tribe of central Sinein which practises polyandry but where inheritance is through the senior husband. The cosmic civilisation of Sinein caused the decay of tribal law; without it there are no safeguards but endless litigation for Vulyar women. They seem to spend half their time in the Administrator's court. In her case, a blood test could determine nothing, since all three were of the same group. This woman was wealthy and employed someone at the University to do some gene signature patterning: it was proved that the child on her left, the inheritor, was that of her chief husband while the other was the child of her newest and youngest husband. It seems that seniority takes precedence even in these intimate matters.

'It would be simple to discover if one, both, or neither is yours; the tests are illegal here of course but that's no real bar, especially considering future hopes . . . tell Magon what I have told you.'

'They both look like him.'

'Day-old babies? Come, come. Who knows what complex ancestry Magon has, and yours – could that be any less convoluted? Alas for Science!'

'Your Science has been preserved in the Archive,' said Cal. 'It is not lost.'

'A simple genetic test would instantly have determined that you are not Rafe Dayamit.'

'I know I'm not.'

Cal burrowed in the bottom drawer of the chest, where his clothes had been laid by Tebora. He sat back on his heels.

'I'm afraid I came as a traveller. No tie.'

192

'Ah! The complete traveller should come equipped for any eventuality. I'll lend you one.'

'How do you know what happened between us?'

'An old medical man? My dear boy! What has life left to surprise me with? But I do admit that you are a surprise to me. Quite extraordinary. And not just a pretty face. I'll leave a tie on my bed.'

Cal pushed the hair back from his forehead and examined his face in the mirror; nothing in his features was remotely like his memory of the tiny babies, nothing at all.

Dinner was formal, the table set with porcelain, crystal, and gold. Cal ate sparingly; after his involuntary fast, food was still a novelty of plenty. He drank one glass of the white wine which accompanied the fish and refused Ceremana. Galabrias asked what ailed him.

'I'm practising,' he said solemnly.

'Have a little,' said Galabrias. 'Go on. Just a taste.'

'You're being deliberately unfair.'

'Will you continue this new frugality if you meet a pretty girl?'

'Yes.' He was adamant. Galabrias leered.

At the end of the meal, Galabrias put a box of perfumed cigarettes on the table, and Cal stretched out his hand to take one.

'That's right. No need to deny yourself everything. You enjoy luxury don't you? The indulgence of being petted by Crinon and dominated by Magon?'

Cal closed the box.

'I might have to follow the Stream,' he said devoutly. 'You are right to tempt me.'

Galabrias lit a long cigar.

'She must be very happy,' he said. 'Your little Dancer. Twins are a rarity in the City; the first children of Mahun were twins, girl and boy, were they not? And Mahuntal is one of Mahun's Dancers! She will be celebrated.

'You don't feel any obligation towards her, do you? Either of you?'

'Magon does. He asked me what he should do if she asked him to marry her.'

Galabrias laughed coarsely.

'What nonsense,' he said. 'She won't. If she chooses to marry again, she will look for a better bargain than Magon, or yourself, my child.

'And what would you say if she happened to ask you?'

'Depthers can't marry.'

'Nor can Beggars choose, remember!'

'I'm a rich man now, Doctor. A salaried professional. Sub-assistant Archivist.'

'Always beneath Magon, eh?'

In the silence which followed the exchange, Cal shut his eyes and saw again the agony of Magon, and the martyr who mocked him from his pinnacle of piety. He closed his being about the few secrets he had left and began to speak of the aesthetes and of Amarant.

'Amarant!' said Galabrias. 'You should be more selective, boy, unless you want to grow diseased like an old whore.'

'Amarant made me,' he said. 'If she could breathe life into her stones, she would be content. She has to make do with living imitations.'

'You seem to have a good word for everyone,' Galabrias grumbled. 'Maybe you could find Chacma's heart of gold. Off to bed now. You tire me out.'

For two days, Cal refused to speak to Galabrias, except of generalities; over the following dek he gave away scraps of information: the furnishings of Magon's bedroom, the ease with which he loosed the inevitable arrow, the way he wrote, the way he cleaned his nails, the manner in which he ate and drank. Of Magon's new excluding love, he said nothing. He had decided that nothing would change: Magon's spiritual inconsistencies were like his own excursions with women, irrelevant. As for Magon, or himself, in the role of father, this was nonsense, and Galabrias had confirmed it. Half in love with the image of himself in love, he went across to Cya's house and looked vainly for a fresh letter, although he knew the courier had not returned. The mountains were a great way away, the precipices of the Mahkra a smudge on the horizon. He walked round to the stables and spoke to Choru, who dozed with tip-tilted hind leg. She turned her head towards him and he walked into the stall and let her nuzzle him, stroking the soft skin between her nostrils. He fetched her bridle.

The horse was fresh, unridden for many days, and she fought with him for control. He rode her along red tracks between unfolding lily plants, until they came to the edge of a remnant of forest which touched the shore. Here, he turned her and let her run herself to a standstill in the dunes; then he made her canter on the hard sand at the water's edge. He rode her into the sea.

When he returned, Galabrias was standing at the gate. He waved with an attempt at nonchalance as Cal went by to the stables and Cal returned his salute. Dinner was rich and satisfying and Cal ate well; but he drank only water. He watched Galabrias light his cigar.

Within him, his soul sat quiet, its intemperate fluttering stilled, its wings folded.

'I shall tell you nothing more,' he said to Galabrias.

He busied himself about the house and garden, helping the doctor transfer seedlings from trays into pots, watching him work amongst the tinctures and modern drugs in his laboratory; he wrote up his conclusions about Balkiss, he went into the kitchen and washed the dishes.

Libraries are shrines, places of silence, contemplation, stillness,

194

profound defiles of shelved knowledge: this is the popular image. In reality, they are gymnasia where the mind wrestles with the written word, auditoria where the soul sings and is shocked into action. In Galabrias's library, in search of a gazeteer, he found a dog-eared paperback, an anthology of Gaian verse translated into five Gunaian languages. The poems had hardly survived the transgalaxial journey and the multiple translations.

' "Bright star," ' he read, ' "Would I were handfast as thou art . . ." ', and ' "I wandered lonely as a bird." '

New cadences stirred him. This was the true, the blushful Hippocrene (he had read the lines and their gloss not a minute ago).

But first I must put off
These, my sky-robes, spun out of Iris' woof,
And take the weeds and likeness of a swain –

A swain? He would be a willing slave, he would prostrate himself before his god, he would dance for a crust. It was nobler than women's greedy love.

About women, these Gaians were confused. They called them roses and violets, they compared them with cherries, pearls, and coral; they promised to love them and die. They grovelled and complained and, usually, their quarrels, from verbal bout to binational war, concerned women: it seemed that women could be bought and sold, and that marriage, for many centuries, had begun with rape. Paris, Helen, and Menelaus; Agamemnon, Chriseis; Achilles, Briseis; Tarquin, Lucrece. In time, after the Armageddon Wars, the survivors of the race had found the souls they had discussed and sought since the beginning – wherever that was. He could find nothing to equal the fixed and certain fact of the City's foundation in the First Year, celebrated in Husu's gracesong. But they had certainly done away with religion, the lines by Antipapa said so, and the last poems – structures – in the book, long polysyllabled words punctuated by single letters and digits, meant nothing, even in translation. Visuals, said a footnote, had become the norm; no wordverse had been composed after 3700AD.

He turned back through the centuries of alien civilisation. Here was passion, the very words were kisses, eager fingers, thoughts which burned – those Greeks, who meant so much to Magon: what were they? A nation, a sex, a class, a school of writers? What was their connection with the painter Domenikos, El Greco, the Greek? He put the book to his nose: with the musty smell of old and yellowing paper, metal, and a cold and unknown perfume, he inhaled spikenard and lemon, hyssop and thyme, the airs of Galabrias's physic garden. He turned the pages. The old fox had been there before him, and a slip of paper marked his place.

He read the lines in one gulp and the hair of his neck and chin stood up.

I held my soul on my lips as I kissed Agathon; for in its misery it came forward as though it would cross over to him.

He was answered; he must go. Next day he looked for Galabrias and, finding him reading in his study, sat quietly on a stool at his feet.

'I shall leave tomorrow,' he said, when the old man closed his book.

'Forty years ago,' said Galabrias, stroking the spine of the book, 'forty long years ago, my wife died. I mourned her for seven years. After that, the whores of Roakn. . . .

'I mourn her still. Every day brings a fresh memory. You don't win the lottery prize a second time.'

'Magon?'

'Unqualified, Horatio. I never fenced in the courts of love; I am not qualified to give an answer. Maybe Plato could tell us, if we could interview his shade. If you were my grandson, I might say, "Children who play with fire burn themselves." It is a Gaian proverb.'

Cal dressed as Shelda rose, swiftly. Choru was saddled and bridled, at the door when he came from a hasty breakfast. He had come to the goodbye. Galabrias embraced him as if he were his own son.

Choru moved slowly through thin fingers of light; the trees bordering the road kept the sun from his head. In Evanul, patches of water, spilled from the water-cart, steamed. He put on his straw hat and turned the mare on to the north road.

The old man went into his house and shut the door. Standing in front of the household image of Mahun, he prayed to her and then, bowing to her, he spoke the second Apology. He turned from her and looked out of the window. 'Master of the four winds, Monos, I greet thee,' he whispered, his voice echoing in the empty house. He came to the end of the prayer and looked round at the unchanged image. Her great eyes were quiet, all-knowing.

'Who knows the soul's secrets, Mahun?' he said. 'Who knows what will be born of Magon's ambition?'

The lily fields surrounded him. For twelve days he saw no other landscape but this, the dark green spikes, the tight buds, the red earth and the stained water in the irrigation ditches. At night he slept in small rest houses, raised on stilts from the ground and the snakes. His regret at leaving Galabrias fell away with the miles and he looked about him as he rode; in his dun-coloured clothes and with bare feet, he felt unremarkable and was conscious that the workers he passed looked not at him but at his horse. He broke his journey twice to visit Huyatt's haunts; in the endless lily fields there was no sign of blue falcons or golden-eyed cats, but he felt that they might be hiding amongst the thick stems, watching him, the pilgrim, the follower of Huyatt Tayal and Magon Nonpareil.

Above Tharamanti the landscape changed: the lilies, the fire of their blooms breaking out, clothed low hills and the straight-edge paths of the flat lands gave way to meandering trails. He followed the upper waters of the Evan until he came to the wide basin where the MiKo flowed into it, bringing down white water from the Mahkra. He turned aside and followed the tributary, sometimes consulting his rough map. When he reached the rainforest that lay between him and the heights, he would have to take a guide.

Tongues of forest reached down between the lily fields. The golden trumpets called him. He walked by the horse, his toes burying themselves in the soft earth of the track, his straw hat hanging by its string at his back.

An image of Mahun stood beside the track and he halted before her. She was protected by a small roof of lily straw and strips of cotton were tied like girdles about her hips. He read the inscription carved into the hem of her maral with amazement: 'Be you goddess or god, Mahun, hear me.'

The sempervirent forests of Upper Vern were watered continually by the MiKo and the streams that fed her, by precipitation from the grey fountain of clouds which hunt every morning along the south-western flank of the towering Mahkra. The forest floor was a sponge which sucked at the foot. Cal followed his guide through the dim glades. The rain had slicked down her hair and made her body glisten but she, accustomed to the weather, walked steadily on.

At the resthouse in KattaMattur, a hut amongst huts, the guide knelt to remove the leeches from his legs. She tipped a green liquid from an old tin bottle on to her hand and anointed each engorged annalid until it shrivelled and released its hold. The leeches fell from his flesh, each leaving a triple-branched imprint and a trail of his blood.

She made a fire, and his meal; only then did she remove the leeches from her own legs, laughing at their persistence as she burned them away with her potion. He saw that despite her self-reliance and stoicism, despite her independence, she served him. 'Fetch my books,' he said, and she fetched them and laid them in a row beside him, her face quiet. But he would pay her well, above the rate.

She unstrapped and spread out his bedroll, carefully removing its waterproof covering so that no spot or speck of rainwater should wet his bed. He took up Huyatt from among the books, intending to read the great passage which summoned the forest from the printed page into any room, but instead he opened the front cover and stared at the mended page. The woman, sorting among his belongings, found the bottle of

Ceremana he had bought, many miles back, in Tharamanti. 'Yes,' he said. 'Open it.' She found the corkscrew he had included, smiling in the City at his own whimsicality; she handed him the opened bottle and he drank from the neck of it and poured the rest on the clay floor, a libation. He lay down on the bedroll, hearing the guide prepare herself for sleep, hearing her whispered prayer to Mahun. Idly, he considered what it would mean to live with such a woman; but he had left women behind him in the City. He did not want her, nor any woman.

He left the forest behind him and climbed alone into the foothills. On his map he had marked the way with a dotted line although the guide had said, 'Follow the road upward. What does a picture of it tell you? It will surprise you with every turn.' He recalled the words of the Law which said, 'Mahun knows the way forward: follow Her', and wondered if the monks of Diridion had an accurate map.

Above him, in front of him, the Mahkra filled his horizon, a grey bulk in the morning cloud. The slope of the road was gentle and every turn of it gave him a veiled view of the loops he had trodden already. He passed a milestone which enigmatically declared 'Evanul 400 miles; the City 4 deks; Diridion→'.

The sun rose. Hidden hues, ochres, umbers, and sepias streaked the golden rock and now he could see above him, secret and amaranth, the dark cleft which sheltered Diridion.

By midday, he was at the top and at the edge of the pale and stony road which stretched away westward to the City and east into Dinoord. As he had seen in Glisa's atlas, it passed close by the precipice and the rock itself sheared upward, topped by two foursquare towers of the same rock. The valley lay open before him. The purple hues had been driven from it by the sun and the rock was pink, water and windworn into folds and crevices. He thought, as he entered the cleft, that this could be a potent shrine to Mahun.

A cry, harsh and wordless, came from the height above him but, looking up, he could see neither man or bird of prey. A moment later he heard a gong sound. The houses, like rocks themselves, were set among rocks atop the cliff and backed by other cliffs; some stood inside faults and caves. At the far end of the valley, where the cliff folded upon itself, were taller buildings, another tower, and a pure white pennant flying.

He gasped when he saw the ladders he must climb to gain Diridion, thirty of them, a zigzag of frail wood lashed together and spitted on the rock. Near the ladders the arm of some winding gear for hauling up animals and goods projected from the cliff. He struck the gong which hung at the foot of the ladders, the lettering on it declaring simply 'Lord of the Skies', and listened to its echo ride up the valley; but already an ant of a man was beginning the descent.

The man was small and wiry and wore nothing beside a loincloth and a soft pair of fur-lined boots. He greeted Cal in the speech of Diridion.

'A fair and fine day.'

'Fine indeed and good enough for God,' said Cal, the rehearsed words coming easily, though he knew his accent was southern and exotic.

The man began to remove the saddle and saddlebags from Choru. He sent them up by the hoist and gentled the horse which, unknowing, tried to pluck a dusty weed from the stones. Choru was strapped into the sling and sent aloft, her ears back and her legs dangling.

'Many of our visitors find this a trying time,' said the wiry man. 'Will you climb alone, or will you be led?'

'I'll climb alone!'

As he left the warm valley floor and went lightly up the first ladder, the wind hit him and matched the ecstasy which had possessed him at the prospect of the climb. The precipice was higher, far higher, than his tower, higher than the Octagon top. With every step upward the wind's buffeting increased and he felt sand in it, the sand of the Tayaal. At the top of the tenth pitch he paused and, looking down, saw the hard rocks below. An eagle rested on a promontory of rock nearby; implacable, she stood over her brood and tore strips of flesh from a hare to feed them. Her mate floated out over Vern. Halfway up, he rested again: there, like the seasons or the three ages, was the pallor of the faraway sea, the loud and verdant green of the vegetation, and the bald stone. He stepped from the last ladder on to solid rock and saw Magon.

He stood apart from the other men who were gathered there, the familiar black robe rattling about his ankles in the wind. He smiled. Cal was dumb, but he held out a hand.

Men moved forward, men of Diridion in high-necked coats, bearded monks in dark brown. It was Arkos who took his outstretched hand, no doddering hermit but a vigorous man of Magon's age and as tall. Cal discovered that he had been announced, like a latter-day Cudbeer, as 'my Assistant'. With Magon on his left, Arkos on his right, and a train of monks and townsmen, he was carried forward into the heart of Diridion, where all the dogs barked.

The meal they ate was a public one, taken in the courtyard of Magon's house, with men and children pressing all around. Magon broke the bread and passed him a cup of water; there was goat's flesh, dry cheese, and a small dish of sweet preserves. Arkos ate only bread and a morsel of cheese. Sometimes a woman passed quietly through the courtyard on the way from her house to the well. When a bell tanged sharply on the thin air, Arkos rose, bowed, and left with his monks. A child climbed up on the bench where Arkos had sat and looked longingly at the ring of bread which remained.

'Take it,' said Magon.

An old woman came out of the house and began to clear away the dishes and the bones that were left. She licked her fingers when they touched the empty saucer which had held the jam.

'We shall walk to see the well and then go up to the monastery. Light a fire when it grows dark,' said Magon in his old, imperative manner. 'Come, Cal.'

They walked along the narrow street, the precipice and the valley floor far below, on their right; on their left a jumble of rocks and houses, the tall orange cliffs. The male eagle watched a cat which sunned itself on a flight of steps. A tide of children followed them, shrieking and fighting amongst themselves. The little girl who walked at Cal's heels sometimes caught hold of his hand. Her left arm and hip supported a sturdy baby. Several boys ran after Magon, one with a kite and others with sticks which they rattled on the rocks. The progress down the street was slow, by fits and starts, but presently they arrived at the well house. A woman left it as they entered, her water jar steady on her head, and the children abandoned them to fling stones over the cliff.

The well house was domed and shadowy; light entered it from an annulus in the roof and illuminated a circle of the clear water. Clearly the building was very old; the stone pillars that supported the roof had once been carved figures, their limbs and features worn away by sand, shoulders, and the wind. Stone troughs for laundry stood near the outer walls, but they would need to be filled with buckets.

The empty well house magnified their voices.

'It's a spring, not a well,' said Magon, 'but God knows how deep the cavern goes. It never runs dry. The only water source in Diridion.'

Cal hung over the wall which surrounded the water. The cavern entrance was irregular, not large, but big enough for light to penetrate some way below the surface and illuminate dark stone encrusted with concretions of lime. The water was as blue as the sky above. His reflection was disturbed by a constant turbulence under the water and a few bubbles of gas floated on the surface.

'Where does the water go?' he said.

'They think it flows into another cavern – just out of sight; but no one has been down there to look. The water is bitter cold.'

Cal, stretching, put his hand in it, and felt the eternal cold of the water from beneath the Mahkra.

'Get me a stone,' he said.

He dropped it and it rolled gently down the slope of rock in the water and slid out of sight. He turned his head and looked at Magon.

'Are you better?' he asked.

'The fever only lasted a half-dek,' said Magon.

'But how are you?'

'Well enough.'

200

A woman and two children came into the well house. She set down her water jar and, crouching on the steps, began to dip up water and fill it. Cal walked round the walltop and questioned her.

'How deep is it? Has it ever dried up? Where does the water go?'

'Who knows?' she said. 'The priests tell us, deeper than the valley floor. They say that Huyatt Tayal discovered another entrance to it but if he did, he never told anyone where it was.

'It doesn't dry up and as for an outlet – God knows everything. There are fish down there, blind, white fish. I saw Father Spiris draw one up last year in his bucket.'

Magon had left the well house and Cal found him at the edge of the cliff, looking up the valley into the eye of the Wind.

'The caves opposite are ancient dwellings,' he said. 'See the carvings? Most of them are disused now, and the people prefer this side of the cleft – but they take the goats round there twice a month. Can you see the green? Samarit thorn. It recovers if it's not grazed too frequently.

'The flag on the monastery represents the pure white of the cloud Monos made Man from.'

Cal listened to him. Even when he spoke casually, like a guide, his voice kept its modulation. His physical presence dominated the dry valley. He put his hands in his pockets and hunched his shoulders. Cal hung back and watched him start out towards the monastery at the head of the valley, the Wind animating his hair.

They heard the monks long before they reached the gate, the power of men's voices singing Monos's praise, the strength of versicle and response.

Magon turned and waited.

'The service is continuous: it has not been interrupted for a thousand years,' he said as Cal drew level. 'They take it from one church to another but it does not stop. Monks leave and join the congregation; the praise is constant.

'Will you come with me into the Moline church or will you see the monastery first? They have a remarkable Huyatt in their library and I have asked that you be shown it.'

'I should like to see the library. How can I pretend to worship your god?'

The gates were shut and a shutter closed the grille in the nearer door. Magon pulled on a tail of rope, a bell rang inside the walls and the shutter thudded back, and a face with narrowed, peering, eyes appeared beyond the bars of the grille.

'Archivist!' The voice was respectful. 'One moment.'

They were admitted and the gatekeeper bobbed towards Magon and retired to his stool.

Brown and grey, monk and novice crossed and recrossed the court-

201

yard in a constant stream. In the centre of the court, a fig tree, symbolic here not of woman's fecundity but of the fruitfulness of prayer, shaded a circular bench. A man rose from it and came to them, greeting them after the manner of Diridion. He was short, ruddy, cheerful, and dressed in the grey robe of a novice.

'I will go in now and pray,' said Magon. Cal looked after him briefly, but his mind was concentrated on the church ahead and he did not look back.

'I am Zander, from Zalcasia,' the novice said. 'Welcome to our community. You are the scholar of the Traveller?'

'I follow him, both to the desert and in his book,' said Cal, wondering as he spoke the resonant Diridian words what awful significance Zander would attach to them.

'Then you want to see our treasure? It is a strange manuscript.'

'I should be happy to see it.'

He followed the novice from the courtyard and through a second gateway which led into a paved alley between high walls. Through the archway at the end of the alley he glimpsed weathered white and yellow stone buildings, but these were not simply tiled in stone; they had massive roofs of green bronze. Speech bubbled from Zander as they walked.

'I have been here four years,' he said. 'And next year I shall take my vows and my place in the brotherhood.' He spoke as if the taking of vows was as common and everyday an occurrence as eating. Cal smiled at him.

Politely, he enquired from what settlement in the Zalcasians Zander came and quoted the passage from Huyatt which began, 'I came to Zalcasia when the snow was retreating; when the glades were loud with the cries of finches and the watercourses sang with their burden of melted ice.'

'Exactly so!' cried Zander. 'Snow, water, and trees, mountain birds: that's my home.'

Thus, conversing pleasantly, they came to the buildings.

The doorway of the first led into a shady corridor and Zander's narrative died. Their sandalled feet made little noise on the worn stone of the floor. Halfway along the corridor hung a picture, in bright and crude colour, of a man kneeling in a garden. He stared upward at a glowing yellow cloud inside which a little group of mean buildings squatted on a mound. There was no pain in the picture, the colours were cheerful, and the man smiled blissfully as he listened to his god. Hung as a pendant to El Greco, it would have shown a different way, and Cal smiled at his wayward thought. Now he was deep inside a monastery, a solemn undertaking.

'The Blessed Ikal,' said Zander softly. 'The founder of this monastery. The picture shows him receiving God's grace and the vision of this community.'

They mounted a wooden staircase and followed it upward for three turns, emerging in a long and empty room.

'This was a dormitory for the first monks,' Zander explained. 'It is used as a corridor now – everything changes.'

The door at the end of the room led into the library. The room was hot with the afternoon sun, its walls plain and whitewashed; the books, few in number, scarcely more than three or four thousand, were crammed into dark bookcases. A circular table with an unlit candle on it stood before one of the windows and near it an old monk sat quietly reading. After a time, he looked round and smiled mildly at Cal and Zander.

'Brother Spinteas,' said Zander. 'He is stone deaf; dumb too. He's eighty years old. Very learned but not very saintly, so he sits up here and watches the books.'

He went up to the old man and communicated with him in sign language. The old man glanced at Cal and made a sign in the air.

'He's blessing you – and your work,' said Zander. 'I don't think it will count for much above. Come on. The Huyatt book is kept in this box.'

The box smelled faintly of lilies and sandalwood. (It surely contained a book richly bound in leather, tooled and lettered in gold and filled with the Tayali's sloping script.) Zander opened the box and took out a small notebook covered in a shiny material. He handed it to Cal.

The book was thin and light. It bore no resemblance to the books he knew and loved for their comfort in the hand, their promise to the eye. He opened it. The pages were thin, almost transparent and slippery to the touch. They were blank, void of writing. Cal was too surprised to speak but Zander, smiling at his expression, said, 'Come to the window.'

Daylight fell on the pages Cal held open and, faintly at first, the sloping strokes appeared, growing and spreading across the page and forming themselves into the handwriting of Huyatt Tayal.

'Mahun!' said Cal. He had not uttered the expletive which first came to mind; but maybe to call on Mahun was blasphemy here.

'It is old, pre-Huyatt,' Zander said. 'Someone must have kept it after the Reformation in the City and given it to Huyatt. It's ideal for a traveller to write his notes in: handy, waterproof, no ink to run. Of course we don't know what kind of instrument he wrote with but, as you see, it works by God's light. Marvellous!'

' "Zalcasia",' Cal read from the page. ' "High granite, pines, finches, an abundance of water flowing, song." '

'She opened the page for me,' he thought. He spoke to Zander.

'May I read it all?' he asked.

'But naturally. That's why you came, isn't it? Would you like to work on it now?'

'My books are in Diridion.'

203

'Then come back in the morning! It is almost suppertime now – come and eat with us.'

The novices' refectory was loud with talk and the clatter of plates. Cal sat by Zander and ate bread and cheese and the soft pink flesh, implanted with dark seed, of a green fig. There was nothing to drink but water. A lay brother moved up the room, lighting the candles on each long table as he came. Opposite him was a man with the hairless face of a forest dweller; others nearby wore, like Zander, the heavy beards of Zalcasians; he saw one young Baian and several men and boys who spoke a dialect of Tlivoornal and must come from the edge of Cheron, where the Ayal rose. He did not ask what drove them from Mahun and the world but listened to them, responded in turn, and watched. At the end of the meal, when a prayer had been spoken and a grace said, he looked up and saw Magon speaking to one of the novices.

'I must leave now,' he said to Zander.

The sun had gone, behind the Mahkra, beyond Zalcasia, from Mahkrein herself, and there was utter silence outside the monastery gate. No light showed in Diridion. The gatekeeper called for a brand and Magon took it from him; its fiery tip glowing and scattering sparks on the wind; but when the gates were shut behind him and they were picking their way downward among the stones, he took out a torch and shone it on the path. Cal carried the brand and played with it, holding the flame into the wind until the shower of sparks became a stream.

'Where am I to sleep?'

'In there. It's the best bed.' He had spoken tersely. He was not completely present, his heart and mind soaring to some other realm where the god listened.

In the inner room, his gear stood on the floor by a narrow bed of wood and rope; he waited. Magon's voice filled the house, although he spoke quietly, private prayers that were low in volume and high in hope. Like a child he named his loves, Mother in her paradise, Crinon, Cal, my son, my daughter, their mother, Arkite, and holy father, keep us from and through the coming night. He began to recite the responses the monks had sung. Cal lay down on the bed. He would not undress. Not yet. It was cold. The blankets were sepia and stained; he pulled them over his legs. When they had come in from the greater cold outside (the blankets smelled of goats and were rough), the house had been full of Diridians, men and children. 'They come every night. I read to them.' He had chosen a simple tale from the Gynarchs, a fable to illustrate his theme. (If I read to them, I would give them drama, high adventure, or something they knew, some drab tale of their stony-hearted god.) They appeared to appreciate the novelty and argued the conclusion; Magon had placed his trap with care, drawing them in, voice and eyes. He would have the souls of the children: the boys would all become monks, and what of the girls? On the forest's fringe there had been yellow fruit, and the guide had refused to pick it for him. For us, she said, for women. It gives us the power to conceive. Only this morning. Leaves and sticks, flowers, stones. The tawny eagle. His step rattled the stones outside the window. His cymar was gone from the hook on the door.

The torch was in the nearest pocket of the nearest saddlebag; he did not need it. Out in the night the stars discovered every rock and shadowed crevice. He put the torch away. Magon's light, dancing over the path, showed where he walked and Cal trod softly after him. He listened for the bell and the creak of the gate ahead of him, and when he heard the gate thud shut, he sat on a stone and watched Eshlon searching for her sister in the north. The satellite travelled patiently, a false star. He rose and came to the gates of the monastery; gently he pulled on the bellrope. The gatekeeper peered at him.

'I'm Magon Nonpareil's Assistant,' he said. 'Can I come in?'

He expected darkness and mysteries; but the long arms of the building were as light as lamps and candles would make them, white-painted and plain. The single painting showed Ikal at prayer. The sacred table stood in the centre, where the four arms met, and on it the Flame burned in its bowl of oil. A sphere of glass held the Water.

He saw Magon's dark head in the midst of the throng and took a place for himself behind the last rank of men.

The never-ending prayer was a tapestry of sound against which every part of the service took place. He was there for all the wrong reasons: here he was the heretic, the devotee of the goddess, the curious tourist, the lover who impatiently waits – he watched Magon. How long? Then, because it was the middle of the night and his body craved sleep, he left the worshippers and sat on the floor, his back against the bare white wall. His head went slowly forward on to his knees and he slept, a cold bundle of emotions in the echoing church. He could sleep anywhere.

Foreshortened, from his viewpoint near the ground, Magon was a mighty statue, the black cymar a pillar of obsidian, the head hewn from granite. He woke, and one of the statue's hands moved towards him. Magon pulled him to his feet.

'What are you doing here?'

'Waiting. I wanted to see what they did.'

'And now? Have you satisifed your curiosity?'

'It's dull. No dance and always the chanting. The words are obscure.'

'That's because you don't appreciate their truth.'

'I don't want to.'

The wind chilled him. He was so tired. He stumbled after Magon. And then Magon, turning to him, pulled him out of the wind into the lee of a group of upright stones. He spoke in the dialect of the Depths.

'I ate dried fish on the road but it had not been cured properly and so I fell ill. When I wasn't vomiting in that malodorous privy (God knows how many children have fallen to their deaths in excrement), I lay on the bed and thought of you in the sunlight of Evanul. I thought very little of God and my purpose in the mountains. I dreamed you were dead; I dreamed that Rafe Dayamit came up the ladders to me. Then, when I could drink water again and had only the fever to rid myself of, I remembered why I had come here; and why I was going into the desert. I got up then and wrote to you.

'I remember only part of what I wrote. Was it all bad?'

The dialect kept strange company with his passionate detail, but it was a gesture, coded affection. He smiled up at the occluded face.

'It wasn't good,' he said. 'You described the prospect you had of the desert from the watchtower; the letter was a desert itself.

'You can see how I came to write what I did. Then I drank your Ceremana and in the morning I went out and tried to buy more of it; but in Evanul they have only lily farmers' tonic. I was carrying it back to the house when a whisperer stopped me. I had three days oblivion before Galabrias found me.'

'I had thought you were safe in Evanul, next door to Galabrias.'

'Nowhere is safe. Whisperers can be found everywhere.'

'Except in the Tayaal.'

'In Evanul, Galabrias and I built a castle of sand; but when he asked me what kind of house I would build myself, I told him that it would be one where you had to beg for admission.'

'You will never build it,' said Magon confidently. 'Come. To bed. It's nearly three-thirty; in the City night has hardly begun.'

Awake by midmorning, he heard the old woman sweeping the floor and, still floating on the soft raft sleep had left behind, remembered the rest of the discourse, the hard words of self-denial blown across the rocks, the sharpness of the stones themselves when he tripped, the omniscient shout of the wind which had entered Magon and driven his heat away. Chaste love. He had heard of it. It was one of the greater heresies, the admission of another love beyond Hers. 'You compel me,' he had said, swallowing his soul, preventing the love which trembled to escape him and fill the space between them. 'If you insist, then I must obey.' There it was, the penalty. This was the expected outcome, the rejection the letter had hinted at and which, during his joyful journey north, he had chosen to forget. But now – he thrust aside the blankets – he would get up and find what other bitter fruit Diridion offered him.

When the wind blew from the south, Cal fancied it carried all the odours of the incense-laden coast, of cassia and anise, of lotus blossom and orange flower, of the smell of the City, her blend of ordure, spices, flowers, and ripe fruit. In the house he smelled candlewax and ashes, the leather bindings of his books, the scent of his own warm body, the unique alchemy that was Magon. Outside the window, Diridion smelt of nothing but goats and men.

The bodies of the monks were rank, smelling of stale sweat, of the grease they put on their hair, and of the acrid oil which fuelled the Flame. Now that the rains had come, depositing the tail of their burden on Diridion, he felt the absence of humidity less. The rain fell in thin sharp gusts, but there was a general lack of water, no lush vegetation, and no insect noise. He missed the broad sea with its constant movement and sighs and, surprised in the midst of his slavish devotion, he missed the beauty of the City women. The women of Diridion were ugly, prematurely old, and their clothing hid their bodies in layers of sheep's hair and painted skins. Among the rocks, although he ate enough every day, there was no sustenance, no physical delight; sex was strictly for others, the sombre men, the unwashed women in their unclean skins, a necessity of relief and generation.

They counted the skin-covered bodies, he and Magon, every one of them, the miserable Diridians of Magon's letter, who now filed through the Allode's courtyard in a silent and uncomplaining line. 'Mahun!' he whispered to Magon. 'The women are ugly!' Magon touched each one on the head and repeated the name he was given; Cal wrote the names in the Register. Afterwards, Arkos took them both to the monastery for the census feast with Krates the Allode. They ate another goat, and they drank the only wine in Diridion.

Clouds covered the valley in the mornings, rolling back at midday to show the rain falling on the hidden forest, cold arrows into a grey void. The people expected snow, and this excited him; but the snow when it came was a sparse scattering of crystals among the stones and in a short time it had become water. He understood why the doors of their houses faced south.

He read and wrote a great deal, often climbing up to the monastery to work in the small high library. From constant use, it became his as once the great Octagon Library had been his to discover and use. Sometimes he remained in the house, sitting at the table there, with his books spread in front of him. If he worked hard, he ceased to see Magon.

Magon moved white shells on a wooden frame. Away from the fire, it was cold, constantly dank, and the dead shells, no longer subject to the tide, made a clicking noise like the echo of civilisation or a painful memory.

'Why do you rattle those shells all the time?'

'It's an aid to contemplation. A series of prayers.'

'How can you think of God in this place?'

'It is not necessary to go into a temple to find God. Doesn't M'untal

207

dance everywhere for Mahun?'

It was the first time he had spoken of her. It was like blasphemy, and the image of M'untal spinning in the Wheel rose in Cal's mind. He heard his own voice: 'Mahuntal. She is one of Mahun's Dancers. She looks exactly like those votive statues of Mayuna.' He saw the lined face of Herkel Galabrias and heard his accusation again: 'You don't feel any obligation towards her, do you? Either of you?'

Magon spoke his next thought: 'They are with Crinon.'

Out of reach, alone in Crinon's garden. He could not speak.

'They will be a year old when we return,' said Magon.

'You gave her a promise.'

'I promised to retrieve her son. I have done so. I promised nothing else.'

'I thought . . . I believed there was magic. I believed in sorcery. But it was only your hypocrisy.'

'My mind, the exercise of intellect. Wasn't it logical for me to select the mother of my son?'

'You could have used the sperm bank; someone in your position could have used the ovbanks they have in Sinein. That would have been honest – and we would know whose children they are.'

Magon's expression dismayed him: the old face, the mask of reason. He had used prayer to stifle the memory of his uncontrolled experiment. No emotion accompanied him in retreat.

'I told you what I wrote in the Register.'

'Your logic is a pretence. It's a disguise you put on, like religion. You have everything: why can't you be content? M'untal is left alone in the garden while you and I sit arguing on this rock.'

Magon moved a row of shells and considered them.

'Imagine that I am Slake,' he said.

'Slake! Slake is an imitation man. I can only act a role I believe in.'

'You will not. Do you think that following the Stream is easy? That it comes naturally? What would be the significance of such a course if it were easy?'

'You speak like a priest these days: in dogmatic clichés.'

They sat in silence, Cal drowning in self-pity, breathless with emotion, Magon nervously turning the pages of the book on his knees. But after a long time, while the fire crackled and the rush of the wind outside marked time, he put down the prayer frame and the book, one on the other, carefully. His step, when he crossed the room, one, two strides, was as deliberate.

'We could pray,' he said, putting Cal's hands together with his own.

'Which god?'

'You could leave.'

'How can I go? – having come so far.'

208

'You are perfectly free. You are not a puppet: go wherever you want.'

'Let go of me.'

He twisted away. The latch had absorbed the bitterness and struck at his hand, the wind itself was a cold gale of regret. His handkerchief was white from the attentions of the laundrymen at home (where his heart was, abandoned to await his return to the City). He unfolded it as he walked rapidly up the track behind the house. His tears had frozen in him, or been wrung out by the pressure of Magon's hands, but the square of linen held his memories, a heavy distillation of Magon's books and the sweet oil with which he polished the saddle to a finish better than the gleaming coat of Arkite himself. He held it up and let the wind make a pennon of it.

The track bent steeply around the drystone walls of the empty goatfolds and dusty weeds clung to it. Three eagles rode the wind, the parents and the strongest survivor of their brood. Below them the cliff built up towards the tattered clouds. A red rag hung from a cranny halfway up the cliff. The kite boy stood on a flat crag above the goat pens, holding a length of tangled string and shedding the tears he could not weep.

'It's gone,' he said forlornly.

'What has?'

'My lovely red kite.'

'That? I'll get it.'

'You can't climb up there!' The boy's amazement stopped his tears.

'I can.'

It was a straightforward climb, no higher than the tower; from below where the boy stood, fingers in mouth, it looked precipitous, but there were many holds. The kite was trapped by its broken string in a crack.

Cal dropped the last ten feet and saw the child remove his fingers from his mouth to gape.

'You flew it too close to the cliff,' said Cal. 'Down there is better: right in the middle of the goat pen. You'll still catch the wind.'

'Have you got a kite?'

'I once had a kite to fly. It belonged to a man called Swan – he taught me to climb too. The kite was shaped like a bird: all the kites in the City are shaped like animals or birds.

'Who made this one?'

'My father. It's a piece of cloth from a bale cover.'

'It isn't damaged. Let's put the string on.'

The struts of the kite had been whittled from dry firewood and its tail was made of coloured rags. Its shape was as basic as its construction. The boy stood close to him while he unravelled the long string and cut a piece from it with his knife to make a bridle.

'It should fly well now.'

They descended to the big goat pen and stood in the centre of the enclosure. The boy held the string and Cal launched the kite into the wind. It dipped twice and then began to climb steadily, as Swan's black bird had soared above the bay, its tail strung out behind it. The boy let out more string and shouted. Cal took the string from him and showed him how to make the kite dance.

He returned with cold hands and the chill on his face turned to a glow when he came into the shelter of the house. Magon was quiet, reading; he did not look up but moved the hand with which he supported and concealed his face, pushing his fingers further into his hair, leaning forward towards the fire. His anger, half born, had been aborted or consumed. Cal shivered. This god of his imposed peace like a hurricane. He had seen Arkite lashed to a standstill when Magon felt diminished by some public and wayward incident with the horse. Afterwards, he would lash himself with cords of self-criticism; here and now the strong priest, Arkos, wielded a mental scourge and held up the mirror.

Cal sat on the other side of the fire and tried to visualise M'untal. All he could see was the lifeless figure of Mayuna. 'Are they mine?' he said wordlessly, willing the words across the miles to the City. Magon gathered his books together: the monastery bell called.

It was close on dusk, but Cal sat still. Magon had gone. He looked about the room. Magon's chest and the locked boxes the packhorses had carried from the City were piled in a corner; on top of them sat the long box which held Chacma's gift, the remote kill weapon. He walked across to it and fingered the lock. Magon kept the key on the ring on his belt.

Gradually the light in the room decreased and the cold began to win the battle with the fire. For a while he lay on Magon's bed. Ten. Afternoon in the City, sleep and lustful dreams. He remembered Dromio smiling at him with a slow sensuality borrowed from the afternoon; how he had turned away to cool his body in the sea. He built a tripod of three branches in the embers and watched them burn away. The Book of Monos lay on the floor. He took it to bed, that separate bed that smelled of goats and mould, and lay curled in a knot against the cold, reading by the light of the candle.

Magon came in and went to bed. 'Reading again?' he said. Twenty more pages of admonition: Cal closed the Book.

Magon slept, turned from the fire, his right hand flung out. It was his habitual attitude in sleep; it was the shape his penitent body had fallen into after the violence of the scourge. Cal stood still looking at the old scars, furrows opened by the nails of the demon he hunted here. The monks armed him by day, but at night he had no defence, falling among the alpha and delta rhythms of sleep with the innocence of a child. His fingers were spread over the Archivist's keys, the dark red onyx of his seal ring massive beside his mother's golden wedding band. It was an easy

210

filch. He never stirred and Cal removed the key of the long box from the keyring. He never stirred: Cal kissed his shoulder and went to bed.

Cal took the small key from his pocket. Magon was out again, walking with his conscience, letting the snowy wind blow into his heart. Cal lifted the long box on to the table. The key turned easily; inside its metal coffin the weapon lay in three parts, a simple jigsaw. The ammunition was in another of the locked boxes. He examined the blunt keys of metal which operated the machine, the smoothed precision of its moving parts, and assembled the gun. It was an old design, for Chacma did not give away useful technology, but it was more accurate than a bow, more effective than a knife, infinitely safer for the handler than the fifty-year-old replicas of percussion rifles they used in the fleshyards; he had heard Magon remark that it could kill a man (or a woman!) half a mile away. He fitted it into the hollow of his shoulder and aimed it out of the window, imagining Hyason Sarin in the sights. He put his finger on the firing catch; the weapon fitted him and he cradled it. It occurred to him that Magon might find it too short. He did not allow himself the ultimate pleasure of pretending to kill, but laid the assembled weapon on Magon's bed.

He imagined Oyno's army concealed in Zalcasia, dark soldiers occupying a redoubt beyond high and unclimbable rocks; a black cloud, the counterpart of the Red Wind, they poured across the shadowed land. They were, in his god's eye view, ants of destruction, and Magon, leading them, rode a white horse.

He returned. His walk to the watchtower had excited him and his step had once more the celerity which, before Diridion laid her dead hand on him, had given his actions a boyish eagerness. He poured water into his soldier's tin bowl and plunged his face in it, gasping at the cold. Drops of water covered his smile, the same indulgent parting of lips and creasing of eyes which used to be his greeting.

'Have you finished demonstrating Swan's skills?' he said.

'I did think of taking the other key so that I could load it.'

'Not yet! You can try it in Zalcasia. When we hunt.'

'Hunt?'

'With Oyno. He stalks the snow leopard every year; there will be time to waste in Binala. The division must have left Roakn by now.'

'What are we doing here!'

'Convincing the monks. The final seduction. Arkos will come to the City next year.'

He flung the towel from him and opened the door.

'Look at that rock: it dissolves in water. Coming?'

Cal, hurrying after him, looked up at the head of the valley. Beyond those precipices, the Tayaal began: stone frayed to dust.

'What about the Tayaal?' he shouted. 'It blows away on the Wind.'
'That's my reward. Yours too perhaps.'

That he should speak of the Tayaal as a reward was simply confirmation of the paradox he was, Cal thought. The desert might be a goal or
a place to be discovered after Huyatt; but it could only reward an overfed
spirit.

Magon halted in the middle of the path.

'Encapsulated death came to us from Gaia,' he said. 'What should
have been sisterly concord became the ritual of two competitors;
instruments of death and torture were traded; the Gaians flattered our
basest instinct. Remote kill was on board their earliest ship, long before
the Golden Age, and *Daystar* brought back its refinements with the
paintings.'

'Death is a condition of life here too,' said Cal. 'The Law says Aash
existed before Mahun.'

'Creation contained the spores of decay; Aash is part of the Wheel.
But the bringing of death had become an industry on Gaia and the
starsailors made their creed universal. The Reformation was an attempt
to halt the progress of the infection but, in treating it, the Gynarchy had
to use its tools. Things had gone too far. The Gaians themselves took
four millennia to put an end to the race no one could win.

'Do you know that Aash exists for the Monoclids? A black shadow, the
counterpart of Monos. And a woman! We will become the servants of
Aash.'

'In the City the only servants of Aash are the Dismemberers.'

'What else will we be when we attack the City?'

In the monastery Cal followed Magon into the Pentagonal Church
and prayed with him and the company of monks; it was clear that a prayer
to the desert god, whom the monks represented as a kindly light, was a
prayer to Mahun and that both were the subjects of Aash.

'All-seeing, all-knowing,' he sang with the monks.

When they left the service, Magon took him to the Allode's room. It
was without the vanity of books or pictures, except for a row of framed
portraits, beginning with the holograph of a plump cleric and continuing
through colour print and sepia likeness to the oils of the present. Past and
present Allodes: Krates's portrait was a miniature in oil on ivory. A glass
of water stood on the windowsill and the light from outside poured
through it and illuminated the dust on the floor. Krates and Magon spoke
of the journey into the Tayaal, and Krates gave Magon the flat polished
box which was Diridion's tribute, the City's tax on her existence and her
mode of life. It was the kind of box which might contain jewels or a small
and rare missal. The Allode and the Archivist prayed together and Cal,
because he wished to show that he understood, joined in the responses.

Afterwards Krates smiled out of his long grey beard at Cal.

'A tamed heretic,' he said to Magon.

'No!' Cal protested. 'Can't you see that the Stream and the Wheel are the same thing?'

Krates laughed gently.

The blue silk shirt which (Xharam'un' had said it, turning her passionate and honest stare on him) transformed him from a beautiful boy into a young god lay disregarded under the rest of Cal's clothes. He had worn it twice: once when they came to compare him with Crinon's painting and once in Evanul.

He piled his books up and spread the shirt on the table. There was plenty in it. He pushed it aside and began to draw flattened cats on a sheet of paper.

The construction of the kite occupied him for two days. Firewood struts were crude, their unevenness would spoil the silk. He remembered that the branches of the goat fodder, the samarit bush, were long and flexible, and went out to cut some. Stripped of their leaves, which he left for the goats, they were perfect. He had to make a paper pattern before he dare cut, drawing in his breath and applying his small scissors to the cloth; it was hard to cut evenly. There was no glue in Diridion: he devised stitched pockets to hold the sticks. At last, the sinuous blue cat lay on the table next to the ruined shirt.

Magon unlocked the mahogany box of Mark dyes and took out black and red. They tested the dyes on a strip of silk: they did not run, nor modify the dye of the cloth they stained. Cal gave the cat a face, long black whiskers and eyes like full moons. Magon took the brush out of his hand and gave the cat fur, a wainy pattern of stripes and bands. They could not solve the problem of the cat's tail: a strip of silk hung limply down. In the end, Cal made it a tail of silk bows and it became absurd and fabulous.

The cat took to the wind. Magon watched Cal fly it, his arms extended, paying out string, unconsciously worshipping the Lord of the Winds. The cat hung over the chasm; it would have mewed and sung if the sun had dared shine. And then the kite-boy appeared, kicking stones. Cal put the string into his hand.

'Now you've got two.'

'It's a cat!'

'She is Mahun's cat: you must call her Plama.'

He saw Magon smile and shake his head.

Below them, the sheep were being brought up from the grazing grounds for counting and slaughter. Another census. That night, when the men came into the house to hear Magon read, they smelled of blood and death and raw meat. Their snow-sodden clothes steamed in the heat. Choru, when Cal had exercised her, riding her up and down the long path that led to the monastery, had lifted her head to smell the clean wind from the desert.

Close to Guna's Zone, twenty degrees above Lutra, the length of day and night must approach equilibrium. It seemed, under the cloud, that night began soon after midday. The candles were doused only when they slept.

For two days, though he worshipped his god in the churches, Magon had been himself. The frame of opalescent shells was untouched, his prayerbooks remained in the pile. Though he could not despatch them, he wrote several letters which he locked in a box. He took a small rkw from its case and spent half a day cleaning and assembling it, playing with each part as though he were a boy again and the weapon his tower of blocks. The separated segments gleamed dully in the candlelight, chunks of ore fused, fired, and tempered into an instrument of death.

Cal, twisting Dayamit's ring on his finger, was content to watch him, an acolyte at a new rite which, though it was not a return, was future usage. When he had spoken of the muscular distortion of the gardeners' bodies Cal, for a moment possessed of his eyes, had understood degrees of rejection. His mother, perhaps, had asked so much that he, responding, had put away both her demands and her love. It was better to have no mother and to keep hold. Yet how could he have admired Dayamit, so fragile and elegant in his tailored clothing, so persistent a speaker after death? The green Mark, whenever he moved his right arm enough to disturb the thick cuff, repeated its message: who? He turned the sleeve back and scratched at it, wishing it unmade.

'He is still here,' he said.

'He is dead.'

'This Mark is his.'

'What about that ring, those gold pens, the chain you wear round your neck?'

'I might have stolen those.'

'And be untroubled? Yes, you are without a conscience, Rat.'

'I shall always owe him,' said Cal, but Magon had ceased to listen. When the parts were reassembled, he tried every control and aimed the weapon at the floor.

'Mind your foot,' said Cal drily. 'I had Hyason in my sights.'

'Not the Nine?'

'I shall kill Hyason. Not yet, but in time. I have plenty of time, all the time in the world. I would have killed her if she had come to torment the Beggars last year. Ask Cudbeer.'

'That's enough! Our purpose is not personal revenge.'

It is exactly that, thought Cal. 'I hate this Mark,' he said.

'If I were to remove it there would be a stain, a blemish like a permanent bruise. You can't erase Mark dyes completely.'

Magon, next day, presented him with a sheet of paper covered in small, stylised drawings of animals and birds.

'One of these will obliterate Dayamit. I didn't know you minded so much.'

'I hate him. I pity him, poor sod.'

'Which design?'

Cal drew a circle in the air with a finger, closed his eyes, and let the fingertip come down. He opened his eyes.

'That one.'

Birds on a mound, one with wings upraised, their long and serpentine necks intertwined.

'That one? Sure?' Magon was laughing at him.

'Do you know the fable of the black partridges?' he said. 'Have you come across the Arbidon bestiary in the Library?'

'Not yet.'

'Read it carefully when you do.'

The preparation burned and he asked if it contained acid. Magon told him that was the Archivist's secret and blotted his wrist with a cloth, mopping up the dye. The green pigment bled into his flesh, a strange, heavy bruise. In the morning, Magon spent four hours masking the stain with the black birds. It filled the time; it was all waiting now, empty spaces on the calendar, before they went into the Tayaal. If the partridges could have lifted their red and blue wings and flattened their crests of gold they would surely have flown ahead.

The monks prayed for them. At the church door, Krates blessed them in turn, laying his hands briefly on each head, even that of the smallest donkey. He took Magon in his arms to admonish and bless him.

'Remember that you are a man and not a saint. And when you leave the desert, remember that Monos forgives,' he said. 'God go with you.'

They were a small procession, a progress of five leading the three animals upward to the desert gates. The guide, Misine, carried the key in his hand. The lock had been oiled against the wind and sand, and it opened easily. The monk swung the narrow gate open.

There was barely room for a horse to pass. Cal, leading Choru, could see nothing for the broad backs of Misine and Magon in front of him. They passed through the tunnel in the wall and he saw the Tayaal. It did not begin at once: for several miles ahead, the ground was a confusion of dry valleys and great rocks, erratics, of every colour from rose to black. The Tayaal was the high red ground before them, a dusty seabed, its sands and humpbacked mountains smoothed by the wind. He knew that the plateau lay a thousand feet higher than the rock of Diridion, the Mahkra massif; that the distant range topped six thousand feet, small mountains beside the Zalcasians; that the desert fathers lived at their russet feet. These were facts. They had little relevance in the face of the

215

smelt furnace ahead, the culmination of his quest and Magon's obsession.

He watched Misine march steadily ahead.

'Have you a map?' he asked the monk.

Misine laughed.

'No one has mapped the Tayaal, not even the Gynarchy in its heyday. I go as Huyatt went, by memory and landmarks.'

By the time they had passed the valleys, the sun was high. He felt sweat on his face, his back, the insides of his thighs against the sticky saddle. They had all drawn cloths over their heads and discarded their thick Diridian coats. His shirt was as wet as if he had bathed in it. He thought of water, of the refreshing coast, of Mahun's fountain, of the icy waters of the deep spring in Diridion. The monks called this the Journey of the Three Hopes.

When they came to the first well, called Clearwater, he eagerly tended the horse, unsaddling her and giving her an armful of the fodder one of the donkeys carried. Perhaps he could lie down in cold water. Inside the well house was a shallow tank of mud. Weeds grew in it, tufts of startling green, and gangling insects like giant mosquitoes lurched there on iridiscent wings. Misine showed him how to cup his hands in the liquid mud, making a fleshy dam. Clear water seeped over his fingers and he drank, his head low over the mire.

They sat in the shadow of the well house and ate bread and figs. Disposed wherever they could find shade, some by the wall, some by tall rocks, they lay down to sleep out the heat. Cal, his head on his arm, looked towards cloud-covered Diridion.

When the sun was a pale sphere, low over the Mahkra, Misine shouted to them. Cal woke slowly. The heat still had the intensity of a kiln; he was moist clay. He wiped his face on his shirt. Zander picked up the dry stalks which Choru had left and stowed them in the bundles of fodder.

'Waste nothing,' he said. 'Give nothing to the Tayaal.' His vitality had evaporated in the heat, beads of sweat hung in his beard. He followed Misine from the camp.

Cal, saddling Choru, was the last to leave. He looked around the empty hollow at the naked rocks and the stone well house, its dark archways sheltering the miraculous spring of fresh water. The sun went down beyond the heart of Vern, over the sea; she would bring day to Sinein. Here was a world of grey without shadows. It would be three hours before Eshtur rose. Choru whinnied anxiously and he got on her and followed the pilgrims.

Soon, it grew cold and he put on the clothes he had shed. Stars covered the dark dome of the sky. Eshtur and her satellite climbed. He shivered and halted Choru so that he could get his coat from the saddle-bag while he wondered how she, in her thick coat, felt, warm by night and

216

intolerably heated by day. But she was a barbon, desert-born. She knew this place. He wiped his hands on her neck, and hair came away.

They travelled along a shallow valley where Tayal houses stood like square rocks themselves. The valley was dry, abandoned since the water supply failed. They ascended again to the plateau, the hooves of the animals clinking on the stones. He saw a slender fox, watchful beside a rock, and thought it winked at him with one of its effulgent eyes. He winked back and would have spoken to it if he had been alone. In the brief dawn he saw the second well, Patience, ahead and beyond it the first foothills, maiden cones as dry as an old woman's breast.

He woke halfway through the day. Zander and the servant boy were bundles on the ground, the animals hung their heads, and Magon lay still as if the heat had axed him. The monk, Misine, held a book in his hands.

'Too hot for sleep,' he said. 'Ikal's words are cool, tranquil like shade. Look to the east: there is a rare sight.'

Cal followed his outstretched arm and saw, treasure in the Tayaal, a sea of glittering water. On its faraway banks, one of the conical hills stood on its head, precarious and weighty; below it, detached from the firm ground, defying gravity, floated a square Tayal house. The white house hanging under the red inverted rock seemed to signal to him, a sign, a flat and ominous portent. As he watched, the vision dissolved and he saw the familiar stony ground, the foothills, and a small settlement of white houses distorted and shimmering in the heat.

'God's mirror,' said the monk. 'It shows us His eminence, His control over the universe: who else could put a lake into the desert, who else remind us so succinctly that we are nothing but reflections of Himself?'

Now that the mirage had dissolved, Cal's attention and wakefulness evaporated. He fell asleep with the image etched into his eyes, a dark red triangle floating above a white cube. The wonder, when he related it later, brought forth a torrent of words from Magon, a flood of physics and metaphysics. He listened to the voice, and saw the miracle. It was the house of Huyatt Tayal in the lee of the mountain, the cube under the pyramid. Huyatt had looked into the mirror. Pausing, where he sat in Alna's high saddle, he had recorded the marvel for all and for all time.

Purity: the village, the well and the community of desert fathers. The cells lay at a distance from the houses of the Tayal village, square and white like them, a world apart. The fathers had to walk half a mile for water. The spring was circular, a wide pool ringed with a wall of white stone and beyond the wall was a green ring of sweet palms and the apricot trees which stood among the houses, caressing their flat roofs with fruitful branches. Water ran into the orchards and vegetable gardens and the bright yellow flowers of cucumbers, melons, and squashes glowed beyond the water channels. There were birds at the well, small, feat, and bright blue. Cal drank the water while they dipped their beaks and bathed in the shallows. And there were women by the well, real women, not the mummified hags of Diridion. They wore coloured garments, garments which hung in folds as far as their knees; from the hem bare brown legs stretched, tangible, visible, female. His heart sang. He went up to the prettiest and asked to be shown the house of Huyatt Tayal.

The building was swept clean. Frescoes of flowering trees among fountains decorated three walls of the single room. The great traveller's furniture had not survived. The place was rather a shrine than a museum and a banner of embroidery pinned to the rear wall proclaimed this. It showed Huyatt riding his white mare through a universal landscape and Cal saw himself and Choru – at the City gates, deep in green Vern, isolated on a pale strand, ascending forested hills, high in Diridion of the Cleft. Enclosed by a green garland in the centre of the panel, Huyatt and Balkiss embraced. The blue falcon and the golden-eyed cat watched them from among the leaves. The border of the piece was a tight design of mythical beasts and birds and he saw the black partridges with which Magon had marked him. The picture made him think of M'untal; its bright colours were hers, and they were the colours of the pretty Tayali who pointed at the embroidery and laughed at his jests.

He began with her feet. They were dusty and their nails were painted with eyes and orange feathers. Her calves were sturdy. The skirt touching her knees – and knees came before thighs – was a kind of enfolding trouser, or maybe a different way of wearing a maral, a tail of cloth pulled through and tucked in at the waist. He could see that she wore nothing beneath her loose smock. Her thin hands – no rings yet, no promises – were painted like her toenails. He asked her about the designs, so that he would have an excuse to touch and hold a part of her.

'Like yours,' she said. 'Old patterns, but mine are only skin deep. Who wished partridges on you?'

She tilted her head, looking up at him with wide eyes, a bird herself, poised to flee.

'They are evil creatures,' she said. 'Don't you know the cock birds tread each other? The hens have to mate with francolins.'

It was an absurd and rural belief and Magon, knowing it from the bestiary, had branded him with it.

'Do they live in the Tayaal?' he asked.

'In Zalcasia, where the women have beards.'

'In Maralis,' he lied, 'where I come from, these birds are called chancers. They bring good fortune.'

'My mother calls,' she said suddenly, took back her hand and was gone, leaving only her footprints on the floor and an unknown and rich scent.

In the fathers' community, the cell they had been given was like the rest, a manmade cave with one door. Magon, stretched on a pallet, was deep in the Book and spoke irritably in reply to his enthusiasm.

'There's a great embroidery,' said Cal. 'Huyatt and Balkiss – and black partridges.'

'Shush!'

He went out again to sit by the well. Maybe she would return.

He had no duties. He visited the Tayali, calling at a different house every day, and treating busy lives as a personal sideshow. The Tayali were patient and answered his questions. They called their town Red Rock and their word for the settlement and the red mountains was the same, Ruht. They walked about it with the assurance of long possession, their practical clothing the costumes of his show, the women in bright colours and silver necklets, the men stark and brave in white. As Huyatt told, each man had several wives but the reality was that several women, sisters in accord, had married one man. Like the Tlivoorn, the women controlled the money: they worked in the gardens and they stitched the intricate embroideries which brought them a living even when the crop failed. The system should have produced a surplus of men but there were many accidents. The harshness of the desert and their own unreliable rifles killed them.

Choru's sisters and brothers champed at dry stems in cool shelters; he watched a Tayali hunter feed his favourite horse with handfuls of sweet dates; he brushed the sand and moulted hair from Choru and lingered in the shade to admire her. The horse was another new love in his canon. He was wary of the dogs, thin, leggy creatures with great chests and tails like whips; they looked as starved as the prowldogs of the City but the hunters told him that a thin dog was a keen dog, and in the houses they were gentle, resting their long chins on his knee and gazing at him with hungry brown eyes. Every household had its screen of falcons, a row of hooded killers, perfectly adapted to their function, and in the courtyards the finest falcons perched on padded blocks. Because they could not see him, they sat tight and he knelt to examine the close intricacy of their feathering, each web an exact tracery, armour fashioned to keep out heat and cold, to help the lift of those long and speedy wings; he looked at their yellow feet, scaly and powerful enough to buffet a rockdove from level flight, grip, and kill, at their hard and sharp talons. When they shifted, the bells on their legs rang, not with the resonance of a chime, but with a dry and magical chink, an invitation to the chase. If life in the City had been returned to the second millennium, then this was the life of prehistory.

Imagining the silken rectangle on the wall of his room, he chose and paid for an embroidery: it was a happy choice, a picture of the desert peopled by animals, the ethereal fennec fox much to the fore, falcons raking the sky and a string of antelopes bounding; behind them the ruddy

219

slopes of the Ruht rose up towards a clear sky. The woman gave him coffee, the first he had ever tasted, bitter on his tongue. He screwed his mouth up as he swallowed, drinking the offering from politeness. It smelled like the bird-girl, but had no sweetness. At the bottom of the cup a blob of palm syrup was a reward.

In the small temple, a dome of the red mountain rock, open to men, he stood and prayed to Mahun. Afterwards, he walked about the dark sanctuary and looked at the statues, Mahun in her many guises, her sisters, and her children. In a dark corner was the pallid figure of a demon, a lumpy white figure, whose skin was scabrous and puckered. Someone had lit the lamp at its feet. He asked the Gynarch what it was.

'Tror,' she said. 'He who tried to take Her from Us.'

He looked again at the image. Like the unhappy Slake, like the rebellious Annon, like the self in his turbulent dreaming in Evanul, it had no testicles. He kept Galabrias's knowledge of this emasculated consort, father of Ingemi, to himself, but, 'Once, he was Her husband,' the woman said. 'You can see how he was punished.'

Magon had seen nothing, no flower, no Tayali, no fruit. He prayed and sat alone for hours, in retreat. Then, one morning, when they rested in the shade of the doorway, a bird began to sing, a sweet warble, a chirruping cadence of pure melody above the sigh of the wind.

'That's a zdu,' said Magon. 'I've heard one before, in Crinon's garden. They come there rarely, blown on the wind, eccentrics like the rest of us.' He stood up and retreated to the back of the room.

If Cal stood in the doorway at night, the small fire in the cell touched his back with its warmth and the cool night air outside refreshed him. The same firelight touched Magon, illuminating his book and his hands as he repeated the gathering prayer, over and over.

'The Name of God is One The Name of God is One The Name of God is One.' It was the undercurrent of this phase, the undertow in the Stream. It gave sense to the night and soothed Cal.

In the village below, the dogs began to bark, and he heard someone shouting at them. He looked at Magon: who could withstand such a din? Magon, unfolding his hands and his legs, got up and came to the door.

'Listen!' he leaned on Cal's shoulder. In between the yelps, out amongst the rocks, a new sound broke.

'It sounds like a chainmaker's,' said Cal.

'It is a forge, a chain of holy men: Desmids from the rocks.'

'Desmids, a chain?'

'The most holy of the Monoclids. They say that the hermits up in the Ruht are nearest to God, but these men try a different way: they have vowed an opposite vow, not to be parted from their fellow men. They are chained together, they are a chain, a perpetual linkage of desire for God.' Magon caught hold of Cal's hand and gripped it in a vice of fingers.

'When you wrote to me from Diridion,' Cal said and looked up at him, 'you were full of the search for your soul, if such a thing can separately exist. The women don't need to split existence into parts: a section for the head, a section for the heart, another room for anguish, another for love. After death the whole being returns to the commonwealth of dust.

'Why must you go on with it? What are you hoping to find? What do you want?

'I only understand desire in one way.'

Magon dropped his hand as if it had been a hot coal. The chain of Desmids went by. The firelight falling from the double row of cells illuminated their procession, and to Cal they were a dance of madmen, devotees of Aash. There was nothing austere in their ecstasy. They were full of sin, for as they ran, the heavy chain coiled twice around each waist, each man beat his own back with a knotted thong.

He felt Magon wince.

'Come inside the house,' he said.

'No. I understand them.'

'They're crazy, Magon. Remember what Krates said?'

'Krates is a gentle man. He has nothing to repent.'

'How can you renounce violence when you plan to force the City?'

'I can't.' His voice became a whisper. 'I can't.'

With their heat and blood and rags, the Desmids had passed. The narrow street was quiet.

'It's done; nothing can be altered. Accept yourself.'

'I can't,' he said again. 'I think I have been cursed with perpetual motion, running between God and you, jolted from spirit to flesh, running and never arriving, running backwards.'

The street was empty, the sun up and burning. Two of the fathers called a greeting as he passed. He was glad to find Zander at the well, dipping a bucket as though nothing mattered but water for breakfast. Zander, mopping his face, began to talk in his customary manner, the words running away with him, of the Tayal gardens and his garden in the monastery, but Cal, a finger to his lips, said, 'I want to ask you a question, not of gardens or reality. Which virtues do you consider the most important?'

'Chastity,' said Zander at once. 'Compassion. Poverty.'

'If you were not a monk, but a soldier?'

'Compassion then – and Justice. How else, after blood, can you face your enemy?'

'Violence might be the means to peace?'

'Can evil be defeated by gentleness? It might be possible; but it is too slow a method for men.

'God works through order. Violence is ours. In the Book, one of Ikal's prayers reads like an earthquake.'

'Don't you think that active penitence is truly the tool of a monk?'

His oblique questions had not deceived the novice. Zander put down his bucket and, with a frank stare said, 'You can't show the light to a blind man, my friend.' He bent to retrieve the bucket. 'Come and breakfast with us. Misine will entertain you with his tales of the desert.'

The small boy from Diridion was tending a fire outside the last cell, where Misine was lodged. Some birds, spitted on sticks, were roasting over the fire and Misine knelt by it, cooking flat cakes of bread on a hot stone. Cal sat on the ground. The birds dripped grease in the flames, spat, and sizzled. Since the monks had discharged their duty by delivering them to the fathers, he had not eaten properly. The fathers gave their guests the fare they ate themselves: bread, dates, and water. This diet apparently satisfied Magon but he was continually starved. He watched the plump breasts and thighs of the birds slowly brown.

'You eat well,' he said.

Misine, turning the bread, laughed. 'We'd be poor survivors if we didn't know how to trap a few rockskippers. They can't fly.'

He gave Cal the first cake of bread, pulling two of the crisp little birds from their spit, and clapping them on the bread.

Misine talked about his life in Sidend, of the mountain air, desire, his young self, the girls he had known; of his skill in making a meal from any animal or plant, of harvests taken from high terraced fields, of the robbers who used to descend on lonely Sidend with the snow. He hadn't given anything up, he said; after all, he was an old man who had enjoyed his share. The monastery was a good deal safer than the margins of Zalcasia.

The boy listened closely, clutching the poker he had made from a stick. After Diridion, a tale of robbers was bliss; and had he not crossed at least a quarter of the Tayaal? But the golden man from the City wanted to talk morality.

'Your robbers must have killed, or was there no resistance? If an innocent man is killed for personal profit – could his murderer be forgiven?' he asked Misine.

'The bandits killed my family. And they certainly didn't ask for forgiveness! Eternal annihilation is the fruit of such a life. But to your question: yes, in time, with prayer and true repentance. Why do you ask?'

'I am interested in this process of repentance,' he lied. 'I have seen the Desmids.'

Zander looked sharply at him.

'Ah – the Desmids,' said Misine. 'They are a different set of dancers. They have pledged themselves to repent every sin of every man.'

'You could use them like a frame of prayershells, to mitigate the punishment for a particular sin?'

222

'No. Nor can the shells be used like that. The moving of the shells is something for hand and eye while the soul operates, a row of punctuation marks.'

Zander walked halfway down the street with him.

'The Tayali say,' he remarked, as he turned to go, 'that whatever you give to the desert will return to you increased. I think that's rubbish myself. Better to get a fruit farm.'

Cal, pondering this, went into the cell. Magon was still sleeping. Cal, in the desert manner, sat on his heels with his arms clasped about his knees, and watched him sleep. He could list his own insights as easily as if he wrote them on paper. And Magon?

So still that he might have been his own effigy, he lay on his back with his hands open and flat at his sides. Cal, frightening himself with the idea of death, though he could see Magon's chest rise and fall, got up and knelt by him. Magon opened his eyes.

'I was a great way away,' he said. 'There is a beautiful place by the sea, a silver kingdom, where – I'm sorry, it's a story Crinon made up years ago. I'm awake now. Is it day?'

'It's midmorning. I have been up three hours and breakfasted with the brothers. Let me go and see if Misine has any more fresh bread.'

'I shall not eat today. I have fed on sleep,' Magon said, but his appearance belied him and he drank the water Cal brought him. 'There are two days left: I should walk in the hills.'

'Haven't you found what you came for, in the shadow of the hills?'

'I fear I have.'

'Nothing changes?'

'That I won't achieve my goal in this life. Yes.'

'You didn't want to see Huyatt's house,' Cal accused him. 'You have seen nothing here but the inside of this cell.'

'I have seen far, too far,' Magon said, but he got up and dressed and went with Cal to the village.

Huyatt's house was unattainable. Seated like beggars on the bare ground, the Desmids filled the alley that led to it. In daylight they had ceased to be flagellating automata; they were individual men, partners in a hideous misalliance. There were eleven of them, all wasted from the heat, hungry, fanatic. The man at the head of the chain had white hair and the heads of the rest were a hierarchy of colour. Their rags had felted on their backs and a stench came from them of pus and putrefaction. Cal tried to avoid their eyes and pulled at Magon's arm.

The third from the end suddenly came to his knees and, reaching out, touched Magon's ankle as he came near. Cal, stepping over the chain, pulled the black sleeve tight.

The Desmid had a solemn brown face. He looked up at Magon and said, 'Are you the man from the City?'

223

'I am Magon Nonpareil. I am the Archivist.'

'I was Benet,' said the Desmid. 'I am the Ninth in the Chain.'

'Get up then, Benet. It is wrong to kneel at the feet of a sinner.'

'You are the man who carries the torch to the great whore; the man who will free us from the tyranny of women?'

Cal, expecting the ironic smile, smiled himself, stood still and heard Magon address the kneeling ascetic like a seer.

'That I carry fire is not in question,' he said.

'Then I will follow you, and break this Chain.' The Desmid picked up a stone and began to pound the chain beside him. The other Desmids watched in silence and two of them prayed but Cal, his fingers still trapped in the cloth of Magon's sleeve, was revolted. The fawning Desmid, in his religious convolutions, mocked love. Wanting the release of action, he took his hand from Magon's arm and, entering the house of the Tayal, shut the door behind him. To still his anger, he stood in front of the embroidered picture and tried to visualise the heavy luxuriance of the rainforest. The thud of the Desmid's stone kept his mind outside with Magon. He sat on the floor and blocked his ears but the rhythmic batter of the stone was too loud.

He was driven outside. One of the Tayali had come with a hammer and cold chisel to break the chain. On one side, the Desmid was free, and on the other, the link was half cut through. While he watched, the Desmid was freed. He walked past the tableau without speaking and went to Misine's cell. The brothers were agog. The news had spread up the track. Zander's questions tumbled.

'Go and see for yourself,' said Cal. 'It's a public event.'

'But no Desmid has freed himself for over twenty years!'

'The Desmids are madmen, Zander. Foul and unnatural.'

Zander impatiently shook his head at him, as he might at a stupid child.

In their cell, Magon spoke courteously, as if the Desmid were a citizen of Diridion or the City herself.

'This is Benet, Cal. He has joined us.'

'What for?'

'To fight for God.'

'To fight? Does he know anything beside masochism and howling?'

He looked at the Desmid as though he were a wild animal, an ape in a zoo, an imitation of man. The Desmid returned his gaze evenly. He smiled. With a half remembered gesture, he held out his hand. Cal's hands remained by his sides.

'Get him some clothes, Magon. Tell him to wash.'

He sat by the door, his eyes on the shimmer in the heated air, hearing with increased acuity each separate drip of blood and water as Magon washed the Desmid's crusted back. The water, flung out, broke up into prismatic drops. Misine came, hurrying down the street, to welcome the Desmid back to the world.

'Some of us,' he said, 'think the Desmids are mistaken; retreating, they insulate themselves from God and rely on mortification to bring them to faith.'

'You are wrong,' said the Desmid gently. 'We spend most of our days in prayer. Let us pray now.'

'Indeed,' the monk folded his hands, 'that would be a pleasure.'

Cal, outside their communion, was afraid, sick and worried by the cat's teeth of jealousy. He looked across the red rocks and wished fervently that the Zalcasian guide would hurry. Surely, in the mountains, the cold heights would act like bromide and end this painful heat.

Snow

. . . and the mountains were wonderful. Zalcasia was the antidote to the poisons he had accumulated in the desert. The velvet green of the tree-line, seen from the valleys far below, had resolved itself into individual trunks. Noble pines. So they were. The air, even before they reached them, had filled with their sharp smell. Magon, in this antiseptic air, had looked across at him and smiled. Then the snow began, thin flakes alighting on needle and bark, on his gloved hands, in much the same manner as those disappointing crystals of Diridion, alighting, awaiting an instant, and dissolving away. But soon these flakes (crowding on his eyelashes) had ghosted the ground with white, were lodged on the shoulders of Magon's coat, quieted the footfalls of animals and men. Feet and hooves made prints in it.

Farewells had been said. Twenty days ago. To Misine and the boy; to Zander. His goodbyes to Zander had been regretful, full of the hope that they might one day meet again. Zander had gripped his hand warmly.

He stretched. Outside, the soft snow fell. He could see it through their tiny triple-glazed window, each flake magnified by the bubbles in the green glass. The headman, Zuhil, had brought them to the guesthouse after Magon had greeted Oyno, his two lieutenants, and a detachment of random soldiery from Zuhil's force. The house was the right size for this cold place, neither large and draughty nor small and cramped, built of thick wooden slabs and lined within with horizontal timbers. Much of it was carved, especially the end of the beams, the doorposts and the flat frame of the little window. A clay animal squatted in the middle of the floor, the stove, rounded and warm. A firebox was buried inside it and a stark metal chimney stuck out of its back. The animal was a crouched bear which held a cub between her front paws.

He was alone, comfortable on the woollen coverings of his bed. Magon's bed was across the room, on the other side of the bear. They had joked about the animals, lying there between them. Magon was with Oyno. He had augmented his prayer books with maps, his prayer with military talk and tales of snow leopards. Together they had leaned over the map-spread table, tracing their route home. Next year after the snowmelt. The soldiers' maps were detailed and exact: proper maps at last. His finger had walked the road home, down from Zalcasia, down into the interlaced Baian valleys and across the pass into Far Maralis:

from there they would be able to see the City.

The bed had carvings along the footrail: a flight of cranes, their wings extending, pointed, triangular, stylised, above the rail. Firelight from the open door in the bear's belly fell on him, diminishing the twilight in the silent house, illuminating the dust. It was warm. In the house he could shed the skin jacket from Diridion, the sweaters, boots, and over-trousers.

On the first day of the snow Cal jumped from Choru's back and picked up a handful of the stuff. It compressed in his hand into a solid ball. He looked for a target and threw it at Benet, half in hatred, half from curiosity, wondering how the reformed Desmid would react. Halting his pony, Benet had gathered snow from a rock and returned Cal's fire, hitting him squarely between the eyes. After that, the game had developed and for several miles they went on playing cat and mouse, hit and miss, with the snowballs among the trees. Choru shied when the snow hit her; Benet had taken advantage of that. Benet's pony was rock steady. Cal had to aim at his long head, ducked inside its hood.

Benet had been sent to live with the soldiers. He was already transformed into a raw recruit, hands clumsy on his new rkw, a shadow in watchet snow fatigues. It was his second transformation. While they journeyed, Magon had treated him as a servant, reminding him of duty and wordly obedience, of his neglected ability to read and write; and Cal had hated him, hated them both. Benet, always willing, always quiet, had performed the simple tasks Magon set him. He kept his deferential distance and Cal became indifferent, watching the snakeskin split. Benet's dissolved vows and new opinions fitted his successive coats; in the last days of the journey he had acquired the mannerisms of the Binalan men and now, in keeping with his fresh character as a soldier, he had learned to swear and his eyes strayed often to the Zalcasian girls in their felt and furs.

And here was a paradox. In Diridion, skins had made sexless scarecrows of the women but here in Binala similar coverings quilted nubile flesh.

They had a Zalcasian servant – a woman!

Last night, dreaming, he had wandered, a midget in a forest of lily stems until, emerging, he had come upon the Tayaal, a palette of red and black, swirling, oily, miasmic illusion. Before him floated a white cube. He had pursued it for a long time.

He smiled, remembering Magon in the tylopod's saddle. The strange black animals had come out of the desert, patiently, to the well. Here they were unloaded: timber, raw metal, a ploughshare, and some boxes were taken from their humped backs. The camels sucked up water as if they could never take on enough. Watching them, he had thought of Hyason Sarin. Her eyelashes were as long as theirs, but they were gentle beasts.

227

He had touched one, rubbing his hand over the tufts of woolly black hair. There were a dozen of them. The Tayali loaded them with green melons and with the embroideries destined for the Alcuon market in Far Maralis. Then the time to mount had come. He was spared. He had vaulted into Choru's saddle, made her circle, and sat there watching. Benet had gone first, seating himself on the hard wooden device, uneasy and jerking as the camel got to its feet. Magon mounted. As usual, everything he touched turned to gold. The camel stood up and Magon, high in the saddle, sat it easily, his feet on its neck, the goad in his right hand. 'You've done this before,' he had said but Magon, laughing, had denied it. 'Not even as a child at the zoo,' he said. Sheeted in the white sandcloth, he looked like one of the Tayali.

They had ridden all night, following the Tayal guide and the two Zalcasians over dunes that even by Eshtur's light were not the lemon yellow of Glisa's map, but dark. Day had shown them the black sandhills of the Negaar. When they stopped in the shelter of a barkan, the black and unrelieved sand stretched before and behind, under them. He had taken out his map and written on it notes of such details as seemed significant, in particular the negritude of the dunes and the delicate tread of the antelope he had seen crossing them.

It had taken three stages to cross the Black Tayaal. Once, before setting off, he had noticed the images of himself and Magon reflected, a multitude, in the little mirrors which decorated the camel harness. The figures were distorted, an army of stunted men. 'The further you travel from this God of yours, the better you are,' he had said. Magon had replied, in mild tones, 'He travels with me.'

The black sand was hot to touch. He laid his skin coat under him and covered his head with the sandcloth; he made shade with Choru's saddle and with a pack. The heat reached up to him. A lizard ran by and stopped near him, lifting opposite pairs of feet up from the burning sand. He went to sleep with the sweat drying on him. Then came Her benison, rain. The falling water woke him. He opened his eyes and saw a trail of grey cloud. The guides had moved into the lee of their camels. The Tayali sang, with a nasal moan, a hymn to Mahun, and the two Zalcasians praised various gods; Benet chanted, a soft pendant to the wild song of the mountainmen. Before he closed his eyes he heard Magon come to his knees and speak a prayer of thanksgiving.

Lying there, water on his face, a taste of salt on his lips and a smell in the desert of green plantations, he saw a far-off circle of light, cones of flame, the crown which sometimes ringed Her head. She was a long way away, but he heard her voice distinctly, calling his name.

'They are all mad,' he said, but she shook her head.

'Strayed,' she said, 'Searching. Only those who wilfully deny me are forever lost.'

228

He slept and dreamed that the harsh sandstone of the Ruht was clothed in green, a new forest grew there; above it were white snows, restful deathfields, constant ice. Where the fathers' cells had stood were orchards, and the Tayali women in bright cottons, picked red apples, their strange skirts swinging against their bare brown legs.

As they left the desert, yellow flowers came out like stars in the black sand, and delicate white blossoms which nodded their heads on fragile stalks; the naked bushes had a film of green and frogs were singing in the refreshed water courses. He saw it as confirmation of Mahun's supremacy and said so while, within, his soul rejoiced.

'It will last a dek,' the Tayali said to him. 'Flower, fruit, and seed, before the waters dry up.'

'But the rain will return.'

'It will return. She knows the day.'

In Sidend, a clutter of houses in the naked foothills, they offloaded the melons, now pale yellow and sweet-smelling in their nets, and exchanged the camels for mountain ponies. They left the Tayali with the fruit, his thin hand waving a farewell. Half a dozen men of Binala were waiting to lead the ponies in the mountains. Magon, astride a dapple grey, pushed it forward into a titupping run, pushed it forward until it galloped for him. Then they went up into the hills, ascending and passing over a rocky shoulder into a high green valley. A lake lay in the centre of it and two waterfalls made rainbows against far precipices. It was one of a number of such havens in Zalcasia, a summer grazing ground. Now, before the snows, the grass was interspersed with wide patches of rosy flowers, and gamebirds called from the shelter of bronzed and dying ferns. Little crowds of black partridges whirred up in front of the horses, but he could never get close enough to them to see if the wonderful detail of their plumage were true or a piece of Magon's imagination. He rode Choru alongside Magon's pony and challenged him to a race. They went half a mile into the green pasture before Magon pulled up the dapple grey. It had been losing.

'Woman,' he said, finding a new use for the sacred word.

'It's a waste of the horses' strength. Look where we have to go.'

Above the tree line, the path bent, giddy and high, steep and stony among overhangs. Higher than these slopes, he saw the twin mountains Darodha and Zelk and, a dream of insubstantial cloud, the snowclad peaks of High Zalcasia, inaccessible country.

'You'll have to keep a tight hold on the mare,' said Magon.

At first the path was wide, easy going as it left the woods, and he rode Choru up it, knowing that even his light weight was too much for her at this altitude, reluctant to trust his own nimble fieet. He looked down. Already the valley floor had receded into a green and gold haze. One of the Zalcasians shouted at him. He got off the mare. Now he had to urge her. The path became rapidly steeper and the surface of it crumbled. His breath came dry in his chest. When he looked down, the mountainside appeared to have no path at all; it was a jumble of barely supported rocks and long patches of scree. The Zalcasians went steadily upward. The horses were allowed to find their own way, pausing from time to time for breath, awkward, stranded, on the uneven surface. He realised that the descent, on the other side, would be worse. Choru jerked her head and made him slip. He heard one of the Zalcasians criticise her and then Ahe, their leader, shouted down to him, his voice harsh in the still air.

'Give her her head.'

He was afraid to release her, afraid that she would fall and break her beautiful white body among the rocks.

'Let her go.'

He knotted the reins on her neck and released her. At once she stopped, hung her head, breathed hard. He stood still and watched her, certain now that she would not climb. But as the horse behind came up, she went on, picking her way up the path. He followed.

The descent was worse. He feared for Choru. For himself, he was elated, joyful, and would have descended easily had he not had the horse to watch. At the bottom they stopped by a tumbling cascade to rest and eat. Refreshed, they began to ascend again, staying one night in a narrow valley. They climbed among the trees, in a vast pine forest; it was then that the snows began. There was one more pass before they came to Binala and they negotiated it in falling snow, the Zalcasians cursing and complaining that they had started out a day too late. But they did not lose a man or a horse and the only thing that fell was a package, torn from a horse as it pushed through a narrow place; the cloth covering ripped as the package bounced from rock to rock and broke open. It was the Archivist's box of Mark dyes; the ink bottles shattered, dyeing the snow with brilliant hues.

'There will be no Marks in the new City,' said Cal, but Magon got off his horse and lamented, shouting a string of curses among the echoing rocks, a string of imprecations in which his own sophisticated oaths were mixed with scurrilous words in Deep and the ugly Diridian words for female functions. He called on Aash to blight the place and the Zalcasians murmured to each other.

'It was my mother's and Ismen Antul's before her,' he said, lame-voiced, his anger gone.

Binala, among its trees, welcomed them, the wooden houses already roofed with snow. Oyno was waiting for them; they saw him, a slight figure by one of the houses, watching their descent through an optic. He walked a mile to meet them, coming up to Magon on the last slope beneath the pines and grasping his hand.

'They are well, all excellently well,' Cal heard him say. 'I had a letter from her last month.'

The courier had been and gone a dek ago, protesting that if he stayed more than a night he would stay all winter. There were letters for Magon, nothing for him. He thought briefly of M'untal, sure that among the sheaf of letters Magon had taken from the bag her protestations were writ large. The matter no longer concerned him. For a moment he saw her, asleep in the folly, and then he let the curtain fall.

He got up to push more logs into the stove. A rush of chill air came in with the opening of the inner door; Magon had left his outer clothes in the porch but the cold poured from him. He leaned on the stove. He was excited; he held his hands against the stove top, where the clay was cracked and broken from the iron box inside, but moved them continually away to gesture.

'They have assembled the large percussion gun,' he said. 'Onyo will try it in the morning. There is a bull for slaughter. Oyno wants to kill something. Zuhil insisted on payment; I gave him thirty bars for it. And the other gun, the corundum cannon – you must see it tomorrow. It requires a power casing the size of my bed: it brings Cheron into the fourth millennium. Oyno believes it will defeat anything.

'I haven't shown him my antiques from the Archive yet.'

'Krates was right. And every day moves you from your anchorage.'

'I'll allow you the pun. But I've not forgotten how to pray.'

In the morning, the house door would not budge though Cal pushed with his shoulder against it. The window was obscured by the inside of a snowdrift which the light barely penetrated. What light existed was diffuse, uncertain; on the table, the oil lamp struggled against the gloom. He heard a shovel scrape stone and presently he was able to open the door. A woman waited on the step outside, their servant, Biyana. She came in and put fresh-baked bread on the stovetop to keep warm. Cal cleared the maps from the table, and sat down.

These Zalcasian loaves, leavened, swelling, smelling of yeast and the hot oven! They tore chunks from them to dip in the stew which Biyana ladled into their bowls. Slakelike, she spoke little, deferential in Magon's presence. When Cal was alone she chattered, speaking of her children, her husband, their cattle. She gave them coffee, carried on muleback over the mountains from Cheron, but he still disliked it. Nor did he like the cow's milk which Biyana, observing his distate, had brought him. It was sweet, but fatty, warm from the udder. He put the beaker down and smiled lamely at her.

'Stand it outside in the snow for a while,' she said.

So soon after dawn the light was ethereal, the sky high, pale. The snow covered everything except the narrow path which Biyana had dug. He set down the beaker of milk. He tried to run, but the snow was as resistant as sand. The drift came to his thigh. He laughed and shouted aloud, making his way through the new hills. The pines had balked the drifts somewhat but, under the four great deodars which marked the centre of the scattered town, the snow had been blown into smooth hummocks and the windward side of each trunk wore a bandage. A bright flock trod the snow, Zalcasian girls carrying cans of milk. He kicked up sprays of snow and whistled when they noticed him.

Magon's voice rang out, but it was Zuhil he spoke to, a resonant good morning. Zuhil waved at the cliff face, dusted and ledged with snow, across the valley of the Binal. A promontory of rock, on which the snow lay like a thick carpet, jutted from the face. Magon's words came clear across the crisp distance between the house and the trees.

'He will be able to segment it with the corundum gun but the other will blow it to bits.'

'Shame!' said Zuhil. 'The pronghorns use that rock to call from in Alcuon.'

'It's a better target than the cliff face.'

'And your City wall?'

'Parts of it are ancient, mud brick or ashlars; the new sections have been carefully reconstructed using the same techniques and materials. There is a partial inner wall but that is of no consequence, a relic.'

'In the City, they are like us. The old ways are best. Surer. Right.'

'Easily circumvented. They are a sitting target. They have neither Darodha nor Zelk to hide behind.'

'They have the seas.'

'Ten miles out, the waters are Chacma's. Our sailing ships and steam vessels are picturesque, and useless. We have chopped off our wings. The City is an anachronism, a counterfeit of the second millennium in the fifth.'

'May she rest in peace.'

'Zuhil!' Magon's hand came down on his shoulder. 'We shall destroy a little but we shall rebuild. It will not be the first time the City has been altered. She will remain herself, the eternal empress.'

'Oh, I shall have no regrets; just a little sorrow.'

Cal, under the deodars, looked up at the tented branches. A flock of orange finches fed from the cones. The sky was obscured by green needles. He walked towards the house. The milk was cold, crystals of ice in it. The rancid taste had gone and he drank, gasping as the chilly fluid went down. His rkw lay where he had left it last night, on the bench near the stove. He had oiled it and practised the smooth movements of loading and disgorging the ammunition. He went out with it under his arm, a hunter in the snow. The dual tracks of Magon and Zuhil led to the training ground.

The place was a fair ringed by curious Binalans. Oyno issued orders, Magon and Zuhil were on their knees beside the two big guns. The barrel of the percussion rkw was trained on the cliff face two miles away; the blunt snouts of the corundum cannon scented the sky. A soldier peered into its guts. Very much aware of his curious and unmilitary rank as the Archivist's Assistant, he walked across the open ground and spoke to the soldier, who wriggled backward, out of the gun's interior. He looked like a Cheronese but must be a man from the City, one of the dispossessed, the husband of a Dancer perhaps – he was short and slender – or a craftswoman. His Mark was covered by his sleeves and his gloves. He banged his hands together.

'Will you be glad to go back?' said Cal.

'I've not been home for two years,' he said. 'But at least it was a straightforward choice; I don't have a woman in Cheron like so many of the others.'

'And in the City?'

'Oh yes, and five children. But they'll be all right. The house is beyond the Old Quarter. Be a shock for them though. She's a bookbinder, peaceful sort of trade. It won't make much difference to us; she's a tolerant woman, not religious.'

'And you were a bookbinder?'

'I was.' He showed his Mark, inch-wide green books in a golden press. 'Some of us were thinking of asking the Archivist to do away with these Afterwards. But I expect I'll go back to it; the Mark will remind me of what used to be.'

The soldier did not question Cal. Magon's shadow protected him and the obscured V was history, while the amatory partridges were a decorative tattoo, his personal Mark and Magon's black jest. He said, diffidently, 'The Archivist would erase it if you asked; but there would be a stain.'

He went away and stood a few paces behind Magon. Oyno approached. His hazy breath outlined his words.

'You are satisfied with the antique and the modern, Archivist?'

'So far. Let us see what they can do. I want the promontory of rock there dissected.'

'We can do that. As easily as we can fell a bull. I shall enjoy broiled beef tonight, an agreeable ending to the demonstration. I shall issue rahi.'

The Binalans were shooed away but Cal could see them peering from their doorways and a group of boys had clambered up the slippery slope of the north-eastern path to crouch among the trees there. The soldiers worked to train the guns and the metal crate which housed the charge store for the corundum gun was wheeled close.

Oyno invited Magon to fire it. There was no sound, no visible discharge, his finger was still, extended over the firing tablet; across the valley the granite smoked and a crack slowly rent it. The noise of the melting rushed at them and filled the rocky field.

'Again,' said Oyno.

The second tube delivered a lateral divide and the rock was segmented like a grey cheese. Cal saw the rock burn. The four sections hung there quaking and the flame enveloped them. A thin burst of cheering came from beneath the trees. Oyno looked round and his eye fell, as if for the first time, on Cal. He beckoned.

'Want to fire the old lady? You'll never have such a chance again.'

Cal inclined his head and wondered if he should stand straight and touch his head to authority as he had seen the soldiers do. He came forward.

'Here you are. It has a lever action, like your rkw.'

His rkw was taken from him. The firing lever of the percussion gun was painted red and an arrow showed the direction of pull. He put his right hand on it.

'Look through the sight. You'll get a better view. You'll feel the carriage move back beside you. Stand firm.'

The rock sprang at him, magnified. He might reach out and touch it. He saw the individual greys of its many faces. The snow had all been melted by the heat from the corundum gun and the new cracks were blacker than the sand of the Negaar. Black and negative. The molten rock had petrified, blobs and wens of granite, giant baubles. The goats would have to find a new belling ground. In his hand the metal shaft was rigid, warmed by his hand. He gripped it. It moved easily; all in the same moment the gun recoiled, alive, the promontory smoked and disintegrated, shattered rock dropping from the place where it had been for fifty million years, and the roar of the explosion assailed his ears. He leaned against the stilled gun and felt an immense satisfaction, a relief. This time, the soldiers had cheered. Magon had cheered too.

The bookbinder, Bashay, adjusted the tubes of the corundum gun, played with the tablet control; the tubes swung slowly round. And a boy led on the bull. He was slow and docile, led by the nose; his brown coat gleamed from a recent brushing and his shoulders were heavy. His value had been in the pendulous testicles which swung between his hocks but now he was old, he was meat; his quiet eye looked on greener pastures.

'Stand aside,' said Oyno, and the bookbinder trained the gun. Zuhil came running.

'No. No.' He waved his arms at Oyno, 'You must aim at his head; otherwise you'll spoil a valuable skin.'

The bookbinder made adjustments. Oyno himself fired the weapon. The old bull went down on his knees, his breath hanging in a cloud above his head; some blood ran from his nostrils and he fell, sudden, heavy, on the snow. His legs jerked. The boy who had led him looked amazed. He approached slowly, knelt down and touched the curling hair between his horns where the light had burned a hole smaller than his forefinger.

'We shall have to cut him up here,' said Zuhil, unmoved. 'If we may disturb your exercise for an hour or two. It's better if he doesn't freeze where he lies.'

Oyno looked at his watch.

'An hour and a half. Entertainment over.'

Cal lingered when the men had gone, and stood by the wondering boy.

'He's quite dead. So quick,' said the boy. 'It's better than a poleaxe.'

'Is it? said Cal. 'Could you fire it?'

'I can shoot pronghorns.'

It was a new type of death. In the City death was a constant; beside the corpse floating in the river, the stranded body below the bridge at low tide, the hunched figure in the doorway, were the sick begging outside the malls. They were not allowed in the Glass Mall, but it was only a few steps away, riches and desolation. On wet days, the porters cleared them from the steps of Hotel Z. By night in Alcuon, the gates of the refinery sheltered them; in Vern, they lined the promenade. He had not seen death on Paradise Hill, but it was there in Crinon's paintings and in the view from the Octagon top: the Domes of the Sleepers with their circling birds. He remembered Swan, sweating his last; the squads of corpsemen and people walking about with rags and handkerchiefs pressed to their mouths, the rats and the ragged, mangy cats.

Cats. The City teemed with the sacred animals and still the rat population increased; the cats fed on the rats and the rats on rubbish and carrion. Both climbed in trash bins to eat. He had once eaten a cat. A white cat. After the rains when Swan was down on his luck. The cat had its head in a bin. Swan had grabbed it and pulled its neck; it had roasted well and was succulent and rank.

And here was this bull, meat for a host of beggars, which Oyno and Magon had killed as a test.

'Who will eat him?' he asked.

'You will, I expect. Father says the Archivist is giving him to the army. He paid a lot for him.'

'I'm not a soldier.'

'I thought you were. You've got a gun. Are you a hunter?'

'I'm the Archivist's Assistant. I'm not a soldier, but I fight.'

Steam rose from the dead animal. The men skinned it and he saw its muscle, ruddy and patched with white fat. They spilled the bull's guts on the ground; the bloody snow was kicked and scuffed, dirtied, and mingled with the straw they had spread. Then the women came, Biyana among them and a girl with hair tied up in icemarts' tails. They took the entrails away in buckets. They gave the mighty heart to Oyno. Biyana and the girl whispered over a bowl of offal.

Magon was walking towards him.

'You haven't been here all the time?'

235

'I have. And now Biyana is cooking his balls for me.'
'My God.'

The snow began to soak into his clothes, melting under the warmth of his body. He would have done anything, gone anywhere, eaten a rat, climbed an icy cliff, sold himself on Cat Street, rather than lie in the snow waiting for Oyno's order, mute under the soldiers' discipline. He wanted to return to his books. He had neglected Huyatt, he had not opened the *Travels* for nearly four deks; his notes and pages of reflection and annotation were in disarray.

'Fire!' It was his turn again; he waited for the other men in his group. It was so easy, far less exacting than the bow. He took aim, the man-shaped target was peppered with his shots; he missed. He put his face down in the snow and did not see Oyno's ironic stare. The sergeant opened his mouth and shut it without speaking. The green flag went up. He did not miss again.

It was midday when they left the training ground. He carried Magon's weapon as well as his own; the Archivist was burdened with a new load of maps.

'Which gun will you use? he asked.

'Both. The ruby is spectacular; so is the sound of the percussion gun. We want to instil fear, we want Annalat to hear it; its din will confirm her suspicions. She will have contacted Chacma by now and found him full of incredulous disbelief. "Your Archivist, Madam? Forgive me, but you do him a grave dishonour. He makes his septennial tour, the man of letters, just as my tigers make their annual manoeuvres, the men of action. Have you no letters from him, the son of Maja Hinoor?" You know how he talks, flowery phrases, little meaning.

'Annalat has received a loyal greeting from the Allode and my despatches. My latest letters will reach her next month, the peaceful state of Zalcasia, the beauty of the mountains before snowfall. My personal letter enlarges on your struggles with Huyatt, the excellence of your projected commentary.'

'You're a bastard, Magon.' His voice was cheerful and he would have knocked Magon's gravity awry with a handful of snow had he not both rkws to carry.

'How did Zalcasia become a client state?'

'We subdued it – in the First Years. Thereafter, custom. Since the Zalcasians are animists, they see Mahun as an empathetic deity. The tribute they pay is minimal and historic – twenty head of cattle and two hundred bars in gemstones. Chacma has set them going this time, but they have always inclined towards rebellion. My mother had a splendid argument with Zuhil's uncle, who was then headman, the last time she came here. It turned on the exact weight of a sapphire which they did not

236

want to part with. She paid them for it and took it. The stone was a star sapphire, and is now in the Temple; I believe it is part of the Vern Mahun's crown. You'll be able to tell me.'

'I will?'

'I shall send you with Zuhil to the Temple.'

'Not to the Block?'

'Oyno will deal with them. He's the professional.'

Cal chewed gonads and reflected; his notes were in order, he had reread Huyatt on Zalcasia and needed to visit the summit of Kiynana. There was a road up it, a way which used to lead into Cheron before Chacma closed it with patrols and barricades. He might have been eating bark, there was so little garlic and ginger.

Ahe had come in, stamping the snow from his boots in the porch, clapping his hands together.

'Zuhil sent me.' he said. 'There is a celebration in his house. His wife was delivered today. Another son. His fifth, Ige be praised.'

'Amen!' said Magon, 'Are we to come now?'

'As you wish. The drinking has begun!'

They shot every morning, the first task, the repetition of an exercise, by rote, always. Turning his head in the interval between his shots he saw the stern mountains, and Magon looking up at them. When he looked again, Magon had gone, perhaps back to the house to pray, perhaps to sit alone and parade the imaginary army. He prayed often, sometimes walking out into the snow-arrested forests; sometimes he was away in the snowfields for two or three days together, a soldier's pack on his back.

It gave him a bleak thrill, the kind of empty pleasure a necrophiliac might feel, to contemplate this new picture of the scholar-saint, the soldier of necessity, the intellectual man-of-the-mountains, kneeling to pray upon a carpet of crystals as perfect as himself; dark, beautiful, and inaccessible, voluntarily cold and remote as the mountain peaks themselves.

The tigers were rowdy. He went with them to bathe in the hot springs. By the water, the snow was trampled and pocked with footprints, and steam hung in low clouds, veiling the naked bodies of the men and making mythical beasts of them. Perfect crystals of ice had formed on the bare branches of the gean trees nearby, winter blossom. He lay in the hot water and mused. Beside him the bookbinder, Bashay, was washing with a bar of coarse soap. He looked down at his legs, distorted under the water. His body was hard, fitter than it had ever been; the leanness came from exercise and training, from discipline; it was no longer the result of hunger, deprivation, meals which were not meals, intermittent, involuntary fasts. The muscle had been fed on the Hill. He was as fit as Bashay.

He considered. He considered Vedara, the girl with the icemart tails and comehither expression, the night of dancing in Zuhil's house, their conversation beside the stove, her ambitions, her body. He might marry her. The unformed thought almost made him laugh. But he could marry her. Galabrias whispered in his ear and he broke the memory and the surface of the water with his fist. He was a bad bargain. He had been too long without a woman, more than a year. Amarant. Vedara, the acquaintance of three days. He would marry her. Since he was in Zalcasia he would have to marry her, and be damned to Magon. What was he after all, but an employer? He would break the contract.

Vedara. She would wait here for him, here in the mountains until the battle was over. He would be one like the soldiers, home to comfort, home to his own. Her children would be his. And when he longed for the City, they would go there. He would buy a house in the Silversmiths' Quarter, one of those substantial villas in a garden, a house like Slake's. His mind was made up. Ironic that he had travelled over a thousand miles to discover that he, like any Diridian, wanted his own woman.

He asked Bashay for the soap, ducked his head and scrubbed vigorously. Rafe's blond cut had gone, grown out and shorn away in Diridion. Vedara's hair was thick and black, confined by the white tails, strung with coloured beads. When she untied it and freed herself of her furs – but he saw Magon praying in the chantry and the fret of curls which touched the back of his neck.

'You're quiet,' said Bashay. 'Something on your mind?'

'Binalan girl.' He could see her now, tapping her feet to the tune of the fiddle.

Damn Magon. He was bored. Magon did not need a nurse; who, having found a god, needs a slave? He would marry her and celebrate the new equality.

'Thanks,' he said to the bookbinder.

'What for?'

'Settling a question.'

'I didn't say anything.'

The snow was exquisitely cold. He danced from foot to foot while he wiped his body on Bashay's towel. A snowball hit him on the neck. Benet was there, already gathering more snow. They spoke together, the cold making their words speedy and breathless. Some of the others were throwing snow, but he avoided them and dressed.

The Book was open on the table beside Magon, a ribbon marking his place in it, but Magon, reclining on the bench, his back against the wall, stared at the window.

'I was thinking,' he said, 'Of snow and ice, frozen water and glass. We are a race of alchemists; we can make a transparent miracle, the free passage of light through transmuted sand, engines, cities, streets, shops, tall buildings, statues in our own image. We travelled the galaxy. But when we touch each other, everything turns to mud.'

'Mud is just earth and water. The first people were made from mud.'

'Or cloud, or water. Religion is the prime symbolist.'

'Rice grows in mud,' said Cal. 'Pots are made of it.'

'And corn grows in irrigated earth. I know what you are trying to say – all flesh is grass and all grass flesh. The separation is temporary, and only lasts one lifetime.'

'You've come back to Her!'

'No. The controlling principle, the spark of creation, comes from God.'

'Rubbish. It's anyone's. Look at Amarant, Crinon, Chenodor.'

'They are subsidiary creators. Monos is the origin. We return to him, we are all pieces of his design continually arranged in new patterns. Fragments of the stars, pieces of the moon, the spawn of the sun.'

'There are huge ice crystals on the trees near the spring. An optic would transform them into stars.'

'You confuse the poetic and the material. Have they gone?'

'No. They were throwing snowballs when I left. Benet was there.'

'Oyno promoted him. He's a corporal now.'

'Will he stay with Oyno?'

'For the time being.'

Cal came forward. A loaf stood on the table, beside Magon's neat papers, the capped pen and closed inkwell, and he broke off a piece of it to eat. He was hungry now. He wished Biyana would come with the midday meal. He sat on his bed and when he had eaten half the crust, he said,

'I danced with a girl in Zuhil's house.'

'Vedara. I saw you.'

'I went to her cousin's house yesterday; Vedara was there. When I was lying in the spring I thought of marrying her.'

He saw Magon attempt to react calmly, drawing in a breath, slowly letting it go.

'It's the only way to have a woman in Zalcasia, isn't it?

'I'm sorry. In Diridion I gave you your freedom, and I had no right to do that, for you never belonged to me. How can one soul own another? Is that what marriage is?'

'Magon.'

'You would come back here?'

'I thought of spending part of the year here, the rest in the City.'

'Yes. You can work in the Archive and write when you are in Zalcasia. This place suits you. If I fail, it is a good refuge.'

'You won't fail.'

'What does she say?'

'I haven't asked her.'

'Good. Zalcasian marriages are strict matters. There is a ritual to observe.'

'What should I do?'

'You expect me to advise you as well?' He smiled, but painfully. 'Well then, the first signal is a gift for her father. Don't go into the house, don't ask for him, but leave your gift in the porch. It must be something you value and something which is valuable in itself; I suggest your copy of Huyatt,'

'I can't give him that!'

'You should. Anything less might convey the idea that you take the matter lightly. But I expect honour will be satisfied – and the gods will certainly be amused – if you give him Rafe's copy. It cost a lot more than mine – yours.'

'Then what?'

'Wait. Don't try to see Vedara. Her father will contact you.'

'I'll go now. Where does he live?'

He found the gold-tooled book.

'He lives in the last house, westward. Take the track beside Zuhil's house.'

Cal stamped his boots on in the porch. The inner door was still open and already Magon had lit the lamp although, outside, it was day. Magon's shadow fell across him.

'Are you sure about this? Cal?'

'Of course I am.' He went out quickly, treading the snow firmly. The sky above the mountains was blue, the blue shadows on the snow copies of their unremitting shapes. When he had delivered the book he walked resolutely back; he had changed the direction, he had moved the world himself. As he approached the house, the smell of the meat Biyana had just carried in came to him, rich with the blood of the bull.

Vedara began to occupy his mind. Her father, returning his gift in kind, came with a leather game bag, sat by the stove and talked to him through Magon – as if he did not speak, read, and write Zalcasian. He valued his daughter, he said, she was clever at sewing and a good cook, he especially valued her work in winter when she skinned the marts and fitchets he brought in. If she must marry a foreigner then, he supposed, a rich one was preferable: but had he any real skills? Words were all very well in their place but no one could eat a book. Vedara was all he had. Since the death of her mother she had been everything to him. And she wasn't ugly.

'My name is Dibor,' he said. 'Like by father before me. And my wife, her mother, was Naya, Shayl's daughter. I don't want Vedara to spoil her own name by marrying a man from the City when she can marry anyone. She has plenty of admirers. She could marry Gesir.'

Under her furs, Vedara could have been ugly, could have concealed

240

any number of blemishes, rolls of fat, sagging breasts, a pig in a poke. He found himself staring at her thick clothes, trying to solve the puzzle, fitting limb to limb. Within a dek she was the focus of his existence. He could not see her without wanting her. She was there when he dreamed.

Dibor summoned him abruptly one night. His house was full of female relatives, Vedara nowhere to be seen. He had been accepted and Dibor led him from one woman to the next. The women inspected him closely and questioned him about his prospects. When they came to the end of the line, Dibor lifted up his arm, as if he were the victor of a contest, and announced the betrothal.

'When he hunts the ounce,' said Dibor, 'he will not fail.'

Vedara walked up to him in the space between the deodars and kissed him openly. There was time to waste in Binala.

'The marriage confirms the betrothal,' said his woman. 'We have to make a start now in case we don't agree.'

'Here?'

'You must walk with me – every day until the wedding. It is permitted.'

He followed her into the forest, watching her duck under laden branches, the snow powdering her boots and trousers. She waited for him and took his hand, bold now as any City woman. Amita had led him among the burning rubbish pits until they reached the banks of the Ayal. Afterwards they had bathed in its nidorous waters. The trees enclosed them in green rooms of sharpened sound, one leading into another. They came to one where the snow was trodden and scuffed.

'Sit down here,' whispered Vedara, 'By the logs. Ssh!'

He obeyed her. In the lee of the piled trunks, the snowcoat was thin. Vedara brushed it aside. He sat where she made him, close against her.

'Now look. Your birds.'

The black partridge strutted to his dancing floor. He was small, arrogant as the miniature jungle-fowls of the City.

Vedara smiled at him. 'Alcuon will soon be here,' she said. 'These are the birds of hope. Their mating signals the snowmelt.'

The hen birds were drab, without the blue primaries and red wing covers, devoid of the bronze crest which stood up like a hayrack. They circled the leck. Another cock entered the arena, and another. They fought like jungle-fowls, flying at each other with legs and spurs outstretched. The hens, scratching for moss under the snow, took no notice. He never saw if the pretty Tayali's assertions were true, because his mouth and his hands were occupied with the woman and his mind with delirious pride because he, the useless man from the City, was her first.

Oyno and Dibor took him away from these rediscovered pleasures.

'The snow's right and the ounces hungry,' said Dibor. 'Tomorrow at

241

daybreak.' He put a fatherly arm round Cal. 'Does my little girl please you?'

The freedoms of the street had deserted him. He blushed.

The snow had a last desperate crispness. Their feet made giant prints in its melting undercoat but, above the town, the snow was still coherent and they moved more easily, Cal and Magon, Oyno and Dibor, Ahe, and the big man, the ounce hunter, Gesir.

Gesir picked up the tracks of the leopard. They ran, as she had done, in a supple line over the surface of the snow; further on, the prints were deeper. She had crept, and the marks her lashing tail had made were wide sweeps in the snow. Snow had drifted and caught in the cracks between the rocks of the bare turrent which the wind swept clean. The Wind blew in his face and chilled him through his heavy clothing. She had eaten, and was resting in a hollow below the rocks, the dark spots in her white coat black patches of melt. Gesir made a brief gesture with his left hand, and retired. The leopard was his, or Magon's. He heard the click as Magon armed his weapon and then the rattle of the disgorger.

The eyes of the snow leopard were yellow suns in partial eclipse.

'Yours,' said Magon. Never first, he looked round and saw the tension in the group of men behind him.

'You are the 'groom,' said Magon.

He raised his rkw. The neck of the leopard, where he had been told to aim, was in his sights, a sea of black catspaws. He moved the weapon and saw her golden eyes again. She looked down the hill, into the tree-line. He heard a mass of snow fall there, far below. Her spots shimmered. She washed herself, licking her paws clean of the last of her kill. All that marked it was a small patch of red on the snow. Then she looked up and he felt her cognition. She looked at him and he heard Magon whisper his name. He sighted again, squeezed, and saw the last leap of the snow leopard. A ragged burst of clapping celebrated it.

'A bit slow,' said Dibor, coming up to clap him, rough, approving, on the back. 'It's always difficult, the first time. I remember my first ounce more clearly than my first woman.'

He remembered afterwards that Gesir's blue gaze had conveyed an unwanted comradeship.

Vedara took the heavy skin from him. The leopard, flayed naked, they had left for the bearded vultures. He would have preferred to bring her flowers, some of the pale anemones which reflected the daylight under the birches at the valley head, or a bunch of those green and white cups which thrust from the snow. She was flushed and excited. She smoothed the spotted fur with a brown and bloodstained hand to which clung the down of the pigeons she had been plucking when he entered and which now lay as naked as the leopard, their pink feet extended. There were pigeon feathers in her hair and he removed some of them and kissed her.

242

'What a skin,' she said. 'What beautiful fur – one for me, at last. A lovely ounce pelt.'

When he heard the adjective again next morning, on his wedding day, it issued from Oyno's thin lips, sighing on the cold air and creeping into Pikat's ear. He passed them quickly so that he would not hear them slander him.

She was lovely. She wore layers of striped skirts, each one shorter than the one beneath it, and when she spun, turning from one guest to another in her excitement, he saw her knees.

The guests made a ring in the clearing. He stood beside Vedara on the ounce skin and felt drops of water splashing from the deodar behind them. The snow itself was altered, a discoloured mush of earth, ice, and water. There were flowers in the shaman's hands and Vedara's hair. Although he never turned, he felt Magon looking at him.

The skin, when it was laid on their bed, became a pleasure ground and he appreciated the differing textures of fur and skin. She was lovely, a beautiful woman. For once, he made no comparisons and they fell asleep like all enthusiastic lovers, with their arms round one another. He awoke with leaden arms, heated in the glow from the open stove and Vedara hot as coals beside him. He examined the ring she had given him, the silver predators which encircled it and his finger above the platinum band he had got from Rafe Dayamit. He had given her the Tayal embroidery which she had held up in various situations against the wooden walls, trying out the effect of its bright colours in the dim light of the – his! – house. He sat in the fan of heat, on the edge of the bed, thinking in warm, sleepy, dislocated images, of Vedara's body and then, as he became cold and wakeful, of Magon, alone in the guest house.

'Kiynana,' repeated Zuhil. 'Your traveller climbed Kiynana?'

He looked at Magon for confirmation.

'You may read it in the *Travels*,' said Magon, 'but – in answer to your next question – he makes no mention of Shalusha.'

'I can't believe he missed it! It lies due north of the peak; you need only round the cairn to see it.'

'If he had no optic?'

'He would see a green valley like any other.'

'Then that is the answer. There are several passages on the beauties of the Zalcasian valleys.'

Cal had listened, silent.

'What is Shalusha? Why is it so important?'

'It is the City's Burnt Lands, the Valley of Corruption, the Cup of Death.'

'Here?'

'Ninety-five miles away. In the old days before the Reformation the

243

Gynarchy sent beggars and deviants there to work out a salvation between the chemical stews and irradiated garbage. The valley itself was burnt – a barren landscape without vegetation. Time has masked the scars but they still send criminals there to eat and drink the poisons, and the indigent population is – as you will see. . . .

'You still want to go?'

'I must. If I don't there will be a gap in the book.'

'Very well. I will come with you and we will take Ahe to guide us.'

Kiynana stood up before them and Cal looked at her rocky shoulders. Snow covered her head.

'Which way?' he said to Ahe.

Ahe indicated the right flank of the mountain.

'There. The road runs east of that buttress. It is not so hard, a better road than the one from Sidend. But we will save the horses. We can leave them at Latun. There is a rest house and my cousin is shaman.'

The shrines they passed were low, built of rocks picked up from the slopes around them, inhabited by little deities, pot-bellied demons and willowy representations of tree and water spirits.

'Kiynana is a little mountain,' said Ahe. 'A child. The adults live in the west. Do you see them, there? They are not clouds or illusions. That is High Zalcasia. I have been there once, but the country is harsh. The histories tell of women who came from the City to climb Herela, but they lie: who would willingly climb twenty-seven thousand feet to risk death and the displeasure of the Great Mother – besides the allmi live in her snows.'

It was a valley like the one which cradled Binala, like the high grazing ground where he and Magon had raced their horses, a bowl of nacrous greens and blues, the central lake a calm sapphire eye. He could hear the birds singing far below.

But high grey cliffs surrounded it, separating the world of Shalusha from the mountaintops which ringed it, distancing the place from the world outside. Magon took the double optic from its case and focused it. 'It looks like another paradise,' he said. 'Guna before strife or sex.' He scanned the valley floor and then, crouched and still, fell silent. The steady brown hands began to shake and he lowered the optic.

'If you want to see perdition, then look by the water. There you will see the effects of poison and experimentation, the unfortunate Surrogates. Some of them were given the hearts of pigs and baboons; in other groups (they live in the farthest reservations) the gene pool has been irredeemably corrupted – so they can never be freed,' he said. He handed Cal the glass. There was no need to alter the focus and he looked into the Burnt Lands. The microcosmos rushed at him. Nothing was burnt. Lush growth masked the lesser iniquities. Flowers grew in the grass on the valley floor and the trees were strong and tall, too tall. The lake was ringed by a gravel shore and small dwelling houses roofed with stones and turf. Three boats were run up on the shore, fishing nets dried on poles. A man squatted near one of the boats, mending a net. His hands plying the netting needle were expert, quick and sure. They were big hands, capable instruments, human hands with six fingers each. When he shifted to ease his limbs, the twisted mass of flesh which was his right foot became visible. Cal's hands were steady on the optic. Anyone could see worse in the Beggars' Reserve and outside every metro entrance, their trollies and begging notices the props of their trade.

Outside one of the houses was a woman and a child. The child held up its arms and the woman, bending and unfastening her shabby cymar in the same movement, took it up and began to suckle it. Her face was marked with brown stains, permanent pigmentation, malfunctioning melanin like the skin of an old white woman. The child, pulling on her nipple with a soft and greedy mouth, had no eyes. He closed his own and, opening them wide against the glass, looked again. Where the eyes should have been was a blank expanse of skin undisturbed by lids, lashes, or brows.

He put down the optic and looked at Magon. Never before had he seen such an expression on Magon's face, a compound of the quintessential bitterness of his spirit and the integral inversion which shaped him.

'The civilisation which lauds fecundity has produced this,' he said. 'And they require Aash and her deathdance as well. Seen enough?'

'No.'

'It's not a peepshow. I don't know why I agreed to come here.' He got up abruptly and walked away.

'I know what it is; I have to look,' said Cal mildly, after him.

The glass discovered more tableaux vivants. A man with pendulous folds of skin about his chest and neck threw a stick for a dog. Two women, supporting themselves on crutches, walked over the grass; a lamb ran at their heels. It was when he saw the man with breasts that he dropped the glass. He retrieved it, admonished himself with a whore's curse, and looked again. The creature was swimming in clear water at the head of the lake, disporting itself amongst the fish, slanting a piece of mirror glass this way and that to admire its doubled set of sexual organs. He bit his lip and looked the other way.

There were many herd animals which looked normal, even larger than usual; but they had the poison in their flesh. The noxious waters spilled over high falls into Cheron, and he watched the rainbow spray. He wondered how much of it found its way into the Ayal and Maralis; if it was responsible for the vegetable deformity he had seen displayed in the fruit market: double tomatoes, corkscrew chillies, peaches and pomelos with

245

warts, tumours of sweet flesh; if it was responsible for the infirm beggars; if indeed the dark and orgiastic wine which Magon drank, the Ceremana from Baia over the knife-edged mountains to the south, was tainted. At the western end of the valley a tumbled mass of rock showed him where the old entrance to Shalusha had been blasted and closed in 450. Since then, the Matriarchy had employed Cheronese airpolice for the final journey. The victims of the Nines were lowered helplessly into their prison, damned angels falling from a pitiless sky. He looked once more at the fisherman's house by the lakeside, but the odd couple and their child were gone, and only a dog stood there, slowly wagging its tail. He put the optic back in its case.

Magon looked into Baia, his eyes on the eternal snows of Mount Bai. Cal put the strap of the optic case into his right hand, and squeezed the hand. It was cold, as if its usual warmth had retreated deep inside the massive frame, a defence against the cold of the summit and the horrors of the valley below. Ahe, at the fire, was drinking hot coffee, and Cal took the proffered cup and drank the bitter liquid: there was nothing else. He sat down and tightened the laces of his boots; then he got out his notebook and scribbled a page of impressions. Magon, when he came to the fire, was brisk, his talk of everyday matters.

Ahe, unhurried, doused the fire. He caught up with them halfway to the village, his even mountainman's stride outpacing Cal.

At home, Cal was silent. Vedara pressed him, at first with kisses and then with words. In Diridion they called it nagging and her gentle, persistent words bit. He described the journey to Kiynana, the wayside shrines and Ahe's bluff cousin who had blessed him and confirmed him in this strange and vow-encompassed state.

Magon climbed quickly. The path had become a variable streambed; runnels coursed around the larger stones and his boots ground into a slurry of water, mud, and gravel. Cal watched him go, diminishing, until he was a black silhouette against the sky, a solitary pilgrim; once he lifted a hand and Cal lifted his own right hand in reply before turning back under the trees, homeward, to Vedara.

Up here, he was redeemed. Above the trees, Binala and the lakes, far higher than the City. He was separate and free, delivered from responsibility, people, the damnable burdens they imposed; for a short time outside the struggle and the scheming, away from Raist Chenodor's schedules, from Zuhil and his irregulars, from Oyno, his practicalities and the army; from Cal. Alone.

He loved solitude. He had four hours to enjoy, a holiday, an escape, the four hours it would take him to walk the seventeen miles to the Oaipe valley, but he would make it five and pause in the liriodendron wood to examine the passionless flowers, the disinterest of the naked branches and the timeless stones among their roots; to listen.

When Magon came to the wood, he closed his mind. The mass of words faded, the clamour of voices, his own insistent conscience and the noise of the past died and he looked at the liriodendrons. Each new flower, and they came before the leaves, was a biting green. They were so different from the magnolias on the Hill, these distant cousins without conscience or memory, grouped in the hollow of the mountainside for nobody's delectation. They were his only because he had found them, his for the time he chose to regard them. Each Alcuon the buds opened and the flowers had their brief season; they closed and died; in late Vern the trees were a shower of lemon and gold. For a season the trees stood dormant until the new Alcuon. Scuffing the leaf fall, as he had ten years ago, he lifted the skeletons, fragile dissolving shapes, and watched them fall into the mould.

Green flowers intrigued him, seeming a perversity of Mahun, as perverse as his own habit of thinking of her – still – as an earth goddesss, the quiescent and accepting counter to the dry intellect and fiery discipline of his desert god. Hellebores, euphorbias, limes, dondia, moschatel, Xhara's pot of orchids, the perfumed tobacco flowers Crinon grew along the woodland path, they all possessed the same ethereal quality, being without the insistent colour of other flowers, secret and subdued. A sparrow perched and shredded some of the blossom. There was plenty. One sparrow would not waste the resources of the wood as his own kind had despoiled the virgin beauty of Vern and Maralis, planting lilies where once the forests had swept to the shore. But he would not think of that; he would listen.

He leaned against one of the trees. The wood was full of noises, vegetable creaks from the moving twigs and branches, water running down the rocks, water sucking and bubbling in the soil under his feet, the sparrow's brittle chirps, his own breathing, and the constant beating of his heart. Be still, he said to his soul.

He was a child again, free to look, to absorb without question, without foreknowledge, prejudice, or fear, in the primeval years before corruption; when the only use for the body is in walking, running, jumping, climbing, breathing; when wind and water, sky and sun, suffice, when a strip of woodland is an enchanted forest; before lust, power, anger, greed, the myriad uncounted words in the Archive, oil paintings from the far side of the galaxy, pretty boys, a god in his own image, the thumbprint of himself on the next generation.

But such a view of childhood was false. As a child, angry with his mother, he had screamed; he had stolen toys from Crinon, lusted after sweets and the cakes the housekeeper made, felt pride in his ability to master any wilful pony, read any language, write with the control and expressions of an adult; he had basked and gloried in the praise of his mother and others, telling him how clever he was, how tall, how strong, how beautiful. And the infinite moment when, his back against the rough tree bark, he and the air, the wood and the water had been one, was gone, many hurrying minutes ago.

At the foot of the Oaipe valley, he sat down on a stone. The landscape closed in above him, the flank of Zelk was near, hanging above him, steep and hard. Above the scree he saw the edge of the green grass field which miraculously grew there, unsullied, ungrazed, a paradise of delicate mountain flowers. The dark mouths of the old shamans' retreats, and the little cupola of stone which covered Xynak, were visible. The tomb of the ancient anchorite was sealed with a block of pink Baian limestone, every word and relief worn from it, but in the granite paving which surrounded the tomb, the single word Monos was cut in Crypto-Maralay and in the Archive was the second millennium copy of a first millennium text which told Xynak's story, Xynak, the original heretic. The valley was a place of lost legends: like every ancient civilisation, his own was rich in countless, overlapping, repetitive tales, stories of buried wonders, hidden treasures, marvellous tombs, petrified queens, sleeping armies and frozen Gynarchs to whom the touch of eternal frost was no more than a brief sleep in the afternoon.

He knew exactly what to do. He had worked so many night hours in the Forbidden Archive. In Zalcasia, he had practised the routine every night through the latter days of Udan and into Alcuon, being alone. If Cal had been present (who else could he trust, beside Crinon?), he would have shared his knowledge. He had modified the Tribute of Diridion, until it obeyed him. He got up and climbed the slope.

The grass had grown tall. He pushed the stems aside. The same yellow flowers were in bloom. He would have shared these fields also, but Cal had chosen to set his feet in another place.

He went straight to the centremost cave. His footprint was still there, in a patch of mud, three deks old. Pausing, he unslung the trooper's pack he carried and unbuckled it. From it he took a torch and the smooth black rectangle which was the Tribute of Diridion. He set them on the ground while he extracted and assembled the small rkw. Then, shouldering the pack and the rkw and taking the torch and the Tribute in his hands, he went into the cave. The box was narrow and light, black plastic, altered oil; he pressed the single key on the face of it and, holding it close to his face, spoke. Crinon's voice rang out, 'Magon,' and while it echoed, 'Crinon,' he said. Their names echoed. The synthesised voice made him his sister's equal. He walked on.

The forbidding entrance was a deception; the cavern was dim and shallow, littered with fallen rocks. His torch illuminated a section of wall and lit up a fold in the rock.

The situation was ridiculous. That fold of rock and himself, alone and heroic, like the chief actor in a moving picture twenty-five centuries ago; the rock was made of moulded plastics and it concealed a rubber-covered switch. He felt for it. They had been consummate engineers, those women of the Last Days. The counterfeit rock lifted like a theatre curtain; behind it was a very ordinary door, larger than a house door, of grey metal (there was a scratch) painted grey. He held the Tribute between his teeth while he took the key from his belt. It was small and wardless, like a lockpick; he had inherited it with the rest of the Archivist's keys. He put it into the lock and the lock, recognising it, emitted a high-pitched squeal. He opened the door.

The passageway was dark, the torch becoming an encumbrance. He felt for the light switch. There it was. The lights came on, white orbs fixed at regular intervals along the wall. He followed the passage until he reached a triple junction. The right-hand tunnel led to the power house, the left to the purification plant. He went straight on and came to double swing doors. The antechamber beyond was floored with grey rubber tiles and the door opposite him was blue: what other colour could they choose but Hers, to safeguard their treasure? To the right of the door was a tiny rectangular grille, and he held the Tribute against it and spoke the words which had waited for him in the Forbidden Archive. His altered voice hissed in the receiver and the blue door slid aside. He went into his kingdom.

The light in the chamber was cold and blue, like the light on *Daystar's* transport deck; the air was chill. There were four hundred and fifty cryomorphs. Enough to take the unresistant City on their own. Four hundred and forty of them lay in the ranks of body bays. Six of the remaining ten, all women, lay on slabs in a separate room with transparent walls and three, one of them male, lay in more elaborate bays, with screens, consoles, and keyboards outside. The six were the officers and the three the medics who would awaken the rest. The last cryomorph, alone on a dais, was the commander, Saissa Hinoor M'una. She was his ancestor, the grandmother of his grandmothers. Forty generations ago she had given birth to the daughter who had continued the line. She looked like Crinon, and he heard a rush of sound in the silent chamber, the involuntary gasp which came from him as he faced her. Her dark hair was stiff and white under the preservative frost, the ice which glazed her limbs and silvered her skin: Crinon asleep outside her time. She was an anachronism, a female solider; not a Temple archer, picturesque and timewarped with her Talong bow and quiver full of arrows, not a security guard armed with a stave, but a woman trained to the utmost, a natural killer, the habitual user of an rkw: he would use the one incongruity to destroy the other. He put his pack on the floor and the voice synthesiser in his pocket; he cradled his gun. He stared at his ancestor for a long time.

Magon walked about among the body bays, from rank to rank. The troopers were arrayed in tens, of many colors and many physical types: flat-chested, sub-mammarial athletic fighters bred for speed and deadliness; full-breasted total women who might wake and live to breed; slender, sculptural virgins, ice-maidens dedicated to Mahun. They were all as tall as he was. Fifty were true agamites, asexual beings, flesh, blood, and bone untramelled by sexual organs. Their body hair was fine, silken floss like the beard of a pubescent boy, but where the soft male flower or the coarse hairy lips of a woman should be was a negation, a smooth mound, a barren construction of flesh over the pelvic bone, the bare china thighs of a doll. He stared at them; here he could linger undisturbed by the presence of Cal, the accusing finger from the Depths, linger to stare at and absorb the enormity of the construction, the presumption of the creators of these experimental primates. He could not think of them as human, but he pitied them as he pitied Slake and the misdirected Depthers and frail Prostitutes.

Twenty-five cryomorphs were male, the corundum gunners. The expression on his face was that of one returned from Aash; the presence of the familiar bodies, well-muscled and straight-limbed, calmed him. One of the gunners had straight brown hair and a sullen expression like an abstracted Cal; but Cal, on ceasing to ponder, would stretch his legs, smile, and give voice to one of his surprising conclusions in that hoarse voice which seemed to have absorbed both the dream and the drug, the powdered lily leaf, perhaps in Maralay, Diridian, or Vernian, using his facility with words, in Deep or in his own teasing blend of demotic and hieratic, every syllable suffused with the accents of the City. The cryomorph gunners had trained like monks. I am as cold as they, he thought, staring at the naked men, ice-cold, love and pain extracted in the desert heat; a reactive fighting automaton, all passion spent.

He had not eaten for seven hours; he returned to his pack and his ancestor and, sitting on the steps of her dais, ate a piece of the composite rationblock Oyno had given him for his five-day retreat. The cryomorphs ate similar food, but their guts had been modified to take it. It was vile stuff, tasting like sweet meat soup laced with fish oil.

13.10. The awakening would take more than a hundred hours and he would be unable to sleep during the first forty-eight of them. For one minute – he timed it – he allowed himself to think deliberately of Cal, the golden boy who swam against the tide, his grace unabated, his tenacity always on trial, of the reality of his tight hold that morning off the Point. And Crinon, a warm and humane version of Saissa Hinoor, would be asleep still, uncovered in the heat of the Garden House, perhaps beside Xhara', perhaps alone. He would wake the male medic first: the women might be terrifying, sisters and spiritual clones of Hyason Sarin.

*   *   *

He made no prayer, but touched five fingers to his forehead in the Monoclid gesture acknowledging submission.

Before he began, he put on one of the protective gloves and, reaching into the central body bay, turned the man's necktag so that he could read his name: MO Dur Kunai M'unor. Once (upon a time) he had known a Kunai, a lissom boy who had passed a Vern afternoon with him on the beach at Evanul. He pulled off the glove with dismissive haste and set his hands on the keyboard.

The system demanded no password; such a code could not have been abandoned to time and chance. He pressed the initiate key and the dark screen filled with light. Letters appeared. 'Welcome, Sister,' said the trustful machine as he read the blue letters, its woman's voice melodious. He laughed, and the tiled walls resonated until the hall was filled with a baritone shout. Then he addressed the machine through the Tribute. He typed carefully: 'Thaw #2.' The screen flashed at him, red words of caution; Illegal syntax, it said, Mistake, and the voice echoed the written word. The system paused; he, waiting there, saw his scheme in ruins, the City untaken, Annalat predominant. He waited for the undetectable shroud of halogen, for the maw of the spiderwoman, the liquid amber, to engulf him.

No one (in the world) knew where he was. He felt blind panic embrace him – but they would find him, eventually, rotting amongst the frozen bodies – except that they could not get in. There would be no release, no gentle Stream to free his soul, not even the beaks of vultures. He looked up from the keyboard at the tiled walls of his mausoleum.

Then – he lived! – the mellifluous voice spoke a gentle prompt: 'Please wake SMO S'an Troya M'una first.' His keystrokes were swift now: 'Thaw #1.' When he pressed the termination key, a temperature chart appeared immediately on the screen. He saw that the cryo's temperature was −70. To achieve a normal body temperature, life, would take nine hours: even so, the thaw was swift, additives to the lymphatic and circulatory systems allowed such acceleration. She was a sophisticated cryo; the troopers, with their reduced intelligence, each took four hours. The three adjacent systems which would monitor her progress came to life beside him. He pushed back the stool and sat down again, to watch the woman awake.

Gradually, the frost faded and he saw her clearly. She was slender, olive-skinned like himself, more than six feet tall. Her legs were strong and straight, her fatless breasts functional on her muscular frame. Except for the close cap on her head, the hair had been shaved from her body as if she and not the cryogenic system were about to give birth. The operatives had done that when they packed the orifices; it made a lissom sculpture of her and exposed her to his gaze.

He looked at the screens. Her temperature had risen, hovering on 80, and her heart began to beat. He saw the first trace leap across the screen, flutter, and settle into a steady rhythm. Yet the heart beat in the unfinished foetus. Presently, she began to breathe. He saw it with delight, the graph on the screen and the sudden change in the nascent body on the slab. She was beautiful. She was his own creation. Without him she would have remained buried in the mountain, not dead yet never living.

She clenched and unclenched her hands. She began to shiver, the tremor taking her whole body; she gagged, choking. Dreamer that he was! He snatched up the long forceps and the metal bowl and stepped into the bay. The packing, cold, damp, clean, came easily out of her mouth, nostrils, and ears. Her eyes showed consciousness. He heard her voice: she groaned and tried to reach her feet with her hands. He took hold of the chill feet and rubbed them. Above the murmur of the extraction pump, he heard his own startled breaths and her even inhalations.

Her eyes moved; she was aware of his presence. Her feet were warmer, damp and red. The bowl and forceps reminded him. He put them near her right hand.

'You had better finish the rest,' he said in Maralay, embarrassed, afraid of the implied intimacy at the heart of her being, that dark labyrinth, the moist female sanctuary he had only once essayed. He turned away and stood with his arms folded.

Behind him, she moved. He heard the forceps clink on the bowl, he heard the swift and efficient sound of drawers and doors being opened. When he turned round, she was clothed in fresh grey fatigues, the emblems and badges of her rank across her chest. She held a hypodermic in her right hand and was injecting the nutrients and stimulants she needed. She put down the syringe.

'What time is it?' she asked, as if she had woken from a good night's sleep. The voice was light and high, a girl's voice, not a woman's.

'It is the afternoon of Fiorin, Isk 35, Alcuon, 4502,' he said.

'Four five o two?' She emphasised the four, and repeated the phrase. '4502.'

Her face was a blank; she looked as though she might cry. Forgetting her limitations, he went to her and held her against his breast, as Crinon had held him when their mother died, as he had held Cal when he was reprieved from death. The cryomorph released herself from his embrace.

'Your voice is deep,' she said, and he knew that he would have to use the synthesiser most of the time. These three medics and Saissa were the most complete of the force. Before her induction, before the processing, her IR had been high. She did not seem aware of his sex, nor did she offer anything, no smile, no thanks, no further words, no questions.

252

'How old are you?' he asked, the irrelevant, obvious question.

'I am twenty-two.'

One thousand and four, plus twenty-two. The centuries' flow had altered her less than wind alters granite.

'Are you from the City?'

'The City? Yes – the City.' She paused. He wondered what images assailed her memory. 'We must work hard to save her.'

His fraternal responses were redundant, irrelevant to her invaded mind. She walked past him, almost as if he were not there, and mechanically began the process which would awaken her two companions. Saddened that his Galatea was imperfect, he withdrew, and watched her operate the machinery with her delicate, programmed, efficiency.

The male medic, Kunai, obeyed him without question, without any change of expression; he walked briskly between the rows of troopers until he came to the bays where the gunners lay in frozen stasis, naked, weaponless. Magon followed him. Hero's story had impressed him years ago, binding the unbegun intention in him. Hero's account of his own awakening was a classic of the fourth millennium; here were twenty-five men who had also lived beyond their allotted span, like the figure of Hero aboard *Daystar*, waxen echoes of reality, except that these were not cast grease but cold flesh to whom the silent medic would bring heat. He had avoided the soldiers in Binala; now he would watch these conjured to life. Their capacity for independent action had been removed, their synapses selectively drained. Innocently, hopefully, they had achieved Talong, they had become absolute action. They would ask no questions. Like the firstborn, Troya, they were especially his and he would lead them. He leaned against the smooth wall, the rkw slung from his shoulder, and watched Kunai work his magic.

The air had warmed by ten degrees perhaps. The tiled halls were no longer silent as Troya and Xanchen woke the troopers. He heard human footsteps, coughs, the conversations of a thousand years ago.

He pulled pen and notebook from the inner pocket of his soldier's tunic. The first record would be pictorial; later, he would catalogue their names. The men woke slowly, each one arrested for minutes at a time; there was plenty of time for his exact pen to record each attitude. He covered pages with overlapping drawings, whole figures, limbs, fine details of fingers and feet, torsoes, muscles, faces, profiles, the divine fingerprints of a spinal column.

The first one was complete, alive, a perfect being reaching for his greybrown clothes; dressing, arraying himself. Others were rising up from their beds. He felt that his fingers, moving the pen, his brain, had made them. It was a long time before they could speak or stand properly. He watched them gather, a silent company. Kunai wiped his hands on a cloth.

253

Magon put away his drawings, breathing on the last page to dry it. He spoke into the Tribute, commanding the men to arm themselves. The gunners moved off, a compact body, along the aisle; at the end of it a broad space was lined with the arsenals, steel-shuttered, barred. Magon spoke into the Tribute, and they opened. Inside, the weapons gleamed. Each gunner took his own weapon.

It was clear from their developing conversations that the events immediately before their entombment had been erased from their memories. They spoke of the City. The picture their words gave him was that of an altered conurbation, as recognisable as reality transformed in a dream. They spoke of high walkways, of plants which spilled from terrace to terrace, of hanging gardens, of the hoppers which sped beneath the aerial pedestrianways; of the spaceport and the airport, of glories now fallen, of the blaze of light in the night-time City, of restaurants, dance palaces, bars, husk, and dust, relatives, lovers, and friends. They spoke of the new Temple building and of celebrations already being planned for the Octagon's first millennium. To this, his response was physical, a shiver born of memory and imagination combined. If he lived – but his would need to be a tenure longer than that of Herkel – he would celebrate its second.

One rkw remained in the arsenal; Magon counted the men and found there were only twenty four. He turned back.

The brown-haired boy had not awoken. Anger overwhelmed him and while he struggled with it, Kunai waited, as unresponsive and patient as a doll.

'What should we do with him?' he asked Kunai.

'He must be left behind; provision was made for the living only,' the medic replied in his unvarying voice.

Magon shuddered with involuntary dread. He had not touched dead flesh for fourteen years, not since the last desperate kiss he had given his dead mother. Now, he closed the boy's unseeing eyes, open so long for no reward. The flesh was cold and yielding, ice no longer, but damp and ready for decay; the sullen mouth would never smile. He should have flowers: hyacinths, narcissi, anemones. His body should be broken and cast on the waters. Now that the sterile caverns were open, bacteria could enter, mould, flies, rodents. He was himself a walking silo of bacteria. He kissed the forehead of the dead boy and prayed over him, repeating the passing office with the intense faith of a convert. He would live again in Monos.

The gunners stood in groups, some at ease, some checking their weapons, their talk still of the City past. He considered how he would use them. Such considerations had filled his dreams and occupied many of his waking hours; now, he had achieved at least a part of his scheme and his main force stood before him, armed with weapons which had no equal in the modern world. He looked at his own weapon: that too was better than anything Sinein or Cheron could produce, who had borrowed the technology of the City and tried to develop it. The weapon was as clean and as functional as on the day he had found it lying beside its five sisters in the depository below the archive. There too had been the manual for the Tribute, a remote communications system, the *Daystar* blueprints, and the extensive files, on paper, concerning the cryomorphs. There had been diaries, and other personal effects.

When he had armed the gun, he had lifted and fired it, the pulse on its minimum setting. The gun let go the light as gently and as effortlessly as he fired his bow. For him, there was no moment of perfect tension before the loose: the weapon did all. With surgical precision, he had melted away the steel bolts, tiny points of liquid fire, in the steel table where the weapons had lain. He had watched the table collapse, a slow adaptation of its rectangular form and a final crash.

He had left everything there in the Forbidden Archive but the manual, the rkws, and the short-range communication module; Chenodor had the bulkbox, and a gun, he carried one subsidiary communicator. He longed to bring the rest into the light, to show everything to Cal, to give Cudbeer the figures.

He spoke to his men in the woman's voice. The anachronism disturbed him.

'Stay here,' he commanded them. 'You may sit, you may speak, you may eat; but remain here.'

Now he could rest. He stretched his arms above his head as he walked away from the gunners, flexing and relaxing the aching muscles. A suite of rooms prepared for her reception lay beyond Saissa's dais – she who should be awake to witness the rebirth of her troops. He went into the second room and lay on the bed there, his eyes wide open, his brain refusing to be quiet. Images fled through his mind; in rapid succession he saw Cal and M'untal, sweaty from their exertions on his behalf; the stiff head-dresses of the women at the wedding of Cal and Vedara, the layered clothes, the decorative ribbons; the face of the dead gunner, his mother's face, the doll Crinon had loved until she threw it in the sea at the age of six, the terrible face of the red ruler in his chess set, the automaton his father had brought from Cheron as a present, Tsiksik stiff in death, his tiny manlike hands clasped, Maja herself, near death, impossible to reach or rouse. He slept fitfully, his right hand on the rkw, his left close against the Tribute in his pocket. When he woke, it was with a sense of loss and urgency; he looked at his watch, and saw that six hours had passed.

It was eleven at night, the 40 Isk, Ingemi. He was late. In the City the hot afternoon was abating and fresh bohea would be brewed to drink with the third batch from the bakeries; outside, among the mountains, Eshtur hung aloft, illuminating each stark peak and the snows that lay on the highest, season by season; below in the quiet forest, green shoots were pushing up. There was no Red Wind in Zalcasia. Even Cal might be asleep, stretched out beside his wife. He pushed the thought from his mind.

The five days were far gone, spent time, beyond the number he had calculated; some of the awakenings had faltered, resuscitation had been necessary; two of the troopers had not awoken, dead like the boy, failed. He had spent two hours with Troya, trying to communicate with her. She learned to recognise him and called him Archivist. He was pleased that he could talk to her without the synthesiser. The troopers needed a commander and, periodically, he had to walk among them and issue simple orders.

He walked up the steps of Saissa's dais. His ancestor, the ice in her heart, lay on a slab which was wider, higher, and more splendid than any of the others. Her life-support systems were finely engineered and silver necklaces and girdles of piping encircled her, each one half hidden beneath the white crystals which coated her limbs and her thick dark hair. Her body, like Crinon's, was magnificent: she was proportioned like an antique goddess, female but not feminine. She, who had been lost to woman and man, would awaken whole. He was both fearful and joyful, anticipating the moment. Her intelligence rating, on the file, was as high as his own and, excepting the thousand-year sleep, she was younger than he. She had been twenty-eight when she volunteered: she would awake with her ambitions intact. He proposed to bargain with her; he would not consider what might be the position should she refuse. He would reason with her: his logic must prevail. He would talk with her and they would plan and fight together. He would talk with her of the Octagon and his charge there, of the disorder in the City and his planned order. He would bring her to the Titian which had once been hers, he would take her to Crinon in the garden. In her the desire to serve Mahun was ultimate: she had left her children for this voluntary death. His mind could not encompass such a sacrifice. He looked at her troops gathering below the dais.

She was so beautiful, the mother of the many mothers whose genetic legacy had produced him; a more intelligent, more lovely countenance he could not imagine in a woman. When she awoke, she would have the rich voice of a Hinoor, the slow smile. The ice, moulded to her contours, marked her like Baian marble, stippling her limbs in a leucous imitation of death. Risking his hand, he touched her and felt the ice burn. He called Troya, Xanchen, and Kunai.

He spoke to the troopers.

'I am the Awakener. I am Magon Nonpareil Hinoor. These are my lieutenants.' The calm Hinoor contralto issued from the Tribute. He named them. 'You will obey them above your officers; above all these you will obey me, but Madam Hinoor is your Commander. I shall wake her tonight.' He felt an absurd wave of affection for the static troops below, each fresh face turned towards him. Though he doubted their ability to follow his words, he spoke to them at length.

'The City,' he said, 'is in peril. Corruption reigns. We bring the renaissance.' He listed the evils of Annalat's tenure as Matriarch. When he looked at his watch he found he had spoken for half an hour and still the newly born faces were turned towards him. He smiled at S'an Troya.

For the twelve hours of Saissa's awakening, the troopers sat still, watching but not, he thought, comprehending. When the frost was melted and the pipes disconnected, he covered his ancestor with the blue cymar he had brought from the City. He stood by Xanchen and watched the screens: many functions were displayed. With Kunai's help, he listened to the steady beating of her heart and when her first breath came and he saw her breast lift the cymar, he moved, near her face, and, as he moved, he set the catch that armed his rkw.

Saissa regarded him with her full, bright eyes.

'You,' she said, 'who are you? You are a man. Did your sister bring you here?'

Her voice was Maja's, intimate and threatening, for him alone. He spoke as boldly as he dared.

'I am the Archivist,' he said, 'I am Magon Hinoor.'

'You are a Hinoor,' she said. The cynical smile dawned slowly. 'A Hinoor and a man.'

'Yes,' he said, 'I am the son of Maja Hinoor, the one-hundred and twenty-sixth Archivist. I am the Archivist.'

Her expression registered alarm and dismay; clearly she had no automatic affection for him although he was one of her heirs. She frowned.

'The state must be rotten,' she said. 'Such a statement is against all reason.'

She sat up suddenly, moving from supine passivity to total alertness with a speed which terrified him and made him grip his rkw.

'Steady, my beauty,' she said. 'I can see that you are uneasy in this hall of women, as uneasy as you are with your weapon. Put it away. You forget that I have woken from death and do not fear to die again.'

To appease her he exchanged the weapon for the Tribute and demonstrated it to her, telling her what he had done, telling her how he had commanded her troops with his altered voice. He was surprised when she laughed.

'In our innocence,' she said, 'we never dreamed that our plan could be so easily circumvented.'

257

'It wasn't easy,' he said. 'It was intricate, convoluted. I worked at night, alone in the Forbidden Archive: I alone have the key to it. It contains the knowledge of your age – its wealth – and all the knowledge which has since been suppressed and forbidden. In 4000 the Gynarchy revised the Law, and the Matriarchy the Statute. The City was closed and devoted to worship alone. We reckon the years from the Reformation: it is 502, or 4502.

'The successive years have eroded the reforms of the year 1, illogically and divisively. What was once sacred is now tyranny and its vices and excesses extend to the Matriarchy, even to the Gynarchs. Privilege is maintained by force and the close control of resources. I myself enjoy ridiculous wealth.

'I made my plans several years ago; others in the City joined with me. The Tribute, the synthesiser, I found in Diridion – but I don't know how it came there, and the monks thought it was a sealed recording. I have studied the cryomorphs, and the years of your Command since 489.'

'Who rules the City?' she asked.

'From the Temple, Justa Edern rules our souls; on the Hill, Annalat Abayon, who was born Heleth Amskiri.'

'Amskiri?' she repeated. 'Amskiri is an Artificer name. Has there been a revolution as well?'

'The Matriarchy evolved a system of replacing one person with another. Surgery and demography were misused to give the Surrogate her new identity. I have used the system myself.'

'You are as corrupt as they?'

'Perhaps: a man of my age, the product of their hierarchy. The Council chose me freely for Archivist, after my mother died. There was no opposition.'

'You have done well – for a man. Thank you for restoring my command.' Her voice provoked him and her smile was a challenge. She sat up and kissed him on the forehead: her kiss was colder than ice. It went to his heart.

'Ah, no,' he said. 'The command will be shared. The City must wake too. This is the fifth millennium: Sinein and Ineit no longer make impossible demands of Guna's people.'

'A bargain?' Her voice was stern, it was Maja's public voice, the one she had increasingly used as he grew older, working in the Archive, reading in the Library, no longer his mother's darling but her ambition. 'Who are you to make bargains with me?'

He did not know if her question was rhetorical or if, after all, the ice had lodged in her brain and killed reason as surely as it had lodged in her heart and killed love.

'I am Magon, Maja Hinoor's son,' he repeated. 'I am the Archivist.

258

'My knowledge is invaluable – what do you know of the 46th century? Outside, in the mountains, I have a detachment of the Cheronese army – five hundred City men – and a corundum gun. As for you, Grandmother, without me, you would still be in stasis. I have completed the experiment.'

'No,' she said, and restored his faith in her mind. 'Without you, we would await another Awakener, maybe a more suitable one.'

She paused; he saw from her face that she wrestled with the implications of his speech. Presently, she sighed and rubbed her smooth forehead.

'I don't underrate you,' she said. 'Clearly, you are one of us, a soldier and a Hinoor. I accede.'

Saissa held out her right hand and he took it, sealing the bargain. Then he helped her to stand.

She stood tall in the blue robe, nearly as tall as he. The troopers got to their feet and every one saluted. They were the new demigods.

Magon watched her. If he could have resisted her challenge, if he could have retired from the battle to let her take the City he might, in that moment, have withdrawn altogether, into a retreat where he could let his ambition die while he turned the whole of his intellect inward to journey amongst words, reading, writing, praying. A house among the liriodendrons. He watched her address her forces; they knelt together to pray to Mahun. At the end of the prayer, he bent towards her and whispered in her ear, 'The gunners are mine; you deploy the rest. Tonight I will show you a map of the City.'

'Very well,' she said. 'But now, we go forth. What season is it, out there, what time?'

'Near dawn,' he said. 'And the first of the Death Days – but no Red Wind blows in Zalcasia. Soon, the sun will rise and we will all go down the mountain to Binala.'

He was weary, he was dirty, sweaty, unshaven. He went to her rooms and ran cold water into a bowl; then he lowered his face into it, slowly, indulgently, until the water filled in the spaces between his eyelashes and blinded him. He dipped his hands into the bowl and scooped water over his head. The towel was sterile, smelling of nothing; he had expected it to be scented like the ancient City with the odours of strange engines, hot metal and glass, of healthy bodies, and the everlasting seduction of spices and flowers.

Emerging, he found that Saissa had instructed the troops; weapons and packs had been shouldered, they were ready to move.

They left the dark halls, the fresh wind blowing dust through the open doors, left the dead boy and the two dead women. Magon stood still in the sunlight and watched the long line of cryomorphs emerge. In the strong light, their blank faces were stern; he was pleased at the uniformity and

259

conformity of expression. They trod on the flowers and broke the grass stems as they walked, but he saw Troya and Xanchen bend to pick a flower each, and Saissa stood by him and breathed in the windy mountain air in great gasps. Then she spoke to her officers, and the officers to the women: order was imposed. He took his own place before the gunners, and they moved off.

The mountains were alive that morning. All the waters the snowmelt had released were singing, and every male bird declaimed. They passed the liriodendron wood in the valley, a mile from the green enchantment, and climbed again to cross a limb of Mount Darodha. Now, it was all downhill. He saw the tree-line and the valley of the Binal. He rested his army; then they went on, the steep slope jarring the foot, pulling at the muscle in the thigh. An hour later, they were close above the conifers and he halted them again. The path snaked downward and disappeared between the trees. He looked into the feathery treetops, wondering how hard pine needles could appear so soft. He took out the double optic to examine the distant leaves; it was then that he heard Cal laughing. He heard the unmistakable joyous bark and Zuhil's deeper roar. Zuhil's men were shouting in the wood, banging the treetrunks. A flight of gamebirds rocketed from the trees and shots rang out.

Then Cal came out of the dark wood, flushed and laughing. The sunlight inflamed him. He stood still; when he saw them, he began to run up the hill, leaping the stones in his path.

When he reached Magon, he was out of breath. He stared at the cryomorph army. The words came quickly, tumbling out of him in a mixture of the Zalcasian he had been speaking minutes ago and the correct Maralayan expressions he wanted to use.

'Cryos! Where did you get them? Sinein? The CoNN starship?'

Below him, Zuhil and the three Binalans cautiously ascended the slope. Zuhil's left hand was held up in a gesture of appeasement, from his right a bronze pheasant dangled.

Magon took hold of Cal's arm and moved him away from the troops, from Saissa.

'They're mine,' he said. 'Frozen in 3498 and entombed under Mount Zelk. Everything was in the Forbidden Archive.'

Cal looked wildly round, over his shoulder.

'Hundreds of them,' he said. 'And who is she?'

'Four hundred and forty-seven, three didn't make it. She is Saissa Hinoor.'

He watched Cal's face; the comprehension was instantaneous.

'I see,' said Cal.

'And you, how did you spend the last days of Alcuon?'

'I got married, Magon. Remember? I have to stay at home and fuck my wife.'

So he was already tired of it: all his jealousy and spiritual isolation were contained in his vicious reply. This marriage he had made would last no longer than his other ridiculous associations with women.

'You might have come with me.'

The only response was a sullen pout; if they had been alone, he would have sulked for hours. Magon turned away from him to watch the Binalans. Zuhil stood squarely in front of the strange army, his fear tempered by his curiosity. The limp pheasant was still warm in his hand. He made up his mind that the soldiers came from Cheron and would not be persuaded otherwise. He said he was not surprised that the Archivist had treated with Chacma for his own force; it must be hard work deferring to Oyno. He had not been aware, till now, that Chacma used female soldiers; but, again, he was unsurprised because whatever they did in Sinein, Chacma copied. Saissa spoke to him and Magon showed him one of the cannon.

'Corundum gun, isn't it? Portable?'

'No one on Guna knows how to make them so small,' Cal said. 'The secret was lost in the Reformation.'

'They've plenty of clever scientists in Sinein,' said Zuhil. Magon invited him to continue to the Oaipe; Zuhil said he could not see any advantage in climbing another thousand feet to look at the tomb of a heretic.

'That central cave is very shallow. I know, I went in there three years ago after a lost ewe.'

Magon gave up.

'Whatever they are,' he said, 'you will think again when we attack.'

The cryomorphs slept in the open, lapped in their all-weather bags. Cal was intensely curious about them; he was up before dawn, leaving the warm bed and Vedara just stirring, lazy, relaxed, and receptive. He walked about among the dark forms. They, who had been absent so long, still needed sleep in which to visit fallen buildings and dead lovers. The pale morning light touched the mountain tops, but where they lay frost and deep shadow covered the ground. He bent and looked at one of the troopers; the quilted fabric was drawn close around her head, her fair hair had fallen across her face. She breathed softly. In sleep, the vacancy of expression which characterised primitive cryomorphs and made them recognisable was gone. She became a sleeping girl, her soldier's bearing shed for the night. He looked into the face of another. She had close-cropped dark hair, was boyishly pretty: he recognised her as one of the medical officers. One of her hands had crept from the cocoon; her fingers were still, close beside her face, bare and ringless. They had no personal possessions, these automatic soldiers; everything had been sacrificed to fanaticism. Because of this, Magon could control them as he

261

could control no rational being, least of all himself. And the commander, his ancestor, was another Crinon in whom understanding and love had been replaced with military zeal. She slept outside with her troops, on the same hard ground, a little apart from them. He dare not approach her: she had all her faculties. He went back to the house.

Vedara, in her nightgown, was making his breakfast, the swelling new tide of her breasts hidden beneath the embroidered pleats at the front of the gown. She had satisfied some of his desires, and given him a kind of freedom; the baby would come in Udan, late in Verrun. By then it would be all over. Lifting the white cloth to touch the new high roundness which pushed from within her flat belly, he forgot the cryos in the chill dawn outside. He pulled her towards him; his penetration of her was a celebratory rite and, here, a right. He smiled into her hair.

Vedara dressed carefully. He lay with his arms behind his head and watched her. She wore practical underclothing, covering her brown skin with fine white wool, stretching the pants around her enlarged waist. She put on her white fur trousers, tighter now. She pulled her shirt over her head and hid her affluent breasts. They were nearly as perfect as Glaver's. The memory had crept from his past. He sat up and swore.

'What's the matter?' She was plaiting ribbons into her hair; the white icemart tails lay beside her hairbrush on the bed.

'Nothing. I must get up, do some work.'

'For the Archivist?'

'No. My own – the *Travels*.'

He dressed quickly. The house was warm, hot in the evenings; but every morning, every time he left the shelter of the bed, his naked body remembered the City's heat. He shivered and sat down at the table, taking up a fork to eat the meat Vedara put in front of him. She poured the bohea she had obtained for him in Binala, somewhere in the isolated town. She sat opposite him, dipping her bread in her coffee.

'You must come with me to the City,' he said unhappily. 'Please. Come with the soldiers.'

'Silly! I can't do that. A pregnant woman with an army!'

He was silent. He looked at her, his safeguard, his refuge, his wife.

'I shall miss you,' he said. It was not a lie, but it was less than the truth. His journey with Huyatt could be finished as a tourist, with short stays in unfamiliar discomfort, but the other world lay beyond Vedara and the book; he knew he had not finished travelling it.

'We shall both be here when you get back,' she said, placing a hand on her tunic, caressing her belly. Mistaking his anxiety for fear, she said, 'You'll be in no danger behind Oyno's guns. And those women. . . .' Her voice trailed into silence. She was afraid of the cryomorphs.

She cleared the table and he spread out his books. He picked up the *Travels*; the familar red binding was limp and worn. The leaf of lemon balm had given its scent to the whole book; he took the leaf from its place between the cover and the flyleaf. It was brittle and faded; fragments had broken from its serrated margin.

'What is that?' said Vedara.

'A memory. A leaf from Vern. Smell it. It grows in a physician's garden there.'

'Lemons and oil; no, lemons and smoke.'

Huyatt had nothing to say about war. In his time the ban on weaponry had been total; for ten years the Temple archers had gone unarmed. In the Tayaal, no doubt, the old weapons were always in use: the sword and dagger, the grip of the falcon, the teeth of the dog, primitive rifles; but less than three pages of the three hundred concerned themselves with the Tayaal.

He skimmed through Huyatt's book. Every page was headed with a sentence. Usually, he saw them peripherally, guides to the content, when he scanned a page; now he read them in sequence.

Look, Traveller, in Maralis the towers are in bloom
Yearning, Huyatt comes to the City
See! In the darkest hour a white sea rides the crescent
Huyatt comes lonely into green Vern
Inter alia, Balkiss . . .

A litany of journeying. The lines read like a hallucination, their logic of the unconscious, all image and, unlike the main body of text, in the third person. He began to copy them, writing one under the other like a long narrative poem.

It was a poem. A grace-song in the metres of Diridion. Surely someone had noticed it before. He would have to check, mining the unending lode again, hearing again the silence in the Octagon, knowing that Magon worked two floors below him, his black robe lending him gravity and the potency of a priest. The last line of Huyatt's long poem spoke of homecoming; he saw, not this little wooden house, nor the high dyeworks tower, but his bed beside the rug which was patterned with the tree of life, the dry wooden back of the St Sebastian turned to the wall. He sighed and let his pen wander on the margin of the page until a forest grew there.

Vedara had gone out unnoticed; as he registered the fact she came in with cheeks glowing, her covered dish, hot from the bakery oven, in her hands. It was time to eat again. He smiled at her.

In the afternoon, he went out and rode Choru a long way down the valley. The Zalcasians were working in their tiny fields, hoeing between long lines of seedlings. It was not his country and he touched his heels to the mare's sides so that her undisciplined gallop would wipe the uncertainty from his mind.

Interregnum

Cal and Choru had reached the summit of the pass. Magon looked up and saw them outlined against the sky, two harmonious and inter-dependent figures in the stark landscape. He set his own face to the mountain. At the top he crossed the flat and broken limestone slabs, weathered from their inborn pallor to a uniform grey; the damp air of the heights had darkened them and gave the vegetation a sombre gloss. He stood beside Cal so that he could share his delight.

So early in the morning, Maralis was blue. There was no detail. The City was a pool of indigo on the edge of the haze and, beyond it, the ocean was an indefinite blur, another cloud. He stood so close to Cal that he could have put an arm around him or a hand on his untidy hair. Cal tried to count the City's towers, arms upraised from a misted lake. Neither of them wanted to use an optic, to dispel the illusion. There lay his City. He would rule her and direct her new compassion. He felt an immense sense of peace: he was whole, strong, his guilt eroded, perhaps in the desert, perhaps in the chilly mountains or the deeper cold of the tomb beneath Mount Zelk.

The noise of Oyno's troops, the footfalls of the cryomorphs, destroyed the moment of unity. He turned round. The men had paused for breath, for rest; Zuhil had begun to brew coffee. The cryomorphs squatted on their haunches, a stick of solidified nutriment in each right hand. Saissa looked at him, but he turned away and took his double optic from its case.

The optic penetrated the mist and gave him enhanced vision in negative; he saw the black silt-choked waters of Kisai, the chain of reservoirs which had once supplied the City, and the white shapes of grazing animals. The arable farmland was an empty chequerboard. After the Red Wind, before the second harvest, the newly tilled soil was both cradle and nurse to the seed. In Nivuna, her streets laid open by the glass, were hurrying crowds and on the country roads, pedestrians and carts rushed towards the town. On the north road a solitary rider led a second horse. He lowered the optic and the near and coloured world loomed, the rocks, a wind-sculptured thorn, the separate strands of Cal's brown hair. He altered the focus of the glass and examined the road. The led horse was his own marvellous Arkite, white as Choru through the glass, and the rider Slake Amskiri.

264

'Slake's down below,' he said in Deep, argot and signal from be.ter days.

Cal's eyes were closed. He opened them. The yellow gaze was abstracted.

'I was trying to count the towers in my mind,' he said. 'Where is Slake?'

'On the road. He should meet me in Nivuna but it's obvious – look there – that Annalat has been advised. I'm sorry: it means more compulsion than might have been necessary.'

Sensibly, Slake had waited on the roadside with the big horse and his own hack. He saluted. It was a clumsy gesture from a civilian, but pleasing. Magon took Arkite's reins from Slake and pulled the irons down the leathers. Mounted, he felt at once isolated and in command; he waited for the column and took his place beside Saissa. The year of journeying was done, but there were still thirty miles to Nivuna.

An animal felt neither regret nor guilt. He imagined himself possessed of the soul of a raptor, an everyday killer, or a cryomorph. He thought of his lieutenants, the sophisticated cryomorphs, in particular of Sondrazan Troya; she had a woman's face, a mask of unreasonable beauty, and taut, athletic limbs. He wondered if she, like Crinon, had declared herself inaccessible; whether she would one day inoculate herself against his sex with the enduring female principle, slow-swimming sperm, derived from a complaisant and dead donor. As for Cal and himself, it was intellect, a wedding of minds; but he knew he deceived himself, remembering the cold green waves which were a prelude to the drama of the white bed beneath Sebastian's abstracted gaze. Between his thighs, the horse was an entity with a will of its own which he had subdued. He dismounted, gave the reins to the waiting cryomorph, and went into the tent which had been pitched in the shelter of a low knoll in someone's parkland, ten miles from Nivuna. They had seen no people on the estate but one of the cryomorphs, alert to movement, had lifted her rkw and converted several deer into untidy heaps of ash and charred bone.

Cal slept in the outer tent. He sat on his bedroll in the sticky heat, too hot, too restless to sleep. Two deks from Binala, two deks of distance, three hundred miles of rock, separated him from Vedara; two deks of growth, Vedara and the foetus within her, twenty days to dull the commitment, the lust and pride; it was not love. Twenty-five miles separated him from the City; nothing lay between them but fields and one small town. On the streets they would all be about their nightly business: Tarla, Dork, and Dromio, Dog, the Bitch. Before nightfall he had seen the Octagon, a dark tower on the horizon, Magon's citadel.

Magon was writing; the lamp revealed his activity in shadow play. He wrote without pause, covering the pages with his even script, the sure black penstrokes his trademark. The pages and the script might be

265

imagined, but never the content: he wrote in the journal with the lock. The light went out.

He had been sitting a long time on the sand but still the tide had not come in and the ribbed sheet of wet sand glittered, empty; the water would take its own time. He came awake slowly, floundering, and moved his body back into consciousness; falling asleep in an upright position was wasted luxury. His neck ached. The dark bulk in the darkness was Magon.

'You must be very tired, to sleep sitting up,' he said.

Cal considered. 'Not tired. Just bloody exhausted. What time is it?'

'Only eleven. You were asleep for a few seconds.'

'Why is it so hot?'

'It's always as hot. We've been too long in the mountains.'

'Too long in the mountains.' Cal echoed his words. 'Too long in the Tayaal; far too long in Diridion.'

He reached for the remembered hand and held it; Magon's palm was sticky with sweat. They sat like conspirators in the dark; Magon's voice was a shadow.

'What a mess.'

'Yes.'

'I wanted to help you escape.'

'I can't escape.'

'Perhaps there is no conflict; perhaps you can live two lives.'

'No. There's only time for one.'

He leaned against Magon and sleep engulfed him, the only retreat.

When he woke in the morning, it was with a changed consciousness. He lay still. His memory was reliable: he had fallen asleep sitting on the bedroll, then he had woken and talked with Magon; he had slept. So little, so much. Magon must have put him to bed; again, the overture had been soundlessly played. The Tayaal, Ruht, and Purity were past. He did not know what he would do about Vedara, about his developing child. By implication and nature he was feckless: did he not come from the Depths? He found his clothes and, just as he pulled the shirt over his head, the tentflap was pushed aside and he saw S'an Troya. She came into the tent, ducking her long and graceful body under the fabric; she ignored his presence, moving towards the inner tent.

'Stop!' he said.

She moved half a step and turned. Her face was a beautiful oval, her lips parted; the bright brown eyes which should have mirrored her mind looked on some other time.

'You'd better announce yourself before you go in there. He is the Archivist; he's not some inert cryo.'

'I have a message,' the cryomorph said.

'For him?'

266

'For the Archivist.'
'Then give it to him.'

The hand on his shoulder woke Magon. He thought it was Cal's and turned over, stretching out his own. But the voice was light and clear, not his.

'Archivist.'

Cal called him many names but never Archivist. He opened his eyes. S'an Troya stood there.

'Archivist,' she said again. 'Archivist,' as he had taught her.

'What is it?' He sat up, gathering the tumbled bag and the day about him.

'I have come because the Commander will not awake. She speaks but she will not wake.'

Cal, in the outer room, listened.

'She speaks of love; what is that?' the cryomorph asked.

Magon's reply made him grin.

'A complication, a disease.'

'I think Commander Hinoor has a disease.'

'People talk in their sleep; maybe even cryomorphs can tell their dreams while they sleep.'

'She does not sleep: her eyes are open.'

Magon erupted from the inner tent, half clothed; such agitation was foreign to him, the disorder of panic. Behind him, the medical officer moved like a sleepwalker, her efficiency gone. She might be able to operate the technics of medicine, she could stitch and plaster, dispense and inject, but she could not reason, could not determine cause and effect. They went by like actor and spectator.

Saissa's eyes were wide open, giving her face the quality of prepared repose which she had displayed in her stasis. Her breathing was shallow and he could hardly hear the words which sighed from her lips. He heard his own voice.

'Don't die. Don't die.'

He touched her: fire not ice, a heat like a cholera victim's or one sick of the sweating epidemic which had taken his mother from him, data replayed.

'She's dying,' he said to the cryomorph, 'She will cease to function.' Had they been taught to recognise terminal states, or only death herself?

S'an Troya knelt beside him and calmly read her commander's pulse.

'I cannot help,' she said, 'It is a malfunction.'

'You must!'

'No. I cannot do anything to prevent death. They told us some would die: the more extensive the modification, the greater the risk. She has been infected by a virus of your time; she does not have the immune

267

system to deal with it: her system is already overloaded with supplements.'

'But she was reborn to rescue the City.'

'She and we others. We all knew the risk when we volunteered. I can assist Aash; but she is not in pain.'

Saissa looked as though she dreamed. He listened to her random skein of words, hearing the names of her children, hearing the ghosts of the memories which waved from the shore, the audible echoes of her visions. She was never conscious of his presence and it was only while he listened for her next word that he realised she had died. He got up and walked away into the park, among the neat arrangements of trees and deer fences, tears of desperation on his cheeks, praying that Cal would not follow him.

When he returned, the body was covered with one of the blue and gold flags and he was able to compose himself and speak a prayer. A party of cryomorphs had been put to work to fell wood for a burial platform and Cal, at his table in the tent, sat calmly copying the day's orders from his own notes.

'The march will be delayed by twenty minutes,' he said.

'I allowed half an hour.'

'Then take your copies to Jahta and Oyno.'

He sat at the table. Saissa had lived thirty days in his world. He looked at his own handwriting, trying vainly to follow the penstrokes without reading the words. As an exercise in control it was useless; he abandoned it and drank a glass of water before he picked up the rest of his clothes, neatly folded by Xanchen, and finished dressing.

That night, he occupied Nivuna. The predatory action of riding into the town, a technocratic army against an unorganised group of women, was not war, he thought. It was distasteful to him, made cowards of them all. The Gynarchs in the small temple had acceded to every demand he made, defenceless except for their spiritual defiance. He wanted to pit his body and wit against an equal adversary: he could not think of one except for Chacma and his own father, and both were too old.

He commandeered the best accommodation. With Olthar Oyno, Jahta M'una, Zuhil, S'an Troya, and Oyno's lieutenant, Pikat, he sat at the rosewood table in the well-appointed dining room of the Justice of Nivuna. He had imagined this final assembly taking place in his tent, the toast from tin cups, and he watched Cal pour Ceramana into the judge's crystal without bothering to suppress his amused smile or the frank admiration which must be visible in his eyes. They were light years from Gaia and millennia from Greece. What was alien antiquity to him, but faraway legend and chance finds in the Library? The starship was long gone and the Gaians' gifts, disparate examples of their art, Renaissance paintings, the English sculptures, the German woodcarvings, the music of Johann Bach and the works of William Shakespeare, the small paperbound Greek anthology, the fat volume of legends – these were only indicators, not texts.

But Cal moved as Ganymedes surely had done, at least in some man's imagination, pouring the seadark wine and bearing it to the new gods.

The walls of the City shimmered, the worn grey granite and the clean ashlars of the newer sections a mergent illusion in the heat, the foreview of their fate. Now Cal would be able to count the towers. Eighteen were visible: in the west the six black columns of the University and the five blue pillars of the Temple. The silver finger of *Daystar*, surely to be counted among the towers, pointed hopefully and significantly at the sky; miscellaneous towers gestured and on the Hill were the three white towers where even now Chenodor would be the agent of panic; last, his own, the tallest, the Octagon. His optic magnified the prospect: he saw the guard mounted on the walls, a full and useless presence armed with staves, with bows and museum pieces, rebored rifles as ramshackle as a Tayali's piece, with spears, even a sword. His rkw was a light and balanced weight on his back. Oyno's men stood calm, anticipating no struggle; Zuhil and his stolid mountainmen had become wild and colourful brigands; and the cryomorphs, the dead alive, triumph of the sciences, lightly held their weapons of the future past. Murder, he thought, we shall commit murder, matricide, in this rude traverse from the artificially sustained past into the universal now. The sun burned the backs of his hands and Arkite fidgeted. He tried to think of Crinon but she danced before him like a mirage and disappeared; eventually, as the slow minutes passed and he waited for Oyno's order, he heard her disembodied voice: 'You taught us, the daubers, scribblers, and illusionists, the recorders of trivia and minutiae, to be the harbingers of revolution and resolution. We are waiting for our moment in history.' He could not fail her.

S'an Troya, behind the main body of the troops, felt fresh currents in the byways of her brain, felt faint. I hope I will not malfunction. Commander Hinoor is dead but Commander Hinoor lives. Sometimes he speaks with her voice. If only I could remember what lies beyond the black screen.

Chenodor brought Annalat into the room. Her manner was grave but unsubdued: she would have abused him openly had she not been absurdly conscious of the fact that she was in fact an Artificer and he the son of Maja Hinoor.

'This is the result of giving a man freedom,' she said. 'I see that Chacma has used you.'

The involuntary abdication must be formal.

'No, Madam Abayon,' he said. 'I used the Archive; Chacma is an adjunct.'

'You were so discreet,' she said. 'How could anyone suspect such a devoted government servant, such a scholar? Your letters lulled me to sleep. I hardly believed the despatches which came from Nivuna.'

'The office of Archivist,' he said, 'was always bait for a revolutionary: my keys opened many doors. Why did you not use the knowledge in the Forbidden Archive?'

'Because it is forbidden,' she replied, her moral ascendancy complete. Then, 'What will you do with my sons?' she asked. So she suspected him of the ultimate evil for – his conscience smiled – the reckoning of his sins must exceed hers, on the last day. The doorkeepers were mute, Chenodor a vast silent bulk hiding his responses in his beard. He felt the tension in his shoulders grow and begin to gnaw.

'They will be given the choice,' he said evenly, 'of remaining at the Academy, or of accompanying you into exile.'

'Why don't you kill me?'

'It is not necessary,' he said, in the same even voice. 'What kind of a focus for dissent is Heleth Amskiri? And I shall know exactly where you are. I am sending you to the villa in Far Maralis: you will have the freedom of its four acres, no more. Give me your left arm.'

He walked round her desk, and fastened the tag on her wrist, covering the borrowed lily, sealing its strap carefully, gently, so that she was not hurt.

'Don't try to remove it: I will know at once.'

He returned to the desk and switched on the control; a soft tone came from the box and the light on it glowed. He switched off the audible signal, and watched the lamp pulse, her heartbeat, her shadow.

'If you remove it – ' he said, and demonstrated its warning scream.

'The spoils to the victor.' She waved an arm at the furnishings, the glass tables, the ornaments, books, and rugs; the silver-plated Gynarch she had made from base metal and stamped with a counterfeit hallmark.

'This will be Chenodor's domain: Administration. I am the Archivist.'

She went out as quietly as she had entered and Gildo brought in her sons, his hands on their shoulders, guiding them. Ishkal had his mother's sensuous mouth. Harendi, being two years older, was defiant and stood erect, his jutting chin recalling the unmoving stance of his cousin, Slake. They confronted him like guilty schoolchildren before authority but he did not patronise them.

'You have been brought here,' he said, 'so that I can determine your wishes and your rights. You both attend CA; next year you, Harendi, will matriculate and CU will be your right. Do you wish to continue your education or go with your mother into exile?'

'Go with Mother,' said Ishkal at once, but Harendi nodded his head towards Cal.

270

'That's a better choice than he had,' Harendi said, his voice reflecting his anxiety, full of animosity.

Magon's unforced laugh made the boy start.

'Ishkal has chosen,' he said. 'What do you want?'

'I'll stay,' said the boy, 'Will I be able to visit Mother?'

'What do you think?'

'No. Can I say goodbye?'

'Yes. Go now.'

At dusk he stepped from the lift into the Octagon and felt the silence and the immutable peace enfold him. His footfalls were deadened by the carpeted floor; the click of his key turning in the lock was an unhushable incursion into the quiet. Inside, the same cool haven: his universal museum, his home. He went to his room, switching on the lights as he went, walking slowly along the corridor and around the turn, inclining his head to each canvas as he passed it. The clock struck eight times: eight, the hour at which Rafe had taken the milk. His ghost had been exorcised, its last gibber a vision in the desert. Absolution. God had spoken to him: he remembered the still small voice and would know it again.

Everything was in order and no speck of dust marred the polish of the wooden floor nor the scarred glass of the great window. Slake had replaced the Martyrdom of Saint Sebastian, the antiphon to Xharam'un's violent abstract. He stood by the bed and looked at the patient figure and the familiar detail of the ruined stonework and the strong sapling, the distant fantastic scene which ignored the saint's predicament. The work had resumed its proper role as fable.

He walked into the bathroom and stood in front of the mirror, surprising his image with the intensity of his stare. He was older by a year, by many more than that in resolution. Thirty-five. The breadth of his body from shoulder to shoulder, as always, amazed him and he stood still for a time trying to penetrate the enigma, the man who looked at him. The reflection frowned, still puzzled, still distracted by life. On the chaotic streets the cryomorphs had killed wherever he thought necessary, culling the population. The dead would be buried with ceremony and honour, courageous, vain defenders. Arkite had trodden on the body of a woman and as he had pulled up the stallion's head he had noticed that she wore green eyeshadow and red lip gloss to court death. He had seen husbands beating their wives. The Law was violated. He, so late, had learned one of Gaia's first lessons.

He walked about among his possessions, pausing to examine the drawings, touching the hand of the wooden figure by the window, caressing the mighty deltoids of the bronze athlete, turning the pages of beloved books. But Saissa would never stand with him before the Titian nor walk among the pools and flowers in Crinon's garden. Alien music filled his head, one of the chorales from Bach's great Passion which he had summoned so many times in the Forbidden Archive:

Commend your way and what grieves your heart
To the love of Him who rules the Heavens.
The Spirit who gives Clouds, Air and Winds their direction
Will also find ways where your feet can walk.

This music, coming as it had in the last cargo to be instantly entombed, was a joy more constant than sexual pleasure, an anthem heard by more than the sensual ear. The music had another dimension, a better function: soul gratification. It was a fresh delight at each encounter; it might be solace in great age or in infirmity. As yet, he must have both. The door was flung open and Cal came into the room.

Part III

CONSEQUENCES

The City is as Huyatt saw her, fairest of all, the bay a perfect crescent, the red and yellow land fertile; on the three granite outcrops which the Gynarchs chose in the First Years, the coloured towers stand firm. The Traveller never mentions the Octagon which dominates them all but it was there in his time, the Octagon of the Archive, pale limestone like the other three on Mahun's Belly, pale stone infused with yellow light, the colour of fresh bread. The foundation stone was laid in 2550OS. When Huyatt came to the City it was more than seventeen hundred years old. Maybe he feared it, this thrusting domination, this tower which contains every record, every book, and every secret of civilisation.

When Magon Nonpareil, the Archivist, came to power in 502AR, the old symbolic and hierarchal definitions came to an end and he replaced them with new systems. Hierarchy became benevolent oligarchy. The new religion of Monos co-existed harmoniously with the old. Magon abolished the Mark, and the social structures of five thousand years crumbled in a dek. When the Nine Judges were banished, a bench of twelve citizens took their place. The Security Corps was disbanded and replaced by a company of cryomorphs, the volunteer defenders of the faith, the frozen soldiery of the fourth millennium. The defence of the new City was given into the hands of General Olthar Oyno and his New Army. The City gates stood open and the citizens went out into the countryside whenever they wished.

The Archivist introduced his new calendar: the Red Wind enforces its five days of chaos, but the remaining three-hundred and sixty were divided into twelve months of thirty days each, a dozen three-dek months named after abstracts such as Justice, Mercy, Clemency, and Order. The new Free Schools and hostels filled with the children of the City, with former destitutes, cripples, and pavement children. The Archive was opened to all. Cal M'unor.Archive,M'unor/Auth 22/Vern 4505OS/505AR/3MN.

Schools and hostels filled with the children of the City, with former destitutes, cripples, and pavement children. The Archive was opened to all.
Cal M'unor.Archive,M'unor/Auth 22/Vern 4505OS/505AR/3MN.

Peach

Peach scratched his belly and then, rolling over on the mat, scratched long and hard at the soft skin between his shoulder blades. Sunlight never penetrated to the dyeworks yard before eleven. It was early, between seven and eight, and he had moved his sleeping mat to the edge of the yard so that he could lie in sun or shade as he pleased. Later, the tower would cast its own long shadow, darkening the yard again, climbing its walls and humping over the roofs of the old manufactory. These changing intensities of light did not seem to harm his plants; indeed, they thrived, the coriander with its leaves like frayed feathers, and the rank oily smell it gave off, chopped and scattered on meat as Cal liked it. Tash had given him the seeds from the handful of spices which Dile had filched. The leaves of the garlic and ginger plants were pointed like blades and, in the other container, an old crate, throve the lilies he had dug up one night in the beds of na Hinoor Circus.

The swifts had returned from their breakfast out at sea; a bickering party of them swept the sky and screamed at each other.

There had been a garden on the boat, a long trough of scented blue flowers. He could still remember it clearly, especially if he closed his eyes, but he could not remember the faces of his mother and father, nor of any of his eight sisters except one, the one who never prospered and who had died.

Peach scratched again and rolled into the sun, shading his eyes with his upturned hands. He moved his right hand to touch his chin, which had still not grown a beard. Maybe there was one hair. He rubbed the place, but could not locate it. The texture of his skin, downy, yielding like a peach, was the reason for his nickname; his given name was Seef, a whistling Tlivoorn word. He had tried to imagine a brown peach, but the images of his shadowy skin and of the ripe fruit would not coincide, except in the picture of the rotten gleanings at the end of a market day. The tribe on Daid's ground had called him Peach right away, from the beginning when Shiny had found him crying after his parents sailed away.

The clock, high above him in the tower, hiccuped; he heard the cogwheels turn and then the music began, chimes which played the City hymn. Magic. All through his years on the streets the clock has been silent; then Cal had come and his persistence, oil, and An's pliers had

275

made it sing. The clock struck eight. Closing his eyes, Peach witnessed again Cal's climb to the tower top, a paper figure against the sharp-edged brick. In the wide spaces between the limpid sky and the hard ground, he dozed.

Feet scraped the dusty stones. Not Cal with his bare feet, nor Prenta's heels. One of them had got in again – but how? He had barred the gates himself, last night. The cryo was looking at him. It halted and gestured uncertainly.

'Shall I kill this one?' it said, and looked over its shoulder.

Peach sat up swiftly and, remembering to pitch his voice correctly, said, 'This one is to be preserved.'

The cryo lowered its hands. It had lost its gun, of course. One of the wanderers, a malfunctionary, an androgyne. They had been the first to break down, replacing the rehabilitated streetdwellers with a new class of scavengers. Its clothing was in tatters, its boots – strangely – whole and securely fastened. He could see its muscular legs under the torn cloth and the exaggerated prow of its blind chest. It had a pretty face and Peach smiled at it. The creature smiled back.

'Go away,' said Peach, and watched the cryo's confusion as it tried to define 'away'. 'Go to Aash. Come on, I'll show you.'

The cryo followed him to the gate. He watched it stride away down the street. Sometimes you could use them, errands and such. The reprogrammed cryos from the Hill and the Block – everyone still called the cryo barracks the Block – shot them on sight. But mainly they were a silent nuisance, skulking among half-demolished buildings, feeding off garbage and gifts, as he had once. He shut the gate.

Now he was up; sleep and remembering had deserted him. He looked up at the tower, a stepped pinnacle of brick rising from the factory front, intact statues of Mahun and her sisters on every corner, and Guna herself, gilded and etched with her continents, atop the tower roof. Once, Cal had taken him up to see the globe, an expedition which had made him shake and vomit. The front door was open and he smelled bread.

In the lower hall, Prenta fed the newest baby with scraps of softened bread. When she thought he had taken enough, she pulled up her shirt and give the baby her breast. Peach stared at the female mystery.

'If you're hungry,' said Prenta shrilly, 'there's bread on the table. And when you've finished you can take Him His.'

He climbed the marble-lined staircase and walked sedately around the carved newel post where, usually, he swung. The old manufacturer had believed in ostentation, the bitch. Marbles and starvation. He passed the open door of one of the rooms, where the tumbled heap on the bed was Hellie, asleep under a sheet, and came to the end of the staircase. Once it had continued upwards in wood, and blind holes in the tower wall marked its former course, high, circling, giddy: the empty well soared above him, the inside of a lantern, its lid made of gilded panels, its chimney a dark window into heaven. The ladder dangled. Peach put the breadrings over his arm and the beaker of bohea in his right hand; his left and his legs would take him up. He climbed easily. A sugar butterfly as big as a plate perched among the bells on their platform. The two floors above the bells, the swift roosts, were dusty expanses, patterned with the prints of Cal's feet and his own and littered with old and new nests. He climbed the last ladder. The clock ticked slowly.

Cal surveyed the City, leaning from one of the landward windows, abstracted; but he held out a hand and took the bohea, carrying the beaker into the window opening. His rings gleamed: a band of platinum, an embossed band of silver and a plain gold ring. He wore tham all on the marriage finger of his right hand, a collection which could have been sold – though they lived, all of them, comfortably, without the small fortune their sale would have brought. They were markers from his past like the white pit on his wrist. Old gifts. Cal only gave him consumable gifts, candies, pickles, cakes, husk; once, a whole bottle of rahi.

'You can eat the bread,' he said now. 'I'm not hungry.' Then, sharply, 'Come here. What do you make of that?'

On Broadwalk, so far and obscured by the haze, they could see shadows, blobs and patches of mixed colour between the buildings; and, against these, a narrow ribbon of black.

'Cryos,' said Cal. 'A line of cryos. What is he about? They're moving away from the Block, east.'

'Here's the optic.' Peach, eager to please, reached out.

'No. They move all the time. Why should today be any different?'

The days passed. Had passed. Today was the one thousand one hundred and forty-sixth. His calendar of divorce was a grid of scratches on the wall and each line marked one more day on which there was no hope of repairing the rift. Materially – he provided for himself and his followers. Spiritually – he worshipped Mahun. Emotionally – there was Peach and a small tribe of sons and daughters who were certainly his. He fingered the twisted Tree which hung always from the chain around his neck. Some of them had seen it as a sign. Even the far away Sineinians showed interest in his fate and came to question him. As for himself, he still regarded the unique landmarks as patternless coincidences, events on someone's road, not his, the road which for him had ended in this blind alley, which had ended at a precipice for Dayamit.

He turned round, away from the many-towered City. Peach was still standing there, the expression in his great eyes like that of a starved dog.

'I told you to get down to the skimmer pads.'

Peach never disagreed with him. Obviously he had not voiced his thought.

'Go down to the pads and meet the journo from Sinein.'

Peach had no difficulty in recognising the correspondent. She had made herself comfortable in one of the chairs in the reception lounge, her bag and box of tricks beside her on the floor. Her hair was tied back in a knot and she wore cream-coloured overalls, the unrestricting dress all visitors from the north imagined practical for the tropics. Her disarmed weapon decorated her belt like a bizarre buckle. Peach hovered.

'Piss off,' she said, in his own dialect.

He stood his ground and spoke solemnly in Citycommons.

'I'm from Cal M'unor.'

'You?' She was surprised.

'He was a street boy too. Shall I carry your bag?'

'Any credentials?' Her own were fastened to her chest, a photoimage and words which he could not read.

'No. Just me.'

'Then I'll carry my bag. Lead on.'

She armed her rkw, he noticed, before she got up and followed him into the hot street.

'Your name?' she asked as they walked.

'Seef – but everyone calls me Peach.' She laughed, surveying him.

'I'm Orel Diran. From Universal.' The name of her network was another credential; even he had heard of it.

Peach pointed out the sights. The street leading towards the old city was crowded with people selling: girls offered hand-crafted necklaces made from melon seeds, carved lilies, toy monkeys on sticks and weighted wooden parrots on swings; there were card-tellers, card-tricksters, and jugglers, their faces made up like clowns'. At the end of the street an old woman in blue robes was praying hard.

'Beggars,' said Peach succinctly. 'All Depthers like me.'

'I thought Nonpareil abolished want.'

'He has opened schools and hostels: I'll show you later.'

'You've been to school?'

'What would I do in school? Besides, I'm too old and they are full: when the City was opened, lots of people came in from the country and then the harvest failed in '7.'

He took her by the tourist route, avoiding the burnt-out Quarter where new pavilions were beginning to arise on the ashes of the old. Even so, she noticed that the metro entrances were boarded up. She was impressed by the Citizens' Court and they paused outside while he told her as much as he knew about the Archivist's new system. The colossal statue of Arbiter Shuma dominated the quadrangle and its own three satellite figures. But she did not seem to recognise any of the sitters.

'There he is: that's him.' Peach gestured at the crouching figure.

She walked all round the monument and returned to the golden boy.

The sunlight emphasised the perfect human form and his absolute nakedness; there was defiance in his submission.

'He knew the sculptor.' Peach spoke proudly. 'He was about my age when she began it.'

The woman had turned away and begun her circuit again. She passed quickly by the shrouded female form of the soul to stand before the mind personified. Magon Nonpareil looked intently back at her, the nobility of his expression alive in the granite. She could see that his exterior was handsome, beautiful even, but what of his mind? She had read all his books, those abstruse studies and lengthy dissertations on words; there were no biographies. Perhaps a picture of the two statues to begin with?

'How long has it been here?' she asked, but the boy, Peach, was stepping delicately from one paving stone to the next, absorbed in a private game.

Broadwalk led into Citadel Street, the costly rewards. There were no Beggars here. They plunged into backstreets and byways and the memorised map of the City was washed from her mind. Peach led her through a warren of filthy alleys, overhung with strings of washing, littered with straw and garbage, populated by busy hens, and then through deserted yards and across wastelands until she wondered if there was a quicker way but he, with the cunning of a Beggar, sought to educate her. The buildings looked as though they might have been factories, old and deserted, fragile archive pictures, massive sweatshops like nothing in Sinein, shelters for labouring mechanical engines. Bats hung, furry stalactites, in dark archways. They crossed a narrow street and he opened one of a pair of metal-sheeted gates in a high wall of brick. There seemed to be no organisation at the place, if this was the dyeworks, M'unor's base commandery. A small woman with cropped black hair, a toddler at her heels and a baby in her arms, looked curiously at her when Peach showed her up the stairs.

She had been prepared for decadence, for decay and tough sinew, for some outward sign of his unique life, a harder impression than the statue gave. He looked older than his image, yes, but only because the lines at the corners of his eyes and tender mouth detracted from the colour of his skin. She had not been prepared for that skin, an echo of the golden limestone, a shadowy gilding; perhaps in him, the original pavement child, every gene mingled in an ultimate cocktail. Race was a memory, but type was still predominant. She herself was white-skinned, pallid, and colourless beside him. Nation and nationality, these had their place, these and the religion which in her own country was secularised, Mahun made into a display dummy. Here religious passion had caused a schism, a clean cut right through the City and the sexes. She shook hands with him, noticing his plain cotton clothing, the magnetic symbol at his neck, his three rings, the white scar of the acid burn.

279

'Please sit down,' he said. The bamboo chair creaked under her. Another tiny woman, very like the first and visibly pregnant, brought tea in glasses, bitter tea which had been sweetened with honey. She wanted to hear the hoarse dry voice again but he seemed – now that she was here, twelve thousand miles and a time-jolting journey from the leaf fall in Sinein – reluctant to speak, almost shy, sipping from his glass and looking at her over its rim with cat's eyes. Perhaps for the popular market, a series of soundpix, City boy, scholar (not much sound there), enigmatic brigand?

'What have you really come for?' he said, startling her, lowering the glass.

Her speech had been prepared.

'Your story, Mr M'unor. Universal has a great influence in Sinein and the System; we publish only truths and we pay well. You have become a force for good in this world: everyone is aware of your struggle.'

'I doubt it,' he said. 'And I've been bought before – how many rkws can your company supply?'

'Universal doesn't take sides.'

'Who says my story is true? Why don't you write it? Independently. Stuff the System.'

'I'm bound by my articles of employment.'

The hot tea, which he had sipped, which she found hard to swallow, had heated her still more. Her face was flushed, she thought, raddled; that on top of the sweat and the journey.

'You carry a weapon,' he said, 'Wise in such an unstable environment. May I see it?'

'Certainly not!'

He dismissed her.

'We eat as soon as night falls. Until then, I'd advise you to rest – the temperature will be ninety-five by noon. I'll send Peach for you when it's cooler.'

Peach was summoned to escort her to the hotel. In the air-conditioned refuge, she scribbled in panic, a flurry of symbols: it was a clumsy beginning.

The alarm buzzed gently at four and she cancelled it, rising to view the City from her window. The sun still blazed in the street below, but the shadows were longer and the cries less muted; a pastoral rattle of cartwheels and hooves and the overbearing, intermittent hum of skimmers rising from the pads. The alarm buzzed again and spoke to her.

'Your escort, Miz Diran. He is waiting in the Rotunda bar.'

Little rat. And he was early: night fell at seven precisely.

'I'll be down in ten minutes,' she said.

Peach, looking scrubbed and prescient with his task, obtrusively neat in the loose trousers they called slops and a blue shirt, was drinking rahi at the bar. As soon as she joined him, a glass appeared at her elbow on the bar and the barman smiled.

'The same,' she said, 'Yes please, ice and water.'

Peach grinned at her and dissolved the illusion of maturity.

'Rahi?'

'We drink it in Sinein. But it's too early to drink, and you have come too early.'

'He told me to take you round the City. The shay'll be here in a minute.'

So she toured the City, sitting comfortably beside Peach on the padded seat, the horse and driver blocking her forward view. The stylus of her recorder transmitted her scribbled impressions to the memory bank in her pocket; her brain recorded the messages from her eyes and ears, her nose. The smell of the City. She thought of it as a commodity which should be bottled and sent north in winter: heat, damp, flowers, spices, rottenness, ripeness, the salt air, even the odour of the boy beside her, an exquisite exotic masculinity. She would allow the sacred City to overrun her, and then extract from her seduction the essence of the place; transmit it to and beyond Guna.

The new Church of Monos stood at the further end of Broadwalk, its stark simplicity proclaiming the unvarnished truth of its faith. The ornate Temple overshadowed it. Nonpareil had gutted the old religion as he had gutted the Quarter, putting it one night to the torch. He had drawn the rotten entrails of superstition and sex, and taken away the licences of the temporal and spiritual prostitutes. His prescription in every case was prayer and the daylight of education. As he had opened the City, so he had unbarred the temple gates and access was free to all, man or woman, sceptic or devotee. To appease the secretive Gynarchy he had left the dark Mamelon and its resident sybil alone.

Orel dismounted from the shay in the Temple courtyard and looked about her.

The guardian statues at the open gates were splendid, especially to one whose faith had lapsed and sunk to empty gesture, an offering of money, on the principal feast days; who for the rest of the year forgot her origins in Mahun.

The golden dome of the Mamelon was a glittering hill, suggestive not so much of a breast as of a shell lapped over and concealing all the elements of life. It had no windows; she could not find a door, no crack in the curved and gold-leafed surface. She told Peach to wait and walked among the worshippers and Gynarchs in their blue robes, veils and golden hoods, on the verandah which ran all the way round the temple. Its multicoloured roofs were supported by wooden figures stiff with red and gold paint. They were all women, not a man among them, sensually beautiful, fifty-five of Mahun's thousand sisters, the

281

elemental forces, powerful and complete.

Orel sat on a cushion in a small circular oratory and looked at the murals: they told the story of Mahun and the Bowmen, nothing intellectual, no sop to the progress of thought and science. It was as if the millennia had passed in a mist of ritual and dance. On the last step in the temple doorway, she found the carving of a ship like *Daystar*, but it read as a stiff and penetrating symbol, force entering a starlit space. In this way, the starsailors, the female majority, had become as men, thrusting towards the heart of the mystery. The oppressive symbolism began to sicken her.

Yet, in the Temple, in the warm and perfumed darkness where polished bowls, oil-lamps deriving their shape from a cleft coconut, or a nourishing mother burned (separate flames beneath the shimmer of rising air), she was at peace, and she sat at the edge of the dancing floor and watched the veiled women of the City enter and sit down. They were at home; her legs, encountering the hard floor beneath her, ached. It took time for the congregation to gather.

A child came out of the darkness with a taper and lit the ring of lamps which surrounded the floor. She went away and there was utter silence. The first sound Orel heard was the chiming of small bells; she had not heard it since childhood for, in the cities of Sinein, the Dancers moved to cubed sound. The Dancers entered and she saw why their elaborate antique costume was hung with so much gold and silver: revolving, the ornaments caught and reflected the light. The Dancers themselves made so many turns, tight circles, smooth revolutions on one spot, that she wondered if they were giddy; she felt herself at the edge of a dream, watching them spin. When she glanced at the women beside her, she saw that their veils had been drawn aside and that their eyes were fixed, intent on whirling colours and far away visions. She became conscious of herself, unsuitably dressed, unsuitably minded, and crept away before the praying began.

Outside, the hot sun hurt her and imposed itself upon her eyes so that she blinked and saw many scarlet circles. Peach had seen her before she located him and ran up with the candies and fruit which he had bought from the stalls in the courtyard. He took her to the beach.

This time, she paid the driver and afterwards moved forward to pat the smooth neck of the horse. It left its scent on her hands, the mark of its animality, the warmth and solidity of a horse, a blessing absent from Sollar and much of Sinein.

A silver tower projected from a dark belt of trees, *Daystar*, an artefact tamed by her grounding and made natural. She should never accuse the heavens with such a gesture; Orel's mind called up the schoolday image: an immense silver cylinder hanging in her cradle below the satellite port off Eshtur. *Daystar* had been a creature of deep space, never the companion of vegetation and the soil. She must be regularly repainted, a shining skin of pigment and oil replicating the original shield, art on science, a monstrous duplicity. She wondered how much they had altered the interior to make a convincing show.

But Peach had wandered on, and waved from the frothy margin of the surf. He led her along the gilt ribbon of sand, alternately slouching and bending to pick up shells for her. Tomorrow, she must make her own way. The boy was bored and on loan; she needed to see other aspects of the City. She was not surprised at his choice of significant situations: the Temple and the bay, both huge theatres of blue and gold. The curtain dropped before they reached the promenade and she walked beside him through the velvet dark until they came by devious ways to the dyeworks.

He must have some means of obtaining money, some influx of cash or goods. Including herself, twenty-one sat down at the long table and four children played on the dusty floor; the small dark-haired woman Prenta held her baby while she ate. There were six women altogether: two of them were pregnant. She thought of them as uncivilised and in some way superior to herself, scarcely educated women whose babies were carried easily and born without intervention. She wanted to be like them.

The men were an assortment, rough, tough, and blasphemous; mostly they spoke Deep, the old dialect of the City's poor which had its roots in Proto-Maralay and the ancient divisions of the Mark. The Marks on their right arms were as assorted as their looks, stylised ploughs, a pendulum, an open red mouth. One of the men – she looked away and looked again – was pretty enough to be mistaken for a woman: the lamplight threw the soft contours of his face into exaggerated relief. Peach whispered in her ear, but the short cognomens meant little; she heard the names of animals and birds. If some of them were Tribers, their dress no longer revealed it and they wore Artisan slops or old army fatigues coloured like the City stones, grey, russet, and gold.

They ate meat, each piece highly spiced, but her itinerant profession had taught her to enjoy variety, and she had tasted the ubiquitous breadrings of the City in its embassy in Sollar; they drank rahi and then light beer from cans stamped with the name of an Ineiti brewer. The cook – she would have accorded him the title of chef for his ingenuity with his limited ingredients – put fruit on the table, coloured, scented, southern fruits still in their market baskets. She liked these casual City ways, where the careless use of an everyday artefact produced an aesthetic effect never intended, more potent than any Sineinian designer could invent. The fat white woman opposite her took no fruit, but pulled a bag from under the table and began to devour cakes from its sticky interior. It was cooler now, though still hotter than a northern summer's day; the fat woman wore two dead foxes around her neck, sorrowful creatures with

283

ears as big as rhubarb leaves, forever pricked in death.

Afterwards, M'unor took her into the small room where she had first encountered him. Transmitting her impressions later in Hotel Z, she was momentarily confounded by her notes; his name translated as 'Mahun's son'. But M'unor was a common suffix; he, lacking a matronym, had merely adopted it to colour his own short bark of a name. The room was a crammed storehouse: books and paper, a wooden image of Mahun, a print of *The City: Noon* from Crinon M'una's celebrated series, maps, a smoking lamp, an unmade bed. She declined his offer of more rahi and sat in the bamboo chair by the open window.

'That came from a matrician house,' he said. 'Sporadic fires, thefts. . . . Most of them have a private camel – there were hundreds on the streets after the Revolution. The government seems happy enough with the situation.'

'Raist Chenodor's party or the Archivist's?'

'All one.'

'Forgive me, but you're out of date. Chenodor's party and the Perseverant Sisterhood have dissolved their alliance.'

'Dissatisfied women – intellectuals, wastrel artists. They change their allegiance with the moon. When I knew them they were flies on garbage. Amarant Abayon, for example – if I had no pride I'd call her a vulture.'

'But Faya Edern – ' she protested. 'Her work with illiterates. . . . And Madam Abayon. She is said to have worked miracles drawing the psychological toxins of the change from child and adult alike with her free expression courses.'

He threw back his head (as Artisan idiom had it), while his unkempt hair flopped away from his neck and his open mouth showed a set of teeth in which the only blemish was a fractured tip on one of the canines. He laughed at her.

'I too,' he said, 'I used to think that the arts should have a practical use.'

She could not expect him to speak charitably or civilly of the wardens of the City; but how could she break through? She knew the recent history of the City as well as anyone.

'Mr M'unor,' she said, 'my readers are well-informed: we ran a short series of articles on City politics last year. But they know nothing of your heart.'

'Call me Cal,' he said, the City accent strong in the rusted voice.

She returned the compliment.

'Orel,' she said, 'my status must have been preordained: it means Enquirer.'

'Yes, I know.' The slow smile was charming. 'I studied Nenian.' He leaned back in his chair and settled his feet on the litter of papers which covered the table.

'Have you heard of *The Travels of Huyatt Tayal*?' he asked.

'A classic, even if it is now found to be fiction and not fact.'

'Then you know its history, and some of mine. A novel masquerading as the truth. A counterfeit of life. Sometimes my life seems an extension of his – a character in another's story. Beware: you may find yourself in the same imaginary land.

'In 501 I travelled in Vern: Huyatt's footsteps, the delusive vanity of a boy. I had always loved the book – that's another story – and when I became Dayamit I was forced to do his work. He had already published one book on Huyatt and a number of essays.'

'Yes. *Huyatt Revisited*, *The Influence of* The Travels of Huyatt Tayal *on the Literary Styles of the Circus Group*, *A Few Words on 'Diridion'*, and *Metrical Novelties in the Odalionsong*.'

'*Revisited* is mine. His book is called *An Inquiry into the Nature and Motives of Huyatt Tayal*'.

'Of course.'

'Later that year I was in Diridion and then the Tayaal itself. What a place! I still dream of it: the dry heat, the red rock, the black sand of the Negaar, the animals – did you notice the desert foxes around Vixen's neck? Living, they are a marvel, nocturnal beasts with huge eyes. Those ears are not for decoration either: they keep the animal cool. Perfect adaptation to the extreme.'

As he spoke, his accent modified itself. He sounded as though he had spent many years in the muted seclusion of a library: as he has, her mind cut in with the footnote.

'Huyatt – I still think of him as a reality – describes a mirage which he, and the monks, call God's Mirror. It's an illusion produced by heat and it occurs rarely and only in Udan. This is what he says: "When I rode Alna home, I knew not the hour nor the day, nor whether my people lived or died. I saw the miracle of Ruht, a sign of my time and their abiding, a scarlet pyramid hanging upside down in clear skies above the white cube of my home."

'That is exactly what I saw. In reality it is a enantiomorphic image of the white houses of Ruht and the red mountains beyond. Usually the traveller sees the whole picture but I saw the most rare, the one he saw: one set, one cube, one pyramid.

'Sometimes I dreamed of cubes, pyramids, the houses, the Ruht; sometimes – I noticed later, back in the City – I drew them in the margins of my notes. I forgot about the vision, almost forgot the Tayaal, except for the picture in my room which shows a string of horsemen crossing the barkans. Then, three years ago, when I was working at the Machine, I happened to glance away from the screen. (You should know that nothing in the Forbidden Archive has been moved since the Reformation: now, years after the Revolution, they continue to add to the catalogue.) On one

285

of the shelves was a section of geometric data, spells for mathematicians, and two labels, one directly above the other, read 'The Pyramid' and the 'The Cube'. The data is stored on complex cubes; also, a pyramid reversed is an arrow, a pointer. I went to the shelves and on the lower one I found a box without a label, a square white box. Inside was a white complex cube; so I binned what I was doing and dropped it into the Machine.

'The first word it spoke was "Congratulations", in their family voice: Crinon's, Saissa's, his through the Tribute. Then "Well done, Traveller. You have found the answer: what will you do with your knowledge? This is the voice of Lys Hinoor, this is my signature." It appeared on the screen. Then followed a series of proofs: drafts, rough drafts, final drafts, pictorial evidence, statistics, even an image of the light-sensitive note-book which is in the monastery library in Diridion. She had begun the book as a diversion, but it grew and took over; she had worked on it late at night when her duties were completed. When it was printed and "discovered" in the third stock of the Octagon Library, she began another forgery, the Odalionsong. That was rediscovered in an attic in Odalion itself. And so on – all Huyatt's work is hers.

"Look again at my *Travels*", she had said, and I remembered my discovery in Binala – that the page headings make a poem. It was so simple, and I and every other scholar of Huyatt so stupid. The initial letters of each line spell out, albeit embedded in alphabetical garbage, her message, "I, Lys Hinoor, the eighty-ninth Archivist of the City of Mahun in Mahkrein, made this."

'I didn't believe it, any of it. I thought it was another of Magon's games –'

Inadvertently, unwillingly, carried along by his narrative, he had spoken the name of his tormentor.

He stood up, so that the interview would end. On the woman's face, he saw her curiosity, her journalist's questing nose.

'It's black dark,' he said. 'Time you were gone. I'll take you back: the lighting's still poor and the streets aren't safe.'

The lanes and alleys of the City were dark as Eshtur eclipsed; but above the canyons, the sky blazed with an intensity greater than that of a frosty northern night. He walked swiftly without regard for her unfamiliarity with the broken ground. They crossed a deserted square and she smelled raw meat. He looked about him at all the black entrances and doorways and took hold of her arm to walk her along one side of the square, his touch asexual and dominating; when he had guided her into another of the myriad alleys he released her.

'Sometimes there are Ironmen,' he said, 'or government cryos off-duty: they managed to reprogramme some of them but at a distance in the

286

dark you can't tell them from the wanderers.

'You were told how to deal with a wanderer?'

'They obey the voice of a woman.'

'Without question. But keep the command simple or you put yourself in jeopardy: part of the malfunction is an inability to contain frustration. They have the strength of a madman.

'There's one. Keep walking.'

He had taken her arm again; this time she felt a tremor in his hand. She saw the cryo clearly as it passed them, the tall silhouette of a beautiful woman in a gown, an rkw tilted carelessly over her shoulder. The scent of rock orchids, rare mountain dwellers, flowed from her.

'Some of them rediscovered sex,' he said. 'And they are more predatory than a falcon – than a hungry Temple Dancer. They have made a new itinerant Quarter.'

Thoughts of sex with the generation of the great starsailors invaded her, an exchange with the past, a fantastic meeting of old and new genes; of a child made from nearness and distance, with the inherited responses of a longhaul pilot and a newly wakened voyager. The hand of her contemporary, this singular man, had remained on her arm, just above the elbow, relaxed now; she was closer to him than she wanted to be. The magic of the night-time City was reality, a perilous now, and she looked after the armed cryomorph, gone down the street to Mahun knows what destination or congress. She remembered that her own weapon was still active and moved a finger to operate the catch.

'Forgot to disengage it? That's bloody dangerous,' he said.

'But I didn't know – ' she began. He would not respond and hurried her down the dark street and into the sudden blaze of Citadel Street; he saw her into the hotel foyer and she observed that the doorman, recognising him, was disconcerted and gave him a salute which was half reverential and half mocking.

Cal loitered in Copper Street. Puddles of light spilled on to the pavement and illuminated the new litter of discarded magazines and news-sheets. Cubed music span and jerked from the bars and, while it excited him, it also disturbed him because it had changed one of the frames, his recollection of the harmonies and silences of the City.

The journo was an odd blend, without the assurance of a City woman, personally diffident, professionally curious, a conformist like every woman, even Crinon; she appeared defensive, strong, trained in her craft, oddly fearful; afraid of him because of the things she had read, been told, about Cal M'unor, the fallen idol, the mendicant king not of a shadowy dreamtime kingdom by the sea, but of a band of Depthers like himself, old whores and Beggars, faded Tribers and transsexuals, of a squatter realm, an area of dirty brick, discoloured stone and asphalt enlivened only by the children, by Peach's flowers, by Peach himself. Until this night and the advent of the woman from Universal he had not thought of Magon as a figure on the world stage; of himself as a supporting actor, an antiDestorio to Magon's Chacma. The drama was becoming farce, the parallel was false, for Chacma was a hideous octogenarian, shrunk from his former strengths and glories, and Magon's father had died five years ago. . . .

He had given the journalist an outline shorn of his rage and hysteria, his tears and abuse, his exposition of Magon's devious plot to keep him tamed and occupied on the Hill.

Magon had been abusive in return. He was innocent, he said finally, the conclusion was false, I gave you more than diversions; and he had left the room and the apartment. When he returned later, he found Cal idly moving the chess pieces of a game in progress, a battle he had joined against himself, an exercise; and with no more provocation than the spoiled game walked up and hit him. The blow raised a bruise instantly; Magon had gone for flannels and ice, applied them to the swelling eye, soothed him and his own intellectual bruises.

'Lys Hinoor,' he said, 'was a genius. I've been looking at her file and her IR was 500. She travelled twice in the Tayaal, once in 254 and then again in 256, between Lilb and Hibornal.

'I have come back so that you can take me down and show me the proofs.'

Two months later, he had begun his reassessment of Huyatt's works, truly Huyatt revisited. Magon had seemed keen to set the record straight and amused to find a forger in his family.

Eventually she would extract it all, another Galabrias, but one who sold her conclusions. Maybe that was more honest. He went into the drugstore and bought five grams of husk, lingering to gossip with the dispenser.

It was raining when he came out of the store, soft warm rain which fell without any of the chill bitterness of an Udan storm. There was the doorway from which Peach had sprung, bearing him to the ground with the enthusiasm of an apprentice robber. He could have escaped all three of them, Shiny and Dove as well, with a simple break, but the injury had prevented him. His wrist ached with remembered sympathy. His cry of pain had come at the same moment as Peach's yell and then Peach, shoving the other two aside, had helped him to his feet, all solicitude, an expression of relief on his face and tears brimming from his beautiful eyes. The invitation issued on Daid's Ground so long ago was answered.

The swan was his, to feed and caress, the black feathers on its head soft as foreskin under his fingers, his to fly, its infinitely long string tied to its dark red legs, its webbed feet dangling over the bay into a plummeting crescent viewed through the wrong end of an optic. It was his to ride, this kite which danced in the wind, shaking its tail of rags. He could feel the bones under the muscle, the skeleton within the flesh. When it plunged, he sank, giddy, delirious; when it soared, he glided, buoyant, delighted.

Deeply asleep, the women excluded, Peach banished, he was himself and inhabited the palace of dreams, his own stronghold. He awoke with a headache and reached for the antidote, the blue bottle beside the bed, for the pinch of husk which, dissolving on his tongue, burning, took away the pain in his head. Galabrias knew nothing of this: it was his own discovery.

'Bitch,' he said, in the habitual voice of familiarity, and saw that he was alone, had slept alone. He shouted for her. There was no answer. She would not respond to the old name. Since Dog's death, dissolution at the hands of a cryo, she would not answer, not make up her face or any other's in the unmistakable fashion and with the inimitable colours of the Faces; but she had come to him and several days later her sister, Hellie, had crept into the dyeworks, with the real fear of a mouse pursued by a cat. 'Prenta. Come up here'.

She brought their youngest child, the three-month old bundle of wriggling limbs, toothless smile, and sweetly foetid odour. The boy lay on the bed and smiled at the ceiling, his hands and feet involuntarily practising deliberate movement, his voice all pleasure, while his father kissed his mother.

'He took me miles,' he told Orel. 'Across the City to the Reservation – it was by the North Wall. I wanted him to find Tarla: she was dead, he said, dead, broken, and consumed.' He watched the stylus move, making the rapid strokes of the journalists' code. 'It would have been better, less painful, to go straight to the physic shop. The jolting of the shay was worse than the agony of walking. Prenta ran across the room but Dog called me several inventive names before he kicked me out: "You're the louse which feeds on the dank undersides of parasites, the arch-parasite of them all," he said. "you're the king of the rent boys, a crutch crab, prick cheese, smegma." Those were his last words, for me.'

Her sophisticated smile concealed her embarrassment.

'So Peach took me to Stone Walk, by the Arcade, and into the pharmacy there. She had more spray and painkillers. I had to go back each day for a dek, then the skin started to grow, white as mould, and she dissolved the plastic and gave me one of her salves, something with bergamot and honey in it. That was worse, in a way, than the burn. I slept with the scents of Galabrias's garden in my nostrils.

'Magon took so much trouble over the design –'

The time of his undoing lived on in his mind with a clarity undiminished by the intervening years.

The door to Cudbeer's old rooms was unlocked. He had seldom been there and not for more than a year, but he remembered how the three rooms and offices were laid out. He pushed open the door, and walked along the short corridor which led to the study. On one side, the room overlooked the western fountain court and the view from the wide window at the end of the room was of the deer park and the fields of Maralis. He saw skimmers above the fields and carts on the newly surfaced road above the gorge, tiny models. On the table lay his Huyatt, the book he had unaccountably been sent to fetch. "I'm sorry," Magon had said, "I left it there." But a head of blonde hair interrupted the view.

'I have waited a long time,' said Hyason, turning towards him. Her white clothes were prison overalls. He halted, halfway across the room. She, reclining on the couch, looked at him with the greed of a hungry cat.

'I thought you were dead,' he said. 'I hoped your death was a painful one.'

She smiled.

'No. Magon saved me. He sent for me an hour ago. Someone who will do what he fears fascinates him; especially if that person is a contemptible woman.

'Come here, filth.'

Behind him, the door shut. He had been aware of a presence in the room; now he saw the two cryomorphs: a pale-haired trooper and the male medic, Kunai.

He turned round and spoke to the cryos.

'Stand aside,' he said. His voice, attempting the higher registers, squeaked and dried. Hyason laughed. The cryos, advancing, caught him up by the arms, anyhow, and dumped him on the couch beside her. She reached out and pulled his head down into her lap. He tried to free himself but with two cryos, it was impossible.

'Amateur', said Hyason, one set of fingers at his throat, the other in his hair. He bit her thigh. She held him closer.

He felt one of the cryos extending his right arm.

Once, as a child, he had touched a live coal beside a traveller's fire; the woman, practical, quick, had plucked him up and plunged his hand in cold water. That burning might have been sensuous pleasure beside the searing pain in his wrist where the partridge Mark was. He could see nothing, smell nothing, but the excited woman. He cried out, a muffled shout which did not allay the torture. He kicked, and Hyason stroked his hair. She pulled up his head and kissed him on the mouth. Then she released him.

The acid had burned the pattern away and made a raw red pit in his flesh; the medical officer dripped an antidote into it. He could not feel that, but under the weal his bones burned. Through his tears he saw the cryo spray a liquid dressing on the wound; he watched it harden.

Hyason stood over him. She spoke to him as an equal.

'You stole his thunder with your incontrovertible genetic proofs,' she said. 'Don't you know him, after all this time? You should have left it alone, let him believe in his virility.'

She put the book in his left hand and then the trooper lifted him bodily, and dumped him outside. He walked a few paces, he walked across the endless floor to the banded door of home. The door was invisible, shut in its surround of wood: his key was inside with everything else. He looked at the faint outline of the door. He heard the distant lift descending as the last reader left the Octagon.

A paper trash sack lay outside the door. He picked it up, holding it awkwardly in his left hand together with the red book. He saw that there were several cryos nearby. They approached. They held him efficiently, carelessly, between them as they took him to the lift.

The fresh darkness outside the Octagon was pierced by silver shafts of light from the great lamps. Above them, he saw the evenstar and daystar together in the sky, one rising, the other sinking. The cryos walked him to the gate.

Outside the iron gates, it felt cold. He shivered, watching the cryos turn back towards the Octagon on the other side of the tracery, bars nonetheless. He walked down the Hill until he could see the south side of the building. The light from Magon's study, high above, was faint: the glass lamp on his desk. Never mine. He walked away, down the long and twisting Hill, towards the City. The last rain of the season began to fall, soaking him with its cold needles as he walked.

When he reached Citadel Street, the Glass Mall a lantern in the rain, he remembered Hyason's kiss. He put down the sack so that he could wipe his mouth with the back of his hand. He knew what was in the bag: a torch, a camel knife, seven frags and eighteen bits. Magon's literal sense of justice would not have deserted him, in this, the final quarrel. He put the objects into his pockets and Lys's novel inside his shirt. The three rings were safe on his finger, Dayamit's gold-cased pencil and the opalescent watch were in the pocket of his shirt, the silver chain and the Tree round his neck. He would have to sell them all to live, items from his personal portable bank.

The City gave him her familiar smell, sweetened by the falling rain. The pain in his wrist had turned into a predictable pulse; at its height, it coursed in all the nerves of his arm and penetrated his shoulder and his chest. Under the first of the new streetlamps, he paused to examine the dressing. The white circle of solidified gel was rimmed with red. He walked down Citadel Street, nursing the arm in his left hand, and passed the Lily Exchange. The building exhaled its old magic. The scent lingered, caught at his clothing. Husk would help him now. He turned the corner into Vern Street, intending to make his way by the alleys and by Copper Street into the Quarter. Beggars had gathered, a tight cluster, in their usual spot by the warehouses, ready to accost the theatregoers and nightcats as they came from the Globe on to Vern Street. So easily had he slipped into his old skin, he had forgotten his fancy clothing, the silk shirt and lambswool sweater. He was one of the Hill people.

Orel had visited the dyeworks three times and amassed many blocks of characters: the memory of her tablet was vast, transmitting as it did to the collection and relay station on the Lutreian archipelago. She had organised some of the data into brief articles, teasing synopses, letters from the City. These were for immediate publication. The remainder, locked in a subfile with a disarming title, she sent directly to store in Sollar Kein, wondering, as she pressed the transfer key, if it gave her subject relief, a kind of catharsis, to rid himself of the troublesome imagery which was the notepad of his inner existence and the legacy of his trauma. He would not be photoimaged nor drawn (she had thought of hiring one of the excellent street artists). For the time being, she abandoned her idea of prefacing the series with a montage of the boy, the man he had become, the untouchable Archivist, and the two statues.

'There are enough imitations of me about the City,' he said. 'Go to the galleries.'

'I shall go to the Octagon,' she said, and smiled when he stood up and said he must leave, now, he had forgotten, Peach had asked him. . . .

She hired a shay and was driven up the Hill. The pale Octagon mounted up to the sky. She read the essay carved on the foundation stone and glimpsed the gardens through open gates.

In the first of the halls she gave her card to a receptionist who laid it in a tray with a host of others.

'May I have a sheet of paper?'

She sat at one of the polished tables and composed a letter to Magon Nonpareil, Archivist of the Sacred City of Mahun. She wrote carefully so that her sensitivity, her knowledge and appreciation of the arts and sciences, her expensive education, and the years at Sollar Kein were apparent in her style and handwriting. She remembered every one of his degrees and titles and wrote them in the correct places and the correct order before she sealed the letter in the envelope she had been given. The receptionist put it in the tray.

Then, she was allowed to walk freely about the vast tower, pausing to look at the sculpture and paintings on the lower floors before she ascended to the first floor of the great Library, to be confronted by the Index. The Machine, she understood, resided in the levels below the ground together with uncounted tons of film, plastic, paper, vellum, clay tablets, wooden tallies, and string accounts. She sat in a roomful of Gunaian literature and thought of Cal, vulnerable and newly delivered from the horrors of the Block. Presently she rose and, for the comfort of the known, consulted a familiar volume, her grandmother's essays on the botany of Eririon. She stroked the name embossed on the spine of the leatherbound book. Here, all the books were real, paper and board.

The reply, which was delivered to the hotel next day, told her with apologies that the Archivist never gave interviews; it was signed Silvanor Cudbeer, Assistant Archivist, and a handwritten postcript wished her every success with her project.

She walked in the City before the heat came, strolling on tree-lined avenues, occasionally entering a shop or a café. Beyond the ancient Artisans' Quarter – a blue plaque told her its history and she saw deserted walks, burnt-out buildings, demolition gangs, and Zalcissa hurrying across the rubble – she found a new square. Remarkable houses surrounded it, a wall of dwellings built in a new interpretation of the graceful style of the old City houses, soft cliffs with coloured balconies and narrow heat-excluding windows. Magon and his famous horse stood on mown grass in the centre of the square, stone witnesses to a resurrection. The horse was lifelike; the man, dressed in the enveloping sandcloth of a Tayali, remained a deliberate enigma. She could not think how to reach him and she walked on and on until she came to the river.

After noon, the City Gallery. The painting had a room to itself and hung on the far wall, protected from the public by a white rope and a dour attendant carrying a handweapon. The canvas was unframed, perhaps ten feet by eight, ablaze with the colour of the afternoon outside the dim gallery. She felt herself diminish and become a grey pilgrim. He burned in the painting, and the white and yellow lilies on the sepia water of the pool were flat suns and moons; his reflection gleamed, the mirror of the perfect body, a watery charm. The older man wore an expression of greed, ageing and ridiculous in his concealment. To hide her blushes from the watchful attendant, she read the notes in her catalogue. 'Crinon Hinoor M'una. Untitled Allegory (portrait of Cal M'unor), 501AR, oil on canvas, 124"×98". On loan from the Artist.' If she had been in the City in 501, she would have pursued him; but she had been far away in Noiro reporting the episodes in a cold environmental war.

He laughed at her description of the chaste surroundings of his youthful fire.

'Glaver has a gown like a pillar of fire,' he said, 'That's Crinon's description. It's the right dress for her, consuming and inflammatory.

'Peach was living with Shiny and Dove in the woodsheds on Salt Street, in hiding from the new terror, separate beds, a roof, and education. I climbed the tower as soon as I got my grip back. My blankets were mouldy and I pitched them out of the window. I should have gone to the cellar. It was cold, Alcuon chill, but I wanted to be up above, higher

293

than the cryos, out of reach in case he sent Hyason after me. The climb
was more difficult because the chantry was being dismantled – they gave
up the restoration when the crop failed – difficult, but possible. I came
down again just before dark because I was hungry and went to Tyler's
where I bought bread at the back door. The girl didn't recognise me and I
kept my right hand in my pocket. I crossed Judges' Bridge and passed the
Dayamits' house. I had to make the City mine again.

'The Old Market was unlit and I thought at first that he had imposed a
curfew. The shops used to be open past midnight. There was no one
about. I couldn't pass Glaver's house without a look. I stood in the street
and looked up at the windows: the shutters were all closed.'

Impelled by no particular desire, but by boundless curiosity – perhaps
she had moved away – he crossed the street and entered the alley at the
side of the house. Washing hung on the criss-cross web of lines in the
courtyard. He touched it: it was damp, rained upon. Its texture was
rough, nothing Glaver would wear, unless she hung out her bodyshield.
The balcony was a shadowy ledge and the window above him dimly lit.
He climbed the housewall and stood on the balcony. The urns were full
of scented flowering plants which silently signalled to the moths,
messages of desire like his urgent need to look into the open doorway at
the end of the balcony, where the light escaped through a thin curtain.

The curtain was made of muslin, a tissue veil appropriate to his role:
he could see her quite clearly. She crouched on her bed with a man
beneath her, a night-rider, an ardent succubus. She had been his
adolescent passion. He listened to her; he whispered her magical
Tlivoorn name: Tsaka, efreet, djinn, spirit. She rolled away from her
lover and dismissed him as if he had been a waiter; the man picked up his
clothes and approached the door.

The priapic cryo passed within six inches of him, crossed the balcony
and disappeared inside the house. One of the gunners, physical
creatures with residual brains: five had gone missing when Magon took
the City.

Cal walked into the room and stood at the foot of the bed. Glaver was a
brown pool, a lovely hollow, a cleft; he did not see a knife but, if she stabs
me now, he thought, it will only be justice and it will end the game.

'I told you to go,' Glaver said. She lay on her back, her lids closed over
her eyes, the marvellous breasts spread and flattened by their own
weight.

'I have never paid you,' he said.

She moved; there was a knife, but her hand, instead of gripping it,
knocked it to the floor.

'The second time of carelessness,' she said. 'If I am ever killed it will
be from my own stupidity.'

He could not wait: he was a moth, dazzled, insatiable. He was unable to satisfy her.

'My friend,' she said, with her inverted Tlivoornal grammar and logic, 'you are a long time without a woman?'

At last he could put his face against her breasts.

'Years,' he said. 'Six of them.'

Her reply was laughter; eventually he had to laugh with her. He saw, as she must, that his tragedy was comedy. Not only had his wings been torn off; they had been cut in pieces.

It took him the remainder of the night to tell her his story, journeying through the years and wild places, to travel all the regions of her body. In the morning, she left him but returned at noon with food and a bundle of invoices. She dealt in other weapons now, she said: knives were the last resort. She could earn ten times more selling rkws and personal impact missiles.

Miel did not disturb them and he did not see the gunner again; but he guessed that Glaver had taken him off the streets and kept him. To ask her about the morality of bedding a recombined cryo would be to define his own status too closely.

'Don't you find it strange,' he asked, 'to screw a man who was born in 3576?'

'He is a man. He is happy: he thinks he has succeeded with a wealthy woman – he has. My chick, he fucks almost as well as you; he has fewer refinements perhaps.'

She laughed.

'Who would think you have spent six years as a woman? You know it is the time Inana spent as a man?'

In her absences, he walked about the room, searching for clues to her heart. The body shield hung in one of the cupboards: she wore a better version, a masculine shaper from Roakn where she had a new house and friends in the army. In another, the costumes of Shiron hung like chrysalids, the scarlet, orange, and vermilion dress dully burning, a satin conflagration of flickering tongues. He touched the silk. Nothing told him about Tsaka. There were no books in the room and only one mirror, a hand mirror on a table; no tubes or pots, but a hairbrush and one piece of her glass, an enfolded cup, a blush rose. Above the table hung a tall painting, the half-size portrait of a woman as pink and white as the rose and wearing nothing but a straw hat from which fluttered a wide ribbon, its title, *Invitation?*, as coquettish as its subject. It was genuine, a rare genre painting of the Craft Revival.

Each time Glaver returned, she restored him with vigorous embraces, the energy of the precise artist of knives. Halfway through the third day she told him, without rancour, to leave.

He walked familiar streets. No cryos or other monsters threatened him; the noise of children escaped from the open windows of the schools he passed, birds waiting for their day. He took to the alleys and emerged on Broadwalk. Nothing but his invisible mind could set him apart from the other wealthy customers at Citybank. The idea was Glaver's. He walked into the empty booth and spoke to the cashier; her super was called and he explained an imaginary plight. It would take them some hours to issue a new wafer but, 'It was handed in, sir,' said the official.

The envelope contained his wafer and a folded sheet of paper with one phrase in Slake's handwriting: 'Yours, not his.' He withdrew all his money and walked back to the knife thrower's house with notes and coins in his pockets.

'Money is power,' said Glaver, watching him count it. 'We learned, we Tlivoorn, that lesson a long time ago. You have seen our men, up to their necks in water.

'Will you entrust your money to a Tlivoorn? I go to Cheron in Ah: my daughter is at school in Roakn.'

He pictured her daughter: a smiling infant, a seductive girl? But she revealed no more of her.

'The bank there,' she said, 'the State bank – Magon Nonpareil is the principal shareholder. My friend is married with the president.'

'And what did you do with the money?' Orel's hand had moved steadily while he related the intimate detail; now it moved briskly. The smell of rotting water from the old dye pits added a burden of decay to the scent of the flowers which had invaded the dyeworks close. She sat among yellow flowers with an expression of greed on her face.

'My affair,' he said.

'I'm not sure if I can publish any of this.'

'It's my truth: duality, constancy, and avarice, those are my character-istics. Make your own deductions. Your word-portrait will be less like me than Crinon's painting.'

'My articles have concentrated on your intellect and your languages.'

'Useless in the Depths. Peach survived as well as I.'

'Peach isn't stupid.'

'Peach is thick. A beautiful clown.'

'I'll have to tone it down, make it lyrical.'

'Glaver is a lyric. You're shocked. You've the sensibilities of a Matriarch.'

'Professional writers don't shock. Nothing in the City could be as disgusting as the stews of Roakn.'

'Which you saw as a tourist. Everyone has to earn a living.'

'At Sollar we were trained to analyse every action and reaction.'

'Like the good doctor. Training is a poor substitute for experience. Galabrias thinks he knows everything about husk when he knows no more than Magon does about women. He thought he had looked into my soul, but he didn't know that I had given it away.'

His mind, when he relaxed, was a tesserate ambulatory of events, dreams, memories, and attributes. He thought about the black swan: he did not need to disentangle the coded message from his unconscious. In the strong light the swan had less substance than the shadows of the dyeworks, than the phallic umbrage of his tower, his reason for remaining, that, and his children. This water was as unplumbable as those secret pools of the inmost garden, the inscape of his mind, a slough for mosquitoes and disease but also a nursery. Orel's hand was still. He had driven her aground.

'Thank you,' she said, her customary prelude to farewells. 'Perhaps I can come again – in a few days' time?'

'Null,' he said in the Facer argot, but she did not understand. 'It means all right, I assent, you may, I'll help you – with overtones of friendship.'

She waved before she turned the corner into Peach's yard.

He prayed sometimes, though he did not go to the Temple. When he prayed, he thought of the statue in the cellar, the buried manifestation of Her harmony. He thought of Tror, the usurped consort, the patient hob. His life and loves were peccadilloes; he had sinned only once.

The idea had been with him since Vedara left the house in the Silversmiths' Quarter, taking his child with her, escorted by her solemn father and her bearded admirer, the man who would become her husband and the stepfather of his child: Gesir, the ounce hunter. He had returned to the Hill. In a sense, he had never left it, working late in the Octagon most days, his dearest possessions still in the room next to Magon's. He cut into the stained sheet he had taken from the linen basket and sent the specimens to Galabrias by special courier. Slake complained of a missing sheet and blamed the laundry. It was harder to get a sample from the twins, but he waited and a day came when both grazed their knees in Crinon's garden. He rushed to mop up the blood.

The revelation came in a small package, three months later, when he had almost succeeded in hiding the guilty secret from the conscience Magon said he lacked. The analysis was lengthy and detailed; he looked at the four patterns, the unique signatures of heredity. Three of then matched: his, Leirion's and Anyal's; the fourth was a stranger. He read Galabrias's brief greeting, which spoke of plants and literature, the beauties of the beach in Udan, and ended with a laconic 'strange new interest for a linguistic genius, but genius takes many byways'. He concealed the papers under old notes in the bottom drawer of his desk and tried to forget what he had done.

* * *

The swifts had nested in Alcuon and raised their broods. The rest of the year was for delight, for aerial play and the screaming intricacies of swift society. Every morning at daybreak they left the tower, shooting from the windows of their rooms, loosed arrows, to fly over the bay in a shifting pattern, their screams piercing the warp of the breakers and the waking City. They dived, closing the scythes of their wings against their bodies, and resurfaced, each with a small fish imprisoned between the hard mandibles of its beak. (He watched them closely through the optic he had bought from Glaver.) Whenever he found a dead bird, a small grey parcel of feather and bone, dried out by the sun, he spread its wings and examined it to see if he could locate the source of the bird's power in flight.

In the heat of the day, the swifts rested in the tower and he, passing upward to his eyrie, would encounter them, open-eyed but motionless, as if they slept, crouched on the beams by their empty and disorderly nests. They returned to the bay in the late afternoon and displayed their noisy haste before they fed. It was a sight the tourists had enjoyed, one now left to the citizens and visiting correspondents. The last bird settled in the tower at the precise moment of nightfall and he could shine a light on them without disturbing their rest. Once he had picked up a swift and cradled it in his hand, feeling the prick of its long claws as it tried to grip, admiring its flexible gape and sharp bill, its saucer eyes, and its grey feathers tipped with black; it was a creature lovelier than the purple swifts of Baia and the Mahkra, a speedy predator which dived into an alien environment for its living. His reading in the Octagon had taught him that the fishing swifts were not swifts at all; but the niceties of birds biology were not appreciated in the City. The birds had been called swifts since the beginning, when they nested on the citadel rock.

Their screaming exit woke him every morning and sometimes, rejoicing in it and the light of the new day, he closed his eyes and slept another hour; sometimes, the activity of the birds infected him and he got up from his bed, the first in the dyeworks to wake, and climbed to the top of his tower to talk with the City. If he trained the optic on the Hill and let his hand, despite the increasing tension and the increased sthenic tremble, move it mechanically towards the Octagon, he could clearly see the entrance court and the closed doors with their bronze reliefs; but Magon's windows facing south and east were hidden from him by the wedge which contained – he could enumerate and list them all – on Level 1, a gallery full of second millennium water colours; on Level 2, a conference room and a suite of offices; on Level 3, and so on, upward through the fine furniture, the heavy fabric of the curtains, the shelves of books and the cool scholastic air, until he was, except for his shaking body, deep in the silence of Level 15 where Lys Hinoor's forgeries and the many commentaries on Huyatt still rested.

Dayamit's watch gave him the day and the time: 25 KiV, 511, 7.07; the volition, because next month the heat would be upon the City and the will stifled. He disdained Triber shams but was forced to operate within their code of insult and retribution. One rkw like his would have settled the conflict for ever, but the conflict had become ritualised almost to the point of idiocy, a crude imitation of the single combat of the First Years. Glaver had a new shipment of knives and other primitive weapons; for him and his concerns she had re-opened a route. It was known that he had her ear and, sometimes, her body. He enjoyed complete ascendancy over the Faces and the Fists; since his advent, the Ironmen had become the underlings.

He slid down the first ladder without using his feet and, on the uppermost floor of the swifts' roost, flexed his arms: the tremor had disappeared. He glanced at the scar, resenting the succession of marks which had spoiled the skin, the proofs of ownership and station which had begun with Dayamit's green Tertiary.

Leirion and Anyal smiled at him, mute forms in his memory. She was not like him, though she had a gold-brown skin which spoke his part; she was a little like her mother in delicacy and finesse, bearing the genes which were the inheritance of his unknown mother. Anyal's face mirrored his. He could understand why no one had commented on the likeness: the boy had dense black hair.

Peach was asleep on the mat beside his troughs, easy in the open air and he responded lazily to his kiss.

On the streets the day had begun, clear and normal as if it were no part of the tedious prelude to the next disaster. Out at sea, swifts had disappeared inside a pearl.

They sat in Tyler's bar and breakfasted on bohea, rahi, and the fresh bread Tyler's son had made during the night. The place had prospered for a while, the solid furnishings which had replaced the old dereliction evidence of the brief time when the fashionable had been seen there breakfasting beside workwomen and the flesh traders from the Quarter. Following Magon's precipitate and retributive burning of the Quarter, when commerce was reduced to night-time dealing in alleyways, it had resumed its old place as a refuge. He bought Peach a bowl of soup and watched him eat it, another repayment for the starvation years.

The news-sheet Tyler bought for his regular customers told him little, though he read every close-packed word on the doubled page. At the Revolution, information had been called the right of every citizen, but Oyno's suspicions had diminished the ideal: the news was of bagatelles. One of the impossible dreams. He was haunted this morning. He looked at Peach and wanted to weep. He twisted his rings and a lock of hair, fidgeted with the Tree and the news-sheet. Tyler, from under his bushy brows, watched him as if he feared another revolution. The boys at the corner table played fivestones as usual but when Zalcissa came in, the child on her hip and her crochetwork in her hand, it was time to leave. He paid the reckoning and left, Peach a hurrying shadow at his heels.

When he had spoken with Miel and then with Glaver, while Peach waited on the doorstep, he plunged into the market and walked for an hour, Peach dawdling at his heels, distracted by the displays outside the shops. He read the signs: the uncollected garbage and the general malaise. Slowly the City was sucking them all in, returning to her disturbed sleep. She did not care. Let them crawl on all her surfaces, the impotent flickers of their quarrels small irritations, flea bites. He bought Peach an ice, a rainbow of frozen syrup, and left him with it while he rummaged in a bookshop, dismayed by the numbers of broken-backed and worthless fictions. Begging had taught Peach patience: when Cal came out of the shop, he was sitting on the kerb, the ice long gone, reading the picture book of the street through the veils of his lashes, his pellucid eyes half-closed. Cal touched him. Sometimes he wondered if he revenged himself on Peach.

They passed by a house whose windows were covered in mesh. Inside, a flock of tiny birds got up and wheeled, panic lifting them from their perches, a cloud of wings in incessant movement. A heap of dead birds lay against the far wall and bowls of dirty water and seed were scattered indiscriminately about the floor. The birds settled. A dozen parrots, manacled to sticks, tried to fly.

'Mama had a parrot on the boat,' said Peach. 'He had to be tied on.'

There was always a crowd on Judges' Bridge. A ramp led down to the waterside and groups of people sat in the gardens there. From the bridge they watched the comings and going on Broadwalk, the straightfaced cryos on guard outside the courts, the traffic over and under the bridge. On the greasy waters of the Uynal small craft plied up and down between the docks and the farms and gardens upstream. They saw a dredger lumber slowly downstream, and the brown sails of wine luggers from Baia. Every trade flourished now that the searchlights, the river guard, and the mole and barrier had been replaced at the water gate by a corundum battery.

He lounged beside Peach on the bridge, conspicuously inconspicuous, his other self stone across the road. He leaned beside Peach on the parapet and they looked into the swift yellow water, down on the deck of a fruit boat and its inhabitants passing underneath. He put his arm across Peach's shoulders and whispered in his ear: Peach laughed. The citizens who recognised him went home and said, 'I saw Cal M'unor today. What a fall from grace.' In the middle of the afternoon a long black column came down from the Hill, fifty female cryomorphs and four gunners marching in order of height and led by a blonde officer with a brassard on her left arm. The same officer, the same terror, a woman like Hyason Sarin. Nothing has changed, he thought; time is truly circular. I am, they are and – he is. Without a future; not reawakened beauty but a killing machine; not a kite nor a swan, no dream companion, but a dictator – the worst kind, a failed idealist. He watched the cryo troop, waiting for its disciplined wheel into the barrack gates; but it came on and passed him, heading straight up Broadwalk towards the Temple, an excited crowd of boys running at the women's heels. 'Go on,' he said to Peach. 'After them.' Moments later, he heard the whine of skimmers rising from the pads and the crack of the gun which signified the closing of the City gates. The carts kept on moving, the citizens strolled; he sat on the parapet and bit his knuckles in delayed frustration.

There had been no time to consider the officer; just time to register the fact that cruelty and force were paramount and Magon, who would be gentle, had failed again. The lust of the hunter returned to him, the retrospective flush of the leopard stalk, himself the small but canny hunter, a match for the big white cat.

Peach returned to the dyeworks after dark, his face grazed, his hair on end. All afternoon they – he and Orel, shoulder to shoulder in the clockroom window – had heard the firework burst of corundum guns from the Temple, and seen sparkshowers and flames. Skimmers bustled in the sky, to and fro. One thing was certain: Magon was not there to see the gilded statues melt and burn, to hear the Dancers scream. He would direct the production from his desk in the beauty and seclusion of the Octagon, the penitent Jerome at his back, the collected objects careful placings in his room, nothing to jar sensibility. And M'untal – but she had married Chenodor and could hide her delicacy and her fears in his broad opinions.

Peach gave him a garbled account of the mayhem: a jostling crowd, fistfights, closed gates and a smell of burning wood. He had grazed his face falling against bricks in the panic of his final flight.

'There's a curfew,' he said. 'The bridges are guarded. The patrols are out.'

He could not attempt sleep and sat crosslegged on his mat, Orel beside him, the first woman to climb to his retreat. The noise from the west drowned the ticking of the clock and Orel, whose machine had recorded the sights and the sounds, put a tentative hand on his arm.

'It was like this in Hayna in '5,' she said. 'I'm all right, but how about you?'

He listened. The noises of destruction had died with the light and he heard only the insects and nightbirds whose city this was. He did not respond to her concern, but sent Peach for bohea. The scalding liquid calmed him. He drank it slowly as if it was a potion against feeling.

'I'm going up there,' he said.

For him, the streets were not channels of fear, but homely alleys. He

301

saw one wanderer sorting through a garbage can, and then he was in the
Quarter, following the kerbstones of the ruined streets, and dodging
through the narrow gaps between the new pavilions. Outside Zalcissa's
tent, too small to be called a pavilion, a flare burned bravely.

The Uynal was a filthy place to swim, little better than the sewers. He
entered the water from one of the abandoned jetties at the edge of Daid's
Ground and set a course upstream, diagonally against the current. Even
so, it pushed him downstream so that he landed south of Helmswoman's
Wharf. On the staging he took off his sodden clothes and wrung the
water from them, shook the river from the casing of the rkw, dressed and
listened. The hymn began, clear chimes across the water, and his clock
struck two. He waited until all the clocks had struck. The City was in
darkness, the only visible lights the tall sentinels which ringed the
skimmer pads; the skimmers slept and the rush of the Uynal was muted.
By two-forty-five, he was at the foot of the Temple wall and he climbed it
at the point where it abutted the lower wall of the adjoining gardens. The
thought that he might encounter Hyason's successor excited him. Reins,
he thought, a curb like Arkite's. Wait. He descended slowly, a careful
shadow dropping silently into silence.

The buildings were intact. He counted them, his eyes straining,
assessing the great arc of the Temple roof and the five tall towers which
barred the starry sky. The Mamelon curved upward, over, and smoothly
down. Over and about them all, as if there had been a great celebration,
hung a remnant of incense, the fragrant ghost of cedarwood. He should
have known, he might have guessed. Magon would never wantonly
destroy an antique. His brain, whose work all the noisy afternoon had
been impeded by sentiment, began to function. The heap of ashes which,
as he approached it, stirred in the cooling air, had been a cedar tree, a
mighty deodar like the giants of Zalcasia. A dreaming cat sat up and
washed her face. He wondered if the cryos had enjoyed their work as tree
surgeons and the subsequent bonfire. Did they dance, abandoning the
discipline which had been bred into their long bodies to caper before the
flames? The grass, so carefully tended, was singed and worn. Real
fireworks, iron and saltpetre, magnesium flares: the evidence, scorched
cardboard tubes and burnt-out cones, was scattered on the grass – and
corundum beams had augmented the dazzling display, fiery writing on
the sky.

There would be cryos at the gates. An easy guess. What a player he
was, to frighten the City and carry off the Gynarchy in a few short hours.
What would he do with a college of saintly women, two hundred lissom
Dancers and a black panther? He imagined a surreal dance, in which the
Gynarchs and the Dancers circled Magon and the great cat, Plama.

The curve of the Mamelon roof began at ground level. His hand
followed it until he came to the door, an ingress as narrow as his hips. It

was open. No sound issued. He thought of the She, her reality and identity masked by her heavy golden head, her terrible face hidden as she fled – or revealed as she was taken, tripped, held, shot.

Lamps burned, lamps of glass and alabaster, a circle around the red dancing floor. The black segments marked the steps of the lunar year and Mahun smiled at him, the Alcuon Mahun, blue and full of hope. Her eyes were sapphires and her maral sheets of gold. From her feet radiated the spokes of the Wheel. There was a door in her belly, a small jewelled panel, on which the single word 'Guna' was engraved. He kissed her enamelled hand. He opened the curving door. Her womb was lined with roseate tourmaline, the two placentas were made from rubies, the double cords from tubes of gold, the twin cauls from crystal. But the foetuses were missing, the twin children, Ingemi First and Ingemi Last, whose birth was the original mystery, whose imitation had been hallowed down the centuries. Leirion and Anyal. He had made them, he and M'untal, the best of Mahun's Dancers, and they lived high on the Hill while he had come to this, to dust and obscurity.

The shadows in the building might conceal a hundred cryos but he knew that no one was there. His torch showed him Mahun's sisters in their niches in the walls, frescoes, stone phalluses, and cats, and the stairway to the ossuary beneath. He went slowly down the steps, moving his legs deliberately forward and counting to overcome his dread.

The bones were piled in wrought iron cages, imprisoning the dead in metalwork ornate with lilies and skulls and the remains of the great, Gynarchs and Matriarchs, poets, painters, musicians, Dancers, the scientists of the Star Age, were laid out in the semblance of entirety, each one named. He sniffed, scenting death; but the overwhelming smell, out-stinking the perfumed sesselid cones which burned to honour the relics, was of cats: shit, urine, corrosive piss, the indelible mark of the sacred animal. He saw the yellow bones of Shelda Hinoor and looked for her great-granddaughter, Lys. Stars and planets were carved on the walls, the death throes of *Evenstar*, the flight of *Daystar*. He listened for rats, for any sound, and heard a shuffle which caused his hands, the rkw, and the torch to shake.

The sibyl sat awkwardly on an empty slab in the last arcade, her robe of golden tissue and her oracular head discarded on the floor beside her. He could not marry the two images. The head had the face of a tyrant, its brows drawn together in a heavy frown, its thin lips parted, not in a smile but to speak, to allow a dreadful prophecy to issue from them. The woman was very ordinary, plain, and middle-aged; she did not scream or panic. In her lap lay the two golden children. She spoke to him.

'This is the worst place to hide.'

He wanted to fall down before her, to let her solve every problem he had and relieve his blind command with her knowledge of what was to come. Encumbered as he was by his gun, he bowed from the waist. She spoke again.

'Magon Nonpareil has taken the Sisters away,' she said. 'They will lose their grace. He will drive out Mahun.

'But you?' she said. 'Who are you? Could you be the last faithful man?'

'Me? I'm a nobody. My name is Cal. I know a place where you can hide until your time comes again. You must leave the Mamelon, and the Temple. The Archivist will not destroy them.'

She held her surrogate children tenderly, as if they were alive.

'Bring them with you. My people need them – they need you.'

She carried the golden children carefully but she left her speaking head and her robe where she had discarded them at the beginning of her journey into the City.

The journey to the buried house was arduous, beginning in the Temple garden and the shallow waters at the edge of the Ayal and ending with the long and filthy trek through the sewers. He led her into the old refuge and began to remove bricks from the wall. His bed had disintegrated into a heap of timbers and some shreds of fabric the rats had not yet carried away. She was calm, weary, and grateful; she wept when he took her into the cellar and she saw the patient images. The clear water flowed from Mahun's vase and he helped her to wash, cupping his hands in the water for her. She laid the golden babes in the water.

'We were misled,' she said and gestured towards the images with a hand from which the consecrated water dripped. 'She justly punishes us.'

'Not Her but Magon Nonpareil,' he said.

'We must begin again. I must cut the first furrow.'

He left her with his torch, which would not run out of fuel, and went by the flickering lamplight through the maze until he could safely emerge in the wastelands beyond the dyeworks. Orel was still there, asleep in the bamboo chair in his room, some kind of an ally.

Peach became his go-between, travelling each day between the dyeworks and the She, concealed so far beneath the City. The She, Alluleya, made the old shrine into her cell, a haven of prayer and a library of the books the boy carried to her, a buried religion. Peach came home singing the prayers she taught him. On the streets the iconoclasts held sway and the Temple became a museum.

His dreams changed. He dreamed of a different world where the swifts flew in a high space and disappeared between the stars; he began to visit an older City, the dustless clarity of the First Years where wheels turned unimpeded, wheels of carts, the mill on the second bend of the Uynal, a wheel of prayer.

*　　*　　*

304

The year ended. It became 512, Magon's eleventh. Orel Diran went away to Sinein. Hellie's child and Malkin's, born within a week of each other in Vern, yelled in unison below. All they want, he thought, is something to boast of, a child or a manuscript to show each other. The City might die and they would still want semen and words. The crying gnawed at him and the strife in the City without felt like a threat. Orel, before she left, had shown him the report from the Council of the Nations and Noiro. Hayla of Hayna had protested again.

When he surveyed her in Alcuon, he saw a city reined in and possessed by a genius of abnegation. Below him, the swifts nested and the tower stank of fish and was loud with the incessant peets of the nestlings, flightless supplicants which would metamorphose in three deks into rulers of the sky.

The clouds which built towers in the north-east sent out scouts to hang over and pry into the City. The morning mist extended to meet them and the marriage hid the day and the swifts from him until midmorning. Through the glass he saw detail, many faces, and the shadows of the retreating clouds ran darkly over the gardens on the Hill. Crinon's retreat was invisible, hidden from him in the valley. The pinewalks, the seat of many follies, were black mazes. Over that sward (in reality a sea of grass and flowers where the deer the Matriarchs had hunted in the old days, driving them to the impasse, had swelled into a placid herd) he had galloped Choru, Magon and Arkite in pursuit. The rough new building he had seen with the naked eye resolved itself through the glass: a stack of stones, golden stones of Baia, the exact hue of his self before the courts, and the foundations of some new structure, perhaps another tower, seven courses of stone. Barrows, heavy chisels, shovels, stone saws, and mallets, a waving kerchief held down by a stone, a bottle; the workers were not there today. A mound of sand and the rainbow face of Magon was as close to him as the end of the optic, dark hair pushed back and edged with violet mist. It was a cheap glass, made in Ineit: his face was flattened and the wall behind him was as close in plane as he was. He was looking up, not at the uncompleted structure not more than twice his height, but at the finished thing. He turned away and Cal, tracking him through the optic, lost him.

Orel returned with a printed script which Cal read, hardly recognising himself in her tale of the adventure and temerity of the golden boy in the wonderful City.

'Why has she come back?' Peach kicked out at the table.

'Maybe she fancies me,' he said and laughed at the boy's expression. 'It's her job, Peach. She's the worm in the gut.'

Orel became part of the circus, a peripheral figure always ready with tablet and stylus and, lately, a smile. On the day which marked the end of his thirtieth year he took a bottle of rahi and Peach to bed with him, or Peach, hard stone at the centre and the blue bottle with a woman's waist, the order was not important, to his bed. He dreamed of Orel, plainly, without any excursions into the wild imagery of his unconscious, and then of locked doors and boarded windows. Deep in there was an entrance but he could not find it. Only later, floating on the tide, did he find himself in the unsullied City among the birds. No men. The blue and black towers were hardly begun, half-columns of intention against the bright sky; but the Mamelon was complete, already gilded. Later he would find the women, safety, and caresses. Later he would discover the kind of men who lived there.

He woke and pushed Peach out of the bed, assuaging his love and his fear with a kiss and a request for bohea.

She had come back, she said, to show him the script and to witness the Red Wind. In Sollar the media were agog with the news of Hayla's declaration and the Council had not been dissolved. He ignored her; time enough.

'Come to the clockroom. I've something to show you: a new horizon.'

She viewed the stones through the optic.

'What do you think it is?' he said.

'It looks like the beginnings of a tower.'

'Who is building it?'

'I don't know: no one at home spoke of building. The talk was all of destruction and threat.'

'Who, would you think? I know, but what do you think?'

'The priests, perhaps – the monks.'

'Close. He is.'

'Have you seen him? Through this?'

Ah! When he had found the entrance, then, she might know it all; when his retreat was secure.

'Wait!' she exclaimed. 'I can see someone . . . it's only a cryo.'

'Give me the glass.' Wresting it from her – she was a true pryer – he unlocked her fingers and, while she sucked and rubbed them, he put the optic back into its case.

He had found his way into the old City. There had been no need, after all, to unblock or force an entrance; it was easy to find if you followed the formula, twice left, once right, after the underground foyer where ancient light posters were black mirrors in the dark, relaying his torchlight and anxious haste back at him. The deep tunnel under the Uynal had a blue sheen, walls of a hard and horny substance like the shell of an old turtle, damp walls which, when he tried to scratch the surface with his knife, resisted the blade. He trembled, under the Uynal and her muddy bed, afraid lest he should be crushed in the tubular space, a man inside a worm. He breathed in air as fresh as Zalcasia's; there was movement in it, a breeze blowing beneath the river. He prayed.

On the other side, he smelled the earth; it was red as cinnabar. Climbing an untrodden bank of soil, he left the underworld and pushed through roots and hanging stems to the surface – where it was night, the same stars and Eshtur utterly alone above the valley. He thought he should turn back to find the Uynal but, crossing a stream, found himself ascending a gentle hill. The buttress of the Citadel Rock was on his left and on his right the land sloped towards the sea. At the top he turned, clear of the trees, and saw the bay in Eshtur's clear light. The City was dark, a deep mystery without lights. He sat down to wait for the day. Magon could not be here, not ever. He was alone yet, in the City, not lonely.

The first light filled the cup with colour. He could make out the Baians, a backcloth to the north, and in the valley, when Shelda rose, one black tower and one blue, a dark mound and the red earth of the fields where crops which were not lilies grew, woodland, a cluster of wooden houses, from which thin columns of chimney smoke rose, beyond the broad and yellow Uynal. He looked hungrily, to remember, for he must return.

He showed Orel how undramatic the Red Wind was, taking her out in it and letting her experience its choking presence. Only with clear skies could wind excite: this, invading every sense, stultified and made the mind dull. Prenta took Orel to her own quarters and washed her, combing and teasing out the ruddy grit from her pale hair.

On the third day of the Wind, when they were settled in his room, the window shut tight and a bottle of Baialt, her taste, between them, he touched her knee. 'Shall we?' he said, as politely as any Sineinian walker. Peach was below, in the sewers, a comfort to the She. Orel laughed, nervously he thought, and told him that such conduct was unprofessional, unguarded, risky. In Sinein. . . . He reached across her for the wooden box with which he had replaced Rafe's jewelled one. She has been in this situation many times before he thought: after the protestation – perhaps without the added persuasion of the drug. . . . He watched her undress and saw the hidden echoes, undeveloped muscle, in her flesh before he focused on the time and her outside, forgot dilute brown and saw her whiteness, the suffuse rose in her skin, her blushing nakedness. She was meant to be clothed, except at such a time, exposed in privacy like the woman of Glaver's fancy, the decorative nude in her bedroom. He must never let Glaver see her. Her depending breasts were treasures from a far country. But he could borrow her body and she his, the tenants of a shared dream. He knelt and opened the box.

'I've never tried it,' she said.

307

'I'll only give you a little: not enough to make your head ache.' He tapped grains of the powder into the paper. 'Right to the back and swallow before you cough.'

'It tingles.' She smiled and rubbed her lips.

'Feel warm?'

'Yes. Sunlit.' He watched her relax in the chair, got to his feet and turned the key in the lock, before he took his own fold and slowly, while his wings grew, took her.

With her he explored the subterranean regions, no sewers these but magical caverns and tunnels of light. She held his hand and they walked on amethyst, twin children in an enchanted labyrinth. The tunnels confused him. 'Which one?' he said. 'Which way?' The mist rose: it was part of him, it was her. 'Am I giving you what you want?' he said. She smiled and led him into a garden. And then they flew.

In the red maral, pleated and folded, she danced and he danced with her. When the dance ended, she soared a little higher and looked down on him. He felt the water falling on his head, green sea water; but it was not water, it was starlight, cold and white.

The room, which had been in another dimension, focused itself and Orel looked down. His brown head was in her lap, his arms spread out, over her, over the chair. She bent double and kissed his back, but he did not wake. She listened to his breathing, studied the receding porportions of his shoulders, back, heels; everything had been, was, gentle; every-thing her colleagues had told her, false. She touched his hair and pretended he was hers.

He woke: she felt his mouth move against her thighs, his hands travel to her waist.

'Panacea for all ills,' he said, the rasp in his voice subdued by her flesh.

'The husk?'

'You were there.'

'With you? No terrors?'

'No: just peace and amethysts and a slow dance.' They moved at the same time, and their voices and bodies collided.

'I don't believe I would want to try it again.'

'But to occupy the same dream! It's a miracle.'

He was the miracle. He made such wonders happen. Not the husk but he, Cal M'unor, was the spellbinder who made women pregnant, made women dream. He had carried a dream for Magon, but he had never been able to tell whether his burden had been accepted for the gift it was, taken from him and swallowed with his soul.

If he was damned, he would not be able to pray. He proved it when she had gone, kneeling dumb before the image on the shelf, feeling the pressure of the women's hands on his shoulders.

*　　　*　　　*

At home in Sinein, the precinct floors hidden under deep drifts of leaves, Orel had been relaxed, hopeful. The paydoctor had commented on it while she cut into the anaesthetised skin of her arm and removed the tiny embedded pack. Her fee took account of the illegality of the operation and Orel, waiting for the bleeding, the confirmation of a woman's body in working order, experienced new sensations, the tiny indications of her gender. Her breasts swelled as if she were already pregnant, subsided, and the blood flowed. It was her eleventh menstrual cycle. In her case, the Gynarchy had overruled the doctors and permitted the implant after the tenth. Usually they made students wait two years. Thus, she had been artificially sterile for twenty years.

She listened to her body and was impatient for the City. She went to the Temple to collect a copy of the Law from the Gynarch-in-charge and discovered a book of rules for busy women, a revised edition shorn of mystery. She searched the antiquarian bookshops of Sollar for an edition in Maralay: none was to be had. In the University library she read the old and perfect rhythms and whispered some of them into her machine. Others, particularly the Star Prayer and the five Apologies, she learned by heart. She visited the Temple again and left it irritated by the secular devotions: the dances were too fast, the music a recording, the Dancers awkward, undedicated, part-timers. Their costumes were synthetic reproductions of the silken maral, and the gold on them was gilt. They had long ago substituted solar lighting for the gentle lamplight she had seen in the City. Only Cal and his people, Hayla, and herself stood up for the old and sacred Wheel.

Her second cycle concluded with its welcome blood-offering and she collected her pass from the office and set out for the City.

He listened to Peach's whine, which was indistinguishable from any other street boy's whine: whatever his legacy from Tlivoorn – that floating paradise, here today, gone tomorrow – it was not in his voice nor in his underfed body where repeated malnutrition had made lean arabesques instead of a fisherman's sturdy flesh. Nor was the heritage in his long-lashed girl's eyes. Maybe it resided in his name, that fluting simulacrum of a waterhen's call: seef, seef.

'You locked the door,' said Peach truculently.

He ruffled the black thicket of hair.

'Just another rahi, just another fold,' he said. 'You can have that room on the third floor, if you like.'

'I can't be indoors: I can't breathe, I can't sleep.'

'Please yourself.' He walked away from Peach and contemplated the dye-pit. The green water crawled about, motion in turgidity, heaved with its burden of bubbles and insects, with floating fronds. The red of the walls contrasted strangely with the green, the stain of civilisation overwhelmed.

'Make me a garden,' he said.

Peach approached him slowly through a forest of oenothera, pliant as they. Like them, he had found home wherever the chance Wind dropped him.

'It's all concrete,' he said. 'Concrete and brick. This stuff's growing on hope.'

But beneath, he knew it now, lay the red soil of the fields and the yellow silt of the Uynal, her two shores more than a mile apart and unconfined by the grey petrified mud of civilisation: roots reach deep. The vats had held realgar and sugar of lead, tin liquor, sumac and malachite green; they had held poison, the yellow essence of the lily: but the flowers grew and the algae flourished. He could see a dozen different birds apart from the high-flying swifts. For an insect the industrial decay was a new world. He sat on a lawn of weeds and opened his book: Peach lay down, sweet spice in the lucent air, one of the bright petals of the primrose caught on his collar.

The old novel drew him in, heart and soul, and he read again of High Zalcasia, the inaccessible white land which he had seen from the barren summit of Kiynana, fatal Shalusha below him, that paradise of mutated forms and bright new perceptions. Twelve fingers disgusted him because he had ten. But what might flower in the curtained mind of the child without eyes? What might have been, before the mutants had received the blessing of involuntary euthanasia?

He could not understand how Lys had immersed herself in Huyatt Tayal, entered his skull so wholly that she was able to describe his bodily sensations as though they were her own. If this was creation's prerogative, then they were all mad; and he thought of Crinon wielding her brushes to outline his persona. He read Huyatt's account of the terror of heights to Peach, stressing the adjectives, explaining them to his reluctant pupil.

The tattered cryomorph disturbed them. Its soldier's boots crushed the weeds and released a scent of lice. Someone had given it a maral and it wore the garment tightly wound, without the covering decency of a bodice. The hips of the androgyne wanderer reminded him of M'untal: the nature of the garment promoted the walk, but the beast's front, not breast nor chest – for who would seek solace or weep there? – without nipples or navel filled him with fear. He stared at the creature with loathing.

'How does it get in?'

'I don't know. It must be able to climb well.'

'You,' said Cal, in the loud and determined voice of someone who speaks to an illiterate alien. 'Did you climb the wall?' His voice, grating on

310

the alto notes, died and he coughed.

'Did you climb the wall, cryo?' said Peach easily, the flute of the waterhen and the treble of the child he used to be combining in a fluid succession.

'I can climb,' said the cryo. 'Climb quickly, climb high.'

'How high?'

'Twenty, thirty feet. I climbed from the chantry into your garden. The lights were out. When is the service?'

'On the forty-first of Never,' said Peach, laughing at his own joke.

The cryo sat down beside him and arranged her skirt, for she was derived from X chromosomes. She sat as still as a mantis and Peach looked at her. He, too, was fascinated by her asexuality though he had no idea how she had been made, no inkling of her conception in a vessel of clear glass, and her slow growth in the rearing lung, while the technocrats tinkered with her responses. He knew that the women of the old days were conjurers: how else could they build towers of blue gems and black glass, an octagon a third of a mile high? Cal read silently on. Vaguely, distantly, he heard Peach engage the cryomorph in conversation.

'Where's your rkw?'

'I gave it to the man who gave me my maral. He functions, it functions, I am worn out. This is my last garment: soon Aash will claim me.'

The movement of Peach touching his eyes and his stomach, invoking Mahun, was a graceful blur on the edge of his vision. Peach had no taste for metaphysics, and death, now that he had a protector, was not even a cloud on his horizon.

'What's your favourite food? Mine're angel cake and ice-cream.'

Great women, the few notable men, were remembered in the Green Cenotaph. It was an old desire this, to visit the place and let his hurt be exorcised by the memorial to Rafe Dayamit. Mounds clothed in short green grass concealed the old walls and fallen towers, the dizzy walkways turned to dust, a coat of verdure over the relics. The green-hedged paths ran straight and true, a grid of observance. He consulted the glass-covered map: path III, plot 3001. The place had the order of expensive death, a composed and perfect end to life, without the rank weeds, strayed flowers and noisy bees of the Friends' Close, where Tarla was remembered, resolute in death as in life. She had died clutching the old photograph, a nymph in the hands of a joyful crone and, when she was dead and the Gynarch (hired at great expense) had pronounced the five Apologies and the Valediction, her friends had burst out singing.

There he stood, the pretty little boy,
A-waiting for his turn, a-praying for a stab
At the goods.
But she

311

Sang

Boys, boys, boys, boys . . . .

He had this from Zalcissa. Tarla's youthful beauty, film embedded in plastic, was now affixed to her memorial, her flesh on free display to every passer-by.

But here, the paths were raked and rolled, grey chippings. Not a weed, no loud bird disturbed the inward-looking mourner exploring his own sorrow. 3001: the digits were black on white, chiselled fine. Fresh flowers lay on the pedestal, pure white damask roses which could only come from the temperate house on the Hill. He laid his own tribute, scalet naias, beside them and knelt to examine the portrait. Dayamit's beauty was preserved there for ever but his body, denied breaking, never power for the vultures' huge span, was consumed and gone. A little drum of sludge, one of the many buried in the Burnt Lands. The photograph was of Dayamit, not himself: he noticed the manner in which the neat beard accentuated the curves of his lips. 'Rafe Dayamit M'unor,' the inscription read, '9 ViU 477-14 LiV 500', and, aping Menander, 'He who is beloved hastens too soon from the feast.' He wondered why Magon had not caused the correct words to be inscribed here: who would understand the ancient Gaian symbols? But Magon, even *in extremis*, was circumspect. He leaned across the monument and inhaled the perfume of the roses, touched their perfect petals and long green stems in case they had been near Magon.

Peach greeted him with a yell. He had been on the waterfront and then at Tyler's drowning his jealousy of the dead secret in rahi. The liquor freed his tongue and gave his voice an accusing tone. Dids't thou not lead him through the glimmering night? Where, why, and when, said Peach, and was she there? These are the forgeries of jealousy. His mind was full of tags and quotations, successions of useless words from the three continents and the nearer planets, drifts of decayed paper, the remember-ings of starsailors and dead longhaulers, unknown poets of past worlds: the plunder of his years on the Hill, when Magon had used his brain to compose speeches, to translate and write popular papers, songs, new text books for the children rising from the Depths. They came soft-footed to him, haunting him with disparate words and emotions in many languages.

Where are they now, the heroines of yesteryear, the reluctant heroes who never returned? And the ship drove on, without wind, without light, without the air we all must breathe. Hylas drowned. She became ice. In Maralis are many mansions, few hearts. She has many skins, iridescence, lapid beauty, a mantle of blue stars. And for her sake I do rear up the boy. And for her sake I will not part with him. The City will follow you. It is always this City you will reach.

'Shoot,' he said to the boy, snapping his fingers.

He watched Peach turn and creep away, and then he whistled so that he would look back.

'Please Peach, would you go to the drugstore? Here! Catch!'

The golden bar spun in the air, distracting Peach from his course. He caught it and was restored; they were both restored.

The light that morning was opaque. The unseasonable rainstorms had lasted for two days, and the water in the broken grounds below the tower, where he had spent the night, made translucent pools amongst the rubble; the dye-pits overflowed with water of many hues. A cloud of water shielded the City; underground, his people had refuge, buried beneath the City of today and yesterday, close to the red earth and the rivers; under the mist the streets were hollow ways populated by tribes of cats. The Uynal rushed, brimful.

He could see the outer limits, ringed by broken blocks and coalesced stone, and, amongst the towers, new towers, tall shapes broken out of the walls of fallen buildings, the blank inhuman constructions of strife, four years of conflict, Hayla's contribution. They all carried rkws now, and their whine and splutter punctuated the eastern music, day and night. A new wild growth, saplings from footings, flowers from timbers, covered the City. She was breaking. The quarrelling tribes had taken sectors for themselves, the airborne fighters of Hayna had taken whatever tall or glistening structure they fancied, leaving a City of isolated buildings surrounded by commonlands of rubble. But his people were safe, unless the waters rose. They had made a new home in the buried houses, those dank and ghostly cellars far below, where the first women had dwelt. He had taken them all in, every terrified Depther who came to him, the circus people, the clowns, even the Rosies, Luce herself. Yet, on the Hill, the towers and the soaring Octagon were whole.

He put the optic down. When he looked, unaided, out to sea, the waters met. No way for a fisherman, for anyone, to see in the fog. The optic showed him the dull-surfaced ship, a white and negative figure, rocking on the swell, her bow pointing east. He had ceased to wonder at her constant presence; inside the cocoon, the sailors must be moving, must rise to eat and follow orders, transmit intelligence and compute the tracks of stars and satellites. She gave no sign of life to the City she besieged. The clock beat steadily beside him. He leaned on the casing and listened to its metal heart.

When he looked up and out again, the arched window framing his view, he saw the cloud in tatters and the stones of the City rose up to meet him. The white towers toed the greenwood and the windows of the Octagon were mirrors. The curtain was up, the overture could begin: he watched the blue light focus, a mutated sunbeam, a superheated blade. He watched it illuminate the Octagon. The knife cut into the cake.

313

When the light touched the building, a red river of glass replaced the pale solid and the Archive bled, millions of paper lives, pages of words, endless torrents of letters, fountains of ink, the passion and the ashes of canvas. He thought only of objects: wood, oils, ivory, porcelain, silver, and gold, the incandescent colours of Xharamahun, Crinon's subtle tones, the precision of the copyist. Lotto's greys and browns, Titian's reds. . . . Yet he always maintained that the sound came first, an implosion which resembled the fall of a ceiling descending into an empty house.

Magon. He spoke the word like the charm it was. There was his ending: in an instant. Over breakfast. He went slowly down the ladders up which he had flown, out of the dyeworks, into the streets. He walked quickly and entered Copper Street; it was there that he saw, reflected in a barber's mirror, his own blanched face and his weeping eyes. The barber shaved on, never noticing the passing vision, but his assistants and all the customers, except the foam-covered corpse in the chair, had fled. They lived on borrowed time. The water was rising. He, Cal M'unor, must lead his people away.

He entered the sewers by a broken cover on Malt Street, so close to a tribal boundary that it was deserted. He slipped into the dark and pulled the cover shut above his head. The torch showed him a steep descent and the old iron rungs. This way was a branch of the third millennium pedestrian system. He walked along the underground road and shone his light on the ceramic floor. Two inches of water in which yellow sediment moved wet his feet.

They were a little dull, his friends, his lovers, his beloved misfits. A few scraps of conversation with the breakfast bread. Even the children were quiet. He went straight to Alluleya, and put his hands in hers before he sat down and spoke earnestly to her. She agreed at once. Her faith was as blind and as true as his. 'I saw it,' she said. 'The light cut me, down here.' And she showed him the red weal on her breast. They sat together, hand in hand, until all the bread was consumed, and then the She stood up.

'My dears,' she said and he, catching his dry breath, heard Crinon in the old and familiar endearment. 'My dears,' said the She, Mahun incarnate. 'Let us be silent, let us reflect together on the days of our well-being. It is time to go.'

He looked at them all standing still, their eyes tightly shut; one of his children peeped between her fingers and he winked at her and smiled. Seven of these children were his. A year ago, Orel and his daughter had moved into Vern. They always left him, the able ones – and the faithless, Nadar, Achille, treacherous An. The weak remained. He shook his head and moved to the window to lead the way. A murmur possessed his followers, a susurrus of conversation and observations as he led them

314

down the stairs and they came to the statue in the water, each pausing to touch her hand as they passed. The water was cold as charity and came to their knees, to the younger children's thighs. One by one they ducked under the low arch and entered the conduit. By the light of his torch, he searched for yellow silt, but found none. He looked back: their lights gleamed in constellations.

Peach whispered to him and the tunnel magnified his voice and relayed it back amongst the crowd.

'Will there be husk?'

'Lilies, growing wild. Plenty of food. You won't need to fly there.'

The cut stones relayed laughter. His light briefly swept the lasered granite but there was no time for archaeology. He walked more swiftly, making waves with his shins.

The walls of the tunnel under the Uynal were awash with yellow and the flexible lining was beginning to split. Slow trickles of river water penetrated. Some of the children whimpered and he heard Prenta calming them.

'Is it far?' said Peach.

'Just the width of the Uynal and a bit more: an afternoon stroll.'

He felt the resistance of the rogue water and the soil in it, but it was no deeper than the waters of the spring. He urged them and the clowns carried the children. The weight of the river flowed above their heads, the everlasting tide swelled by the unseasonable rains and the liquid snow running down from the mountains. Peach had exhibited such self-control that he was not surprised to see him tremble and to feel the hand which suddenly came up and gripped his arm. He turned his head and for an instant directed the light so that Peach could see his face and his smile.

They left the water behind them and mounted steadily between the red walls from which the roots of trees broke out. He smelled the damp promise of fields after rain; and then Peach cried out that he could see the light and they all began to run.

The birdsong moved him most of all, bright webs of sound streaming from the treetops, that and the unsullied light, the magic of the City magnified a hundred, a thousandfold. He stepped into the green valley, and let Peach slip past him into the undying City, for an instant touching his hand as he passed. They all passed him, the colours bright upon the clowns and the acrobat, the reds and pinks bursting with the renewed bodies of the Rosies, Prenta in her new yellow maral, Hellie, Malkin, his children, every Triber. And the She carrying her golden relics. They seethed and clamoured in the valley and the children rushed to explore. Peach led them now and he watched them pass on into the misty distances. His face registered his sorrow, but he had no regrets. He pulled a branch of naias from the nearerst bush and turned back into the tunnel.

315

She might choose to claim him now, or she might free him for the epilogue. He met the rising water uncertainly; but he could pull himself through it, though it tried to overturn him. The old cables on the walls helped him. Somewhere in the tunnel he lost his flowering branch. The clear water of the spring welcomed him: he walked upstream and let Mahun's stone presence refresh him before he climbed the cellar steps, and ascended the stairs. In the sewer, the water had overflowed the walkway.

The heavy cover shifted grudgingly. He had to use all his wasted strength to move it. He emerged among the feet of hurrying refugees on Citadel Street, as grimed and sodden as any sewer rat.

The Hill was steeper then he remembered. As he climbed, he caught glimpses of the shattered Octagon and, below, a new vista of the lambent City held hostage by water. The nearer fields of Maralis were lakes. A sheet of paper blew against his legs and stuck there, so that he had to bend to remove it and send it on its fluttering way.

Panic inhabited the Octagon; here, too, water had taken the place of fire. He could get no sense out of the women rushing loaded, hither and thither. No one questioned him, no one queried his presence there. Filka, someone told him, she had been up there, and three of her staff; they were still trying to ascertain . . . he left the confusion and walked on.

The rain had refreshed the gardens. They lay open for him, wide as ever, filled with flowers and tamed water. Repeating the old custom, he let his grimy fingers trail in the three lead cisterns as he passed them, once for Magon, once for himself, and once for the future. He unlatched the gate.

He shut out the world. The latch clicked, settling in its groove. Tall hedges – they had grown another two or three feet – concealed the garden from him. He stood still, debating which path to take. There was no need, his heart knew the way and he went through the forest, his bare feet making prints in the muddy path. He listened for the parakeets and soon they came, a cloud of them, a red and yellow scarf of feathers laid along a branch. She had persuaded some bromeliads to grow. He could see their fleshy excrescences high in the trees and all along the path scented green trumpets grew beside white clarions, her own mystical composition. Young trees marked the end of the little forest. He walked on a grass plat, and there she was, almost as if she waited for him, bending and stretching, picking peaches, clucking and murmuring over the damaged fruit and placing the whole ones in her basket. Perhaps she only sought peace and a task to occupy her in this, the subscript to her brother's life.

'Crinon!' His voice was now a mockery of the old, the harsh cry of a heron or the coarse shout of a fisherwoman. But she recognised it and turned, leaving the basket, dropping the fruit she held. She held him;

they both wept. He did not know what to say; the frozen scene in her kitchen, her tears when Vedara left him. He was surprised to see her smile.

'He's up at the tower. He wasn't up there,' she said incoherently. 'She failed; she destroyed a lot of books, but she failed.'

'What tower? He pulled it down.' He shook her to bring her into the present.

'He built again in Maralis. Without the City, he believes himself without the influence of Mahun.'

Since he had come to mourn and was now required to rejoice, he continued to weep. Crinon led him from the orchard. They were all there. They had grown older, and some of the children were strangers, others adults: a tableau of the past with fresh additions, a well-loved building on which vibrant new limbs have been grafted. Four children played with the dolls' house. Slake was there and S'an Troya; M'untal, kneeling before a map of the City, looked up at him. Someone had coloured in the flooded area on the map. Her face had lines which should not have been there, the echoes of her tears for Chenodor, furrows for her father. The golden mirror-image was Leirion and Anyal; he saw his doubled self in her lovely face and his beautiful body. Gildo looked from the twins to him and held up his arms in a gesture of hopelessness. A small girl clung to Xhara's hand.

Faya was the first to come forward, and as she came she picked up two glasses of wine, handed him one, drank to him, smiled. Then Gildo embraced him and the wine was spilled. The glass in his hand prevented him from being overwhelmed and made M'untal's hesitation seem refinement. Indeed, he stank of his passage through the sewers. He stood drying on the steps, a pied and ragged figure, streaked with yellow mud and stained with the old red earth.

Later, when he had bathed and heard their tales, they dined. His hands shook throughout the meal. To spare them, he left the table and the room, and privately swallowed the pinch of husk which kept his equilibrium. For joy and flight he needed a good deal more than this meagre seasoning of his melancholy. He looked into the second compartment in the little box and calculated the number of flights which remained. Faya had poured him a fresh glass of bubbly. He leaned back. The chair was comfortable and the company of the close group, where he was now a stranger, agreeable; there was no hurry. All the time that was left him remained to be filled.

'Don't you remember,' said Crinon, 'that Magon opened the gardens? There was a ceremony, refreshments, musicians. Fifty people came; ten of those return regularly. . . . A new gate leads into the gorge – it was meant for the provincials. He did try; he goes on trying. He won't give up.

'But who appreciates him? He was right. Nobody cares.

'When you go to the tower, take Choru. She's an old lady, so treat her gently.'

He had become a tourist, a new Huyatt, a fifth millennium Lys, writing his own story. The anguish was past, that and his time in the City. Without her, he would find his soul again as once he had found Magon, journeying among the rocks, the sand and the high peaks.

In the garden after the meal, Crinon read him Xharam'un's fate.

'She locked her paints away; she never touches the flute. The child is her life.

'It was one of Magon's gunners – a dark night in a dark street. She had given a concert and decided to walk home instead of waiting for the carriage. She forgave him. She said it was never his fault that he had been made into an animal; even his consent to the alteration – she forgave him that. No one could have guessed, she said, what outrage would be done. He as much as she was the victim.'

Xhara' herself, he guessed, after the first outpouring to Crinon, never complained; he had seen her new silence, her devotion to a different art.

'What happened to the gunner?'

'Magon had him castrated. No one has dared tell Xhara'.' Her arm was a brace across his shoulders.

'He is married, my dear,' she said, as carefully as if she opened a trap to free the animal suffering there. 'He married S'an Troya two years ago.'

He thought of the regiment of women he had maintained and smiled gently. Even Magon.

Crinon let the garden speak, filling the silence with its own music. He wanted to stay there, to remain with her and plant slips and seeds until the end.

'What does he do? I mean, when he is himself.'

'Many years have passed. You forget. He has changed. No, I misrepresent his endeavours. He has grown older: he understands more. Let him speak to you.'

Choru recognised him, her animal love without discrimination, or the consciousness of the passage of time. The mother of many foals, she had become sedate and gentle, her spirited gait worn away. Yet riding her was a continuation and not a new beginning.

Of the first tower, nothing remained but a low mound. He paused there, got off the horse, and sat for a while amongst the tall grasses thinking of the past. Time had stopped. Today his hands obeyed him. But if he had stayed here, he would not have found Orel; he would not have saved anyone, nor discovered the City's treasures. Peach would have died.

A wide wooden gate at the head of the gorge was open and the road led downward in a broad curve which made him giddy. Only the height, he thought, and shook his head to clear it. He was glad to be so far from the water. The sun came out as he rode and showed him the Alcuon growth struggling to free itself of rotted leaves. Too much rain. Was it possible? The gorge smelled of it and the rocks were coated with moss and slime. The clouds which were piled in the north, hiding Baia, moved forward, bringing shadows with them.

He found the road and the track which led from it across uncultivated land. The tower was hidden by the wood and he anticipated thorns and shadows, the cobwebs of forgetting and the red rust which too soon dulls bright steel, a penitent beast transformed. Saint or madman, it did not matter. Somewhere in there, his horse neighed and Choru answered it.

Omega

Immersed in a time-denying trance of concentration, Magon continued to write. He wrote until the clock struck eleven. The hall clock answered it. He pushed back his chair. The translation was finished. Stray words lingered in his mind; he was dissatisfied with his rendering of serpent as treachery. The word implied hypocrisy, a double tongue; snakes – they were the smooth, dry creatures the physicians had taken as their sign. Venom could heal. Am I treacherous? Reality pushed between the words, darkness into the lamplit circle: no, he would not consider his actions. He rose and fetched a thesaurus from the shelf. Treason, that was the word; that was his crime. Hayla would never forget that he had overthrown her Goddess. The knife dug in and twisted: a great cavity yawned. What was a drop of acid? They had once used such means themeselves to obliterate their Marks. What was a dressed burn and hurt pride? An eye for an eye, retribution, the righting of his wrong. He sat still and imagined the pain in the seared wrist. He remembered the conflicts of the past eight years; no, he remembered only the times when the love he had expended had been returned, given again in such small commonplaces as a look or a sympathetic laugh. Damn him, he said, echoing Dayamit, we are all committed to Aash and Hyason Sarin is her chief evangelist. Is, no. Was. She had voluntarily taken the milk, though he had given her a choice.

Now he was safe. In his own world, in his own chair, the desk and the work before him proof of his status and invulnerability. He sat still, considering pain.

Its nature was invasive; it was a condition of life. One might anticipate it, fear it, sedate the brain and avoid it, seek it or enjoy it. To Benet, endlessly circling the Tayaal, it had become mundane, of as little account as hunger and thirst, themselves its concrete forms. Xynak had called it vanity. Its obscure magic had forsaken him but thought was pain made abstract, a prospect of temporal desolation to precede the after-life he had assured himself by his conversion.

In Shalusha pain had ended in oblivion, a wiping clean of the slate. He had watched the rocks tumble into the crater and seen the mighty cloud which, hanging for days above the mountain peaks, had marked the cessation of pain for those incarcerated there. Cal had known pain before he migrated into luxury: it was a condition of life on the streets. His birthright was restored and the desolation he would feel when the burn

320

had healed was a fitting punishment for his crime of betrayal. He had used the correct instrument; the City would solace her own.

He saw his own reduced reflection in the belly of the demon on the inkwell and recalled the demoniac possession of his anger. His hands were clean – he spread them – but his spirit was as distorted as the limbs of the imp. He was a sadist by proxy, and the soul he had swallowed choked him.

His personal experiments had failed. Only Crinon remained, the once and future consort, Crinon and the dutiful adulation of the cryomorph, S'an Troya. He paid cash for Slake's slavish devotion. Rafe was past experience. Cal was gone, past tense also.

He had succeeded in awakening a response in his own body: sweat poured from him, he was as hot and as wet as if he had run the long way round the plantation. He rose and adjusted the air-conditioning; he took out a handkerchief, towelled his face and his neck with the white square until it was grey.

His body, tuned so fine, had failed him. He was without music. His vanity was exposed. He looked at the counterfeit shelves. She has precognition, he thought. The plants, her lilies, and the quiet garden have given her knowledge beyond mine. The half-run hour glass, the skull, the drawing with the single word already crumpled and rejected. Nonesuch. Nameless Cal has heirs. Nonpareil, traitor, serpent. Farewell, thou art too dear . . . .

He sat down and read through Hayla's invective again. In a paragraph he had been tempted to delete, she made play of his sterility. He did not intend to reply to her charges, nor to respond in any way, but when Pikat went to Sollar for the next Council, he must avoid the pitfalls.

Benet's body had disgusted him, the memory of the whips and the scars had terrorised his nights. He had dreamed of flesh and rotting sponge, of discoloured water. The weals were hideous. They brought back the day when the gross Ineiti had moved close and pressed against his pure boy's body, on Cat Street, so long ago. Every thought had the same destination, returning him to the catechism of the golden skin and the betrayal in the yellow eyes.

But he could expect no less. He had asked for it. His addiction had become a vice somewhere on the ascent. The sequence had its own logic, and dissembling and lies were part of it. Yourself, Magon? Do you mean yourself? His self was cleft – he felt the raw division and rasping where the two parts fought. Not me, he said, but Cal who was exiled; and exiles do not return until there is a change of government. Love is not love which alters where it alteration finds. He would give orders, ensure that no one mentioned that name in his hearing; he would close and lock the doors of his room and let the dust cover everything. On his way in, hours ago, before the brute expulsion, he had encountered Slake in the kitchen.

He was sorting the washing, Cal's vermilion singlet raised in his hand between the piles on the floor. The moment would not vanish, the jumble of dirty clothes, his and Cal's, and Slake's brown hand holding up the slip of cinnabar cloth. He let go the breath he had unconsciously held in as, in the kitchen, he had tried not to inhale the combined odours because of the memories they woke. He closed the folder and called for Slake.

When Slake had gone, muttering in an incoherent and undisciplined way foreign to his characteristic resignation, he unlocked his journal with warm fingerprints and took up his pen. First the date: 21/12, the Sineinian style; then his innovation, Clemency, 6MN. He winced at the irony and his pious pretension. Those vain periodic names, chosen in the heat of victory – but it was done.

Slake would not speak directly to him for deks; questioned, he spoke inaudibly. He carried out his tasks with a grudging haste.

His own recovery was as gradual, a slow banishment. He gave himself no time. If there was any, a moment on waking, a time between tasks, he contemplated the phenomenon of Troya waking. From the first physical awakening, when he had watched the ice release her, to the light of today, she was his. He knew her secrets. Her virgin mind was his to tune and attune.

Sondrazan Troya M'una, born City, 22 Mahun in Alcuon (the month of his birth) 3476.

(Her mother had been ambassador to Southern Ineit and afterwards Representor in Sollar Kein; her donate father was Ies Kuni (thus), the only male artist of note in the first quarter of the third millennium. His work, shelved in the Forbidden Archive, awaited the attentions of Silvanor and Filka.)

Hair brown; eyes blue; blood group A+. Genesig (attached), IR 440. Med. Hist.: childhood ailments, norm. mens. @ 12.4, hysterectomy Alcuon 3493, ovect. Vern 3493.

(She, unlike himself, had voluntarily joined the legion of the childless, innocently and zealously offering up her body to the City.)

Hormone implant 7KiV 3494 (Surgeon's Report attached). Cryomorph induction, 22 MiA 3495. Sex. Profile: Het./Virg. Relig.: standard. Ed./Quals: CA, Matric, SScCU, CadMed 1st Class. Mil. Profile (cont. assess.) begun 1LiV 3495.

And so forth. He leafed through the printout, pausing only to study a photograph taken in her sixteenth year, before she had given away her womb and her store of potential children. She still looked like that, lissom as a reed – no – like Masolino's awkward Eva on the Gaian discs. He could not think of a parallel. The Mahunian literature was full of words like round and fertile, ripe and full – but she was a straight arrow, a sterile shell with the neat face and the secretive sex of a liriodendron flower. There had been ovaries once: he turned to the surgeon's report. In those days the City had an ovbank. A batch of her eggs had been labelled and frozen; and then – the large letters of his history primer restated their message on a page of his memory – in the second year of the Reformation the bank was closed and the building which housed it dismantled stone by stone. Even the pens and the bohea beakers had been destroyed. All S'an had left was the slow-release pack of hormones which preserved the beauty of her plundered body.

When she next came into the room, a tablecloth over her arm – for she had voluntarily adopted some of Slake's duties – he beckoned to her.

'Do you know what this is, S'an?'

She came towards him, her walk still without art, that of a sexual innocent.

'No, Archivist.'

'It is your life, your story. It tells me everything about you.'

'Everything, Archivist?' (He wished he had not taught her to use his title. When the time came, he would teach her his first name.) 'Does it tell you the name of my favourite flower?'

He was tempted to lie.

'Not that. Let me guess: hay-maidens.'

'Archivist!' Her little laugh was delicately provocative. Perhaps he was wrong. He walked an unknown territory. He had everything to learn.

'I love casqueflowers. You know how they hang in thick clusters by the Eshlon Steps.'

He said nothing, listening intently to her frayed memory.

'They've a scent like honey and orris. It overpowers you. You can smell it twenty metres away. And the flower itself – as blue as Her Ingemi maral and with a heart as red as Vryon's, or mine.' (Who had Vryon been, to touch her memory so? He would find out.)

'We picked the flowers for Race Night. To wear one means so much! Loyalty, sisterhood, dedication. A future beyond the stars.'

'And the boys?'

'Oh, them. They went to the Quarter.'

'Tell me.'

The tablecloth was a bright banner over her arm; she was arrayed in righteousness and her reply was a lesson learned by rote.

'Cadets do not go to the Quarter. The Quarter is for Subs. Once a month, flesh trade fees to be deducted from allowance. The Quarter is not for cadet officers. Mahun has provided it for minus ratings.'

'I see. Did you never go there? Just once?'

'Oh, no.' She unfolded and shook out the blue cloth. 'Once, I did. I never told anyone. Everything I saw made me feel dirty. The place smelled so and an Artisan woman followed me. I walked quickly but I didn't run in case she did. Then, in Copper Street, I ran until I came to the Fish. It's a café. We used to meet there. I wanted his sympathy, but he wasn't there.'

'Do you think I should destroy the Quarter?' He felt that the thought was hers, not his who had paid the tigers' rate on Cat Street.

'Some people need it.'

She spread the cloth and replaced the bowl of flowers. Since Udan, he had put flowers on the table, often choosing them himself in the glasshouses, for no one except Crinon picked the flowers in her garden. He had picked these pyxidiums; their harlequin colours matched his mood and recalled the laughter Cal had once induced. Some of their fights had been the amiable scraps of boys, or young lions.

'Is this all true?' he asked, tapping the file. 'Are these the facts, these words in your file?'

She came to him again, stood close, reading the first page.

'That is true. What these words say is correct. But they are bones. I have a heart. My mother knew it.'

'What do you know of your father?'

'His name.'

'Ies Kunai, the photopainter. I shall bring you his life's work.'

Suddenly she bent and kissed his hand, spread on the desktop beside the blotter; as briskly, stook up straight and saluted.

'Commander Hinoor, may I leave now? The transport is ready.'

In places, the glue had not set; the ivory was still unshaped. It was time for the lesson.

'S'an,' he said. 'Look at me. That's right. Listen to me.

' "I am S'an Troya. He is Magon Nonpareil. I am a woman. He is a man. This is his room. This is his City." '

'Now say the words. After me: "I am S'an Troya. He is Magon Nonpareil – " '

When he went down to the city, he travelled in a closed carriage. The choice was not made from modesty or fear, the carriage doors bore his distinctive rebus, but because he wanted to preserve his memories. He sat behind the blinds and listened to the City, hearing, over the new din of music and skimmers, the rattle of the wheels on the Hill, and the clatter and whine of the rkws as the cryomorph guard outside Citizen's Court saluted him.

The carriage stopped outside the church. He went into it and stood in his place near the priest, who spoke of compassion. He listened, turning the teachings over in his mind and balancing them with his own thoughts.

His hands hung down by his sides; thinking that his attitude revealed his indecision, his irresolute state, he clasped them. The prayers began again and the water was passed. He took the chalice from Benet, and drank. Benet wore his new grey robe, the novice's dress. Magon watched the flame, the slow combustion of the oil in the flask. When the calling prayer came round for the third time, he left his place and the church, pausing in the chapel to pray in front of the icon of Ikal blessing the Water. One Substance, One God. As the carriage took him back to the Hill, his reason echoed the sacred words: One God, One Duty, One Ruler, One City.

Charity (Kriy), 508

During the night he remembered. He had dreamed that he was asleep, afloat in the great bed on peaceful waters and, waking, did not understand his relationship with time and space. He got up from the bed and stood by the window, watching the copybook of the stars. The cold worlds gave enough light to see the dark shapes of the two canvases and the new painting he had purchased, a deep grey rectangle, on the wall opposite the window. Vryon na Hinoor. The echo came from the Archive below.

He lay down, stretching his limbs and emptying his mind to still it. But he could not sleep. The sheet was damp and rucked beneath him, the pillows flattened. He dressed, left the silent apartment and descended through the mysterious starlight. He moved with the ease of familiarity through the Archive Index to H and found the cross-reference. The cube was black. He pocketed it, inside its protective layer of film, and went to the Machine. There was a host of them, na Hinoors, offshoots of cousins of his family in the third and fourth millennia. Twenty-five of them had been named Vryon. He narrowed the frame of reference to the year 3495, and found him. A student of physics and astronomy, he had been something of a composer, a player of the glass harmonica: abstract sound from glass tubes and spheres. Not understanding the definition abstract sound, he called up some of the music and let it spin webs of ice around his isolation.

Vryon na Hinoor was hardly a relative: he had as many traits in common with Xhara', Cal, Dur Kunai, S'an herself. From student to cadet to officer, his progress had been rapid. It was clear from his profile that he enjoyed the attentions of vigorous women, that he would soon have lost interest in the sterile and dedicated cryomorph volunteer. His physical profile was interesting, six foot three and a hundred and eighty-six pounds, an athlete who had learned to draw the Talong in the days of touch weapons, who kept horses on his mother's estates in Upper Vern. But his hair was straight and light and his eyes a clear grey; his voice, despite his education, still held on to the broader vowels of Vern. He had sailed from the Eshtur satellite aboard *Daystar* to discover new worlds and new horizons for himself, fresh minds and the receptive bodies of a race like his own. He had not returned, dying of a Gaian viral invasion on the voyage home, a white-haired (they had not learned to prevent breakdown of melanin until two years after he left Guna) centenarian with the body of a twenty-five year old. His burial canister and memorial was a tiny star in a new constellation, five light years away in a graveyard outside time, where the crystal music of his imagination had given way to the ceaseless music of the spheres.

S'an Troya lived in the Block. Each day she made the journey up the Hill, climbing into the open carriage at eight and leaning back against its leather cushions to enjoy the birdsong and the lively clatter of hooves. Xanchen sat opposite her, her long face always in repose; it was not clear if she thought or merely responded to fresh stimuli by instinct. It was not clear if she heard the birdsong or the noise of the iron shoes on the stone road or if the heart of her being was always elsewhere.

'Listen, Xanchen.' S'an could see an orange bird which, with wide-open bill, delivered its challenge to the morning. 'Look.'

'It's a bird,' said Xanchen, and relapsed into her otherworld.

The tower on the Hill, the great Octagon; that had been there before, in the other time. It had been the dominion of blue-clad women, a serious and mighty Matriarch at its head, a scholar who appeared on feast days and delivered a speech to the assembled students: the Archivist's Address. Today, there was another being, but it spoke with several voices and oppressed her with its talk of the past. It was a Hinoor, but it was also Nonpareil and she knew – from what remote corner of her mind had the fact come? – that the word meant without equal in the first language of Cheron. This being, Magon Nonpareil, was male and she called him Archivist. He fascinated her, this reverse image of the boy she had loved; he made her heated and confused.

'Xanchen,' she said again, 'the right stimulus – ' But it was useless. She could not hold the kind of conversation she needed with a cryomorph; nor could she, herself, find the hidden thoughts.

The new canvas filled him with delight. Its colours were those of the illuminated ocean, the colours of sea anemones revealed, bright jewels of paint, yellow, scarlet, vivid rose, a singing blue, a green as virulent as an arsenicane dye. These amorphous forms, pure colour, these brushstrokes were scattered on the pure white canvas like random thoughts, happy accidents, and amongst them, punctuation marks, were ideograms, the jottings of the mind, pictograms which lost their form when concentrated upon. Some were like flowers, some like the harsh instruments of an indefinable tyranny, some like grotesque beasts and men with superabundant limbs. One brushstroke made a swan, Cal's silent black swan which rode the wind above the City and was the harbinger of dreams.

The sale had massaged his ego. The tiny room off Font Street was crammed with the art of the three continents, objects from lifelong collections. It was a sale of effects, the dazzling companions of a judge, the temporal solace of the deposed President of the Nines. He pitched his first bid deliberately low to allow the price to rise and be haggled down before it settled at a suitable sum, and the referee began his cant. He spoke his second bid with his usual firmness and decision. It was not challenged. This was, after all, a contest in which he held the sharper weapon of unlimited resources.

'Colours of the Mind, Julla na Faraja,' announced the referee. 'The Archivist, fifteen hundred bars.' The sale was a good advertisement for her, the scarcely known painter, whose work Nina once had the wisdom to collect, who was working now, in the turbulent City, unknown to Crinon and her circle. It was another feather for him.

He had communicated his interest in the amber by letter, and an assessor was waiting when he entered the vault. The woman came forward to unlock the case and place the carvings, one by one, in his hands. He borrowed her eyeglass to examine some of them more closely. He had known of this collection and had coveted it since he was nineteen and seated by his mother at an endless dinner party in Shuma's house. Thoughts of the amber had sustained him through the speeches. The vervet was very fine, one of three. If he bought the collection, he would have two of them. The scarcity of amber explained their great value. It took a polish as delicate as a smooth skin under artificial light. He disliked the pieces which were artful sarcophagi, turned and polished traps which had once held fast frantic legs and wings and now preserved the broken delicacy of the insects for ever; but there were only three of these. The rest were made from clear amber, the bubbles in it used to reinforce form, to underline; as an eye for example, or a tear of resin welling from a plum. They were all golden, the colour of the best bohea, of honey, tragacanth, sandarach, dammar, mastic. . . . They had none of the cold display of mined gems.

'That one,' he said to the expert. 'Could one have that mounted, perhaps in a pendant annulus of fine gold?'

'One could.' She was horrified. 'But, and you will forgive me, Archivist, it would be a crime to turn such work into a mere jewel.'

It was a fingernail-sized windflower, pale child of northern woodlands. The colour of the amber gave it force, supernatural power – a sunlit moly. A speck of some mineral – the soil of its home? – made its black root. It would lie warm against the skin and might protect her.

327

He named a price which would satisfy the assessor and her firm's greed and renown.

'That is more than acceptable; indeed, quite overwhelmingly generous,' she said.

The box arrived in the apartment before he did. He was not free until nearly ten and he ran from the lift to the door. Slake was still there, patiently tending his drying dinner.

'I've eaten,' he said. 'With Chenodor. I'm sorry: eat it yourself.'

'Yessir.' Slake could be insolent while preserving the appearance and the tones of servility.

The box stood on the low table near his desk. He knelt to unpack it, lifting each tiny carving from its nest of shredded packing.

Beauty. He would always need it. He must be surrounded by objects made to please, artefacts which demanded his noblest responses, beauties which did not accord with his chosen inner life, the raw quest of the spirit. And colour, from the absolute harmonics of the Martyrdom to the anarchy of the new Faraja. Vanity made him clothe his own body in dark colours: it needed no enhancement. He had chosen Slake principally because his solemn brownness did not obtrude; the need to save what was left after the unthinkable punishment came later. Sollar and Sinein had a programme of social restitution, a chemical regimen; here, in the remorseless City, castration was mutilation, just retribution. With Slake in place, a permanent fixture, he had been forced to give these fearful matters consideration.

Beauty, not ugliness, no more the expedient axe. In his new scheme the place of S'an Troya was still undefined but her obscured light persuaded him and some pervasive demon drove him to consider an alliance with the woman, with another soul he could attempt to heal, a girl he could dominate, as the peaks of High Zalcasia rise above the peaceful valleys of Baia. His IR was 504; hers an insignificant 440.

There were twenty-one carvings. They would all have fitted in a cup. He put the windflower to one side and examined the rest. The vervet monkey pleased him least because pure greed had motivated its purchase. The horse – he had to love it, because it was a horse, the noblest of God's creatures, and his first love. He knelt there a long time lifting and moving the pieces, absorbed in their perfection. The windflower he put with his papers for tomorrow's meeting with Chenodor and Oyno. While they argued and he mediated, the knowledge of its presence in the room would soothe him.

Mercy (Tra) 512

The latest meeting had altered nothing. For the time being he must remain one-third of the triumvirate, biding his time; but he noted how

328

Oyno and Chenodor found points of disagreement in every item on the agenda. Oyno had never believed in his power to alter circumstance, from his first cynical examination of the cryomorph chambers to his present grudging acceptance of the solutions offered by the Machine.

Chenodor had been irritable. Mahuntal's husband for ten years, he remained unhappy with the chance mores which forced him to discuss arms and administration with his father-in-law and the putative father of two of his wife's children. He had no vanity in him. He worked hard for the new City and neglected his family and his art equally. He had worn his beard in the same style for years; the creases seemed as fixed in his clothes as his body was fixed in a state of deliberate slovenliness. His nails were usually dirty and the areas on his face which were meant to be clean were covered in a three days' stubble, relics of his once-aggressive heterosexuality. His interest in the Dancer had been apparent for years and his wife had divorced him on the last day of the old law. Magon had experienced disquiet when M'untal accepted the sculptor; not for himself, he reasoned, while he concentrated on his entry in the Marriage Register, but because she was delicate and fastidious. As for Chenodor, he had seemed content with the wedding, both the new ceremony and the irregular arrangements for the yearling twins. Himself, he denied nothing and added nothing. Everyone had heard, but not from him. of Cal's part and of his researches with blood, semen, and gene signatures. He knew how they gossiped – Crinon passed on the circle's tattle. No one challenged him, nor spoke of it in his hearing, and he used their system to suppress the talk, although he had always despised the need which drove his fellow creatures to destroy each other with words. Everyone knew that Leirion and Anyal called him Father; everyone knew who paid for their education and amusements.

When she had taken the great bunch of kyani and merythian from him, in the colourful room that smelled of her perfume and of the two babies cradled together beside her bed, she had buried her nose in the flowers and murmured, 'White kyani! How did you persuade Nan?' before she held up her face for a kiss. An antique dressing table against the farther wall had carvings he would have liked to examine. Perhaps he had loved M'untal a little before he had taken refuge once more in prayer, his vain attempt at resolution and, after the catharsis of the desert, in the return to Cal.

White was the colour of mourning. He had blundered again but M'untal, delighting in the freshness and the scent of the flowers, had not noticed. Nan should have warned him. He remembered his unreasonable irritation at the absent servant's omission.

White was the colour of the building where she hid herself away and welcomed Raist Chenodor every night. The sunlight gave it a stark purity and the blue of the distant bay was extravagance behind it. The Snow

Palace, the building was called. As a child he had pretended it was Meloura, the planet he navigated by on his journey into the galaxy.

He had come straight out here from the meeting, these days without the pressing sense of guilt which once drove him to work every day from eight in the morning until well after nine at night. At this time of the year, the grass was tall and still green except in the paddocks where the horses had cropped it and needed a supplement of pellets and bran. The grooms would have tended Arkite. The old horse was weak and could no longer be ridden. But his daughter and successor was ready and when the rains came and the indoor school became a haven instead of a stuffy prison, he would go down and try her himself. Leda. She was a white and willing swan. Planning her conception, he had juggled names and attributes and made a choice: Arkite had covered the Dinoordian mare, Rafe's legacy; Choru was too small, he reasoned, and the elder of the two. He must have a strong animal to carry him into old age.

The uncropped grass was in flower. He came up over the low hill which hid his tower from the south side of the garden and saw that they had made some progress. He called it his tower of prayers, each golden block a wish which would raise his aspirations another five feet nearer God. Every one bore a single word from the long skein of the evening and morning prayers, carved on the curving inner surface, so that a worshipper could read them as he mounted the stairs, from the first to the last.

'If I made a prayer for every seedling I raise,' Crinon had said to him, 'I would have a forest in heaven.'

He had felt then that she treated his ambitions with the impatient, affectionate dismissal she had accorded his childhood enthusiasms. But she was true.

For this task, he employed only men. The powerhouses of his chosen religion would build his statement on the highest point of the enclosed land, the crown of the City. Had he not thrown the gardens open to the general public? It was not his fault that so few chose to climb the Hill and claim their right. He could not build to match the Octagon, but that was his domain already; because he built on rock, the highest outcrop of the underlying granite, on the tower top he would stand fifty feet higher than the Octagon's flags.

The foreman unfolded his plan. He had first drawn out the design in his journal: divided circles, segments of a whole, forlorn towers overlooking empty plains. He had augmented his skill in drawing with the construction modules in the Machine but, even so, the design had not been finished until late in 507 and Cal never saw it, having destroyed his right to confidences less than a month later.

'Yes,' he said, in answer to the multitude of questions. 'Do as you think fit. I know nothing of stone-cutting. But you've been slow.'

'It's the money,' said Hasi. 'They're never satisfied. They want a supplement for the time they spend away from home.'

'Then give them what they ask: you know the total allocation. You were hired to run the project.'

He looked out from the first window, an unlined gap in the wall, and saw the spread of the gardens and the low roof of Crinon's house. It was too close to his home. His dissatisfaction mounted as he climbed and he saw ghosts, the unfinished height, a prospect of months or years of wrangling. He looked out over the City. The curious structure of the old dyeworks tower took his eye, a ponderous pile topped by another Octagon. The lesser Octagon. At first he had looked anxiously at every report from the City Wardens, expecting a death, the distorted corpse of another addict, one more gone too soon to God, a slight and wasted Beggar with the mark of an old wound on his wrist. Later reports told him of a renaissance of derelicts, a new Beggar king; he had kept the happy news to himself and locked them away, assigning to one of the Wardens the duties of spymaster.

His strong tower would make thirty – as many as Cal's years. Time had passed and been lost to the inevitable progress of the years. He had reached and passed the awful milestone of his fortieth year and now, beginning the second half of his fifth decade, he sometimes encountered Aash, feeling her soft breath on his neck, hearing the rustle of her skirts. How many years would it be before he could stand on the tower top, build there his altar to the Master of the Winds, safeguard his soul?

Five days of next month were set aside for Arkos's visit, and he wanted to show his old mentor how much ardent progress he had made. Arkos wrote from Diridion of snow and a private passion.

It was slow, so slow, this intricate business of revolution and innovation. When he had rejected the glamour of celibacy, all those years ago, he had committed himself to building. The secular arm of the church, consisting of the people of Diridion and a handful of old and desperate City men, had been weak. He believed in the new community. Today, the resistance to change was weaker and the congregation numbered three thousand; but the church was poor. The distribution of wealth continued to favour the women: many had sent their money out of the City, to Hayna, to Roakn where no one enquired, and whence came a third of his wealth. Some money had travelled as far as Sinein. He could enact laws but he could not rob Citybank, nor could he preach what he did not practise. Cal's plundered account was still open.

His own reserves increased, the absurd salary, income from shares and sales conducted by the brokers in Roakn, the rents from his estates, *ex gratia* payments, gifts. It did not trouble him, yet, this well into which he dipped a glass, occasionally a bucket, but it gave him the advantage in every transaction. In the matter of S'an it gave him the power of a slave-trader. He had received the jewel from the goldsmith in Udan of 509; he kept it in a drawer in his office, a secret charm.

Power was something he wore, an old garment, and time and the three-part rule had not diminished it. They all, even Chenodor, saw him as both key to and repository of precedence and fact. His province was learning; he was the jealous curator of the secrets of the City.

She was ready. Able to perceive. He had measured her IR several times because he did not believe the figures. His fifth calculation still gave the sum of 452 and the Machine had verified it. He took Kunai's box with him. It was not large, about seven by eleven inches, made of a hard, unknown substance, not glass and not plastic. In dim light it looked black, in lamplight fathomless blue. The light also revealed an inscription on the lid: Kunai's Illusions. When he tilted the box, gently so that the contents were not disturbed, the letters reflected the colour of the box's surroundings. In the lift, they were silver: above, as he walked towards his door, striated ochre. He entered his study and they changed to gold. It was the last light of course, and the glass valley outside the study window was in shadow.

She was there, sitting on the edge of a low chair with her hands clasped round her knees, staring at nothing. An untasted cup of bohea stood on the table beside her. Slake had served it in his translucent cup.

'You haven't touched your tea.'

'Oh – I was thinking.'

Yes, she could. How could she? He sat opposite her, the box on his knees; smiled a prompt.

'Long ago,' she said, 'when I was a little girl (what were his terrors of the inexorable years, beside hers?), I never noticed the Octagon: it's too high. I saw the cats on the doorsteps and the cracks in the roadway. My mother took me out at night to see the Illuminated Skyway. She showed me the stars.'

'If your father had been there and not an existence in the past, he would have taken you home and made a new heaven for you.' This was the time to plant. He had not looked into the box, but he knew it must contain some logical trickery with light. 'Here. This is Kunai's life.'

She took the box from him, copying his careful movements; she laid it on the floor. He watched her. Though he had seen her naked, she was an enigma. The grey uniform screened her as effectively as a carapace. He wondered if his own black cymar made others puzzle. The lamp shone on the box.

' "Kunai's Illusions",' she read. 'What is in here? It can't be a disc.'

'I don't know. It belongs to you.'

She opened the box. Nothing sprang out, nor cowered in the darkest corner. The box was divided internally, filled with myriads of thin rectangles like identity wafers. She extracted one and held it out, under the light.

'Oh. Look.'

In her hand she held the edge of the forest, the moment where the familiar fields dissolve and the unknown begins. They both halted there and looked into the dim spaces while time stood still and the clocks (in another world) struck seven. Sunlight broke through the canopy and crept into the wood from behind them. Their two kneeling shadows lay across the forest floor. Her hand trembled and awoke a cloud of insects which boiled up and over into the light. He moved, closer, his knee touched her heel, and his shadow fell across the illusion and destroyed it.

She sat back on her heels.

'Which one now?'

'Any. Close your eyes.'

She took the first wafer her fingers found. It was thinner than a pocket mirror but it contained a great space. It was Maralis, the City's towers on the horizon; a view like the one he had seen from Goldencap Pass before he took the City. Except that all the land was tilled and the villages and Nivuna clean, no middens, no dross, but wooden houses laid out along broad streets and open grassy spaces where children played. He thought he could hear their shouts. Reservoirs, broad plains of green and blue water and everywhere, fields and woodland, not a lily, not yet the invasion and the tainted greed.

'Another.' He took one from the centre of the row, held it to the light and almost thrust it back into the box.

'No, no.' Her laugh was an arpeggio. This was a picture for adolescents to look at secretly, by torchlight under the bedclothes. The woman lay on her back; when he moved his hand, animating the scene, she rotated her hips and spread her legs.

'I look like that,' said S'an.

'You are thinner.'

'The growth hormones are responsible for that. They stretched me but they didn't fill me out.'

How literal she was, childlike and direct. He suspected that the picture was one of a series and he replaced it, selecting the next from the parallel row: a seascape. They looked at twenty or thirty more and his head began to ache. S'an, he thought, would have knelt there all night. The blunt fringe of hair she wore had grown lately and it had fallen over her eyes. He pushed it gently back for her. She was studying a nias flower and the intimate kiss of a bee.

'You carry on. I shall be back soon,' he said.

He ran down five flights of stairs, dispelling his ennui in the rushing descent. He took the lift and sprinted from it to the office, fumbling the great bunch of keys in his haste. The return could be slow, the amber anemone safe in his hand.

She sat in the pool of lamplight; everywhere else had grown dark, the room, the sky outside; and there were clouds which covered the stars. She was grey, a long thin body in cerecloth, a living body with frozen emotions and surely without a soul – for where could the soul go when the body was neither alive nor dead? The man who had made the illusions and half of her had been dead for more than two millennia, her mother for a thousand years. He put the anemone in his pocket and thought about the next communication.

'I'll call Slake,' he said. 'It's late: you'd better go home.'

'I'll leave the illusions. They're not really mine: they are yours – or the City's.'

Slake took her away from him. He sat in his chair, the uncovered box at his feet. Later, he took out the erotic arcana and spread the fifteen miniatures on the table, moving the lamp about so that the couple moved, a masque of copulation. In his mind, he heard their grunts and squeals. But when he slept at last, he dreamed of Cal: not as a friend or a lover, nor as beauty dressed in the borrowed robes of myth, but simply that he slept peacefully in the next room and when morning came would rise and begin the day beside him.

Piety (mid Ah) 514

That year, the heat of Vern oppressed him. Instead of running, he swam, letting the cool seawater wash away the sweats and humours of the night. He supposed that his reaction to the heat was another sign of the unstoppable years, a pointer to eventual decay and bodily weakness, the intellectual desert of senile dreams. Sometimes he thought that the grey which had invaded his hair was a sign of wisdom, sometimes that it was another pointer to the beginning of the end. Crinon had been amused when he cut his first wisdom tooth at the age of fourteen; now she teased him with images of the false distinction his grey hairs lent him.

With the cryomorph, he was either employer or teacher, and the amber anemone remained where he had secreted it, in a box beneath the cabinet which housed the remainder of the collection. Then, a dek before the coming of the rains, he woke from a long night of dreamless sleep, unexpectedly refreshed. Breasting the tide off the Point, he rejoiced in the strength of his body.

His perceptions sharpened. He looked into flowers and noticed the antennae of insects. He saw that Slake too had grown older and displayed a strong devotion to S'an Troya. He saw the long white streak in Crinon's black plait and remembered that next year she would be fifty.

The tower preoccupied him. Slowly it had risen to twenty feet. There were endless problems, and no work would be done during Udan. When he had time he added paragraphs to his monograph on the dialects of the Ruht. Crinon had completed her canvas of battling archers and was adrift; Xhara' had suffered her sea change. Of the Sisterhood, only

Amarant had regular employment teaching self-expression in the City. He had attended the latest exhibition, causing a flutter and a stir amongst the orphans and disabled gathered in the hall; he had wept (almost, feeling the symptoms and turning away from the crowd) at the reality around him and the manifestation of it in the pictures where stiff Tribers with knives and cryomorphs with rkws paraded under blue skies full of skimmers and bright showers of gunfire, Mount Bai a stern grey shape in the background. Faya sat all day on Crinon's verandah, stitching at a large piece of canvas. She was tired, she declared, exhausted by her mission in the City. They could all write now and she could not: she would write nothing again unless someone commissioned a report. The novel she finished in 512 would be her last. Age had withered her and the swan's throat had become the neck of a vulture; but a kind and tolerant old vulture, who loved and amused that child of Aash, Xhara's fourteen-month-old daughter. Faya fed on gossip and had a new and insatiable appetite for telling the cards. When her fingers had grown sore from the needle she spread them before her and looked into the future.

'You, Magon,' she exclaimed, breaking his concentration. 'You have turned Justice on her head. And Balked Ambition, that's here.'

He inclined his head in her direction, politely – she was his sister's oldest friend – but he kept his eyes on the text. The word ambition was in the next sentence. He thought about the tower and his reasons for building it: it seemed to him vaunting ambition, venal pride, that apart from the obvious symbolism, the salve to his disappointed vitality.

The child of violence approached, trailing a toy horse on a string. His horse. He recognised the worn red paint and the pits he had gnawed in the ears.

'Dog,' said the child, 'Dog. Dog. Dog.'

'It's a horse. Horse.'

'Dog.'

Faya held out her arms. 'Come Anlie. Come to Faya.' The child, safe in her arms, stared at him with the persistence of a lunatic. 'Dog,' she said again.

'All animals are dogs at the moment,' said Faya.

He looked at his hands, expecting to see them altered, after the manner of demons, into hirsute paws, the strength of his thumb converted to a fragile dewclaw. He looked at Faya: once she had had the elegance of a greyhound. Undeveloped brains, idleness, ambition, unfinished towers; these occupied the afternoon with the fevered logic of Vern, when even Crinon's garden threatened to spill into the calm waters of the pool.

The child still stared. He fancied she had the fanatic eyes of her sire, the Grade B gunner; he was no less useful without his balls. The chance that he understood his loss was small and, if he did, it was a concrete lack and not, like his own, an invisible poisoned hope. He, Magon Nonpareil, was glad that he would pass nothing down the chain of inheritance. All he would hand on were ideas, patterns of the mind; nothing concrete, no blemishes, no rotten chromosomes, no passion. And S'an too was as empty as a discarded eggsac on the beach. The union of the past and the present which was made real in Anlie filled him with despair. There were already too many children, too many born to suffer disillusionment. In such moments he regretted the zeal which had led him to Diridion, to Mount Zelk and the cryomorphs.

He rose, leaving his book open on his chair, and went into the house. In the kitchen, Xhara' boiled an egg and broke bread into small pieces. He went on into the studio and let the essence of the place seep into his lungs. Crinon sat astride her stool, brushless, her hands on her knees. The canvas was filled with jutting shapes, shadows of a new idea. His silence harmonised with hers. She began to talk of her work.

'I must paint one. They're so different, so much the same. The archers were just a beginning. But where's the beauty? Is there any left?

'I'll have to exclude Xhara'. She must not come in.'

'Xhara' can endure anything.' He stroked her arm, brown and clean of paint for once; he pretended to brush away her golden lily Mark. 'She is boiling an egg in the kitchen.'

'I know. Every day at four. An egg or cheese. Anlie marks time by the state of her stomach.'

The communion of acceptance which had replaced their old optimism, the passions of his conversion and her first figure paintings, was acceptable, suited to ageing and the time. He glanced out of the west window: the plants looked thirsty, desperately in flower, waiting for water.

'I know what it is,' he said. The answer was plain. 'The tower is in the wrong place. It should be outside the City.'

When he went to the meeting, he had purpose. Chenodor was inclined to argument and division. He soothed Oyno, and watched his new manoeuvres, the outwitting of Chenodor, the steps which would lead his administration into chaos.

Laughter came from his kitchen, an unreasonable noise. The door was open and he approached it with determination. Slake had uncorked a bottle of icewine, nectar of frozen grapes from the highest Baian slopes; half of it was gone, poured into and drunk from his finest Vikkutrian. Sarcasm might deflate him, sarcasm and distance. A frisson of rage spiced the moment.

'Did I ask you to open that, Amskiri?'

'No sir. It's only an '89.'

S'an slid past him, a guilty exit. Her cheeks were dark red: alcohol, not blushes.

'89 costs twelve frags a bottle.' (You should drink table wine.)
'Deduct it from my salary.' (I earn enough to buy my own anyway.)
'Don't be a fool.'

Slake recorked the bottle and shut it in the refrigerator. He turned his back on Magon and became absorbed in the careful washing of the crystal. His words, when they came, seemed to escape him without being spoken.

'I can still raise a gallop.'

He swallowed. The challenge had come from the most unexpected quarter.

'I believe that's one of the penalties of castration.'

His exit would end the confrontation. The study was no refuge for S'an was there, standing near the walnut table, a hangdog figure in front of the window.

'Surgery would help him; I've examined him. He wanted to make me happy in return,' she said.

'He can't make you happy. This is 514 not 3498. He was gelded. He is powerless; your nostrums will not restore his creativity. Besides, you don't want to marry a servant.'

Relief came when he had spoken the words. Now it was out of his hands and custom could take over. He opened the box and retrieved the hidden amber. It had the quality of her skin, an oily translucence. He fastened the tiny catch and kissed her cheek. He kissed her lips, but not her, not S'an Troya, searching for a current between the twin flaps of flesh, the gates of her being. He could not ask Slake to escort her. She sat opposite him in the carriage, silent, apparently content. He considered his proposal and her calm response, the ritual, the gift, the eventual marriage and its consummation. They were as nothing beside the building of the new tower.

Tranquillity (Verrun) 514

What have you done, Magon? The voice was not his own. The tower would not crumble. He hefted the pick again. A creditable performance. And unrehearsed. The voice was hoarse but the lips were warm. They were open. It's the best bed. There's only time for one. Mahun, the women are ugly.

He opened his eyes and focused on the dark ceiling. Dreams, disturbed memories, false conclusions, were the province of the uncontrolled, the demon of excess, the nightmare; nobody, nothing rode him. Once, he had seen the creature who called himself Pulchrinella, a made-up travesty, as pretty as a painted doll; he knew men who had handled him/her. What have you done, Magon? The voice came from the back of his mind. He had enough to do in the unfinished city. The lily trade, poverty, justice, the estates, the Wardenage, Hayla, Chenodor, Oyno. They rode a children's carousel, the abstracts spinning with the gaudy protagonists. He laboured at the badly geared wheel.

It was six-thirty, the sea dark as the land. He would reach the shore with the light and extinguish his fervid fancies.

Justice (Mahun) 515

They were married on his birthday. Benet assisted, Arkos married them. S'an sipped the water daintily and passed her hands quickly through the flame. He had told her, in a comprehensive heresy, that Mahun herself sanctioned the ritual, that it was part of the Wheel. He promised to honour and protect her. Afterwards, there was a private breakfast at the Garden House, Amarant, Faya, a composed Slake, the clergy, Silvanor and Filka; Crinon wept openly. They unwrapped some of the expensive gifts people give each other on these occasions. He watched the stranger he had married. She knew nothing; the room was full of viciousness, the gossip and speculation of kites like Amarant and Gildo. For the record he had added her old and new ages and made thirty-five. Their reflections, side by side in the studio window, were distorted by the old glass: he was a monstrous dictator, she a waif in silken trumpery. A wife. The voice of his conscience nagged. Passion had abandoned him. He had written the play: they must act.

He had chosen Vikkutra because he had only once been there; it was free from associations, free of perilous memories, self-devouring shadows of the old world. He could see that she was very tired, bewildered by the long ceremony and the noisy crowd. The carriage took them away from the inquisitors. She slept, leaning against him, an ancient innocent. He was afraid that her thin body would be impenetrable; he was frightened of hurting her. She slept an hour in the resthouse and they continued the slow journey. She sat close to him as if she enjoyed his newly sanctioned proximity; he remembered how nervous M'untal had been. Remember that you are a man. The picture of the Allode appeared. Monos forgives. But he was alone and it was a mistake to call up that memory; Cal had been beside him watching the chaste religious embrace with his usual unreasoned jealousy. S'an was reality. Her sleeping hand moved under his. He closed his eyes and called upon her father's illusions.

He was determined to court her with an elaborate supper, to drink just enough icewine and to ply her with the chef's finest creations; with husk or dust if necessary. The house he had borrowed had once been a fort and the scale of it was too vast for an amour. But when they entered it, and he had closed the heavy door and shut out the stars and the noise of the sea, he found that its solidity gave him comfort.

338

S'an, called into the mist of her second existence, had seen the man and ignored him. Yet he had persisted, this image of strength and intelligence, the guardian of the Octagon, throughout the succeeding years of repetitious tasks and reawakening. He had summoned her to aid and accompany him. Now he was present all the time, had been there during the long hours in the bare white building, the hurried breathless time in the house in the garden, the hours of conveyance through evergreen forests. She had married him and Vryon was dead. She had promised to solace Magon until Aash delivered him. She had observed and understood the differences between them: her smooth skin, the roughening of his face as the day wore on, her round hips and his broad shoulders, her light pipe and his marvellous voice. She remembered some of the old transformations and how clever Rann had become an automaton, forfeiting his mind and independence to become an extension of the weapon. And now the gunners belonged to Magon and the diminished City was his too. The black screen was a veil, a film of gauze whose torn corner flapped, blowing in the wind.

Two glass vases stood on the table, one as clear as day in the mountains, the other pale yellow, the echo of the beautiful flower he had given her. She picked up the vase and looked at the room through it. Everything was transformed, afloat on a golden sea, and Magon had become a dwarf. She, like Kunai, could make illusions. She put down the glass so that she could smile and turn to him. The medic, pushing the long needle into her arm, had been gentle, his rich brown eyes on her nakedness, so that, when she awoke and saw the same intent brown gaze, she was confused. He, adrift on some tideless sea, was as vulnerable as she was. She tugged at the complicated knot the women had tied in her girdle, and the garment slipped from her for, after all, it was nothing more than a length of silk.

The innocence of her naked body, freed from the frost and rising from white waves of silk, woke echoes in his mind, long paths of words down which he had wandered alone. Aphrodite, Eva; Isis, Eshtur; Bella and the Snow Queen: women constructed from words, the collective syntheses of legend. If he closed his eyes, he could touch her, still in the timeless gardens of the Hesperides, find her and enter the labyrinth, first with the sensitive fingers of a gardener. . . . There was no clue to grasp and no golden fruit. When he woke from the brief sleep which overcame him after the crescendo, a different fear accosted him. He thought of her inhabiting his bed, a fixture, and he got up from the rug on which he found himself to fill a glass with the cold green wine with which he would have begun his own seduction.

Next day, they walked about Vikkutra. He talked incessantly, pouring facts into her, any facts, for she must learn. He told her the history of

Vikkutra and spoke of her trade and her wars. The sand of the beach was as white as S'an's maral. He told her how it was conveyed to the kilns and converted into glass; he bought glass for her and boxes of plump raisins; he kissed her until she complained that her lips were sore, yet she returned his kisses. It seemed that she approved of him. He had made her mind: he would shape her sexuality; he would have no more of Maja's smothering and no guilt.

At the end of the dek he was so tired from the intellectual effort of making love to her that it was he who slept in the carriage which took them home to the City.

Charity (Lilb/Kriy) 516

Leda freed him: he took one day out of every crowded dek to ride. The mare carried him precipitately through the drying countryside. The white swan and, at home, Slake. He never asked what S'an did when he was absent, working, searching for the site for the ultimate tower of prayer; but sometimes she brought home silverware and bells or he observed a weighty exchange of glances betwen her and his servant. When she had been down to the City, she was animated as if by fear and – most likely – that was all it was: she had sought and found excitement on the dangerous streets. Or with Slake. It was she who had hired the surgeon from Ros Kein. When the strife is over, when I have overturned both Chenodor and Oyno and calmed Hayla, he thought, I will build her a house there: I will build her a colonnaded palace, a garden for her own delights. She was secretary and wife; they were friends – but he never confided in her. She functioned well, spoke clearly, wrote with style; her thoughts cohered except during those stifling episodes when her freshening brain faltered. To paper the cracks, she had devised a beguiling technique: she knitted everlasting garments and when her mind failed her and the blush came to her cheeks and drops of moisture to her brow, she took up her work and moved the needles until her memory returned. As he grew older, she stood still. She receded from him, her body caught in the stasis her mind had escaped. She looked like an ageless girl. She was the essence of the cryomorphs: he saw Saissa in her frown and the seductive attitudes of the beautiful gunners in her walk. Crinon admired her and persuaded her to sit; he was permitted to watch the portrait grow.

And the new tower grew, mounting higher inside the belt of woodland he had chosen. Arkos had sent Zander to oversee the work, and under his direction the old works had been demolished, the stone transported, and the footings dug in the bare red earth. If the tower represented none of his pain, it held his latest aspirations: he would prevail. Bird and insect song and the stifling heat cut off the place, enclosing it in an invisible

340

paling. He tried to prevent the monks from crushing the lilies which flourished where the trees had been felled; he laid some of the stones himself, lifting and trowelling with the rest, before he returned to the Octagon, to the City and the political chicanery.

Given enough rope, he thought, the old image more potent than those of the needle or the silent gun: Chenodor had broken the law, a technical trangression as rash as Rafe's, no deliberate flouting, but a sin of omission. It concerned his bodyguard, a licence, and a number of rkws. He issued neither threat nor reminder, but signed the warrant and left the rest to Oyno. That left one. He had not expected that Oyno would die so soon and so ridiculously, falling from the riverside emplacement to the hard deck of a passing boat, and he considered that it was no more than God's will that M'untal should lose her husband and her father within one month. In the church he prayed for their souls and, returning with the carriage hood open, saw the destruction and Hayla's ship, waiting beyond the roadstead, on a tide of hope that he would again trangress the unwritten laws of the Council of Nations – and Noiro, one should never underrate a developed country. To be sure of Pikat, he recalled him from Sollar to show him Oyno's body and Chenodor's death certificate.

Udan-Alcuon (Joy-Compassion) 516/517

During the rains, which were heavy and prolonged that year, he visited the tower frequently and, while the monks lifted stones in the downpour, he sat alone among the building blocks, raising questions and considering alternative solutions. The Machine squatted beneath the Octagon, a silent sybil of unchanging reason. With this brain, he could play as never with his own: he could see into the future. Already he knew the crops which would grow best in the red earth and replace the ignoble lily trade. Trees would grow well. Grasses could flourish, and cattle ate grass. Wild horses would crop anything. Once, they had inhabited the forests and might be set free again to roam and start new forests with their seeded dung. He would begin with his own lands.

If no one needed a martyr, the world needed an exemplar. Hayla – to overcome her by force was the simple solution; she was a composite, every successive Haynian queen was called Hayla so that treating with her was treating with history. He intended to meet the woman face to face. Through the magic window of the Machine he watched Pikat in Sollar stumble against the first words he had written and, gaining confidence, catch and speak the rhythms of his passionate address.

Playing there, beneath the stones, the books, and archives, he moved his hands to call up the various journalists who conveyed their messages of panic and prejudice to an apathetic world. Famine, war, pestilence, death; Haerth, Sowash in Noiro, Alut, Maralis. A rainlashed blonde addressed him (and how many million more?) in a clipped Sollar accent. She, he noticed, had lost her red CoNN triangle and spoke unverified rumour. She told him that his time had come, and he laughed. 'The citizens say that the rain is a sign of Mahun's displeasure,' she finished, jubilate. 'This is Orel Diran for Universal Prime Time from the City on the last day of Alcuon 517, or, as the Archivist has it, the thirtieth day of Compassion. We shall see.'

He deleted her. Tomorrow, the Red Wind blew.

The rain stopped, but the Wind did not blow. The clouds he had hoped for, they approached, but they brought more of the terrible water, no searing and cleansing turbulence. 507, the failed harvest: that had taught him the function of the Red Wind. The grey cloudbank hung over Maralis, waiting, and when he went out to mount Leda and ride up to the tower, he wrapped himself in waterproofs.

He saw it from Leda's back, the technological lightning bolt which preceded the storm, and did not know which way to turn – home to pick up the pieces, or onward to the other topless tower. In the Tayaal, in the liriodendron wood, riding Leda through the crowded forest, he had thought himself free; but now he was released. No more paper, no more ink, no more books to make me stink: the schoolday chant filled his mind with its hammering, idiot insistence. Terror seduced him as he watched the incandescent firework falter and smoke out. The hazard system had probably done for the public ostentation and the treasures in his office – a puddle of tempered bronze, Jerome drowned, the ivory apple and its tenant worm washed away by the jetting water. He found himself lying along the neck of the mare, shaking with hysterical laughter. The tower was nearer; he collected the reins and touched her sides with impatient heels.

They had the news. He could see it in Zander's agitation. The monk shook the relay as if it had bitten him.

'Sondrazan?' he enquired, surprised into an appropriate reaction.

'With your sister.' No need to speak of her nightlong absence and Slake's temporary desertion.

'She arrived there last night,' said the monk, relishing his rank morsel of the folly of secular relationships.

'I remember now,' he lied. 'I worked late . . . Crinon invited her.'

He sent emollient messages of concern and strict orders and slept on one of the monks' pallets, hearing the rain fall between his dreams. In the morning, the sky overhead was clear and light blue, reminding him of the late winter dawns of Northern Sinein. But the clouds had not dispersed and Zander fretted while Benet asked for leave to send a courier into Tayaal. If God had sent rain to the desert. . . .

342

The work of placing the stones, one on the other, of climbing down for a stone and up again burdened with its bulk, filled his mind and the sweat which poured from him in the dank afternoon was a cleansing agent. He had slept badly in the hut. He would return tomorrow, return to Crinon since he, the Archivist, had nowhere else to go. Silvanor, from somewhere in his widower's anguish, would have called upon his talents and organised a lodging. The old house, or Hotel Z, maybe, where the hawklike journalists roosted by night. But he would go to Crinon. In any case, his wife was there. And Slake.

Arkite answered another horse. Probably he had imagined it, since they were ten miles from the nearest farm and three from the road. He bedded the stone and looked up to wipe his face. There was a bottle of water in the undercroft.

The shadows at the edge of the clearing were green illusory shapes. As he had once stood bewildered and shaking in the office, so now he stood under the trees, the surreal projection of a tired fancy. The shadows obscured whatever marks time had made on his body. Magon waited. One of them had to make the first move. So slow, so shaped, had the days become that the acceleration of his heartbeat startled him.

'What do you want?' he said.

Cal came from under the trees. In the daylight – he saw it with sorrow and the insight his wife and the years had given him – the marks the drug had made were apparent. He was gilt, spent, a remnant of himself; his state of being announced itself in the dirty fatigues he wore.

'I was afraid,' he said. 'I had to find out. I was looking at the Octagon when it came.'

'You took your time. Hayla loosed her bolt yesterday.'

'I had responsibilities. I slept at Crinon's.'

He looked up at the tower, at Magon looming on the scaffolding. Magon wiped his hands on a rag.

'Would you like a drink?' he said, old concerns invading him. 'If you've come from the Garden House, you've had a long ride.'

He seemed even shorter, shrunken and dessicated by the lily. The drug had dried his voice as well and its attractive hoarseness had become a permanent rasp; he had a habit of clearing his throat before he spoke. He smelt like an Artisan, of garlic. Magon offered him the bottle of water and drank from it himself. How to begin, to close the gap? There was no doubt but that he had come to stay. They could hardly talk of straws.

He watched Cal prowl the undercroft, looking up at the arches and the coursed stonework. Sometimes he ran his fingers through his mud-coloured hair, and rubbed his papery skin. Those rings must irritate him, the same three rings: his ten kilobars had preserved them. But Maja's ring, which I missed, wishing to give it to S'an, will soon return to me.

He looked exhausted, his ending preordained by his addiction and his

343

devotion to the goddess and the City: no ship exists to take you from yourself. They had read the ancient poem together in the garden.

'You have made better progress with this tower,' said Cal. 'How could you hope to build a tower to Monos within the city boundary?'

He was right. It was his own conclusion.

'I have Zander to direct the work,' he said, to turn the talk from such close scrutiny.

'I saw him. He was mixing mortar.'

'I am married. And you?'

At one time the reply would have been raucous laughter, and Cal's lips twitched.

'Crinon told me. And you've no need to enquire: I know who spies for you. Go and look in the Archive.

'What made you pick a cryomorph?'

'She is wiser than I am.'

'I know cryomorphs. One of them drowned itself in my dye-pit and one of your gunners killed an old friend.'

His sleeves were rolled back: the scar was a ragged patch, white as the face of Aash, bright as moonlight on the Uyal. Let me see. No, he could not say that; he could not remove it, nor unsay any one of his harsh condemnations, spoken, he remembered, with ceremonious distance, in Maralay. His face had the same mixed expression of sobriety and insolence: his smile would not have altered. Yet, I remember him more handsome. He was sensuous to the last degree, and that lit up his expression. So long ago. But he is still alive; still here; here, beneath my tower.

He could not bear it, this visitation, this invasion of his private space by the ghost of his beautiful handcoloured memories. Where could he be lodged when his own haven was destroyed?

'Haven't you a following in the City?' he said, grasping at shadows. 'Peach and the women, your children: they must wonder what has become of you.'

'They have gone. Into the City.'

The drug had taken his intellect too.

'They don't need me now.'

He must mean that they had drowned.

'Look,' he said. 'I can't take you back to the Garden House. I don't know where I shall sleep.'

'I'll stay here. I've been looking after myself and two hundred others for a long time. And I shall enjoy a gossip with Zander.' At least his grin was unchanged, the same bright banner of jaunty composure.

Waking in Crinon's bed, for she had taken the hammock, he felt S'an's hand on his chest. Last night, after dinner and its attendant discussion,

344

she had curled up beside him, her absence still a mystery. She had not explained it. He felt abused, hurt, and displaced by the combination of events and the women's determination. Crinon had berated him for leaving Cal at the tower.

'Your boy has come back,' said S'an.

'My boy?'

'Cal. Beginning and end, first and last.'

'Don't speak like Gildo, in tired metaphors.'

'I don't. But I now how to nurse a husker. Shall I help you?'

'No.'

Coffee restored him, coffee and Crinon refreshed, a stimulating breakfast blend. He watched the steady rain and the gathering of the birds, which flitted from the trees to the verandah rail, rousing their sodden feathers, waiting for her. The python which, in his opinion, Crinon regarded with superstitious awe, made her slow and winding way among the shrubs.

Crinon brought his bread, warm from the oven. Some of the birds bowed to her and she chirruped at them, feeling in her pockets for their seeds and scraps.

Mama went out,' he said. She looked relieved, holding up her hands to the birds. The parakeets perched on her wrists and shoulders. When they had eaten, she came back to him and kissed the top of his head.

'Master juggler.'

'I feel like a wrestler. It must end.'

'Only when you do.'

Alpha

Continuity (Late Ah) 517

The capricious rains had ended in early Vern and the lily crop had struggled with the chokeweed. In Maralis, wherever he rode up to the tower, late vegetable crops were being harvested; neither the Machine nor the forecasters could tell him if the rains would come again, at the proper time; but a roof covered the unfinished tower and there he had made a home, three basic rooms and three-quarters of a stairway which led nowhere. The monks were building an oratory in the garth below, where the lilies he had preserved now dropped bright petals from seedcases like purses. He counted the days until Cal would be unable to make his unsteady way about the tower.

On good days he was lucid: one could hold a conversation with him, as fine and detailed a conversation as any from the happy days in the Octagon. It was almost possible to recover their shared hilarity, an alliance against petty stupidities, the daily nothings of a life together.

When the subsidence began, Magon had sought the cause in the Archive. Sewer maps existed, some of them in detail, but the record was incomplete or undiscovered and the geological data showed solid rock beneath the Church of Monos. The engineers had blasted into it when they began the foundations. He gave orders for propping and underpinning.

'What do you expect?' said Cal. 'She tolerated you for so long; now, she devours you.'

'There must be a cavern from an earlier time, some structure which the floods have disturbed.'

'I never found one. Let me draw you a map.'

'It would be a fiction, an imagined maze; the labyrinth of your mind.'

'Then tell me, Magon, how you are so certain that another *Daystar* will come from Gaia?'

'I have begun to find truths in the Machine: the fables and the reality are joined at the root only, like the scales of a lily bulb. Once you know that, it's possible to tell them apart.'

'Have you heard from the Gaians? Has CoNN spoken to them? Aren't these thrice-blessed people of Gaia projections of yourself, figments of your faith, just as you say my City is a product of the grit and not Her revelation?'

Once, he had heard the voice of God. He waited. He could not speak of these things to an unbeliever, nor could he in all compassion tell what the Machine revealed, the lies and shadow plays, the elaborate masques it had first given him, and the dead others, as truths. Computer-generated actors had played to him and become a part of his memory, real substance on which he had based judgement and subsequent action. The *Daystar* shown in the City was a sham, and the death of her sister ship an illusion; their true existence had been in another dimension, one into which only a cryomorph or a longhauler could leap from Eshtur's satellite, 'Nyon, the old departure station.

'I know,' he said. 'Just as you knew that Lys spoke the truth about Huyatt.'

In his transcendental phases, Cal leaned hour by hour on the sill and Magon, returned from the Octagon, drew up a stool and sat beside him.

'Tell me what you see.'

Outside, in the sun, the trees continued to wilt, and it did not rain. He could see the white, truncated finger that was the Octagon, pointing into a cloudless sky. Cal appeared to look in the same direction.

'The eternal City. There are new houses on the west bank of the Uynal. I see Prenta – she's wearing green today. She looks well. The children have grown. And they have begun the third tower of the Temple. What audacity, to build so high from wooden scaffolding!'

He had spoken in Maralay, his broken voice adding pith to its cadences; but his next words were in one of the dead languages, Proto-Maralay. He had never been a classicist; his talents were with living languages and their bright and burgeoning nuances. He must have heard recordings in his days of brilliance on the Hill, the days when his tongue and his mind, interlocked, had produced his most fluent and skilful translations and his most original work.

'My City, my mother, my hope, my ending,' he said, and then, 'I never see Peach. I think he must be dead.'

Orel Diran's long letters, essays on Cal and his catholic love, had told him more about Peach than the brief communications of his agent, An; but he did not intend to reply. Cudbeer would do that, a polite message of acknowledgement. Her words had touched him; clearly, she was as dependent as once he had been – was still – but she had escaped both the man and the City to raise her daughter and write her book in the relative peace of Vern. She called herself Orel Diran M'unor in a vain attempt to retain what was lost. Even before the letters came, he had written the instruction which would give her access to his diaries when the time came. He looked at Cal; here, in the dark interior of the tower, he appeared almost whole.

347

He had become a servant and Cal was the master who endured his careful touch. He would not accept S'an's offer of help and struggled with his nursemaid's tasks. When Leda neighed at daybreak from her shelter in the wood, he remembered how Cal used to ride Choru on the beach at Evanul, slender muscle astride fluid strength; afterwards, he tasted of salt and iodine.

S'an visited him, reminding him that it was he, the City's Archivist, who was trapped in the stressful prison of the sickroom.

'My head aches,' he said.

'Sit down.' She had not allowed her new concerns to detract from her healing skills. She removed his shirt with a swift professional touch.

'Be still.' Her fingers moved in his hair, slid over his face and shoulders. He must have slept. His first waking sight was of her, his shirt in her hands, looking out of the south window.

'What can you see?'

'Once, I would have seen the topmost walkway and the roofs of the Chimeraton. The Octagon's the constant of course. The water has almost gone, just a lake about the lower Uynal and the bridges. It looks blue today. They have mounted a flagstaff on the Octagon; the flag is flying.

'You are due there tomorrow, Magon. The Archivist's Address.'

'I know.' He smiled. His promotion of her interests had brought its rewards. He had gained an ally, because she understood him.

'When Cal – ' He hesitated. He could not speak the terrible word. 'Later, would you?'

'Would you?' She smiled.

On bad days, when visions invaded his mind and his body was lost in a sthenic fit, the hours stretched. There was nothing to do – he cancelled all engagements – but sit and watch him, try to guess where he was and weigh the pros and cons of giving him a gram of the drug to calm his excited system against the sum of the harm it did. If he flew, his eyes rolled, despoiling the beautiful yellow gaze. Magon had grown used to the distress he saw and the pain it evoked in him, but once on a clear day and after walking the circuit of the unpopulated rooms, he had bent and kissed Cal on the lips and whispered, 'Take it back.' Instantly calm, Cal slept and none of the poisonous powder was needed.

This was the time to plan and consider new strategies. The trumpet lily should be banished, except from Crinon's garden and the garth, where it might remain as a memorial. He filled the hours beside Cal's bed and sheets of paper with columns of figures and notes on crop rotation, breeds of cattle, horses, and the climate of Southern Mahkrein. The activity dulled the pain; he had only to look up to remember. Even God cannot change the past, he thought, but I will alter the future until I am satisfied.

Herkel Galabrias had travelled a long way and his old body ached, although his mind was a bright star. Like all the Hinoors and their near kin, age hardly reduced his mental activity. Recently, he had finished his greatest work, the assessment and interpretation of the chronicles of the First Years; last month he had begun work on the Tayali Tapes, transcribing and translating as he listened. But the journey in chilly Verrun, away from the mild coast of Vern, had called up the echoes of past infirmities: the joints of his fingers were sore, his left elbow had become painful again and the hair of the wispy beard he had grown in his seventy-fifth year was falling out. He sipped vinefire from his flask (at eighty-eight, one has earned one's pleasures) and smiled at his cousin's daughter, quiescent and composed opposite him in the jolting carriage. He had responded at once to her call.

The carriage had left the gorge and was climbing the new road amongst the hissing of the ground skimmers. The horses didn't seem to mind, why should he? He had been glad to abandon eastern modes of transport and settle into older and better customs, a slower pace.

Crinon returned his smile. Her mother is there in her face, he thought, the grave demeanour of maturity, the reward of coming to terms with this terrible life.

The countless stars were reflected in the receding waters, reality and the symbols of reality. They, he had told the Diridians, were the souls of the damned, condemned to revolve endlessly in empty space, faint lights eternally without God, transmitting their messages of hopelessness across space, the flickering light of yesterday with us today. Moving amongst the stars: it could not be possible. The gaps between them were so vast; yet he could cover them with a fingertip. He held up his hands and covered a million stars, worlds too hot, too cold, too poisonous, too airless for men. From Gaia, he had read, the majority of her ten planets were invisible to an unaided watcher; of the ten in Guna's own system, four were visible from this broad continent, Mahkrein, but only Hibornal and the Mother herself were inhabitable. Ky, he knew, was the yellow eye, a champagne diamond, a topaz in the Udan sky and begetter of legendary tigers. Meloura was the red one; far away Zelt held her course. He located them. The false star 'Nyon had risen, the artificial world of technicians, cryomorphs, and uncertain hopes. Her appearance heralded Eshtur; and Gaia too had her moon, which was once called Diana and Aphrodite, the mother of all the arts.

He had wanted to return the paintings and sculptures, to send them home. Now it was impossible. They were part of Guna's atmosphere. He wanted to live until the *New Daystar* homed on 'Nyon, landed and disgorged the mysterious travellers, a scene of unparalleled fantasy, suited longhaulers and himself, in his black gown potent with his years of service to the City, gravely accounting for the loss of the Gaian's gifts and apologising for the wanton savagery of his peer, Hayla. Using his fingers like a child's counting frame, he numbered the decades: six until she comes, and six plus five equals eleven. Eleven decades. An impossible tenure. He too would be dust among the planets.

The moon rose and the carriage arrived, a black silhouette on the grass below. Benet, lowering the steps and helping the passengers to alight, seemed also a black paper cutout. He ran down the stairs to welcome his mother-cousin. The old man's cheek, under his lips, was velvet. His sparse beard scraped. He was smaller, shrunk by his great age into a disproportionate child with a glistening bald head.

'Why Magon,' said Galabrias. 'You are quite grey.'

How you have grown. I expect you have begun to shave off that fluff. I remember you in your cradle. In – let me see – 468, I saw you at your mother's breast, greedy boy: dear Maja, how she would laugh if she could be with us today. Herkel marked each infrequent visit with one of his absurd statements, a calendar of an altering relationship.

'A grey head is the proper crown for a scholar,' he said lightly. 'Now.' The ground was too rough, the stairs too steep for the wheelchair. He bent his knees and picked up the old man as if he were indeed a child. Benet followed with the chair and Crinon with baskets, a long sheaf of white lilies, and her current sketchblock. Aash, she was callous.

He was asleep. They wheeled Galabrias to the bedside and stood back to watch the shock register in his lined face. He said nothing, but a small sigh escaped his lips. Regret or impatience. The old physician lifted one of Cal's hands and found the racing pulse.

Cal opened his eyes. There were no more zy trees but he could shape the stones of the ceiling into anything he fancied, a golden dawn, the white expanse above the great bed, the vines which overhung the folly. The old turtle had come. He would try to speak. He moved his lips, licked them, but the heat in his chest was too great. Magon held his hand and the board and he chalked in ragged capitals: SOUL OR BODY DOC? He could still grin.

'I see,' said Galabrais, 'that the soul is in place, and that body and soul belong to Mahun. I was wrong. You, even in 501, knew the outcome.

' "Now the Medicine of the Soul is made out of four ingredients," ' he quoted, ' "and these are Weeping of the Heart, True Confession, Real Penitence and Good Deeds." You have never been a penitent; but three out of four, seventy-five per cent, that's not bad for a sinner. Magon won't do as well.

'I have brought you some of my oil.'

350

The physician leaned back in his wheelchair and watched Magon uncork the bottle. The room filled with a scented requiem of sunwarmed blossom and the bruised and blistered coats of oranges. Magon covered the ochre skin smoothly, with long, deft strokes and Crinon's reed travelled over her paper. His horror at her determination had abated: he understood her need to draw here. Something would grow, beauty would arise, from the hopelessness of death. Later, he would show Galabrias the three finished rooms.

He pushed the chair and the old man in front of him around the circuit of the upper floor. Beneath the unfinished shaft, Galabrias held up his hand for the forward motion to stop.

'Where does that go?'

'To the stars; up into the light. I shall build an altar there.'

'Magon's folly?'

'As you wish.' The old demon chuckled and rubbed his hands together with delight as if he had been hired to clown.

The length of the night was infinite: time had been inflated, yet it raced. At three in the morning when all systems ebb and Aash wakes, daylight seemed as far away as Gaia and also about to dawn. Crinon had spoken the Valediction four hours ago; and he, without disturbing the unbeliever who breathed so lightly, had inwardly chanted the liberating words of the passing office. With luck and God's good will, they might also free him.

The old man slept in his chair in the outer room, his chin sunk on his chest; he did not dream but, when the sun rose and warmed the garth below, he woke and peered out. The greens without had a reluctant quality, faded by the successive heat of long, slow Vern. Next month would bring refreshment. He thought the buds and fresh young leaves of Udan the most delicate and intense of the year; in his garden even the withered oriental herbs put out shoots, tender beginnings. He could not see the City. Rain trees – he could smell them: vanilla sugar, new-mown hay – and a sky like Her banner were enough; age loves a quiet landscape in which to practise its mental acrobatics. The sun, the ultimate furnace, burned her way across the sky and his eyes filled with tears; his head nodded and he slept again so that he never felt the hem of Aash's robe touch him as she passed nor heard Magon cry out.

Tranquility (Hibornal) 518

' "If my art could convey her manner and her mind, there would be no lovelier picture in the Universe." ' Crinon did not hesitate to commend her work. He stood close to his sister in the Director's office, a celebratory glass of Ceremana in his hand. Beyond the massive door murmured the crowd which had come to view Crinon's portrait of his wife. When they

351

walked out into the concourse, Crinon on the Director's arm, Xhara' and himself a pace behind, the crowd of spectators, confined by coloured ropes, turned as one woman. He smiled. Why not as one man? He had not been able to overturn that supreme absurdity, a sex-based language; yet his experience had as much validity as that of the City mothers. He had not wanted to overset that beloved absurdity and break the perfect rhythms of Maralay and all her sisters and distant cousins, Citycommons, Trav, Deep, Diridian, Tlivoorn. . . .

'This is unprecendented,' said the Director sharply, as if she apologised for the changeable enthusiasms of the crowd.

'It's gratifying. It's flattery.' Crinon's strong voice carried. 'It is because S'an is his wife.' He saw smiles illuminate expectant faces in the crowd.

The door into the gallery gleamed with a new, post-flood coat of paint. There was a dark stain on the marble of the walls, three feet above the floor. They had been silent pools, these rooms, hollow cisterns filled with the excesses of last year's Herelian storms. Obsequious art lovers, the ones with complimentary tickets, circulated. They cluttered the long room and obscured his view. S'an, of course, was absent. She had declined the invitation and the publicity; in the empty and unpainted salon of her new white house he had installed a link with the Machine. She sat there now, a dedicated acolyte. The house itself was a shell, a frame for her beauty. Whispers in his ear: regrets, compliments, Madam Nonpareil, very like, it transcends the material. He made the gestures politeness and etiquette demanded and retired to the couch in the middle of the room, the centre of an impromptu court which rivalled that before the painting. Eventually, the crowd cleared, drifted away, and they began to prepare the room for the public. He viewed the portrait through a shifting screen of attendants with ropes, posts, and empty glasses.

Crinon had set her against a background of High Zalcasia and Mount Zelk, her second birthplace. The painting was not a true grisaille; there were subtle blues in it, the world seen through an optic at night, or in mist, colourless colours which the imagination could imbue. S'an blushed easily yet, in Vikkutra, she had been as unblanching and composed as a matron of fifty. Through a glass darkly: the greys interfered with the perception of form; but S'an's head, as stark in outline as that of an archer on a millennium medallion, was not obscured and her harmonious features, straight nose, wide mouth, wise eye, the dark coif of her hair, were presented unadorned. He had seen paintings which awoke longing in him, the cousin to physical desire, to meet and know the subject, or the artist who could make such work, to become, himself, one of the enchanted group in a canvas, the charmed circle which included the invisible painter; but this, of his wife, only astounded him with its craft. He would need to return to it, again and again, before he could understand it.

His own visits to Zalcasia in 504 and again last year had been empty pilgrimages. Mount Zelk's peerless meadow was scarred by skimmer treads and the cryomorph chambers were full of dust, broken tiles, and discarded bottles; the white floors were sullied with the footprints of the workers who had cannibalised the machines and crated the parts. The dead, the two women and the exquisite boy, were gone. Relenting in his devotion to Monos, he had given up their bodies to the restored and shrunken Gynarchy for dismemberment and exposure on the Domes, pawns in his game with the Council of Nations.

In the City, the footings of the new cryomorph centre had been dug but the cautious request, both written and verbal, from Leirion and Anyal had suprised him; he considered that their youth made them ambitious, the same youth which allowed them to lay aside the thought of death. He would reserve time to weigh the pros and cons but ultimately he could not prevent them from suspending their short lives in the hope of visiting Gaia. Maybe their wayward genetic legacy had programmed the desire. M'untal had made a personal visit and begged him to forbid the sacrifice: in law he was still their father, under his law his was the ultimate decision.

Crinon had spent two months in Zalcasia in late Alcuon and early Vern, the seasons of S'an's physical awakening. Crinon's eccentricity would have amused the stolid Binalans; he knew that his vision of her drawing in the mighty landscape, rugs across her shoulders and knees and heavy boots on her feet, a flask of coffee laced with ichor to hand, somewhere close by a patient attendant and two hairy mountain ponies, was accurate. . . . He glanced at her. She had exchanged her crumpled shirt and slacks for finery and was arrayed – there was no other word for it – arrayed in a loose eastern suit of raw russet silk. She wore amber earrings and the rope of uneven amber beads he had brought her from Noiro. High heels too, frail stilts which elevated her – she was taller than he was. Or Sondrazan; tall and heavy and magnificent. Xhara' must have dressed her.

In Binala, he believed, she had spoken to Vedara; since Crinon was involved, there were certainly tears, and gifts. Kahil would be sixteen; he had made sure long ago that forty-five bars reached Vedara every year from his own coffers, bypassing the suspicious and no doubt wholly admirable person of her husband, Gesir. He pulled the journal from his pocket and began to write in it, sitting there in the centre of the hushed gallery while the citizens shuffled past. From time to time he was aware of the consternation he was causing and of the precipitate summoning of a pair of cryomorph guards. Which part of me do they value, what do they protect? Answering his own questions, 'The person of the Archivist,' he murmured, 'Not me.' He had begun to carry the journal soon after Cal's death; it was better thus, it acted as a buffer, as now; better to pause and jot down than to call up memories alone at night. One of M'untal's letters

was tucked inside the notebook, a creased and dog-eared marker. He
had read it many times. It was her valedictory letter, written on the eve of
her marriage to Chenodor. He unfolded the paper. The handwriting was
neat and upright: she had probably copied it from a draft. He would have
preferred the draft, immediate and unedited like a drawing. He would
have preferred to read a scrawl, the product of emotional disarray, and to
experience again (God's name, for only the second time!) her need of
him. The letter began with a quotation from the Law.

19 Verrun in Udan, MN1

'Whoever loves as I do turns on the Wheel.' [She was correct;
Tellon, Cal, himself – Cal and himself? – Chenodor and now
another misfit, an Ineiti entertainments producer who was in the
City to make capital out of distress.]

Dearest Magon,
 Alna says I shouldn't write. I loved you, I love you. Tomorrow I
marry Chenodor but that's separate like next year. Will it be hard
for you, writing it in the Register? I hope not – I hope so. We could
have had some more children, brothers and sisters of Leirion and
Anyal, the two of us alone.
 I'm rather drunk and my friends have gone home leaving a heap
of gifts on the couch. It's not good to be alone at such a time. I wish
you happiness, so hard to find.
 I love you.
 M'untal

For a long time he had pretended that he carried the letter as a charm
against self-delusion. He knew now that he carried it because it said
farewell for him to the unrealised dream of a world he could not enter.
He had never asked her how she had known that their few hours at the
Folly would be their only hours; that he was desperate for probation, for a
son, even a daughter; that, like herself, he believed excorporeal conception to be evil. She had worn her fool's maral printed with lips as scarlet
as the old emblem of the Gynarchy, a gluttonous vulva, unwinding it
slowly from her slender body and skipping to her own music; and Cal,
who hardly ever wore more than slops and a shirt, had been provoked as
much by his own nakedness as by his recent radical discovery. She had
greedily taken him afterwards, as much a harpy in the end as Amarant,
woman commanding: give, give. It was true that she had marked Cal's
death with full mourning, a white maral for two seasons and wreaths of
touch-me-not, but she had not disobeyed his request to stay away from
the funeral. That, he could not have managed with her beside him to

revive irrelevant memories.

In another pocket he carried the old red Huyatt and the battered Tree, not caring now that the book weighed down and stretched the fabric of his elegant suit.

When they had gone, all of them, and he had sent the cryomorphs into the anteroom, he let his gaze rest on the cold snows of Zalcasia behind his wife's shapely head. Along the bare branches of the liriodendrons white ribbons of snow would lie, and the highways would be impassable – but this swift way, the time machine of the imagination, the sevenleague boots of fancy, gave him perspective. The attendants were here again, and workmen. He beckoned them and watched them continue with their work. The other painting was brought in and hung. He hardly needed to look. He knew it so well that viewing it was like going home.

When at last he was ready to depart he rose from the leather couch and saluted each canvas with a swift glance of summation and – he was alone – a brief bow, hardly more than an inclination of the head. Cal had always disliked cryomorphs; he continued to stare into the water, trapped by his sun-bedizened reflection, and Sondrazan Nonpareil looked on icy summits.

He had reached the glass doors which led into Broadwalk before the director and the cryomorphs pounced together to bring him back from the dangerous street outside, to pour a last soothing glass of the smooth red wine, to call for his carriage and the outriders.

Justice (late Mahun) 519

For him, sex had never equalled diversion: commitment, pain, overwhelming joy, relief, it might be one or all of these. He had bathed and was shaving, his mind running between the portrait, the tower, and the rejuvenated Quarter, when he remembered the tranquil and intimate, above all Slake-less dinners in the harmonious months which had followed his marriage. He called for his servant.

He would not have the intrusion of bells or buzzers in the apartment. His private suite of rooms, furnished in the Octagon taste, the impersonal best, was a lodging. The tower was his home, if he had one. A dozen books and his clothes were all his possessions here. At the tower, scarcely more. As for S'an, her house had been finished a week ago. He would like to see it; he should see it.

Slake had to leave the apartment in order to use the relay in Cudbeer's office.

He dried his face. There he stood, his reflection staring incuriously back at him, the man who flirted with God, an ageing scholar and the most powerful man in Mahkrein. His face grew more like his father's every day. He had outrun Destorio and outwitted Chacma; Cheron was split, divided between the factions which followed Chacma's eldest son and one of his own half-brothers. His mother would have approved, might even have ventured a short sentence in his praise. His body had acquired a tough and sinewy grace. He was proud of it. When it decayed, then so should he; but he had no idea who to mark as his successor. How many more years? Ten? Twenty?

'Seven-thirty for eight,' said Slake through the door.

His delirium lasted almost six deks. With the ponderous certainty of the earth-moving machinery which was, even now, transforming the estate in Dinoord, the days rolled on. He spent as wildly as a boy on his first love, bringing her perfumed silks and roses, and offering her his competent verses. No matter that few of them had been written for her. She tolerated his enthusiasm; she might have been amused by it. It was hard to tell because she smiled often and, sometimes, inappropriately. Too soon, he began to miss the deep silences of night in the Octagon when he would awake and feel the mass of books above him and be conscious of the strong foundation of knowledge beneath; when he lay alone and thought, with the poignant expectation of a dismissed lover, of the Machine in the cellarage, waiting for his touch. He must return. The small auxiliary of the Machine, which he had given S'an, met his complicated requests with an unequivocal 'Unauthorised'. Again, it was S'an who restored his intellect and cooled his passion; who made him leave. 'Magon,' she said, Maja's gold ring gleaming on the finger with which she admonished him, 'once again, you have forgotten yourself and the City.'

He had dissipated the last of his sorrow, emptying the dregs into her compliant and compassionate body. This is the last time, he thought, and did not care. He could live on memory, although he had found it unreliable, exaggerating every past event until it took on the livid colours of a decaying acetate image. Yet, 'Remember me.' That would have been his command, if he had been able to speak. The white stone on the headland was a memorial which, in time, would weather and decay as much as the ancient Domes across the bay. When the Gynarchs had set the body down and ripped the grey cloth in which it was sewn, Crinon's neat stitches continuing where his own had faltered, they had all gone into the Necrarium for the final, restorative meal.

He sat for a long time when they had gone, the crumbs, the emptied dishes before him, a smear of red pigment on Amarant's glass. Eventually he would pluck up the courage to return to the domes, where *he* was. He walked slowly along the path, pushing aside the overgrown branches. He could hear the birds calling: warning, possessive yelps; later the blood voles and rats would come. The white blossoms of the umbrella trees appeared to float, divorced from their dark green parents; weeds grew on the terraces. The sky was grey.

They used knives, he belived, those grisly anatomists, the Dismemberers, the surgeons of Aash. The broken body was covered in birds. They had a utilitarian beauty, the ungainly kikiks mantling over their portions as if they were fleet desert falcons which deserved a reward. He waited under the last tree, watching the violation. But they had done and they soared all together, the barbs drifting higher than their ignoble cousins. He looked at the scattered bone, all that was left, and then up at the destroyers. How much more gentle was the Stream. One of the great barbs, rust-coloured, wing feathers taut as pennants on the wind, circled above him. He saw her talons open. Whatever had dropped near him in the grass, missing the fallen stone by inches, was no physical remnant. The bird landed uncertainly upwind, holding out its wide sails. He knelt, and found the Beggars' Tree, bent to new angles and smeared with a fatty deposit, a scrap of chain still threaded through its ring. He took out his handkerchief and wiped it clean. There, kneeling in the grass, the birds of death about him, and the clouds above releasing their promised rain, he was able at last to vent his grief and weep.

Eventually, someone came. He did not see her at first, and she waited until he had composed his features and attempted to wipe the grass stains from his knees. A novice in a pale blue cymar. She carried a tall basket and had a virginal smile. She climbed to the first terrace and began to collect up the bones. For a time, he watched her, awed by her lonely and disagreeable task, her determination, and her grace. Then he climbed to the terrace himself and touched the bones; he took one fragment up, and a second, dropping them one after another into her basket.

It that was a kind of absolution, so was his expenditure in S'an's body. Only his irrational sense of the pressing past had prevented him from bringing her back to the Octagon.

He spread his hands over the mute plate and spoke to the Machine.

He travelled in a desert where the level sands became blue sky at the horizon; his travels were detailed excursions from a red stone to a dry, white twig, to a sloughed snakeskin bowling gently along before him, each of its scales as sharp and definite as his senses. Although there had been no rain, no water, and no flowers for years, something grew there, a limb which stuck up from the sand. It had the shape of a tree, a naked thorn. He could see it clearly and every fine detail of its bark and hollow thorns, but he did not know if he was there in the landscape or if it hung before him over the desk, some distance above his hands; he knew that he and the Machine had brought it to life. A flower burst from the bare wood, swelled, and became a fruit, dropped into the barren sand, put out roots, shoots, leaves, and began to mount above its arid birthplace, overshadowing its parent. He could feel the roots pushing against his hands but, when he looked down, he saw only those hands, and the lines and creases and hair on them, the cut across his right forefinger from the

357

broken plate last night. Then she spoke.

Hers was not the small voice he had heard before, nor the voice of his mother. She spoke from the Machine in tones which made him want to bow his head, or open the lid of his desk to hide behind it from her unwanted attention.

'Magon,' she said, 'I wish you would acknowledge my existence. It's one thing to lose the soul of a believer in a straight conversion, but to have a sceptic float in the kind of limbo you occupy is quite another.'

He looked up; of course he could not see her, but he could imagine her blue robe and the cane she would raise if he got the question wrong. Automatically, it seemed, his first finger extended and he touched the orange interrogation sector beneath the glass.

'Do you think that I, the Lady of this, my City, and Empress of this, my world, am incapable of using and inhabiting a machine?

'What do you want to know?'

He could test her, ask for some straighforward miracle and prove her existence in the Machine tomorrow. But she would know; deception, dissembling and manoeuvring were out. He could ask her a personal question: will Slake Amskiri and his mechanical prosthesis take away my discarded wife? My Lady, please tell me if *he* is with you.

He watched the flow of alphanumerics as the Machine encoded his question.

'How long will I live?'

The Machine answered him. A blunt 'Unauthorised'. He heard Mahun laugh somewhere in the room, near his shoulder, behind him, overhead. The Machine sighed, as always, when he overloaded it with his unanswerable demands, a soft blend of hissing and light, and he saw, on the screen, an array of maps: Dinoord was a green plain and in Vern and Maralis the lily fields had changed their shape. He moved the window and expanded the frame, until he arrived at the sea. The maps were undated, he was lost. He moved the window swiftly until the colours blurred.

Usually, when he could not concentrate, he made a swift tour of his kingdom, greeting his staff with friendly queries (he had the deserved reputation of knowing them all by name), touching some of the books like good luck charms as he passed, taking tea with Cudbeer, descending to Level H to view the work of conservation, constant as the painting of Arbitration Bridge. Now, he prowled about the Forbidden Archive, seeing the laden shelves through a mist and troubled by the insistent thought, 'When?' Tired, unanswered, and believing himself the victim of an antique joke like Lys's or of the onset of a fever, he committed the unthinkable and left the level, forgetting to shut down the Machine. One of its quiescent brains whispered into the silence, roused in a brief display of concatenating light, and broke the circuit.

It was comic, this thing they called age, which had drawn deep furrows in his skin and taken away its elasticity and the colour from his hair. He looked like a dissolute angel, a wasted rake turned too late to religion, with his white curls and the sinewy limbs of the ascetics whom the Gaian Theotocopoulos, El Greco, the Greek, had painted in a land called Spain, so many aeons, so many light years from this place, this hot moist continent, this woman's world, where he had been born. Does one grow to resemble one's loves, he thought? Is this gaunt shape the final revelation and resolution of a life? I am no golden centaur but a mortal sceptic, turning from desire to hope, tossed between the Goddess (he now accorded her a capital letter) and the God, a stranger in my land and an impostor in my city – that ultimate City, the last resort.

She had a shape the first settlers would have recognised, seeing the plain of roofs between Temple Hill and the Citadel Rock, the thrust of the black towers of learning and the blue of faith, the diminishment of the wide green acres and their imprisoning by fences and walls, a forced conversion into tranquil parks. He had rebuilt as much as he could, some of it stone in the old style, some of it painted compounds in the new, unstressed fashion.

Underneath, the land endured. Beneath the fields lay bones of hard granite which broke down slowly into rich, red, and shallow soil. The forest encroached, ten thousand saplings planted in nourishing stands between his new fields. He had planted melons and their near cousins, pumpkins, squashes, and gourds, using the methods of the old agriculturalists, the lily farmers, to raise wholesome fruit in place of poison. The methods were not dissimilar. In Alcuon, the chokeweed grew, consolidating the fragile earth, then planting, myriads of infant plants started in the barns. Throughout Vern, the thirsty fruit drank from the irrigation ditches, a succession of ripe colour and sweet flesh which would satisfy any glutton; but he had ceased to be greedy, turning his old intellectual and bodily passions into a love of cultivation. There was enough for the City, enough for the farmers and a surplus to sell in the east. The Machine displayed his crop piled in foreign markets, cradled in nests of shredded paper in Sollar's most exclusive stores, being relished by the workers in cold Noiro.

His moonlit walks among the fields of Ruht had shown him the sleeping fruit; at least, it seemed to him that the green globes slept amongst their coiling stems, sheltered and warm beneath coir mats. He had knelt amongst the plants, hearing the fennec fox bark and the rock rabbit scream, to lift the rough blankets and peer at the fruit underneath. The moon coloured everything from her sparse palette and he saw blue fruit and shadows of indigo; paths of white light and stark walls where, in the silent laura, Cal was asleep and never knew how the future had visited his Nestor.

Sunlight gave the fruit a different form. When he saw the ripe fruit by day, he wanted Cal beside him, to load his graceful arms with the plenty. His farmers grew Banded Planets, Roakn Loaves, Sweet Hives and Snake's Eggs in their garlands of lobed green leaves, juicy fruits whose eccentric and traditional names were suggestive of rotundity and fecundity. He travelled in Vern to assess the first crop and, on the Dayamit estates, was entertained by Melada who, stooped now and as white as himself, treated him as close kin and begged for his reminiscences to buttress the memory of her beloved son; here, he had picked a ripe melon and cut into it, to reveal the dense rope of fibre at its centre, the nest of its flat seeds; he had cut a thick slice and eaten it, marvelling at this natural construct of simple sugars and water. The girl who followed Melada Dayamit about the estate and carried her parasol was one of the grandchildren, he was told, and, emulating Crinon, he made solicitous enquiries about her aspirations, schooling, and identity. 'Why, Rafe's!' Melada exclaimed. 'Posthumously. One of my neighbours agreed to bear the child.' He felt the shadow of the guilt which had once consumed him, shivered, and touched his belly in the automatic gesture which honoured Mahun; looking again at the girl's langsat complexion, he saw other shadows and followed her grandmother into the house, out of the glare.

His horticulturalists had named several varieties for him: Nonpareil, the Archivist, Magon Hinoor. Was this fame, this gentle tribute? Crinon had shown him the way; it seemed that her last year had been spent in discussion – of soil types, temperatures, propagation, methods of irrigation. Without her, the Garden House was an empty theatre, a memorial to former times, a museum in truth: Xhara' had remained in Evanul. Sometimes, he went to the house with Slake to dust the countless objects, replacing every item he touched exactly where it had been, to inhale the pungent smell of her studio where his unfinished portrait was a jigsaw of black and umber; or he sat alone on the verandah, relishing his solitude and reading Crinon's letters. On her desk lay a half-finished letter to Xhara' and, beside it, the bitten rosewood penholder from which her words had leapt, a hand both bolder and more generous than his own, the writing of someone who had wielded a consummate brush.

8 KiV 530

Dearest Xhara',

We have supped on the verandah, Magon and I – cheese, fruit, and wine. Just like old times. When the lamp was lit, I closed my eyes and pretended we were ten and twelve again. Only the hooting of the owl family convinced me I was older, much older – in

Mother's garden we could hear the night hawks which roost on Citadel Rock chitter as they fed, flutes, organs, and the shouts of the ice-cream sellers from the City.

I am sending you Anlie's books; Faya brought them up this morning.

I took cuttings from the vine. I know it's the wrong time of the year, but I think they'll do. The soil of the short bed is so hard, whatever I try. The feather grass struggles on the margin of the little pool. It I didn't know better, I would believe the carp nibble its roots or else that one of

Nothing of consequence, no profound thoughts; but the small concerns, the gestures of sodality, love expressed, with which she had seasoned her life. His memories of her were tender and absurd, smiles over a new flower successfully raised, tears – real distress – over the scattered corpse of a bird when a cat, evading both the gardeners and their traps, had got into her garden.

Sometimes he made Slake call City Gallery in the morning; after lunch the carriage took him there, and he strolled in the cleared rooms past an acreage of water colour and a desert of transitional cubism until he came to Crinon's two portraits. To S'an and her snows, he gave considered attention, standing back to admire the composition, moving close to peer at the brushwork; and then, always the same ritual, he closed his eyes, turned, and felt his way along the central couch, to open them on the other world which Cal inhabited, ardent, alive, and young in the everlasting afternoon beside the pool. He had not deserved to die; no one deserved that merely for following the primrose path. Three and a half decades were not enough for all his memories; the eight crammed and turbulent years together were a wavelet in the tide of history, scarcely more than a long afternoon.

There was no portrait of M'untal. Perhaps (old age was making him superstitious) because she had no personal vision of death like Cal, rent by his addiction, or S'an, reborn out of ice; like the painter herself, the sudden victim of a coral snake. Crinon's tragedy was that of every accidental death. She had forbidden the snake-charmer entrance years ago because she believed the vipers had all fled when the python came. Crinon would, he thought, have come to M'untal last because to give life to the stiff figure in its silks and gold would have required all her artistry. Easy to paint her with her children, laughing at last. She had left the City early in 519, sixteen months after his first bereavement. He was still in mourning. She had gone, as effectively as if she had died, sailing for Ineit the long way with her producer and three of her children, pregnant already, expecting a miracle. She had left him their two frozen children, the icy statues which were his in name. Leirion and Anyal would wake

361

one future day and bring their true father's vitality to a different planet, Gaia herself. He could imagine the triumph. She had left him her temple costume, the red silks, the silver bells and the leafy head-dress; all the jewellery, lustrous and symbolic with its display of trigonal and triclinic crystals. He needed a three-dimensional image. Amarant's figures were mighty and inappropriate to his purpose, but she produced for him a City girl, Acanta, the daughter of a self-made Artificer, who could carve wood. She had made a woman painted like the Temple figures but in exquisite detail. He had helped her dress the figure, watching while she arranged and tied the maral and placed the jewels, smelling M'untal's beloved flowers in the sweet breath of her garments; he crowned the figure, placing the coronet of trembling leaves on a head of hair as abundant as M'untal's own, a wig of the tresses from some whore glad to sell it to the Gynarchy and prosper. So M'untal dwelt in the Temple, dancing for ever before the Vern Mahun, her delicate face solemn, her hands eloquent, her feet for ever treading the Wheel, changeless and immortal like her companion, the clay figure of the legendary Dancer, Mayuna.

And Mahun, in her ninth aspect as the fount of all wisdom, had blessed him and at last given him a figure: a hundred and ten, a century and a decade; forty-seven years more in which to accomplish the aim he still regarded as his. He like to think of her asleep there, beneath the Octagon, appearing to him when she chose, tolerant, forgiving, and sharp as a nail.

'Give me your soul, Magon,' she had said. 'Let me have your immortal soul, and I will free you. You shall see 550 and 577; you shall see the men from Gaia.'

He thought she had bent over him and whispered, 'You shall see Cal,'; but of this, he was unsure; in these years of epilogue he had learned to dream by day as well as by night.

He never consented aloud; he never touched the green panel, nor gave her an affirmative answer, but he felt the Wheel spin beneath him. In the last week of Bey, he rode up to Diridion, climbed the ladders, and confessed to Arkos.

Poverty (Verrun) 577

So, while he acknowledged her omnipotence, he continued to bow his head to Monos, and to swallow the tasteless water in the church; he was the monks' patron; he debated as a student in their seminars; he stood on the tower top and heard Zander dedicate the bare block of stone the novices had hauled there. He felt the wind blow from the south, from the City and the sea, and veer east to stir the black and cinnabar sands and take another millimetre from the Ruht. Next year, he vowed, forgetting –

he felt strong in the forceful wind – he would stand there and watch the Red Wind tear across Vern until it buffeted his face, filled his eyes with sand and tears, and lifted the sandcloth from his mouth; he would experience, he would see and rejoice in every turn of the wind.

To celebrate the Octagon's second millennium he had uncovered every item which had been made in 2550; the citizens perambulated in dark galleries filled with subordinates of the Machine whose screens glowed with pictorial and written records, births and deaths, marriages and divorces, starship dockets and starsailors; in the galleries on Level 3, he showed the people marvels: clocks without clockwork, pebbles from Meloura, irradiated fruit, the teeth of dragons; in the countless processions, at receptions, in temple and church, he wore his graduation gown and silks, rainbows for his languages, white for the arts, grey for the humanities, an epochal octogenarian. People held street parties: he could not imagine why, when their connection with the Octagon was at best half-a-dozen entries in the Register; he was presented with the third amber vervet monkey to begin again the collection he had lost. In 552, he remembered, he had sent the carving to Ishkal Amskiri to be rid of it. Ishkal was a diligent scholiast and published a volume of his commentary on the Law every decade. Exile had become retreat; he never left the villa where his mother's bones lay in a reliquary of lead. As for his brother, they had met two or three times, acknowledging the mutual attraction, they had dinner together . . . . sixty-five years ago. Harendi, that was his name. He had wasted his education, idled, and fled to Sinein.

The Gaians were brought to Magon in the New Citadel. When he stood at last before them on the dais he understood why he had rid the City of Annalat. The women looked up at him. He had grasped a century and wrested it from their clutch. Sondrazan stood on his left and a little way behind him, her clumsy title of Matriarch-in-Council an indication of future tense. What was time? Time was not even necessary; it contributed nothing to thought and had no significance, since Crinon and Cal were gone. He had served a long penance. His distance from 508 was immeasurable. The years stretched their length between the Octagon's bimillennium and the coming of the starship, and the two events were blurred, melded together like silica and ash in a furnace; like a doublet in which the colour of the gem permeates the glass and the colour of the glass, the jewel. The City's leading families were there, and her finest produce; dozens of bottles of Ceremana had been opened and bubbly, for toasts. But the longhaulers from Gaia would touch nothing.

One of the bearded men was named Smith. Another was named Batuta. There was rivalry between these two and spiritual tension. They spoke in English and remarked that his pure sixth millennium accent differed from their own; after all, he said, feeling a need for justification, there has been no face-to-face contact since 3775. He asked questions about the ship and the crew; action and thought suspended, cold, they had travelled through time itself, dependent on the ship's systems. Several expensive lives had been lost and Smith had woken to the stench of death in the cabins; he had cleansed the slabs alone and then climbed up to the control to dock the ship off 'Nyon; when he woke, Batuta had insisted on piloting the Sineinian shuttle which carried them to the City.

Did they therefore fear to put their trust in ice and machines? 'I put my faith in God,' said Smith. ' "Does there not pass over a man a space of time when his life is a blank?" ' said Batuta stoutly. ' "We have created man from the union of two sexes so that We may put him to the proof." ' It seemed to be a quotation from some Gaian law, and Magon turned to question him more closely; but Smith, the other captain, wanted to talk of practicalities. They had each brought an assistant, a cook, and a supply of sterile food. A medic was in constant attendance. They bore gifts, new weapons, old fabrics, antique holograms; he thought of the lost paintings. One of the wafers showed a naked woman; but she would not move like Kunai's base dreams. *Daystar* did not carry women. 'She's not an ice crate. She has room only for the crew and five passengers. Three slabs are empty: I offer them to you.' Smith had bowed stiffly, as if he were unused to formal gestures, bowed again at his response, 'Any ship that sails from Guna takes women as a matter of course,' and the eight men left abruptly without, he thought, any appreciation of his culture, to ride back to their capsule for decontamination. They were there now, locked up in Space Park, preparing their reports; they were in the City, these scrupulous strangers who regarded him as an alien. *Apollo* had brought them: cultural invaders, cryomorphs themselves, they had not appreciated the miracle of S'an.

The familiar City and her citizens surrounded him. They walked and ran and breathed the impure air and the breeze from the sea. They rode about and laughed in their incredible rout of conveyances, alighting from a skimmer to ride in a shay. He rode, not now astride a horse but seated behind a pair of them, connected to their wilful spirits by taut reins. He rode to Dinoord taking as many days as he needed for the slow journey; time had as much meaning as it did out there, beyond the planets, frozen days without sensation. In Dinoord, the soil was as red as that of Maralis but deep and knit together by the grass which had fed the blood horses and now put fat on his cattle, and on the cattle of the landowners who had followed him. The grass fields had increased; they stretched in a level green park almost as far as Taimiss. He could drive the drag for miles across the new plain, delighting in the fluid movement of the horses but forced by the infirmity of his hip into his wheeled and unstable shell. He drove a pair of dapple-grey Dinoordian pacers and thought of them as an old man's choice and of the drag as an old man's conveyance. The rattle and shudder hurt him, but he refused to acknowledge it as he refused to travel by skimmer, to be translated from place to place without the interval and preparation of the journey between.

The giant ploughs had come from Sinein. He loved to watch them tearing up the soil, preparing more seedbeds. More grass, more flesh, almost as many cattle as there were stars.

The *New Daystar, Apollo 505*, was a pale star off 'Nyon. At night he looked up to her and saw Leirion, Anyal, and the third Orel, cold among the stars, arrested in stasis and unconscious of their journey. His ship, too, lay in the roads.

S'an and he, they were the only ones left. Using Mahun's Law, she had divorced him on his sixtieth birthday; it was an expected gift and he had welcomed it. But she did not marry Slake; like him, she lived alone. And the rest, they were scattered and dispersed about the continents, the worlds, the heavens. They had become clouds, thoughts, abstract lemures which appeared by night, real only in his faulty memory. He could parade them through the Machine as if they lived: Galabrias with his ruddy cheeks and stick to knock out weeds (Cya had planted a memorial in his garden); Crinon laughing with his young, black-haired self; Rafe dressed like a demon in scarlet silks at a masked ball. He did not often look for Rafe. M'untal laughing, happy for ever, her tiny hands held up, her skirts a bell; Maja in a brief moment of informality at a reception; Orel Diran. He watched her walk towards him, her daughter and granddaughter at her side. Cal, his terrified expression trapped by the photographer and animated by the Machine, the topaz eyes staring, the dark pupils stretched wide by the drug; Cal, beyond the void, somewhere in the eternal abyss which was the abode of the Goddess, filled with her unthinking ritual, with words, dances, fogs of obscurement and clouds of

(Tranquility (Hibornal) 577)

unknowing, the mist which this morning hid the City, covering even the blue towers and the golden Mamelon which She (for he believed wholly in her influence) had helped him preserve – though Cal was gone, and Crinon.

In the last light, the Octagon gleamed, whole, as if it had never been violated. It contained everything he loved and valued. The tower was redundant. The Machine would not speak to him again, and She had gone; when she returned, it would be for his incorporeal, immortal shadow, his transparent soul. He was too far away to hear the music, see the dancing in the streets, speak with Sondrazan. The sun fell at great speed, its orange disc dropping at such a rate into the sea he thought an audible splash would not have come amiss, and he smiled.

The circus had come to town; a new-old entertainment for the City. It was wholly appropriate that the gaudy splendour of the circus, with its bizarre Gaian customs and the melodies of the City, should mark his last hours. Clowns, telling old and wistful jokes, would mark his passing. In the City, tales abounded. If space was time why should not time be space? They claimed to have travelled far but from whence they would not say. A Traveller on the road from Nivuna had encountered them and, recognising his own kind, had come up with the vans and spoken with the leader of the troupe, a long-faced clown. The road, the Traveller swore, had been an empty white ribbon a moment before. It was late afternoon; the sun was setting and dazzled him. Someone else told how the circus came out of Vern, not by the highway, but by the old and weedy road. There had been a Facer woman, seven children, and a beautiful Tlivoorn boy. But there was a rational explanation; time was not circular, it was linear and the past could not be the present. Clowns, acrobats, dancers, the old illusionists; amongst them was a fortune-teller named Alluleya, a woman in her middle years who, when pressed by the curious Gynarchy, led them to an empty wild beast cage, pulled aside the straw and revealed the golden figures of twin embryos, full-term, perfect children, Ingemi. There was a rational explanation; for every event which appeared supernatural there was a scientific rationale. Thieves – how easy it must have been for an accomplished thief to climb into the Temple enclosure the night he took away the leopard and the women and, availing himself of the disorder, remove the Mamelon's treasure. There was a rational explanation. Even for Mahun.

Flying to Noiro, his wings the metal blades of the stratocruiser, he had looked down into a sea as clear as that of the Bay. It was a glass in which he sought his airborne reflection but he saw, instead, the communities and landscape of another world, amethyst jellyfish, silver spars and shoals of brown weed. The shadow of the cruiser darkened the water and made the creatures invisible. He looked ahead and saw jewelled islands lying low in the sea and justifying their poetic name: Noiro, at the back of the North Wind, the Land Beyond. The shadow of the craft was shaped like a swift with its wings laid back to dive; on the ground in Roakn it appeared unstable and incapable of flight. He thought its name had been *Shiron*, or maybe it was *Shion*, which was Cheronese for dart. One of the women Cal used like the drug, something to take him out of his earthbound body and up into the clouds. He would have scorned this prisoned flight, powered by sluggish fusion and cased in metal. In 500 – he was certain of the year – he had searched the empty ballrooms for Cal and M'untal; that evening (his anger and frustration had been a knotted scourge), he had watched Shiron fling knives at a pale man and surround him with haloes of reflected light; she was so swift and sure. Her man had acquiesced, standing perfectly still, passive, against the spangled board, letting her perform, aware of and indifferent to the deadly blades. At the climax of the act his eyes had widened; but he gave no other sign and the last knife sunk into the wood between his thighs. It was perfectly clear that she could have castrated him if she had wished.

Yet they were glass, the women, brittle and beautiful, often shattered by circumstance. Crinon's tears over Maja; Xhara' screaming in the dark street, screaming still in the bar they called him to, screaming in the hospital. And then refusing. Shipwrecked, drowned, yet refusing. No douche. No drugs. What will be, will be. As strong and as yielding as glass in the furnace. No intervention. Pride. My daughter.

Glass when it broke became a chance mosaic of spiked remnants, nothing like the solid it had been, scattered for ever on the stones. He had almost dropped one of Shiron's pieces at the sale in Roakn, a new acquisition, a blue libation bowl from the first millennium which had cost her two consignments of rkws. Broken glass worn by salt water and honed on the seashore made gems for children, jewel mines at the water's edge. He had chased many dreams in and out of the waves, believing that a half-hidden piece of red glass was a ruby, searching for amber.

Islands are bits of coloured glass, the shards of dreams. The chief city of Noiro was Traumesse, Dream City, where they manufactured anodyne visions for the masses. It occupied one of the midbelt islands, but he could not remember which. He had become so tired, so old; memory was mosaic. The island had many lakes of dark brown peaty water which mirrored the clouds.

Cal's vanity had been revealed by mirrors. He stared often at his own reflection, not amazed or awed, but in love; watching him admire himself had been an attempt to preserve transience in the archive of memory. The painting told all; but there was no gold in Noiro, except when the sun set in its slow and poignant northern manner; there was amber. Noiro was the mother of amber and the tears of pine trees lay in the shallow waters off Longbeach, waiting to be rolled and polished, once-pliant resin become stone; amber. He held S'an's moly, the delicate warm windflower, in his hand; but it would not be effective against the enchantments of Mahun. Her City was a ragged contour beyond the glistening rain trees, far away; he smelled damp earth, honey, and flowers.

This was the last night. The stars moved, time ran. He watched the moon rise and illuminate the distant City.

Appendix 1
Chronology

Year	Event
1	Foundation of the City. The first Gynarch, Elfara Kiden M'una, and the first Matriarch, Lara Shuma M'una, elected by the First, the Council of Origination.
1–500	The First Years, the subject of Herkel Galabrias's study. In 479 Zalcasia is subdued and becomes a client state.
500–1000	Consolidation and expansion into the Provinces. The Hinoor dynasty establishes itself, following the expulsion from Mid-Ineit of Anyala Hinoor.
901–910	Brief flowering of an early form of the Monoclid religion in Vikkut, ending with the execution of the heretic Xynak.
1500	In return for a yearly tribute, a primitive form of Monoclidism is allowed in Diridion which becomes a client state under the protection of the City.
Late 1900s	Experimental near-spaceflight.
2000 plus	The Golden Age. Development of spaceflight, both near and deep. First contacts with Gaia. Building of the Octagon in 2550.
3000 plus	The cryomorph era: deep spaceflight normal, planetary mining and remote observation of other lifeforms. *Daystar*'s first flight.
3498	The cryomorph Defenders of the Faith are interred.
3700	*Daystar* sails for Gaia.

3852	*Daystar*, carrying the gifts of art and remote kill in her holds, docks (for the last time) off 'Nyon.
3999	*Evenstar* explodes on take-off.
4000/1AR	The Reformation. The City (but not Guna) voluntarily returns itself to a pre-hightec age: air and spaceflight, genetic construction and recombination, and cryogenics cease. Scientific knowledge is buried and the Forbidden Archive begun. The City is rededicated as a shrine and religious centre, protected by international treaty and the Law.
1–280AR	The Silver Age. The arts flourish, Shelda and Lys Hinoor and Huyatt Tayal amongst their chief exponents; there is some neo-technological development. The City becomes dependent on its trade in husk and dust.
465AR	Birth of Crinon Hinoor M'una, the painter of the City, to Maja Hinoor M'una, 126th Archivist of the City of Mahun, and Destorio Nonpareil of Roakn, Cheron, General and Principal Councillor in the Revolutionary Government of Tikan Voal Chacma.
467AR	Birth of Magon Nonpareil, 127th Archivist of the City of Mahun, the son of Maja Hinoor, Archivist of the City of Mahun, and Destorio Nonpareil of Roakn, Cheron, General and Principal Councillor.
473AR	Suppression of the uprising of the heretic Annon.
482AR?	Birth of Cal?
502–577AR	The Custodianship of Magon Nonpareil.
577AR	*Apollo 505* arrives from Gaia.
577AR onward	The Counter-Reformation under the combined Matriarchy and Gynarchy of Sondrazan Troya Nonpareil.
650AR	*Apollo 505*, the *New Daystar*, docks off Gaia; on her cryomorph decks, Orel Diran M'unor III, Leirion and Anyal Kiden Nonpareil.

657AR/   Orel Diran III completes her translation of *The Archivist* in
6088AD   Islington, London.

Appendix 2
The Players

The table below gives English equivalents of Gunaian names. The reader may therefore pronounce them as she pleases: but the first syllable of Magon should be pronounced to rhyme with 'day'.

Unless otherwise differentiated, all names except those of nationals born outside the City and the Five Provinces have the suffix M'una, daughter of Mahun (sometimes spelt M'unah) or M'unor, in the case of males.

Cal M'unor, m.
Magon Nonpareil, the Archivist, m.

IN THE DEPTHS

Tarla, an old Prostitute, Tarot and dream reader, f.
Glaver, Tsaka, Shiron, a knifethrower and arms dealer on the rim of the Depths, f.
Miel, her assistant and target, m.
Nadar, a notorious cut-throat and male Prostitute; he runs a real laundry business and is known as the best launderer in town, m.
Niska, a classy female Prositute, f.
Ala, another female Prostitute, f.
Zalcissa, a female Prostitute, friend of Tarla, f.
Pulchrinella, Dork, a droll, a transsexual, an old friend of Cal and a friend of Rafe Dayamit, m.
Kondar, a male Prostitute, m.
Jakes, a supplier of adulterated black market drugs, m.
Toomy, a supplier of black market husk who works in the husk packing depot, m.
Dromio, a catamite, friend of Cal, m.
Achille, another catamite, model to Amarant, m.
Peach/Seef, a pavement child, an abandoned Tlivoorn, m.
Dove, another pavement child, Peach's friend, f.
Shiny, another pavement child, Peach's friend, m.

Bind, an old husker who has escaped from the City, encountered in Odalion by Cal, m.

Tash, a husker who has escaped from the City, encountered in Odalion by Cal, m.

Tyler, owner of an eating house in the Quarter, m.

An, an Artificer, Magon's agent, m.

Meleager, a clown, m.

Loy, his apprentice, m.

The Travelling Woman, billed as 'Sierra and the Rat Queen', she came from Ineit and visited the City and the Five Provinces in Alcuon and Vern, 500, with her show. Nothing else is known about her.

The Rat Queen. What is a rat queen? On Gaia, several rat kings have been displayed since the mid-second millennium: six or seven rats joined by an untiable knot in their tails. Various theories have been advanced, but no one knows how they are formed. They are objects of superstition and dread.

THE FISTERS

Fil, encountered by Cal in prison, m.

Dile, a Fister, m.

THE ROSIES

Luce, Luciana Tisal M'una, sometime lover of Glaver, chief Rosy, f.

Morn, f.

Star, f.

Stella, f.

Aurora, f.

Dawn, f.

THE FACES

Dog, leader of the Faces, m.

The Bitch, Prenta, Dog's woman, a tattooist, Artificer, and body painter, f.

Mouse, Hellie, the Bitch's sister, f.

Horse, a drummer, m.

Ax, a drummer, m.

Malkin, singer, in screams, the Cat's woman, f.

Jill, f.

Cat, m.

Tod, m.

Vixen, f.

THE IRONMEN

The Ironmen were originally iron smelters and workers. Their Mark is the outline of a smelting furnace crossed by a hammer.

Bale, leader of the Ironmen, m.
Stoker, Bale's agent, who extorts money from the City's shay drivers, m.

ON THE HILL

M'untal, Mahuntal Kiden M'una, matrician lady, Temple Dancer, mother of Luth, Leirion, and Anyal, f.
Crinon, Crinon Hinoor M'una, Magon's sister, painter of the City, f.
Destorio Nonpareil, father of Magon and Crinon, a Cheronese, counsellor to Chacma, m.
Annalat, Annalat Abayon M'una, the present Matriarch, a Surrogate, Slake's cousin; once Heleth Amskiri, f.
Ishkal, Ishkal Abayon M'unor, Annalat's youngest son, born about 491AR, m.
Harendi, Harendi Abayon M'unor, Annalat's eldest son, born about 489AR, m.
Justa Edern M'una, the Gynarch, chief priestess of Mahun, f.
Luth/Ister, M'untal's son by Tellon, m.
Fiora, M'untal's adopted daughter, Lorilla's daughter, f.
Leirion, M'untal's daughter by Cal, twin, f.
Anyal, M'untal's son by Cal, twin, m.
Cudbeer, Silvanor Cudbeer M'unor, Magon's assistant, a mathematician and statistician, m.
Estila Morion, the Assistant Archivist, f.
Lonie, M'untal's aunt, f.
Parstrie, friend of Malajide, f.
Tressa, Taressa Kiden M'una, M'untal's sister, f.
Verelustra Tain, Verelustra Tain M'una, Lector, a professor of languages at City University, f.
Tellon, Tellon Celth M'unor, M'untal's first husband, former husband of several Dancers, m.
Malajide, Malajide Kiden M'una, M'untal's mother, Oyno's wife, f.
Alna, M'untal's nurse and personal maid, her family are silversmiths, f.
Lorilla, a silkweaver from Far Maralis, Luth's adoptive mother, f.
Filka, the Assistant Librarian and Chief Translator, later marries Cudbeer, f.
Slake, Slake Amskiri M'unor, Magon's personal servant, castrated for alleged rape of a Gynarch, m.
Chacma, President Tykan Voal Chacma, of Cheron, military dictator, ally of the City, protector by treaty of the City, delegate to the Council of

Nations and Noiro, m.

Nan, the head gardener on the hill, f.

Xharam'un', Xharam'un' Han M'una, Xhara', Crinon's friend, companion and lover, a flautist, abstract painter, and revolutionary, f.

Faya, Faya Edern M'una, a romantic novelist, close friend of Crinon, and revolutionary, f.

Chenodor, Raist Chenodor, a sculptor and, later, member of Magon's government, close friend of Crinon, leading revolutionary; marries M'untal, m.

Gildo, Doos Gildo, a writer and poet, an uncle of M'untal, close friend of Crinon, revolutionary, m.

Amarant, Amarant Abayon M'una, a monumental sculptor, close friend of Crinon, reluctant revolutionary, f.

Ayli na Shuma, a principal Councillor, Chenodor's wife of many years; divorces him in 502AR, revolutionary, f.

IN THE CITY

Mother Serilla, head of the Hospice, nun of Mahun, f.

Sister Shelda, a sister at the Hospice, nun of Mahun, f.

the She, Alluleya, oracle of Mahun, a Gynarch, f.

Cyrra, Cyrra Ankit M'una, a pharmacist in the City, friend of Herkel Galabrias, f.

Orel Diran, native of Sinein, comes to the City in 511 to write about Cal, first author of *The Archivist*, f.

Orel Diran II, Orel's daughter by Cal, born 512, second author of *The Archivist*, f.

Orel Diran III, Orel's granddaughter, emigrates to Gaia, translates *The Archivist* into English, f.

THE DAYAMITS

Lissa Dayamit, Lissa Dayamit M'unah, a prosperous weaver, factory owner, Rafe's aunt, a widow, f.

Lota, Lissa's youngest daughter, f.

Nila, Lissa's eldest daughter, f.

Fleish
Lifad } Lissa's three sons, m.
Welch

IN THE BLOCK

Hyason Sarin M'unah, First Officer of the Security Corps, f.

X.T. M'unah, a prison doctor and Lector, f.

Y.K. M'unah, another prison doctor, f.
Arbiter Talamun Mahud, an arbiter-at-law, puts Cal's case to the Nine Judges, f.

IN VERN

Melada Dayamit, Rafe's mother, a lily farmer in Odalion, Vern, f.
Hysan, Rafe's sister, f.
Lia, Rafe's youngest sister, f.
Kinas M'unah, bookseller in Odalion, local government official; Cal stays in her house, f.
Galabrias, Dr Herkel Galabrias M'unor, physician, soul-doctor, antiquary, expert in addictions, author of several medical books; native of Evanul in Vern, a cousin of Maja Hinoor, m.
Tebora, servant/housekeeper to Galabrias and Cya in Evanul, native of Evanul, f.
Erys, a whisperer and husker in Evanul, f.
Cya, Cya Han M'una, Xhara's sister, a musician, owner of the house in Evanul next to Galabrias's, f.

IN DIRIDION

Arkos, a senior monk in Diridion, a Zalcasian by birth, Magon's mentor and teacher, m.
Krates, the Allode of Diridion and Father of the monastery there, m.
Smintias, an elderly deaf mute, looks after the monastery library in Diridion, m.
Zander, a friendly novice in Diridion, a Zalcasian, m.
Misine, a monk of Diridion, expert traveller in the Tayaal, native of Sidend by Zalcasia, m.

IN THE TAYAAL

Benet, a Desmid, Magon's disciple and a soldier for a time with Oyno, m.

IN ZALCASIA

Oyno, Olthar Oyno, M'untal and Taressa's father, Malajide's husband (he has another wife and family in Cheron), senior mercenary with Chacma, ally of Magon Nonpareil, m.
Pikat, Oyno's lieutenant and aide.
Zuhil, a Zalcasian, head man of the town of Binala and of a loose

federation of Zalcasian villages, m.

Vedara, a Binalan girl, daughter of Dibor; Cal's wife and, later, Gesir's; mother of Kahil, f.

Kahil, the son of Cal and Vedara, m.

Dibor, Vedara's father, a widower, hunter, and trapper, m.

Ahe, a trader and leader in Binala with Zuhil, m.

Bashay, a soldier with Oyno, a City man, a bookbinder by trade and Mark, m.

Gesir, a Zalcasian, a noted ounce hunter, Vedara's second husband, m.

Saissa, Saissa Hinoor M'una, ancestor of Magon and Crinon, the cryomorph commander, f.

Sondrazan Troya M'una, cryomorph Senior Medical Officer, becomes devoted to Magon who marries her in 515AR, f.

Dur Kunai M'unor, Kunai, cryomorph Medical Officer, m.

Xanchen M'una, Xanchen, cryomorph Medical Officer, f.

THE DEAD

Hero, a cryomorph and painter, Chiara's husband, voyager on *Daystar*, m.

Chiara, a cryomorph and poet, Hero's wife, voyager on *Daystar*, f.

Mayuna, a Temple Dancer, subject of many votive figurines, f.

Annon, executed leader of a male and Monoclid uprising in 473, m.

M'nah, a Beggarwoman, Cal's first protector, f.

Swan, a thief, known as the King of Thieves, a cat burglar, who cared for the child Cal after the death of M'nah, m.

Diment, a Beggar, m.

Huyatt Tayal, one of the Tayal, author of a famous travel book and other works, m.

Balkiss, Huyatt's love, f.

Shelda, Shelda Hinoor M'una, Silver Age poet, f.

Hibornal na Mahun, endower of a small chantry, now deconsecrated, in the old industrial quarter, f.

Maja, Maja Hinoor M'una, 126th Archivist, mother of Crinon and Magon, wife of Destorio Nonpareil, f.

Lys Hinoor M'una, Archivist in 250AR, a writer and ancestor of Magon and Crinon, f.

Rafe Dayamit, trader in trumpet lilies, wealthy, executed in Cal's stead, Magon's lover, m.

Ies Kunai, holographist, active 3rd millenium, S'an Troya's donate father.

Ahia na Ahia (1502?–1599OS), considered by many to be the City's foremost writer, a playwright and poet, inventor of the ambulatory terpsichorean tragedy. *The Tragedy of Vikkut* is probably her greatest work although the incomplete *Ila and the Demons* has almost as many advocates.

THE GAIANS

Joseph Smith, co-captain of *Apollo 505*, the Gaian ship, a Christian.
Imran Ibn Batuta, co-captain of *Apollo 505*, a Moslem.

DEITIES

Mahun, the supreme deity of Guna and guardian of the City, f.
Ingemi, Mahun's twin children, f., m.
Tror, Mahun's deposed consort, m.
Monos, heretic male god worshipped in Diridion and in the laura at Purity in the Tayaal, m.

OTHERS

Hayla, Chacma's rival, hereditary queen of Hayna, north of Mahkrein, f.
Arkite, Magon's horse, a 17hh bay bloodhorse, s.
Choru, Cal's horse, a 14.2hh grey (white) Tayali-bred, Barbon, m.

Appendix 3
Quotations

Direct quotations

pages 37, 71, 212: *The Book of Monos*, first recorded in Diridion in 10AR, supposedly copied by Ikal from a (lost) Second Millennium version.

page 87: Pindar, *Theoxinus*, translated by 'Angharad', Gaia, 1988AD.

page 120: 'The Unco Knichts Wowing', *English and Scottish Popular Ballads*, F.J. Child, Gaia, 1882AD.

page 134: 'Always Together', unpublished short story (Archive HIN/ CHM/479/600dep) by Crinon Hinoor M'una, possibly derived from 'Annabel Lee' by Edgar Allen Poe, *A Third Gaian Anthology*, City, 3500OS.

page 136–137: 'The King and the Scholar', *Zalcasian Folk Tales*, City, 425AR; *Folk Tales of Far Maralis*, Nivuna, 460AR.

page 146: XXii, XXiii, *The Law: The Life and Teachings, Prayers and Precepts of Our Lady, Mahun*, numerous editions beginning with *The Drynoptera*, City, Foundation Year, 1OS, 4000 Before Reformation

page 187: *Hamlet*, William Shakespeare, Gaia, 1599–1600AD; *Hamlet: A Gaian Tragedy by W. Shakespeare*, Sinein, 3453OS.

page 187: *The Travels of Huyatt Tayal*, second edition, City, 249AR.

page 195: *Starsailors: An Anthology of Gaian Verse*, Sollar Kein, 455AR: John Keats (1795–1821AD), 'Bright Star', his last sonnet; William Wordsworth (1770–1850AD), 'The Daffodils'; John Milton, 'Comus', 1634AD.

page 196: Plato, 'Agathon', translated by 'Angharad', Gaia, 1988AD.

page 202: *The Travels of Huyatt Tayal*, scholars' edition, City, 456AR.

page 272: J.S. Bach, *St Matthew Passion*.

page 285: *The Travels of Huyatt Tayal*, first edition, City, 247AR.

page 350: *The Book of Beasts*, T.H. White, Gaia, 1954, translation of a twelfth century (second Gaian millennium) bestiary in Latin, one of Gaia's 'dead' languages which, like Proto- and Crypto-Maralay, has influenced later languages. Compare *The Arbidon Bestiary*, manuscript, Archive, PM/T21/500OS.

page 351: Martial, c.38–104AD, inscribed on a portrait of Giovanna

Tornabuoni by Domenico Ghirlandio, 1488AD, Gaia.

I am responsible for putting these words into Crinon's mouth.

ODM III.

page 354: The *Carmina Burana* poet of Benediktbeuren, Gaia, c.1300AD.

page 364: *The Koran*, a Gaian book of rules for men; it is a little like *The Law*.

Embedded quotations

page 89: Homer, *The Iliad*, Gaia, c.850–800BC. *Note:* For those unfamiliar with the Gaian method of dating historic events, famous writers, etc., BC means Before Christ and AD means Anno Domini (Latin), In the Year of Our Lord. Both terms refer to the Judaeo-Christian God Jehovah in one of his manifestations as the Son of God.

ODM III.

page 312: W. Shakespeare, *A Midsummer Night's Dream*, Gaia, 1596AD. Ahia na Ahia, *Starborn. Gaian Tales and Legends*: 'The Voyage'. Ahia na Ahia, *The Tragedy of Vikkut.* W. Shakespeare, *A Midsummer Night's Dream.* C.P. Kavafis, 'The City', *Penguin Book of Greek Verse*, ed. Constantine A. Trypanis, Gaia, 1971AD.

page 344: C.P. Kavafis, 'The City', *Penguin Book of Greek Verse*, ed. Constantine A. Trypanis, Gaia, 1971AD. C.P. Kavafis, 'On a Ship', *Penguin Book of Greek Verse*, ed. Constantine A. Trypanis, Gaia, 1971AD.

page 367: Christopher Marlowe, *Dr Faustus*, Gaia, 1590sAD; there is one edition of his works on Guna and it is, oddly, in the main City Library.

I have not, except where given above, acknowledged the many and varied debts we three Dirans owe to the Gaian, Shakespeare, and to our own Ahia na Ahia, and do so here: scraps from their laden tables fall into every mouth. ODM III